The Tyranny of the Blood

By Jo Reed

To Mum

Very Best Wishes

Jo Reed

A Wild Wolf Publication

Published by Wild Wolf Publishing in 2009

Copyright © 2009 Jo Reed

ISBN: 978-0-9562114-1-5

www.wildwolfpublishing.com

Acknowledgements

Writers are mad creatures. Most of the time they live inside their heads, and it takes a special bunch of people to drag them into the light of day. My heartfelt thanks go to my dear friend Carly, who started this whole thing off, and to my long suffering readers, Deb and Ang. Glen, my thanks to you, for having faith, and making a sailor of me (and Roger, the cheque is in the post)! Thanks to all my fellow writers who have poked, prodded, critted and shared – you know who you are. Finally, special thanks to Liz Williams for her unstinting and generous support, and to a certain lady who has forgotten where she lives now; bless you, Lorraine.

For Chen and Tom

CHAPTER 1

My first abiding memory is of the chain. My every waking moment was dominated by it, and often it touched my dreams as well. It was, I calculated, some six feet long, a heavy thing made of iron, so heavy that I must have been four years old before I could lift it off the ground. By the time of those first recollections, it was already a part of me, a burdensome extension of my being as familiar as my hands and feet, so that I could not imagine what life might be like without it. At one end of the chain was an iron ring, which was placed around my right ankle the moment the birth fluid had been wiped from my newborn body. At the other end was my mother, shackled as I was by a similar ring around her wrist.

It didn't take me long to understand that my mother loathed me, her firstborn son, as much as she loathed the chain that bound us to each other. Never once did she speak directly to me, and she only looked at me when she had no alternative. I suckled, so I am told, in silence, with a cloth over my face so that she would not have to see me at her breast. When she went around the compound I was slung on her back, the weight of the chain as it dragged on the ground causing the fetter to cut into my tender flesh.

Babies grow of course, so every week or so a man, a servant of Lord Corvan, my father, would come to examine the ring, replace it if it became so tight that it might damage my leg. At the same time he would run his hand along my body, using his gift to shelter my fragile bones from harm. He never smiled or spoke, but his touch was gentle, his coming one of the few things that gave me pleasure. Apart from those few minutes every so often I was never free of my restraint, and the ring around my mother's wrist was never removed.

Some time later, when the gift came to me, that man was given to me as a servant in my own household. I think it was a deliberate act on my father's part. Lord Corvan knew, I am sure, that my curiosity would lead me to seek out the images of my first years, draw them from the mind of the man who had once been my only comfort. Thus, I observed my early struggles from the vantage of the intervening years, through the memories of one who witnessed them. On reflection, perhaps I should have let them lie undiscovered.

As I grew and began first to crawl, then to walk, I learned quickly to keep pace with my mother's purposeful stride. If I didn't I was simply dragged along until I was able to scramble back onto my feet. Her only acknowledgement of me was the scraps that she threw from her plate and which were my only form of sustenance – that, and the occasional dousing in a bucket of freezing water when I became too filthy to ignore.

I remember the time when I realised that other children were not restrained as I was. I would watch them running and shouting in the courtyard from my place a foot or so behind my mother, where she wouldn't have to look at me. None of them ever spoke to me, which was just as well, for although I understood speech well enough I didn't use it, and I would have had nothing to say to them in any case.

I say I did not use speech, but that is not the entire truth. I didn't know it then, of course, but my bloodline had bestowed on me an unusual intelligence, a thing that was later to become both a blessing and a curse. Having nothing else to occupy my time, my days were spent listening intently to the talk of the women. At night, when my mother fell asleep, I whispered the words to myself, remembered the expressions, the cadences of the voices, and so I learned the language of adults rather than the childish prattle of others of my age. When my mother was awake, silence ruled my life, and the result of my breaking it was usually the sting of a well aimed stone.

In due course I began to wonder why I had been singled out for such treatment. The fact that my mother hated me I took for granted, but search as I might I could not think of any reason why I should have incurred such displeasure. The other women might have been able to tell me, but they seemed afraid of us and seldom came near, although I often caught their pitying glances as they passed by. It was to be many years before I learned the true cause of my mother's bitterness. Now, when I look back it is with admiration for her, and understanding, although forgiveness is perhaps beyond my reach.

My mother's name was Mira, and she was beautiful, the most beautiful creature in the settlement in those times. She was the younger sister of Amala, the only woman ever to leave the Family. I say 'leave' – the truth is, she did the impossible – she escaped from what must have been the most closely guarded place on earth, and ran straight into the arms of the man who was to become our sworn enemy, Derlan, the leader of the most gifted of the southern tribes.

When Mira was born, no one could doubt the source of the seed that made her. If the strength of her gift were not evidence enough of Corvan's blood, the honey tint of her skin, unusual in females of all but his line, was an indisputable proof. She was a small, delicate thing, as all the women of the Family are, with her mother's golden hair and bright green eyes. As soon as she was born she was closely guarded, her unwanted protectors keeping watch over her day and night. It is not surprising, given what had happened to her sister. In Amala, Corvan had glimpsed the beginning of the fulfilment of his ambition, one with the gift to cross into the future and foresee events. But at the very moment of his triumph his prize had escaped him, and he wasn't going to let it happen a second time.

As soon as Mira's gift appeared she was confined alone, with only her guards for company. From the start it was clear that she was a woman of extraordinary power. It was from such women that our kind was named – Dancers, after the skill to enter and navigate the great Dance of life, to see the delicate balance of events in places way beyond the boundaries of our human senses. Her mind ranged far beyond our borders, and she could follow the threads of many lives at once, even, it was claimed, across the water to the Western Isles.

I am told that she was possessed of the gift of memory, and that she found her long dead sister Amala, the source of all

9

my father's rage, and spoke with her. Thus she learned of her sister's unique gift to see what had not yet happened, and realised that she was destined to be mated with her own father in his attempt to regain what her sister had denied him.

Such was the fate of many of our women. The furthering of the blood could only be achieved through the distillation of power from those of the greatest gift. Whether brother, sister, parent or child, it made no difference. The nature and the strength of the gift were all that mattered.

Three decades passed before Corvan finally came to Mira. Even then she was young, according to the measures of our people. They say that when, finally, my father took her, she resisted so violently that he had to call on his servants to hold her still. When she conceived she threatened to do all she could to ensure that the monster inside her was not born, and that if it was she would refuse to care for it, or throw it from a high window to its death. In response Corvan immediately picked out six women, all with child and all of lesser blood. He brought them before her and told her that should she seek to carry out her threats both they and their children would be put to death. So it was that one savage Highland winter's night, two years following the succession of the Roman Emperor Hadrian, I was born and, on a whim, remembering Mira's last words, my father had us chained together.

My life continued thus for some seven years, spent mostly trying to remain as invisible to my mother as I could, until I saw my father for the first time. My mother was sleeping, and I, as usual, was curled up under a blanket at her feet. I heard the door open and the sound of the two guards walking away across the courtyard. That was unusual, as we were never left alone. Then came the soft click of the door closing, and an almost inaudible tread coming towards us, stopping just by my head. I felt my mother stiffen, and huddled under the blanket trying to keep still. A hand grasped the blanket and pulled it away, and then I felt arms lifting me to my feet. I looked up and found myself staring straight into Corvan's eyes.

Even now I find it difficult to describe the thoughts that ran through my young head as I stood there gazing at the man who was my father. Many have tried to describe him but none, I think, have done him justice. It is easy to say that he was handsome, as indeed he was, tall, with blue-black hair that shone like polished ebony, flawless skin the most perfect shade of pale gold. His whole posture was one of extraordinary grace and elegance. The sight of him took my breath away, and the longer he scrutinized me the more embarrassed and ashamed I felt, for I was filthy as I always was, and naked save for a coarse shirt that just about covered me. The chain, of course, prevented my wearing much else. He held me at arm's length, looking me up and down as if trying to work out what kind of creature I was. To fall under that gaze I can only describe as like being pierced with daggers of ice. I just kept staring back at him, too young then to be afraid, and thoroughly unused to anyone looking at me at all.

Eventually he set me down carefully with a slow nod of the head and turned his attention to my mother. She hadn't moved an inch, and was staring at him just as intently as he had been staring at me.

"Tell me Mira," he said, and I was surprised by the softness of his voice, "has it not been an honour to raise a boy as perfect as this one?"

She said nothing, but I felt a shiver pass through her and she sat up, her expression a mixture of hatred and contempt, much the kind of look that she usually reserved for me.

"Now that he is weaned," he went on in the same silky tone, "I think perhaps it is time that you provided me with a daughter – one with your sister's attributes would do very well."

He crouched down beside her so that their eyes were level, and as he did so I saw my mother draw back and with all her strength spit right into his face. I think I must have closed my eyes, because the next thing I was aware of was something warm and wet dripping down my face, soaking into my shirt. When I opened them it was to see the dead body of my mother lying back on the sleeping rugs.

Meanwhile, my father's attention had shifted from her back to me. If he wanted some reaction he was disappointed. I had long since learned that to betray any emotion was dangerous, and besides, what was there for me to grieve for? Not the loss of a mother's love, of that I was certain. If I had known then what I know now I might have wept for her, but it is probably as well that I did not, for such weakness in my father's eyes might have signalled the end of my life as well. As it was, he smiled and nodded his head again.

"Perfect," he murmured to himself, subjecting me to yet another intense examination. For a moment I felt that my head would burst, the red hot needles of his thought burning into me, laying bare the nature of the man I would become. Had my father discovered a single flaw my life would have ended before it had truly begun. He was satisfied, however, and very carefully he removed the iron ring from around my ankle and stood me back on my feet. At the same time I felt his hand move slowly down my spine, checking, I suppose, for any sign of deformity. He nodded again, then walked to the door without a backward glance and beckoned for me to follow. I took a step and stumbled, landing on my knees. I had never walked without the chain and without its weight I found it hard to balance. I tried again and the same thing happened, my father watching my struggle with growing impatience.

At the third attempt I managed to stay upright and totter unsteadily to the door. When I reached him he took my hand and led me out of the compound, supporting my left side so that I didn't appear to hobble as we walked through the gates and down the wide cobbled pavement to my father's house. Here he handed me over to another man, and without a word turned his back and ascended the staircase to his rooms above.

My new guardian stood still until he heard the click of a door closing somewhere up above, then turned so that I could see him properly. His face had a gentle look, with none of the coldness that characterised my father's expression. His eyes filled with concern, which is not surprising, as I must have looked frightful, grimy as I was, spattered all over with blood and shivering with cold. At once he took off his cloak, and wrapping me in it picked me up and carried me back outside, along the pavement, and into another house. There he put me down in front of a log fire and set about heating water.

It was the first hot bath I had ever had. I had, naturally, watched my mother bathe many times, but I had never been permitted to join her. For some reason the prospect set me shaking with apprehension, and when the man saw this he rubbed his chin thoughtfully, then went over to a sack in the corner of the room and pulled out a huge apple. Taking a hunting knife from his belt he cut it into small pieces and held one out to me. I stopped shaking and stood, frozen, mesmerised by that piece of apple. It was no more than a yard from my nose. I could smell it, and I had to swallow to stop myself from dribbling. Yet I could no more have reached out and taken it than I could have flown up to the ceiling. When he realised that I wasn't going to move he smiled, pressed the titbit into my palm and gave an encouraging nod. I stared at it, still hardly able to believe that it was mine, and then, in one swift movement, I stuffed it into my mouth and swallowed so fast that I almost choked.

The man seemed to think that this was amusing, because he smiled again and made little shushing noises through his teeth. It was the first sound I had heard him make, and I started to wonder whether perhaps he couldn't actually talk. He held up another piece of the apple, but this time beckoned for me to come closer. I took a step expectantly, and he reached out with his free hand and stroked my head, making shushing sounds all the while. I was strangely calmed by it, and this time held out my hand to take the apple, making sure that I ate it a little more slowly.

By the time I was crunching my way through the fourth chunk of the fruit I was almost oblivious of the fact that I had been relieved of my old shirt and was standing naked on the hearth right next to the bath tub. I watched, fascinated, as the next piece swirled down to lie tantalisingly at the bottom of the tub. I took a deep breath, and gritting my teeth plunged my arm in, right up to my shoulder, and fished it out. The water was warm, almost inviting. To reach the sixth piece, on a low shelf behind the tub, I

13

had no alternative but to climb in. I hesitated, but desire soon got the better of fear, and with the man's gentle hand supporting me I clambered into the water.

I can't describe how wonderful it was, to sit in that delicious heat, dipping pieces of apple in the water to warm them, munching away while he rubbed me with all over with a rough cloth. My next treat was a pile of soft, black juicy berries. He fed them to me one by one as he cleaned my hair with vinegar. I whimpered once when the foul liquid stung my eyes, but I was altogether too intent on my next mouthful of berry juice to make too much fuss.

I was similarly distracted as he set about the long task of smoothing out all the tangles in my hair. It hurt frightfully, but just as a wild animal will submit to a painful touch that it knows may save its life, I held myself still, snivelling quietly because I couldn't help it, but not daring to open my mouth to scream in case I lost my precious supply of berries.

When he had finished he put a blanket round me and left me to dry in front of the fire while he went to fetch clothes. They were proper clothes – a little too big, but luxurious compared to the coarse gowns that my mother had dressed me in. There were deerskin trousers, a thick, warm woven shirt and even some boots, although they were several sizes too big. He saw this at once and disappeared for a moment, returning with two thick leather mittens with which to cover my feet. He helped me to dress and I rolled up the sleeves of the shirt, which were twice the length of my arms, while he tied the trousers securely round my waist using a leather thong. Thus attired, I sat down to a bowl of hot deer meat and a hunk of fresh bread, my senses reeling from the procession of luxuries that were being laid out before me.

That was the moment, I think, that I became my father's creature. Young as I was, I reached out for that brief mind contact he had given me, and held it to me as I would grasp a solid rock in a shifting sea. The strength of my blood had been proven by my survival, my mind already trained to endure all hardship without complaint. I came there fully formed in his image, hardened to pain, ignorant of love. My heart was locked deep within me, impenetrable, invisible. I was his perfect son, ready to be moulded as his heir.

Although I could not have voiced my feeling then, I was filled with gratitude for my release, just as I burned with hatred and contempt for the women I had left behind. Perhaps he placed those thoughts in my head during our brief communion. It is more than possible. Whatever the truth of it, I had but one ambition – to be like my father, to please him, to make him proud. From that moment I belonged to him, body and soul, and my yearning to see him again, to hear him speak, to feel his touch, made my stomach almost rise to my chest.

My host, meanwhile, waited until I had finished eating and was lying back contemplating the sensations of being both warm and full, and then he spoke at last. His voice, like my father's, was surprisingly soft, although it was clear from the words he used that he had little experience of speaking to children.

"My name is Morlain, son of Sovan, who is Lord Corvan's brother. I have been entrusted with your care and education until such time as your father sees fit to relieve me of that duty. His instructions are quite precise. We will begin tomorrow morning. Meanwhile, you may ask me anything you wish."

It took me a moment to absorb the fact that I had been spoken to directly. Moreover, my host was awaiting a response, an idea that filled me with dread. As I have said, I had been well schooled in the art of silence. Also, although I had heard Morlain's speech well enough, and understood the words, I did not really grasp his meaning. I did understand, however, that I had not felt so comfortable ever before in my life, so I cleared my throat and prepared to put to use the years of whispered practice beneath my blanket at the end of my mother's bed.

"Will I have to go home?" I asked, stumbling just a little over the words and flinching slightly at how loud my own voice sounded, but at the same time feeling a burst of pride at my achievement.

This made him roar with laughter, and for a moment I thought that my attempt at speech must have failed. When he had mastered himself, however, he became quite serious and said gravely, "If, by home, you mean the women's rooms, then most certainly you will not return there, at least not until you are a great deal older. That is no place for a son of the Family once he has no more need of his mother's milk. This is now your home, for the present, until your father decides otherwise."

His answer put me a little more at ease, but still unsure I asked, "Am I safe now?"

I half expected him to laugh at me again. But he did not, and said, "That is a question I cannot answer. No one is truly safe, the sons of our Lord perhaps least of all. But it is late and you need to rest. Come, enough questions for tonight. I will show you where you will sleep."

He got up and led me to a small room at the back of the house. It had its own little fire burning in the hearth, and a pile of thick furs in a corner, just under a small window. I suddenly felt wearier than I could ever remember, and sank down into the soft heap. He made sure that I was well covered and then, to my surprise, I realised that he was going to leave me alone there, that no guard had been called to watch over me as I slept.

I had never been alone before and I began to panic, but he came back to me and said, "Don't be afraid. See – the door is open, and my room is just along the hallway."

So saying, he left me, but I could not sleep despite my being so tired. After a while I got up and crept out and along the corridor until I reached his door. I did not dare to open it, but I could not stay in my room alone either, so I ran back to fetch one of the furs and curled myself up outside his door. There he found me, fast asleep, the next morning.

CHAPTER 2

It was a little before dawn when I was gently shaken awake.

"Come," Morlain whispered. "We have much to do."

It took me a moment to remember where I was, and that I could move freely about, untethered. He waited patiently enough, and I followed him as quickly as I could to the big room where I had bathed and eaten the night before. I was directed to a tub of cold water and shown how to wash myself and clean my teeth with a sharp stick. Then I was handed a comb and instructed in the correct arrangement of my hair, and how to tie it back in the proper manner.

This last procedure was completely beyond my capability, but Morlain showed no impatience as he watched my pitiful attempts to drag the comb through my hair. After five minutes I had only succeeded in creating fresh tangles, in between frequent glances at the sack in the hope of the appearance of more apple. Finally he relented, but to my disappointment made no move towards the sack. Instead he put his hand over mine and guided my efforts, being careful not to dig the comb's sharp teeth into my scalp. Then, moving behind me, he fiddled for a moment or two until I felt the weight of my hair resting firmly on the back of my neck.

"Don't worry," he assured me, patting my shoulder as he moved back into my field of vision. "You will have plenty of time to practice."

He helped me to dress, and then gave me a large hunk of honey bread and a cup of warm water containing some kind of herb with a strange but not unpleasant taste. Seating himself across from me, he began to outline the rules of my new existence as I ate.

"The sons of our Lord," he began, "must be perfect in every way. You and your brothers are the pride of the blood, and at all times you should present yourself as befits your position here."

He could see from my expression that I had no idea what he meant, so with a sigh he explained, "It is expected that you always appear clean and properly dressed. You should tie your hair as I have shown you, for it is the mark of your line, and distinguishes you from those of lesser blood. Each morning you will wash, and every evening you must bathe and oil your skin. Everything you do should be done without haste and with grace. In general, speak only when you have something of importance to say, and never betray your feelings in your voice. Always look others in the eye, and when they bow acknowledge their courtesy, but show no deference. To this rule there is one exception. You must never look directly at your father unless he commands it. To him alone you should bow, and then with the utmost respect. Now, you have much to learn, so for the moment you may speak freely to me and to any others that you meet in this house."

He stopped talking, and I must admit that I felt no more enlightened than I had before. I took a sip of the herb drink and asked, "When am I going to see Father again?"

"When it pleases him," he replied at once. "But not, I think, until you are fit for his eyes, which may not be for a time yet. He has ordered that you remain in this house and not be allowed to go abroad until you have gained some measure of elegance. After breakfast every day you will exercise until noon. Then, until the evening meal you will learn those skills that will prepare your body and mind to receive the gift, and to act in accordance with our law."

He was about to go on, but thankfully was interrupted by the appearance of a boy in the doorway. The newcomer was, I guessed, twelve or so years old, and I noticed that his hair was arranged in a series of neat twists held fast by an interwoven leather thread, the style that Morlain had earlier described to me, and presumably had arranged on my own head. Morlain got up, and to my surprise gave the boy a shallow bow.

"Welcome to my house, Ilvan. You honour us."

The boy nodded in return.

"The honour is mine." He turned to me and bowed. Although his face was almost without expression, I caught something that might have been humour in his eye, and wondered for a moment whether he had meant the gesture seriously. "I am honoured to meet you, brother Rendail," he said.

I was about to get up when Morlain reached across and put a hand on my shoulder.

"Remember what I told you," he whispered, and so I remained seated, inclining my head slightly and trying to keep the curiosity from my face. Morlain threw me a brief smile of satisfaction. "Good. You should learn quickly. I must leave now. I will return at sunset, and meanwhile Ilvan will guide you through your tasks."

Without offering any further explanation he disappeared, leaving the two of us alone. Ilvan stood in silence, waiting while I finished my breakfast, and then brought me a bowl of water so that I could rinse my hands. I could see that he was as curious about me as I was about him, but he said nothing. Things were becoming a little awkward, so in the end I asked, "Why won't you speak to me?"

He looked slightly embarrassed, even a little nervous as he answered, "Forgive me, brother. I would be happy to speak with you if you wish it."

"I do," I said, confused. "But why can't you talk unless I tell you to? Is it the same with everybody? Morlain didn't ask me first, and he's been talking a lot."

I saw Ilvan start to smile, but immediately he fought the impulse, and said, very seriously, "Cousin Morlain has been given leave by our father to speak to you as he wishes. I have not. Your rank is greater than mine, and it would be impolite of me to speak without your permission, unless it is about your daily tasks."

"Well, I want you to talk to me," I said, wondering if all my encounters with other boys would be like this.

"Would you like me to sit?" he asked, and I nodded, so he came to the low table and sat opposite me. There followed another silence. I was still very new to the art of conversation, and it took me a minute to realise that he was waiting for me to say something. I grabbed the first thing that came into my head.

19

"Do I have any other brothers, or are you the only one?"

"You are Corvan's twenty-ninth son," he answered at once. "I am his twenty-seventh. But of those there are sixteen living, including we two."

"What happened to the others?" I couldn't help asking.

He fidgeted a little, then replied, "When the gift comes, our father looks to see what we can do. If he thinks our blood useful he prepares a mate for us. If not ..." He shrugged. "I do not yet have the gift, but it will not be long now. Then he will decide whether or not I am pure enough to mate." Seeing my puzzled look his brow furrowed thoughtfully, then he added, "We all have the healing gift, but that is no longer enough to satisfy our Lord. We must also display greater strength and show that our power can extend far beyond our own bodies. With each mating he hopes for more and it is our task to try to please him, for the good of the Family."

I don't think Ilvan had any more idea of what that really meant than I did. There was a silence in which I thought about it, then I asked, "But if he doesn't decide until the gift comes, why is it that I have greater rank than you? I won't be old enough for a long time."

"Because in your case there is no doubt," he answered. "You have the purest blood, and when your gift comes it will be far greater than mine, or anyone's. At least, that's what Father says. Now he can't sire more offspring from your mother because he lost his temper ..." He stopped and looked away, blushing, then carried on, stumbling slightly, "I mean, he has decided that you are very precious to him. He has told us all that we must show great deference, but at the same time we must make sure that you are trained correctly in all aspects of our life. Those are his wishes at the moment, until he tells us differently. Now, if you will forgive me, brother, cousin Morlain has made it clear that you must complete all your tasks before nightfall, and if you fail I will be held responsible."

He rose and bowed his head again nervously, as though terrified of making a mistake. I followed suit, but remembering Morlain's words I simply nodded, which seemed to please him.

20

He asked me to wait and disappeared down the corridor, reappearing a moment later carrying a length of rope onto which had been threaded several small iron weights. To my dismay he proceeded to wrap the rope around my left leg, from the top of my thigh to my ankle, but not so tightly that it was uncomfortable. I sighed with relief when I realised that he had used the entire length, and that I was not to be led about by the rope as I had been by the chain.

"It is to help you balance," he explained. "You need to make your left leg stronger so that you walk correctly. You must wear the rope every morning until noon, and begin each day by climbing the steps to the top of the house four times."

Now it was a tall house, arranged on three floors, and to me the twisting stone staircase seemed endless. I took a few nervous steps, but was surprised to find that the rope was not too heavy and it was actually quite easy to walk. At least it was at first. It took me the whole morning to accomplish my task. Ilvan walked beside me patiently but gave me no help as the weights on the rope began to feel heavier and heavier and my leg began to ache so much that I could hardly move it.

I finally collapsed at the bottom of the stairs just as the sun rose above the highest window, signalling that it was almost noon. I was both exhausted and hungry. I lay still for a moment or two, and when I had recovered enough to sit up Ilvan carefully removed the rope.

"When can we eat?" I asked hopefully.

"Not until evening," he replied. "Our father was very precise about that."

I had to struggle to hide my disappointment, despite the fact that I was quite used to going without food. Water, however, was permitted, and I gratefully drank almost a full jug of it, resolving to eat more at breakfast the next day.

Then began my introduction to the intricate rules of Family life. I spent the afternoon practicing basic greetings, which changed from individual to individual depending on rank. There was the question of how to bow, and to whom (which in my case was not that difficult), how to respond politely, how to interrupt a conversation – in fact a formula for just about every interaction imaginable.

"Watch," Ilvan said, and walked to the far end of Morlain's long reception hall. "I am Morlain, and I have come to visit you in your house. Your servant lets me in, and he bows, like this." Ilvan dropped his chin almost to his chest and inclined his upper body. "Then the servant says; 'You honour us,' and lets me in. He conducts me into your presence, and bows again, then he waits in case you wish to give him further instruction." Ilvan repeated the bow. "Morlain doesn't bow to the servant, but when you look at him, he will bow like this." Ilvan repeated the gesture for the third time. "Do you see the difference?"

"No."

Ilvan had to go through the sequence several times before I noticed that the final bow was not quite as deep as the others.

"Good," he said, when I told him. "Now watch my eyes. When Morlain sees that you are looking at him, he will look back at you, just for a moment, then he must lower his eyes as he bows. Do you see? The servant must keep his eyes lowered all the time."

I nodded. "What if I don't look at him?"

"He will wait until you do. It is very impolite to interrupt someone of higher rank if they are thinking."

"How will he know if I'm thinking?"

I heard Ilvan let out his breath in a small sigh.

"He will know because you are not looking at him. Now, when he bows, he will say; 'You honour me, Lord.' You must not bow, but you nod, and you say; 'The honour is mine.' Then you may both continue to have a conversation."

We practiced this for half an hour, Ilvan first pretending to be Morlain, and then to be me, until he was satisfied that I understood.

"What if Morlain came to see you?" I asked, when we finally stopped for a rest.

"Ah! Then it would be different," Ilvan replied, clearly pleased with the question. "Although my rank is higher than Morlain's, it is not high enough for him to call me 'Lord'. If he

22

came to see me, his bow would be as deep, but not as long, and he would say; 'I am honoured, Ilvan.' If I were to visit him, as I did this morning, he would say; 'You honour me, Ilvan.' In either case, I would only give him a small bow, and say; 'The honour is mine, Morlain.'"

"What if I don't want to see him?" I asked.

"Then you would tell your servant, and your servant would give your greeting, and either ask him to wait or to come back later."

"What if I'm not in?"

"Then Morlain would not come to see you." I caught just a hint of irritation in Ilvan's voice, and decided to change the subject.

"What if I had a house and your mother came to see me?"

For a moment Ilvan looked aghast.

"A woman would never come to see you. It's not allowed. Women can never leave the compound. If men want to see them, they have to go there."

"Well, what if I went there, then? Or what if Morlain went there? What would he do?"

Ilvan shrugged. "Nothing. He certainly wouldn't have to bow."

When I asked why not, Ilvan's placid features formed themselves into a frown.

"It is not something I have ever asked myself," he admitted. "I suppose it's partly that females can't use their gift to cause harm, and so are no danger to us, as we males are to each other. But mainly it's because they simply exist to serve the blood. They have no other function. We care for them as we care for our horses, and it would not be sensible to speak politely to a horse."

As he finished speaking, Morlain appeared and announced that the evening meal would soon be prepared, and it was time for me to bathe. This time the water was cold, but I didn't mind that too much, and when I had finished, and Ilvan had helped me to comb out and arrange my hair, I was brought a flask of fragrant oil which I had to rub well into my skin all over. Fresh clothes had been brought, and I found that they had been made to fit me perfectly.

While I was dressing, Morlain questioned Ilvan on the progress I had made, and especially on how I had fared with the weights. I was made to walk up and down the room several times, after which he nodded his satisfaction.

"Good. In a month you will be able to walk with the proper grace. That will please our Lord."

Ilvan, to my disappointment, then bade us both a formal farewell and went off into the dusk. I was quite ravenous by this time, and would have fallen on my food, cheese and cold meat, like a wolf, had Morlain not forcefully reminded me yet again of the need for grace and lack of haste.

"Your body is the vessel of the blood," he said sternly, "and at all times must be treated with respect."

I curbed my enthusiasm and ate as delicately and as slowly as I could while he tested my memory of the forms of speech I had learned that afternoon. When I had finished he carefully examined my legs, and massaged the left one gently to ease the aching from the morning's exertion. Then I was ordered to my room and told firmly that tonight I was to stay there, for I had to get used to sleeping alone.

CHAPTER 3

So my new life continued, day after day of the same routine, sometimes supervised by Morlain but most often by Ilvan, who appeared during breakfast every morning, leaving as the evening meal was served. For some six months I was not allowed to leave Morlain's house, and by the end of that time I was almost unrecognisable. I walked perfectly with no sign of dragging my left foot. I was able to tie my own hair correctly and could use all the proper responses quite naturally without thinking about it.

At last, one morning, I was told that permission had been granted for me to go out into the settlement. My excitement was mixed with a good deal of apprehension, for my only sight of it had been on the evening that my father had led me out of my mother's room, and then it had been quite dark. So, when Ilvan announced that he was to accompany me I was inwardly relieved, and set about making myself look as perfect as possible. Morlain finally agreed that I looked presentable, and together Ilvan and I set off down the pavement in the direction of the south gate.

It was a fine morning in late April, and for several minutes I was almost blinded by the brightness of the sun. Everywhere there was noise and activity as the men went about the daily business of the place, some on their way out to hunt, others fetching grain, wood and water. The movement was dizzying, and several times I had to stand still to get my bearings. Ilvan stayed at my side, giving me time to get used to my new surroundings.

When we reached the iron gates to the central compound I stopped for a long time. I had never seen the place where I was born from the outside of the fence, and my first thought was how big it was. The great three sided building towered up around the courtyard, which was shaded from the sun except for perhaps a few hours of each day in summer.

There were several women in the courtyard, talking and drinking together, and children of all ages running about, coming and going quite freely through the gates, laughing and shouting to each other as they played. To my surprise some of the men joined in the games as they passed by, greeting the children by name and treating them with great care and affection. For a moment I felt an overwhelming urge to be a part of it, but a glance at Ilvan confirmed what I already knew, that such behaviour in one of Corvan's sons, and especially in this one, would be both inappropriate and dangerous.

We moved on, slowly making our way to the gate. The rough cobblestone pavement, so wide that it took me thirty strides to cross it, ran in a great square round the central compound. The distance from one corner to the next seemed vast, the pavement narrowing into the distance before turning to follow the line of the compound down to the next corner. The houses of the men, three storey buildings of roughly hewn stone, also formed a great square, their doors facing inwards towards the compound, the pavement in between. The favoured sons of my father and of Sovan each had their own house, Ilvan told me, together with personal servants and advisors that generally lived on the uppermost floor. Others of high rank would be granted an entire floor to themselves, while the weakest of our males, those in whom the gift showed little promise, lived two or three to a room and performed the settlement's more menial tasks.

The settlement had three entry gates, to the east, west and south. Ilvan explained that the west gate was seldom used except for the gathering of fuel, as it opened out onto a wide expanse of peat marsh, beyond which great purple crags stretched for mile after mile to the west and north. I wanted to go and see, but Ilvan politely refused, saying that it was a long way, and he didn't want to make me tired. The east side of the settlement was bounded by a wide valley through which surged a great, fast flowing river, fed by the rain that streamed down from the high crags. In places the river separated into smaller, shallower streams, and it was from these that we were able to gather abundant supplies of fish. The river was also a perfect hunting ground for other game – deer and the occasional boar that came out of the forests and down to the banks to drink.

The far bank was bounded by dense woodland, beyond which the crags rose again, serving as a perfect defence against intrusion by the neighbouring settlements, but more importantly to my father, as a barrier that prevented unwanted attempts at escape, particularly by our women. Such politics were way beyond my understanding then of course. The east gate, however, was on our route, and Ilvan took me to look out over the valley, the vastness of which made me feel quite giddy. There were gatherings of creatures on the near bank of the river, more than I could count, and all the size of rats, I thought, from my high vantage point at the gate arch. Ilvan explained that they were horses, and that we used them for riding and pulling loads. The idea puzzled me, but I didn't question it. They were left to roam the length and breadth of the long valley, constrained by the river and the crags, but twice every year they were counted, and the most promising caught and taken to the southern meadows to be trained and put to use.

We continued on our way, and every so often people we passed would bow their heads in greeting. Although no one was so impolite as to stare, I could feel their thoughts directed at me in curiosity. At last we passed through the south gate and made our way down to the grazing fields in the valley. Once more I find myself struggling to describe the thoughts that went through my mind as I first saw, then touched the grass in the meadow.

The earth was soft, so unlike the stones of the pavements or the floors of the houses, and the trees that had looked so small from the east gate arch towered above me, the woodland growing denser on the far side of the well fenced fields. It all seemed very unreal to me, and I was sunk in fascination, so much so that when a full grown horse trotted towards me I did not notice until it was only a few feet away. I caught the movement out of the corner of my eye and looked up, only to be overcome with terror at the sheer size and power of the beast, which could easily have crushed me with just one stamp of its hoof.

I leapt away and must have cried out, then, seeing that Ilvan had not moved and was regarding me with a rather contemptuous smile, I drew myself up shamefacedly and

27

composed myself, trying to stand still and not tremble. Ilvan realised that I had seen his expression and immediately turned his head away. At the same moment a man jumped over the fence at the far end of the field and strode purposefully towards us. At first I thought it might be my father – he was about the same height, and held himself with the same air of easy authority. But as he drew nearer I saw that it was not so, although he was very similar in appearance, and the three twists in his hair signalled that he was of the same line. He stopped in front of me and bowed curtly.

"I am Estoran, son of Corvan. I am honoured." I nodded in return, and formalities out of the way he rounded furiously on Ilvan. "You dishonour us, brother! It is not your place to pass judgement on Rendail, and I will make sure that our father hears of your lack of courtesy."

How Estoran had managed to see Ilvan's brief expression I had no idea, or perhaps he had taken something from my companion's thought. Whatever the case Ilvan turned quite pale and fixed his eyes on the ground, not daring to say a word. In the silence that followed I felt my own temper begin to rise, and before I knew what I was doing I said, being careful not to raise my voice, "No you won't."

Estoran froze, forgetting his manners completely and staring at me with his mouth open.

"But …" he began, and I cut him off.

"Because if you do," I went on, "I will tell him that you let a horse loose in the field and that it nearly trampled me to death. I don't think he would be very pleased to hear that."

The effect was dramatic. It was Estoran's turn to look apprehensive. He took a pace backwards and bowed, although I could see that he was controlling himself with an effort.

"I was … unmindful," he said quietly. "Please forgive me, brother."

Ilvan raised his eyes and looked from one to the other of us uncertainly, until Estoran finally nodded towards him and said, "I spoke in haste, Ilvan. Please forget my words."

"I would be honoured," replied Ilvan, returning the nod, while I stood by, amazed at the power I seemed to have to order everyone about, even a brother as old and as powerful as Estoran. At that time, of course, I had no experience of the capriciousness of my father's moods. Later I would learn of the very real dangers that lurked behind even the most trivial slip of the tongue or wayward glance. Everyone, it seemed, even Estoran, had been ordered to treat me according to the protocols governing interaction with a high ranking adult, regardless of how I behaved in return.

My anger meanwhile had leaked away and I was becoming quite fascinated by the horse, which was now standing quietly eating grass. It was a beautiful creature, muscular and glossy black, and I could see from the fine intelligence in its face that it would not have harmed me.

"May I see?" I asked Estoran, and he smiled briefly, telling me to stand quite still and watch. As if in response to a silent command the horse stopped eating, raised its head and walked slowly right up to me.

"You are quite safe," he said, patting the animal's neck affectionately. "I raised him from a foal, and he will obey any command I give him without question. If you wish you may sit in front of me while I ride him."

I did wish, very much, and said so. Estoran leapt onto the creature's back and pulled me up in front of him. As the horse broke first into a brisk trot, then into a canter, I think I experienced my first glimpse of real happiness. My only thought was to be up on a horse of my own, alone, guiding it silently with my thoughts as Estoran did with such skill, not even needing a rein to control its movements. I was bitterly disappointed when, after half an hour or so, I was lowered gently back onto the ground.

"When will I be able to have my own horse?" I asked, still mesmerised. Estoran smiled approvingly, and when I glanced across at Ilvan I saw that he was smiling openly as well.

"As soon as you wish," Estoran replied. "Lord Corvan requires that you learn all the skills of our people as rapidly as possible, and it is very necessary that even our young boys ride well. You may choose a pony now if that is your wish. But be careful, for it is said that the qualities a man chooses in his horse reveal much of his inner nature."

Looking at Estoran's beast I could quite see that this could be so. Both were lean yet muscular, handsome and graceful – his was a horse for fast riding, not one for carrying burdens or trotting in front of a cart.

"I chose him just hours after his birth," Estoran explained as we walked across the fields to the stables. "As soon as he was weaned I took him from his mother and trained him to respond only to my thought. Now it is as though we were one creature, and he obeys my commands almost before he hears them. My life has spanned that of some fifteen horses, but I would go far to find another like this one."

We skirted round the main stable block and came to a field just behind in which a dozen or so ponies were frisking in the spring sunshine. They were all lean and sleek just like Estoran's horse, only quite a bit smaller, more suited to my size. I wanted to go into the field, but Estoran explained that the ponies had only been gathered from the valley the previous day, and that until they became used to the touch of men they might be too dangerous to approach.

My eyes were immediately drawn to a pure white animal right in the middle of the field. He was slightly taller than the others, and when the sun shone on his mane it shimmered a startling blue. My brothers followed my gaze and Ilvan commented, "Yes, he is by far the finest of the gathering. But I judge he has a fiery temperament and will not be easily broken. What do you think, brother Estoran? Brother Rendail is still very small for such a powerful pony."

Estoran nodded and considered for a good while. Finally he said, "It is an impressive choice. Lord Corvan has already singled this one out for breeding and has said that he may not be ridden. Nevertheless I will inform him of Rendail's choice when he comes to the stables tomorrow morning, so that he may make the decision."

Reluctantly I allowed myself to be led away, and we spent the rest of the afternoon touring the stables and watching the horses in the neighbouring fields. We arrived back at Morlain's house as dusk was falling, and I could hardly eat for wondering what my father's decision would be.

Unable to keep silent I confided my preoccupation to Morlain, who simply shrugged and said, "There is no purpose in letting your thoughts be taken up by events that you cannot influence. Such things use valuable energy and make you weak."

Nevertheless, all night long the image of the white pony tossing its head, its mane glinting blue in the sunlight, remained before my eyes and I hardly slept a wink, or at least that is how it seemed. The next morning I was up almost before the sun and had already breakfasted and groomed myself by the time that Ilvan arrived. He was actually very late, which made me even more anxious and put me in quite a temper, although I was careful not to show it.

"I am commanded to say that you must gather your belongings and follow me," he said with no more than the most cursory greeting. It was clear from whence the order had come, so I did not argue but went to my room and gathered together my blanket and spare clothes, which were the only things I could have called mine. Morlain had already left, and I asked Ilvan how long I would be gone, and whether I would be able to tell him where I was.

"He will know," Ilvan reassured me, and so we set off once more in the direction of the stables.

Set at right angles to the main block was a long row of dwelling houses, all just one storey high, their doors facing out onto a large earth yard fenced off from the fields.

"The guardians of our horses live here," Ilvan explained. "They oversee our herds, control all aspects of an animal's preparation, and as a rule decide to whom a particular horse should be given. Brother Estoran is the greatest of our horse masters. We have been ordered to attend him at his house."

When we reached the first door, however, it lay open and it was clear that Estoran was not at home. Ilvan shrugged and walked in quite confidently, down the long hallway to a door at the other end of the house. He opened it and stepped aside so that I might go first. At the back of the house was another small field, and as I walked through the door I felt my heart leap. Estoran had the white pony on the end of a long rein, holding firm as it kicked and stamped, tossing its head against the restraint. He turned and bowed to me, gesturing for me to keep still, and I did so, still clutching my clothes wrapped in the blanket.

I stood, completely absorbed, as Estoran played the animal gently and patiently, shortening the rein little by little until finally it stopped its protests and came to rest no more than three feet from his hand. It was still unsure, I could tell by the nervous movements of its head, and he made no move towards it in case it should become startled. He stayed quite still for a long time, then carefully gestured for me to put down my bundle and slowly come to join him in the middle of the field. It was not until then that I realised that Ilvan was no longer behind me. I was too eager to meet the pony to wonder about it though, and did as I had been bidden, walking up to my older brother as smoothly and as quietly as I could.

We stood together for a while until the white pony was quite calm, and watching us without any sign of fear. Then Estoran, holding tight to the rein, stretched out his arm to stroke its neck. It shied away at first, but seemed to learn quickly that it was not going to be harmed. Within minutes he was able to walk right up to it, and to my surprise the pony craned its head forward and pushed its nose into his hand. The reason soon became clear, however, when he revealed a piece of apple on his palm. I saw then that he had a pouch at his belt filled with berries and tiny apples. I was reminded of the way Morlain had coaxed me into my first bath, and I suddenly felt an understanding of the beast flood into me, touch me in a way that none of my own kind had done up to now. We were the same, the pony and I, both learning the rules of a strange new world. We would learn together.

"Come, Rendail," Estoran said in a low voice, and held out an apple to me. I moved up to him and held out the treat as I had seen him do, keeping my hand flat so that the pony could take it easily. I fed it apples and stroked its neck, or at least as much of it as I could reach, while Estoran kept a tight hold on the rein in case it should take fright again and rear up. After a while he said, "We should leave him be now. I have worked him since dawn and he needs to rest. We will do more tomorrow."

Reluctantly I nodded, and watched from the doorway as Estoran removed the rein and my glorious white pony cantered off to the far end of the little field, kicking high to celebrate its regained freedom.

Once inside, Estoran picked up my bundle and showed me to a comfortable little room with a window facing out onto the field, where I could watch the pony from the small window. There were coarse woven mats on the floor, a small low table, and a large pile of furs one corner.

"You will sleep here," he said, and then beckoned for me to follow him into a much larger room, where we sat on the floor next to the hearth, and he poured me a large cup of apple juice. "As you have probably gathered," he said when we were both settled, "Lord Corvan has consented to your choice. I believe, although I may not presume to voice our father's thoughts, that he found your choice impressive."

I felt suddenly proud that my father should be so approving, and at the same time filled with a longing to see him, to show him how well I looked, how clean, graceful and well mannered I had become.

"He is aware of all that happens to you," Estoran went on, answering my thought. "He will see you when he desires to do so. Meanwhile, he has decided that you have learned enough from Morlain, and that your time would be better served here with me. There is more to survival here than appearance and good manners. We pride ourselves on our skill with horses, and in the hunt. Unless we have no alternative we do not use our gift to provide us with sustenance. That is a matter of honour."

So began the next stage of my education into the ways of the Family. Estoran, I learned, was more than three hundred years old, the oldest of my living brothers. His blood was strong and he had a powerful gift, but great as it was it had shown no sign of any other enhancement. In addition to his being the oldest of us, he was also, or had been up to now, our father's favourite. That he had been accorded the rare honour of being able to mate freely with whatever woman he chose was proof of his position. He had, by his reckoning, seven sons living, and nine daughters, all of whom were considered to be of good blood. My appearance must have been a terrible blow to his status, but for the most part he showed no sign of it. Throughout the years that followed he constantly pushed me to the limit of my endurance, but at the same time he ensured that I was well cared for, that I became skilled in all that my father desired me to learn.

CHAPTER 4

For five years I remained with Estoran and the horse masters. They were hard years, and in the beginning lonely ones. The warmth and comfort of Morlain's house were gone, but more than that I missed the company of my brother Ilvan. The emotion of loneliness itself meant nothing to me, being, as it was, beyond my understanding. I did understand, however, that Ilvan had provided a window through which I could view my new world, and that without him I was, initially at least, plunged back into darkness.

On the first day, I left off the task that Estoran set for me, of preparing a stall for my new pony, cleaning and lining the floor with straw, then trimming and polishing a new leather rein for its bridle. Ilvan had not appeared after breakfast as I had come to expect, and so after an hour of raking straw I left the stables and went to wait at the foot of the path leading back up the hill to the south gate. When Estoran found me he did not seem unduly surprised, and gently ordered me back to my work.

When dusk fell I returned to his house, hungry and exhausted, to find the evening meal set out, but no sign of my guardian. His servant, a stable hand roughly twice my age, politely informed me that I was to wait in my room until his return. I waited for what seemed a lifetime, tormented by the scent of deer meat broth warming on the hearth, impatiently wishing that Estoran would come back soon so that we could eat. When he did finally return, however, he gestured for me to follow him and walked out and down to the stables.

When we arrived at the stall I had prepared he turned to me and said, "You must know, brother Rendail, that Lord Corvan is aware of all that you do. He has asked me to make clear to you that when I speak it is with his voice. If I command you, it is his command. To disobey is to act against the Rule. Do you understand this?"

I nodded, not quite sure what was coming next.

"Yes, brother Estoran, I understand."

"That is good," he said. "Today, you did not obey my command. Our father expects you to be perfect. He is very angry that you went against the Rule. Therefore," he went on, and as he spoke he took down the newly polished rein from its hook on the wall, "he has commanded that you have no food until the morning, that you are to be whipped, and that you must sleep here in the stable tonight. In the morning you will wake ready to strive for perfection. That is, if you do not wish to disappoint him."

Later that night as I huddled in the straw hardly able to move, my stomach growling with hunger, I resolved to prove to my father in any way I could that I was perfect. Now that Ilvan was gone, the only solid thing that remained in my life was my desire to see Lord Corvan again, to show him that I was worthy of his attention. I shifted slightly, biting my lip as the cruel welts across my back burned like fire. The pain was oddly comforting. It was my reassurance that my father watched over me, was aware of everything that I did. However hard my life was going to be, one thing was certain – I was not going to disappoint him.

When Estoran came to the stables the next morning, dawn was still some way off. In answer to his question I admitted that I had been unable to sleep. His eyes narrowed, and at once I felt ashamed that I might have broken yet another of my father's rules. He did not seem angry, however, and knelt beside me, telling me to keep quite still. Very carefully he placed his hands on my shoulders and at once I felt the pain start to ease. I realised that he was using his healing gift, just as Morlain had done when he had nightly soothed the ache that the leg weights had caused my strengthening muscles. Estoran's gift, however, was much more powerful, and within minutes the soreness in my back had all but disappeared.

"Our Lord requires you to ride," he said, matter of factly, "so you must be well rested." He reached into the folds of his cloak and produced a flask of water, followed by a large hunk of bread into which had been pressed a thick slice of cold meat. "Eat," he said, "and sleep. I will wake you when all is ready."

As I drifted into sleep my mind was filled with only one thought. My father had commanded that I was to ride my pony.

He was no longer angry, and had given me my heart's desire. I would ride my pony, and I would be perfect.

It was many weeks before I was finally master of my white pony, and at the end of it my brother had mended my broken bones more times than I could count. Estoran was not unkind, but neither was he companionable. He had clearly been given leave by our father to speak to me freely, just as Morlain had done, and just like Morlain, Estoran was always polite, but firm and distant. Unlike Morlain, however, Estoran had also been given leave to beat me whenever he felt like it, or so it seemed. Even on those numerous occasions he always bowed his head politely as he outlined the nature of the latest imperfection that had caught my father's attention.

When I was not riding or hunting I toiled at the stables, cleaning the stalls, preparing the mounts of men who came down to hunt, feeding and watering the beasts on their return. I might be called at any hour of the day or night to help tend to a sick animal, refill mangers or water troughs, or join the night watch who stoked the perimeter fires, keeping vigil against marauding wolves. In addition to those duties I was tutored every evening by Estoran in the use of bow and knife. I forgot the meaning of fatigue, learned to take sleep whenever I could at any time of the day or night, to do without food, and drink from handfuls of snow in the winter. Even the slightest failure resulted in the swift sting of a rein across my back, but I do not remember feeling any resentment, only the burning desire to do better, to make my father proud.

By the time I was eleven years old my body had become as hard as hazel shell, my honeyed skin stretched tight over a fast growing frame of bone and muscle. I was tall for my age, and broad shouldered, but not gangly. I was quick and supple, a better rider than many of the men, and at the tender age of nine I had brought down my first stag. Since the beginning I had been the only child outside the compound, at least the only one that I knew of. The youths that were sent from the compound to the stables began their adult lives when they were twelve or so, plucked from behind their mothers' skirts to stand trembling in the stable yard, in fear of their lives as the horse masters outlined the rules of their harsh new world.

That fear was not unfounded. The country beyond the settlement was wild and unforgiving, blanketed in snow sometimes for six months of the year. A hunting party in winter might be gone for several days, and it was not unusual for an inexperienced young one to fall behind, get lost and freeze to death in the snow. Occasionally an enthusiastic but foolish boy would try to impress his masters by bringing home fish, only to fall and be swept away by the swift currents underneath the ice. When the thaw began in spring it was the task of the younger ones to wade chest high into the streams to drive the fish towards the hunters. Deaths from shock and creeping cold were not unknown. Yet more of the unwary were taken by wolves, the only creature that even a grown man would not confront alone.

These losses meant little to us. They were merely a part of the natural selection process, a culling of the unfit. For those who survived the physical rigours of their first year in the adult world, however, another hurdle to manhood awaited them, one that was even more dangerous and unpredictable. Every newborn child born within the settlement was examined by Lord Corvan for signs of development in the nature of the dormant gift. Those who survived that examination were subjected to another at age thirteen or so, when the onset of puberty forced their gift to the surface. If a boy failed that test he was never seen again.

The fact that the same transformation would soon happen to me was not something that I thought about often. When I did, I can't remember feeling anything more than a mild curiosity. I had but two ambitions; to please my father was one, and the other was to become a master of horses, like Estoran. His gift to control the beasts was beyond compare, and I envied the ease with which he could command his own treasured mount, without either word or movement. The only creature for which I had any depth of feeling was my beloved pony, and I longed for the power that the gift would give me to shape its thought to mine. I knew nothing of the process of transformation itself, and so did not fear it as some did, nor did it ever occur to me that the coming of my gift might also signal the end of my short life.

These children – for so they seemed to me, although I was still younger than any of them – would stare at me in awe as I flaunted my skill in the training fields, standing on my pony's naked back to shoot arrows at apples hung in the tree branches as it galloped and plunged over dead trunks and ditches.

I knew that Estoran did not approve of my habit of providing the young ones with such entertainment. For one thing, it kept them from their work, and for another, I laid myself open to public failure, something that I vaguely knew would anger my father. But I was young, and strong, and the thrill of stretching myself to the limit exhilarated me. The pleasure did not last long, however. I was out just before dawn on a particularly cold morning, showing off to a small group of boys detailed to break the ice on the water troughs. The frost caked grass was treacherous, and my pony lost its footing and threw me as it slithered into a section of the perimeter fencing. I landed badly and twisted my ankle, much to the amusement of my audience. I don't know which was worse, my sore ankle, or the humiliation of being tittered at by youngsters, most of whom wouldn't survive the coming winter.

I was sitting, ruefully trying to decide the question, when Estoran appeared out of nowhere. One look at his face told me that up until then, I had really not considered just how bad things could get. He was shaking with rage. It occurred to me then, that as Estoran was solely responsible for everything I did, my father would hold him to blame for any mischief I might get into, sanctioned or not. He strode up to me and pulled me to my feet, at the same time calling for all the stable boys to be assembled in the yard. I gritted my teeth against the pain in my ankle as he dragged me through the gate.

Once there, he called on two of the older grooms to tie me securely to a post and stood by, his face impassive now, as the pair of them took it in turns to give me the most terrible thrashing with thick, tightly plaited whips, the kind we used on stubborn carthorses. Even the boys who had secretly wished for me to be knocked down a level or two stopped grinning and stood silent, their faces pale with shock and terror. I knew that if I made a sound my humiliation would be complete, so I pressed my lips together and kept my eyes on the stony figure of Estoran as I felt the blood streaming down my back.

I was left alone, locked in my room, for the rest of the day. When Estoran came to me in the evening his anger seemed to have dissipated. I even saw his brow furrow slightly as he surveyed the damage. As he worked on my ankle he told me of my father's pleasure at my show of discipline and the skill of my horsemanship, and as I listened, I felt my heart almost burst with pride.

Not long after that, I was given leave to explore the settlement alone when I was not busy elsewhere. The only place I was forbidden to go was to my father's house, which, I found, was guarded day and night by two watchful servants at the door. It was understood, of course, that it was not permitted to enter the central compound, and I admit I had no particular desire to do so given the nature of my early life there. It did not occur to me to dwell on the sudden and violent death of my mother – indeed, I saw it only as a good thing, a service that my father had done me in releasing me from my captivity among creatures of less worth and interest than the horses.

I was forbidden to enter my father's house, but not to look at it. Quite often on these rare excursions I found myself drifting towards it, walking slowly past, trying to look as though I was on some errand or other. I would never have dared to stop and stare, but always secretly hoped that Lord Corvan might emerge so that I could catch a glimpse of him. He never did. My only memory of him was of the night I left the compound, and that memory had become almost lost over the years.

His house was the largest in the settlement, and had an arched entrance with two great wooden doors that were always kept firmly closed. Two tall servants kept a constant watch outside, chosen purely for the strength of their gift. It was clear that they took their duties seriously, for their eyes were never still, but flitted constantly along the length of the north pavement, alert for anyone approaching the doors.

Once or twice I felt their baleful gaze on me as I walked past, and found myself trembling even though I had a perfect right to be there. I did notice, however, that the north pavement was generally not as well used as the others, except by the men and servants who lived in the other houses. Morlain was one of these. His house was some six doors away from my father's, in the direction of the east gate. It was a great honour to be accorded the right to dwell close to the head of the Family, although also, I later found out, it was an honour not altogether appreciated by some of the inhabitants.

Morlain was the son of my father's brother, and he, together with one or two of his older sons, had been shown favour so that my father could keep a better eye on their comings and goings. I did not know it then, but it must have irked Morlain considerably to be put in charge of the welfare of Lord Corvan's chosen heir.

The first time I went past, I had a sudden urge to see my old tutor, to look on the place I had called home, even if it had only been for a short time. I stepped towards the door, and at once it opened, as if his servants had been watching me from behind the cracks in the shutters. They bowed low, and we exchanged the usual courtesies, after which I was shown into the room where I had experienced my first bath, and the gentle touch of another human being. I felt an unexpected dizziness. I was asked to wait, and found myself thinking how small the room looked now. The stairs, that had been my only exercise for all those months, one leg weighed down by lumps of iron, didn't look as intimidating as I remembered. I could have run up and down them all day, now, without even breaking a sweat. I hadn't seen the place for more than four years, of course, but in my mind I had expected my perception and memory to be the same.

I was so lost in my recollections that I didn't notice how long I had been kept waiting. It was only later that I realised it was far longer than would be considered polite. At last, Morlain appeared, his expression almost blank. He bowed, and said, "Lord

41

Rendail. Your presence honours me. Is there something you require?"

I don't know what I had expected. A lump rose in my throat at his distant greeting. I had wanted him to do what I knew he could not – smile, perhaps take my hand in greeting. I pulled away from my childhood self and bowed in return.

"The honour is mine, cousin Morlain. I thank you for admitting me to your house."

He didn't reply, but gave me a cold, shallow bow, just on the right side of politeness. I realised that he was waiting for me to state my business, but all of a sudden I had nothing to say. This man had bathed me, fed me, cured my limp and prepared me for the outside world. He had been more of a father to me than Lord Corvan, or Estoran, and as I watched him, I knew with certainty that he hated me. If it had been within his power, he would have struck me dead. As he gazed at me, his look was one of utter contempt. I swallowed, and forced my voice to remain even as I said, "I simply wished to see these rooms – to refresh my memory. It has been a long time …" It was a feeble explanation, and we both knew it. I saw his lip curl briefly in a dismissive smile.

"You are welcome to tour my house, Lord. You will forgive me if I do not join you. I have urgent business, a matter that your father has asked me to attend to."

"Of course," I replied. "Lord Corvan must not be kept waiting."

He bowed again and, turning, strode out, leaving me with the servants, who fidgeted in discomfort. I gave them a curt nod, and with a last look round the room, strode out and quickly up the pavement to the next corner. Once there, I collapsed against the wall, dizzy with the effort of containing my emotion. I had not realised I would be so affected. I forced back the tear that had unexpectedly come to my eye. I would not shame myself in my father's eyes, even when I was alone. And I was alone, completely. I understood that now. I straightened, took a breath, and walked on.

I also met a number of my brothers on my travels up and down the pavements. Castillan was Lord Corvan's twenty-sixth son, a gentle creature, handsome, lean and graceful, who never looked anyone in the eye when he bowed. He reminded me of the cows that we kept to provide us with milk – always groomed until their hides shone, their large eyes blinking innocently as we reached for their udders to relieve them of their milk. Kyrolan, just two years older than me, was a pale, thin boy who had been given as a servant to my father's third son, Safim. He scuttled down the pavements like a little hairless rabbit, constantly glancing fearfully behind him in case his master should be watching.

Once, the boy stopped to bow to me, and I saw Safim come running out to hurry his servant along by means of a volley of well aimed pebbles. Kyrolan, caught between the two of us, simply froze, quivering pitifully, and it was only when Safim strode furiously up the pavement that he noticed me and stopped, unsure what to do.

Having dismissed Kyrolan I made full use of my status to give Safim a voluble lecture on elegant behaviour and good manners, ending with a thinly veiled threat concerning my interest in Kyrolan's well being. The next time I saw the boy he seemed just a little better fed, and held himself with a greater air of dignity as he gave me his bow. Estoran told me that my father had only suffered Kyrolan to live on Safim's request, the reason for which puzzled me until several years later. I was still young then, and in many important respects ignorant of the ways of men. Another year went by, and finally, when I had just passed my twelfth birthday, Estoran came to me with the news that I had awaited for so long – I was to make ready to greet my father.

CHAPTER 5

I stood alone in the great entrance chamber of my father's house. The doors had closed behind me and the only light was from the torches on the walls, whose flickering turned the shadows into all manner of threatening shapes that lunged towards me out of the darkness above. I had never been frightened by the dark, but here in this house even the stones under my feet seemed possessed of their own menace. Estoran had been gone a long time. He had told me firmly to stay where I was before striding confidently up the broad staircase to my father's rooms above. I began to think to myself that it was strange how I had so longed for this moment, and yet now that it had come I wanted to be anywhere but where I was.

At last I heard footsteps, and Estoran reappeared.

"You are to go up," he said, and with a nod walked past me out of the house, the doors closing behind him. I took a deep breath and slowly climbed the stairs.

The door to my father's room was shut, but as I approached, it was opened from the inside and I was momentarily dazzled by the bright sunlight that streamed out onto the landing. When my eyes had become accustomed to the light, I saw that I was not the only one to have been summoned into the presence of the head of the Family. With a little jolt I recognised Ilvan – it had been he who had opened the door – and realised that it was the first time I had seen him since the day he had left me at Estoran's house. He was five years older now, and his eyes had darkened almost to black, the sign of the coming of the gift. I remember feeling slightly surprised that I was almost as tall as he was, and equally as broad shouldered, despite my being five years younger.

He gave no greeting save for a deep bow, his eyes lowered as though he had been forbidden to look at me. Standing in the centre of the room was my brother Castillan, who was just a year or so older than Ilvan, and it struck me at once how similar they looked now that Ilvan had grown. They stood aside as I entered, and I stopped just inside the doorway, staring straight ahead at the imposing figure of Lord Corvan himself, who stood by the window with his back to me, seemingly unaware that I was there.

There was a long and heavy silence, but at last my father turned his head and flicked me a glance, then resumed his study of whatever had caught his attention outside.

"You honour me, Lord," I said, and bowed, and waited.

There was another silence, in which I began to be afraid that I had not spoken correctly, or that there was something else I should say. But finally I heard a sigh and he turned round, fixing me with a stare so intense it made me shiver. He raised a hand and beckoned for me to come forward. I obeyed, and when I was within arm's length he gestured for me to stop. He proceeded to examine me closely, lifting my chin to see my face, prodding my arms and shoulders to test the firmness of my body, running his fingers through my hair.

His perusal went on for at least five minutes, ending with my walking up and down from the door to the window and back several times, before a gesture once more bade me stop. Then, at long last, I heard his voice, low and sweet as I remembered it from that night in my mother's room.

"Stand beside me, Rendail. You may call me 'Father'."

"I am honoured, Father," I replied, and did as I was told.

"Now," he said, putting an arm around my shoulder and lowering his head so that our eyes were level, "there is a decision that must be made, and I have decided that you must help me."

"Yes, Father," I said, wanting to please him more than anything else in the world at that moment.

"Good. You see your two brothers here?" I nodded, and looked at Ilvan and Castillan, who were standing side by side now, quite motionless, their faces betraying nothing. "They are weak in the blood," my father went on. "They are an insult to my line. However, today I am feeling generous. One of them may live, and it is for you to decide which of them it shall be."

Whatever else I had prepared myself for, it was not this. I looked from one to the other, horrified. There was no appeal in

45

their eyes, no change in their expressions. I realised then that both had entered the room with no thought of ever leaving it. Castillan I did not know well. We had greeted each other now and then, he behaving always with perfect politeness towards me, but we had never held any sort of conversation. Ilvan, on the other hand, had been my almost constant companion for the entire time I had stayed in Morlain's house. But that had been a long time ago, at least it seemed so, and as I have said, we had not met again in all that time.

Nevertheless, my mind told me that if I had to choose, as my father had commanded me, then his would be the name on my lips. But I couldn't utter it.

I tried to look as though I was considering, then said, "Please forgive me, Father, but I don't have your wisdom. One may be a little stronger than the other, and I might make a mistake in my choice."

My father tilted his head to one side, his eyes becoming just a little harder, if that was possible. Then I saw a faint smile, and he said, softly, "You are a very clever boy. You impress me. But you have made your choice, have you not? I see it in your thoughts. They have seen it too. Is that not so, Castillan?"

"Yes, Lord," my brother replied in a gentle whisper. My father was still looking at me, his arm around my shoulder. I felt a little shock run through me, and heard the dull thud as Castillan's body hit the ground.

Lord Corvan got up and stood aside. Ilvan looked as though he might collapse at any moment. I don't know how he managed to stay on his feet, but somehow he did, his face rigid with concentration.

"You owe your brother a life," my father said calmly, addressing Ilvan.

"Yes, Lord." Ilvan was unable to hide the slight tremble in his voice.

"You now belong to Rendail," our Lord continued. "He may use you as he wishes, for whatever purpose he desires. Your continued existence is within his gift." Then he turned to me again. "I have prepared rooms for you. Come, follow me."

46

With that, he swept out of the room without a glance at the dead body of Castillan, and I had to almost break into a trot to keep up with him. Ilvan stayed where he was until I realised that he was waiting for my command. I beckoned to him, and soon the three of us were making our way down the pavement to what was to be my fourth home since I was born.

The house was just three doors away, and the entire first floor had been set aside for my use. There was a large living area, soft matting stretching from wall to wall, and a low table in the centre. The big window looked out over the great crags and the northern end of the valley, just like the one in my father's house along the pavement. There were two other rooms for sleeping and a smaller one used for storage of pots, blankets and water jars – all the things that were needed for comfortable living. I was introduced to two men whose task it was to ensure that I always had sufficient food, water and wood for the fire. To a twelve year old boy used to the frugal manner in which the horse masters lived, these simple rooms seemed luxurious. There, my father left me, with instructions to attend him two hours after dawn the next morning.

As soon as he had gone I felt suddenly awkward. My two servants, assigned to me from my father's household, towered over me, one on each side of the door, while Ilvan hovered behind me, his eyes on the matting. For a full minute no one moved. Realising that no one was going to unless I did something, I drew myself up, and ordered the servants to bring food for Ilvan and me, and enough wood to last until morning. After that, I told them, I wanted to be alone. To my relief, they both bowed at once and disappeared.

The food arrived quickly, and as soon as we were alone again I gestured for Ilvan to join me at the table. He obeyed, reluctantly, and I noticed that he had untied his hair, removing the three twists that denoted his position as one of Corvan's sons. The table had been piled high with bread, meat and cheese, but it was only when I saw it before me that the events of the morning took shape in my mind, and suddenly I no longer felt hungry.

47

Neither, it appeared, did Ilvan, and we both sat for some time in uncomfortable silence.

Finally, Ilvan's voice broke in on my brooding.

"Am I permitted to speak, Lord?"

I nodded, but kept my eyes firmly on the table in front of me. The image of Castillan, alive one minute, dead the next, filled my whole vision. It was not as if I knew nothing of such things. I had awakened many times to find a familiar face missing from the training fields, or seen one of the young ones struggling to fulfil his duty to his masters, knowing that he had not the strength, that his days were numbered.

But Castillan was a son of Corvan. He had enjoyed my father's favour for as long as I could remember, and I had often been filled with envy that my brother had been taken to live in our Lord's house, that he had seen him, perhaps spoken with him every day. It had not saved him. My father had plucked him from the world as easily as he might pluck an eye from a cooked fish at table. What was even harder to swallow was that it had been my choice to send my brother into the void. What if, when my gift came, my father was disappointed?

"Do not be concerned." Ilvan's soft voice broke in on my thoughts. "It was what Castillan desired. I felt his relief that your choice went against him. I, also, am grateful, for unlike Castillan I did not wish my life to end. It will be my honour to serve you, Lord, in any way I can, for as long as it pleases you."

The fact that my older brother and former friend addressed me as though he were speaking to our father made me very uncomfortable. However, I understood enough to know that as far as Corvan was concerned Ilvan was no longer of his blood, but simply my personal servant, and that Ilvan spoke only as protocol demanded. He seemed quite at ease with the situation, unlike myself, but of course his outward demeanour meant nothing, and as yet I had no gift to see beyond his calm expression. What he had said, however, made me look up, startled.

"Castillan wanted to die? Why? He wasn't much older than you – than me – not even grown up. I don't understand."

Now, in my short life I had witnessed many things that in other places would be considered unimaginable, but not once had it occurred to me that anything might be so terrible as to make me want to end my life. But that life was only just beginning, and in those days I had much to learn.

Ilvan had not answered my question. He sat still with his eyes lowered as though he might ward off my curiosity by avoiding my gaze.

"You must tell me," I insisted after a long silence. Ilvan became uneasy.

"I don't think Lord Corvan would permit ..." he began nervously, but I cut him off, suddenly angry.

"My father has said that you belong to me. He has said that you must do as I command, and I command you to answer me."

Ilvan raised his head and, for the first time in the eyes of any man of the Family, I saw sadness there, a deep well of it that he couldn't hide despite his efforts to remain impassive. Instinctively, I lowered my voice.

"Please," I whispered. "You must."

I had no idea of the dilemma in which I had placed my former companion. He was my servant, and to disobey my command was to act against the Rule. To obey me, however, would mean to speak of my father in a way which was also against the Rule. He hesitated, his dark eyes studying me intently. He was using his gift, weighing up the risks that lay in his unenviable choices. I waited, not understanding his struggle, but anxious not to get our renewed acquaintance off on the wrong foot.

At last he nodded, his decision made, and began, haltingly at first. As he went on, though, his voice regained its calm, the sadness melting into a glow of recollection as he told me of his own childhood and that of Castillan, our brother.

"We were of the same mother, Castillan and I. We were born less than a year apart. From the beginning he was a gentle, sensitive creature. Everything frightened him. Even the distant howl of a wolf in the night would make him wake, shivering. He loved our

49

mother deeply, and was hardly ever away from her side. She knew, I think, that life for him would be brief, and so she strove to make what time she had with us as carefree as she could. I was around eleven years old, Castillan almost twelve, when our father came to see us for the first time.

"Castillan was so terrified at the sight of him that he lost his mind. He screamed and kicked, and to our horror struck out and caught our father's face with his fist. Lord Corvan, though, simply laughed. When he had calmed himself he said, 'I will take this one. He amuses me. In one year, send the other to me.' Castillan pleaded to be allowed to stay, but of course it did no good, and we watched, helpless, as he was hauled away.

"Some two months before the day that would signal the end of my true childhood, Estoran came striding into my mother's room. My first thought was that Castillan was dead. He was not, but my initial relief was short lived. Estoran had been sent to fetch me and I was to join my brother at my father's house. Something was wrong, but what, he wouldn't say.

"I was hustled up the stairs and into Lord Corvan's private chamber. There, I found him pacing up and down in a fury the like of which I had never seen. When he saw me he stopped dead, fixing me with the most terrible glare, so frightening that I almost forgot to bow. When he spoke it was not to me but to Estoran, his voice a deadly whisper. 'Fetch the boy.' Estoran disappeared, and a moment later he returned, dragging Castillan behind him.

"At the sight of him I almost wept. He was in a pitiable state, half starved, his eyes bright with terror. He was trembling so much he could not stand, but fell to his knees the moment Estoran released him. For a moment I forgot that our father was there and, lifting Castillan gently to his feet, I tried to reassure him. But Lord Corvan yanked him away, and holding him upright by the scruff of the neck turned to me and hissed, 'Do you know what this creature has done? Not only has he refused to obey my command, he has sought to end his own life rather than fulfil his obligation to me. He has insulted me and dishonoured this Family. It is intolerable.'

50

"He twisted my brother's head round so that he was forced to meet the eyes of his tormentor. 'You will not die,' our father said, 'however much you wish it. Your brother will ensure that you don't. Your brother will also ensure that you follow whatever command I give to you. If you do not satisfy me, I will hold him responsible. Do you understand?' I saw Castillan desperately nod his head. 'Now,' our father said, turning to me, 'take him out of my sight. He will eat and make himself presentable to me. He will be ready when I call.'

"'Yes, Lord,' I managed to reply, and found my brother thrust into my arms. I almost carried him along behind Estoran, who led us up a flight of stairs to a small room at the top of the house and left us there, Castillan clinging to me, his body heaving with despair, while I sat, wondering what was going to become of us now.

"We were brought bathing water, clothes, perfumed oils and trays of meat, cheese and bread. I managed to get him into the bath, which seemed to calm him a little. It wasn't until I had helped him to dress, and made him eat a little, that he calmed down enough to tell me what had happened."

Ilvan paused, and looked at me apprehensively. It was clear that he was unsure of me, and even though I had commanded him to speak he was consumed with fear of what our father would do if he learned of the disclosure. Given what I had heard so far, I well understood his reticence. As I sat, thinking over what he had said, several things struck me at once, not least the fact that despite my apparent position within the Family I was probably no safer than any other member of it. When the gift came to me, it was as likely to be the cause of my downfall as of my survival. I couldn't have said at that time that what I felt was any kind of affection, or even friendship, for the boy who had been my brother and was now my servant. Those terms meant nothing to me then, having experienced neither in the way that these two brothers had done. I only knew that I felt less alone when Ilvan was present and that I wanted him to stay close to me, to act as my source of understanding of those things beyond my knowledge, just as he had in that short time all those years ago.

51

We had been left wine, well watered of course, and I poured some for myself and my companion.

"My father has said that you are weak in the blood," I said carefully. "He has said that you are no longer his son. What he has decided is the law in the eyes of the world. But here, in this room, when we are alone, we are brothers, and I wish us to speak together as brothers, as equals. You will know my secrets as I will know yours, and perhaps in that way we can help each other."

Ilvan looked up at me, once more intent. I knew that this time he was using his gift to divine whether or not I was trying to draw him into some kind of trap. I met his gaze steadily and waited, until at last he acquiesced and murmured, "You honour me, Lord."

"It isn't a matter of honour," I replied at once. "I need you. Tomorrow morning I must attend my father. If I know what our Lord might want of me I can be prepared and less likely to make a mistake. I don't have to remind you," I continued, perhaps unfairly, "that you are now my servant. If I fall from my father's favour, then so do you. So, will you help me?"

Ilvan's eyes widened, surprised perhaps by my stark statement of our position. There was much that I didn't understand, but I was certainly no fool. At last he bowed his head.

"I can give you no advice as to our father's desires," he said with a resigned shrug, "but I will keep nothing from you, even though what I say might turn you against me."

"Why would it do that, if you tell me the truth?" I asked.

Again he held my gaze, his expression that of a stable boy who hears the soft tread of a wolf and knows that his next step will be his last.

"Because what I am to tell you concerns you as much as your father, and when you learn what was in my mind you may not think so well of me, or wish us to remain brothers. But I believe that already you are wiser than our Lord, and value truths that he can't perceive."

Now, I will not deny that I was shocked by this statement, but it also showed me that Ilvan had taken me at my word and for good or ill had placed his trust in me. So I nodded for him to go on, and after a deep draught of the wine he continued.

"Two nights before, Castillan had been called to Lord Corvan's private chamber. That was not at all unusual. In the time since he had been taken away, our father had used him as a servant in the house, calling him at all hours of the day and night so that he was hardly able to sleep for more than two hours at a time.

"On this particular night, another of the servants was sent to fetch him, and he was told to bathe and put on fresh clothes to attend his master. This he did, and found our Lord sitting quietly in his room, alone. He was told to sit and given a cup of wine. Castillan became frightened, knowing that our father would not offer such kindness without a price. Our father didn't take his eyes from Castillan as he drank, but looked him up and down, then walked around him, studying him closely.

"Finally our father sat down, and said, 'I have an heir. At last I have sired a son whose blood will be pure. Through him the gift that I have desired will be revealed, and my ambition will be fulfilled.' It was as though he was talking more to himself than to Castillan. He sat for a while, his thoughts seemingly far away, then he suddenly turned to my brother and went on, 'Therefore I have decided that it will not further the blood to take another woman. My line is assured, and any other offspring that I might sire can never be as perfect as Rendail. You are a pretty enough boy, and so I have decided that from now on your sole function in this house will be to attend to those needs that I can no longer satisfy elsewhere.'

"At first Castillan did not take Lord Corvan's meaning. Such things were way beyond his grasp. But as it became clear what was now required of him he panicked completely and tried to escape from the room. It was useless of course, and when it was over and he was finally released he was escorted back to his own room and instructed to rest all the next day in case his Lord should require him again.

"As the day wore on he became more and more agitated, and when, after nightfall, he was commanded once more to attend

53

our father, he couldn't bear it and tried to hurl himself from the window of his room. Naturally he was prevented, but at least, for that night, his protest had the desired effect. Our father was so angry that he simply beat him and left him chained to the wall in the corridor outside his room. It was the next morning that I was summoned, and so there we were, together, placed in the most impossible of situations, with no way out of it that either of us could see.

"As Castillan spoke I could see a change slowly come over him. The fear seemed to leave him, to be replaced by a calm that worried me more than anything I had seen so far. 'All my life' he said, 'you have looked after me. I am the elder of our mother's sons and it should have been my duty to care for you, my younger brother. Now I have placed you in danger because of my weakness. You love life, Ilvan – I would do anything to end it. But it is my turn now to protect you, and if I can do that, perhaps my life will have value again. After all, it's not so bad a thing that I am being asked to do, and perhaps our Lord will tire of me soon and we will both be released, you to your life, and me to the end of my miserable existence.'

"I pleaded with him, but to no effect, and I watched as he dressed and anointed himself with the utmost care. From that moment on all his terror seemed to disappear. It was as though he gained, almost overnight, a dignity and grace that I would never have thought possible before. It was true that he was a most beautiful creature, and when the gift came to him less than a year later, he was much admired throughout the settlement for his physical appearance despite the weakness of his blood. Everyone knew of the services he performed for the head of the Family, and he quickly became known as 'The Lord's Folly'. Nevertheless, Castillan was left untouched now, except when Lord Corvan desired him, and was not required to do anything but tend to his appearance, for it was common for him to be called at any hour of the day or night. So things remained, and while outwardly my brother was the very image of perfection, he confided to me often that he wished it all to be over so that he could gain his much desired freedom from life.

"Around a year after I had joined Castillan I was called to attend Lord Corvan. He told me that he had a special task for me. It was the day that you were released from the compound and brought to Morlain's house. We all knew of you, of course, and of what you had endured since your birth. We also knew of Mira's fate, and Castillan in particular was filled with admiration for her defiance and her cleverness. She had deliberately provoked our Lord, and unlike my brother had been successful in fulfilling her desire to be free of him. Lord Corvan was naturally incensed that he had been so manipulated, but by then it was too late – your mother was dead, and you were removed from the compound before your time, to be raised by the men of the Family until such time as you were ready for your father's attention.

"I was told that I was to become your companion and tutor for the time that you remained with Morlain. By the time I got back to our room I had decided what I should do. I said nothing to Castillan, but my path seemed clear to me. You were the unwitting source of all my brother's suffering. If you did not exist, our father would once more seek his pleasure among the women in the compound. So, I decided that at the first opportunity I would kill you, and then, one way or another, Castillan's trial would be ended."

Ilvan paused again, and his eyes met mine with an absolute calm, so that for a moment I thought I must have misheard him. But I hadn't, and I whispered, "Why didn't you?" I thought that if I had been in his position I would not have hesitated, no matter what the consequences to myself. I knew that it was not a question of courage either. Ilvan had already shown me that he possessed more of that than I think my father understood.

For a second his face melted into a smile. "When I saw you," he said, "I realised that you had already suffered at least as much as Castillan and me. More, I thought, because for a short time we knew the love of our mother and the freedom of childhood. You had not asked for the strength of your blood You were dangerous, even then, but you were also the source of great hope. Supposing I had done what I had planned? Lord Corvan might have sired more offspring, and perhaps one with your strength but without your wisdom. For you *are* wise, Lord Rendail. I can't help but let my gift see your mind, and when it is your turn to rule you will take account of more than simply the purity of the blood. When the gift comes to you, you will understand a great deal that is hidden from our father, and fear will not be your only weapon.

"Even then, before I could see such things, I somehow knew it, but more simply than that, I realised that no matter what the cause I could not harm an innocent child, much as I loved my brother. When you went to Estoran and my time with you was over I told Castillan what had been in my mind. I was glad then that I hadn't acted, because he made me see just how ill conceived the idea had been. Lord Corvan's reaction to your death would have let loose a whirlwind, and who knows how many other innocents might have been hurt. 'One life,' my brother said, 'is not worth so much destruction. Besides, if you are right about Rendail, the future of this Family will rest with him, and we must think of all those who are not yet born.'

"And that is how things were until last night, when Lord Corvan called for my brother for the last time. As they lay together afterwards, our father said to him, 'Tomorrow, Rendail will come to this house. If he is to rule after me, then it is time that he began to learn the ways of power, and I must devote myself to his preparation. Therefore, I release you from your service, and your brother also. Go now and spend what time is left with him. In the morning, my heir shall decide whether or not your greatest wish shall be granted.'

"Castillan came back to me and we spent the rest of the night awake, knowing that it was to be our last together. We both believed that neither of us would survive to see out another day. In our father's eyes we were not strong in the blood, and I had seen brothers of a much greater gift than ours removed forever from Corvan's line. When we learned that one of us was to live I felt Castillan's joy, for he had no doubt as to which of us would be chosen. I felt happy for him, and in the last moment, with his silent voice he asked me to give you his thanks for your choice,

56

and to tell you that he gave his life willingly for the furtherance of the blood."

There was a long silence in which I sipped my wine and watched Ilvan as he took some cold meat and bread. His movements were elegant, almost feminine, and I could partly understand how it was that my father had found Castillan an attractive companion. I also realised that Ilvan had given me a most precious gift, one that my father had not the ability to recognise. In speaking as he did, my brother had placed his life in my hands, not through fear or any kind of coercion – he could have lied to me, or at least not revealed the entire truth – but as an offer of loyalty, a signal of trust. I bowed my head.

"Your words honour me," I said. "I am grateful."

"It is I who am honoured, Lord," he replied, "and you should not speak so to one who is your servant, even when we are alone. But will you permit me to suggest that you take food now, for you have not eaten since early morning, and it is getting quite late."

CHAPTER 6

"What should I do?" I asked, as I combed out my hair and watched Ilvan tend to the fire. I wished that I could take him with me, but of course it was impossible. I had been instructed to attend my father alone, and not to put too fine a point on it, I was terrified. Hard as it is to believe, it was my first real experience of the emotion, and I found it very distasteful, to the point where I was beginning to get quite angry with myself, or at least with my body, which did not seem to be paying any heed to my mind. When the gift comes, I thought, it will be different. But at that moment I was not altogether sure that it would be. Ilvan turned to me, and putting down the poker went to the table and poured me cup of herb tea.

"Do you mean, how should you behave in your father's presence, or what should you do about your fear?" he asked, settling himself on the mat and regarding me steadily.

"Both," I snapped, then, realising that he was trying to help, I sighed and sank down opposite him, and muttered "neither," then, pathetically, "I don't know."

"You should drink this, Lord," he said, and I took the cup from him grudgingly. I swallowed, and at once both my temper and my nervousness receded a little.

"What is it?" I asked, taking another mouthful.

"A mixture of herbs, Lord," he replied, "with just a little mistle leaf. My brother used to drink it often when he knew he would be called before Lord Corvan. It helped him a great deal, I think."

The mention of Castillan sent my stomach into a riot again, and I had to put the cup down to hide the fact that my hand was trembling.

"Please, Lord, don't be concerned," Ilvan said at once. "It was not my intention to imply that you suffer in any way from my brother's weaknesses."

This was ridiculous. With an effort I mastered myself and drank another large draught. Ilvan was right – it was helping a great deal.

"My advice, Lord," he went on, "is simply to do everything that your father requires you to do, no more and no less. However, at times it can be difficult to know what precisely it is that Lord Corvan requires. If that is the case, you should not seek to understand his wishes, but respond openly in the hope that what he hears pleases him. He will know a lie before it is spoken, and that will anger him."

"Well?" my father demanded, pacing towards me, hands behind his back, an almost contemptuous smile paying about his lips. It was difficult to make a careful consideration with his eyes boring a hole straight through my head, but I resisted the temptation to say the first thing I thought might be acceptable, and after a pause I said, "I want to see my pony. If I could be anywhere at this moment, I would be at the stable, with Estoran."

His eyes narrowed slightly, then I saw him break into a broad smile.

"Then tell me," he said, raising an eyebrow questioningly, "why is it that you would prefer the company of your horse to that of your own father?"

"I did not say so, Father," I replied bravely. "My pony is valuable. You said so yourself. I don't trust anyone else to look after him as well as I do. If anything happens to him you will be angry, because he is to be put to the mares this spring. I want to see him, but I would like it better if you came as well. Then I would not have to make the choice."

There was a short silence, after which my father gave a short exclamation of delight, and said, "You please me, Rendail. Tell me, are you afraid of me?"

"Yes, Father," I answered, because it was true.

"What makes you afraid?"

"That I might not please you."

"Then you have no need to fear. Would you like to hunt with me today?"

"Oh yes, Father."

"Then come. You are right. Your pony is very valuable to me. We will go together."

My father's skill both with a horse and in the hunt was breathtaking. I had never seen such elegant mastery of an animal, nor such speed and accuracy in the chase. He made no allowance for my age, nor for the fact that my pony was so much smaller than his great black gelding, so my head was spinning with exhaustion when at last we came to a halt on the edge of the pine woods across the valley. It was late afternoon and still early in the year, so the light was beginning to fade rapidly. In an hour or so it would be quite dark. Together we had cornered and brought down a young stag, and in addition to that I had contributed half a dozen rabbits.

I was sent to fetch firewood while my father set about skinning one of the rabbits. I suppose I must have wandered a little further than was safe. Under the evergreen canopy it was already hard to see more than one or two feet ahead in the gathering gloom. My only warning was a soft rustle behind me and somewhere to the left. It was enough to make me swing round in alarm, just in time to see a great black shape leap towards me, blotting out what little light there was left. Tired as I was I managed to hurl myself backwards, throwing the bundle of sticks that I had gathered towards the creature in the hope of confusing it. For a vital second it seemed to check itself in mid flight, and instead of landing right on top of me I heard a thud as it hit the ground beside me. At the same time a terrible pain shot up my right leg, so that I cried out in shock.

I had no time, though, to think about what damage might have been done, as the beast was on its feet and I found myself staring straight into the eyes of a huge wolf, its great fangs bared, its jaw so close that I felt the hot saliva dripping onto my face. What happened next I am not quite sure. I remember somehow finding my hunting knife in my hand, and I lashed out with all my strength at the thing, my blade tearing into its neck, but not deep enough to find any vital parts.

60

It was enough to make it draw back, but only far enough to gather itself for another attack. It was in pain now and too enraged to be turned aside. I gripped the knife tightly in both hands, knowing I would not get a second chance, and as it launched itself at me I closed my eyes and thrust my arms straight up into the air above my face. I felt the blade sink itself into the animal's flesh, the weight almost wrenching my arms out of their sockets as the body quivered and fell sideways. I didn't let go of the knife, and when I finally opened my eyes I found myself lying across the belly of the corpse, my knife buried to the hilt in its chest.

I think it must have been some time before my senses returned to me. I felt weak and dizzy, and had to force myself to even move my head. Surely my father had heard the struggle, I thought. Surely his gift would have told him that I was in danger, that I was injured? But I heard no sound, no help coming to me through the dark. I knew as well as anyone that where there is one wolf there are many, and that I had to move, get to somewhere safe before this one's pack mates arrived to avenge their comrade's death. I forced myself onto my knees, gritting my teeth against the awful pain in my leg. I did not look, but I knew that I was losing a great deal of blood, and it was that as much as anything that was making me light headed.

Refusing to leave my knife, I tugged at it until it at last came free and stuck it into my belt. Believe it or not I then set about gathering up my sticks. It became of paramount importance to me that I should not go back to my father without them. Perhaps it was delirium, perhaps instinct, but slowly and painfully I managed to gather up a good armful before hauling myself upright and trying to see which way might lead back to the woodland edge.

I was about to give up and sink once more to the ground when my eye caught a faint gleam of light. At first I thought I must be dreaming, but as I made my way towards it, there was no mistaking the flicker of a flame a few hundred feet away through the trees. I desperately walked on, and as I drew closer caught the unmistakeable scent of roasting meat. A moment later I emerged into the clearing to see my father sitting calmly by the little fire, tending to the cooking rabbit.

He turned to me, annoyance clear in his expression, his eyes daring me to let show any sign of weakness. I was certain then that he had followed my struggle from start to finish with his mind, and that he would have let the wolf tear me to pieces rather than come to my aid. By an effort of will I stayed still and returned the stare, until finally he gave his attention back to the rabbit, gesturing for me to put down the sticks and come to the fire. I obeyed, and lowered myself gingerly onto the grass. For perhaps an hour we stayed there – my sense of the passage of time had deserted me. My father handed me some of the meat, and although I had never felt less like eating, the nourishment helped to clear my head a little. My leg had lost all feeling, and it was as though there was a cloud all around me, obscuring both my vision and my hearing. Eventually he got up and kicked earth over the fire.

"Come," he said, "it is time we returned home."

So saying, he leapt up onto his horse and spurred it immediately into a trot. I wasn't sure I could stand, let alone mount my pony, but I knew I had no choice, and so somehow scrambled up and urged the beast to follow. I have no memory of the ride. I only know that my thanks went out to the creature that knew my mind better than I did, carrying me faithfully homeward, taking care that I did not fall. When we reached the settlement my father dismounted at the stables, and not waiting for me to do the same he handed the rein to a waiting groom and set off on foot back to the south gate. As he passed, he said quietly, "It was a good hunt. You please me, Rendail. Rest tomorrow – the day after, attend me at dawn." The last thing I remember as everything darkened around me was being lifted from the pony and laid on the cold grass.

"My Lord?" The voice seemed very far away. I felt a cool touch on my forehead, and opened my eyes. It took a moment for the room to come into focus. The shutters were closed and there was a warm fire in the hearth. I tried to sit up, but felt dizzy and sank back into the soft pile of rugs.

"Not so quickly, Lord. Let me help you."

Ilvan raised my head gently and put a cup to my lips. The infusion of herbs was fragrant and hot and I drank gratefully, then let him put folded blankets behind my head so that I could sit up.

"How did I get here?" I asked, surprised at how little strength was in my voice. Ilvan lowered his eyes, blushing, an answer more eloquent than any words. "You carried me? All the way from the stables?"

He nodded. I could imagine what a struggle that must have been, for he did not have anything like the strength of a man like Estoran, or my father. Yet when he spoke, it was to say, "You must forgive the weakness of my gift, Lord. The wound was deep, but touched no vital parts. You only need to rest now for a while, and eat, and you will feel better. Another might have brought you back to your strength much more quickly than I."

"There was no other," I replied. I had a sudden urge to embrace him, but he quickly got up and went over to the fire. He brought me some warm broth and bread, and as I took the bowl he brushed my hand. Our eyes met, and in his I saw a clear and urgent warning.

"You must remember, Lord – I am here only to serve you, nothing more. That is my honour, and your father's wish." The last words were spoken with a slight emphasis and I understood at once.

"I will remember," I said quietly. "I will survive, and one day I will rule, and I will not forget."

"Why?" I asked. I had slept, and eaten again, and it was getting on towards evening. I felt much stronger and was examining the long, rapidly healing wound that ran right from my hip almost to my ankle. I had been lucky. Had the wolf not been deflected in its flight it would have taken my leg in one bite. As it was, my flesh had simply been torn by one of its sharp fangs.

"I cannot answer, Lord," Ilvan replied with a shrug. "Perhaps you should ask your father that question."

And so I did, the next morning, when I presented myself before him as I had been commanded. He fixed me with his customary stare, the eyes entirely without warmth, without emotion of any sort.

"Tell me, Rendail – what are you feeling?" he asked, reaching out and stroking my cheek. "Are you fearful, or are you angry? What lies beneath your voice?"

I thought for a moment. It was true, I felt more anger than I did apprehension, but aside from that, there was something else that I could not quite place. I closed my eyes and studied the sensation, tried to capture it, recognise it. My mind wandered back to my earlier conversations with Ilvan, and with a suddenness that made me gasp inwardly, I realised the full meaning of what he had been trying to tell me. What my father despised above all else was any notion of attachment, of affection.

For the sons of Corvan the bond of brotherhood was of all things the most forbidden, the most dangerous. My mind drifted back to my first day at the stables, of the cruel beating I had received for venturing forth to look for Ilvan. For the first time I understood the nature of my imperfection, and why I had been punished so severely for it. And of course, between father and son the very idea of such a relationship was unthinkable. My father's world had no place for friendship, or loyalty, or love. The society that he had created was ruled only by the blood. All other considerations were of no value to him.

In my inner heart, I had entertained the idea that my father was a man to whom I could offer the faintly stirring spectre of affection that Ilvan had awakened in me. As we hunted together I had found myself drawn to him, as a son, in the normal way of things, might be drawn to his father. But within the Family, such offerings were not the normal way of things. I also understood, in some vague way, that my father's gift of Ilvan as a servant had been – and very likely still was – a test of my worthiness, my suitability to rule. I had dared to touch a thing that, if I was to survive, was untouchable, so having touched it I closed my mind to the possibility and returned my father's gaze.

"I am surprised, Father, that you should risk the loss of such valuable blood. What if I had been killed by the wolf, or died on the journey home?"

"Then," my father replied, "you would not have been my son and your blood would have been valueless. As it is, you pleased me greatly, and you also learned a valuable lesson. Never allow yourself to become unwary, even in the company of those you trust, for you may be sure they will betray you, if not by design, then by misfortune."

We were walking down the pavement by this time, and after a short silence he asked, "How do you find the servant I gave to you? I trust he satisfies your requirements. If he does not, you have only to tell me and he will be removed."

Whether or not this comment was in some way linked to the previous one I could not tell, but knew instantly that I was on dangerous ground once more.

"He serves me well," I answered non-commitally. "You honour me with your gift, Father." I paused, and then, deciding to take the risk, I continued, "But surely, Father, as you gave him to me to do with as I wish, should I wish him removed it would be my task and not yours. I must command my own household, just as you command yours."

At this, my father laughed out loud.

"That is true," he said, his eyes showing a rare glimmer of delight. "The gift will be with you soon, Rendail. I can tell. And when it comes, you will command more than just your own household. I see that I chose well. Your brother Estoran has great strength, although yours, I am certain, will be greater. But of all my sons none possess your cleverness, and that will enhance your gift still further."

We had reached the gate of the compound, and my father casually seated himself on the wall, motioning for me to join him. We sat together for a while watching the women in the courtyard. Children were playing nearby, but I no longer felt any desire to join them as I once had, on the first day that I had walked outside with Ilvan. I got the feeling that some of the mothers would have called their offspring inside if they had dared, but none of them wished to draw our attention to them and so they stayed as far from us as they could without appearing impolite, every so often glancing uneasily in our direction.

My father seemed to enjoy the effect of his presence on the women, and when a stray child, a boy of around three or so, wandered up to us, he carefully picked it up and sat it on his knee, much to the consternation of its mother, who I saw half rise, her face stricken with anxiety. He stroked the child's head and looked into its eyes, then very deliberately put it down again and watched as it toddled off to safety, the mother trembling with relief.

"Estoran's youngest son," he commented lightly, at the same time fixing the mother with a cold stare as she gathered the boy into her arms. "He should not have taken her. The child will be of no use, neither to me nor to the blood. I will give him another year, and then I will decide. Perhaps I should dispatch the mother with the child, for I fear Estoran is too attracted to her. To mate too often with one woman is dangerous. Tell me, Rendail, what would you advise?"

"The boy may have a use," I replied, thinking of what might have happened to me the day before, had it not been for Ilvan. "The woman is not important. But I think you should not allow Estoran so much freedom. He mates with anyone he chooses. When I am older, I will be more careful and not take the matter of the blood so lightly."

My father stared at me for a minute, then nodded thoughtfully.

"You are right. The distinction between quantity and quality is something that my son appears to have forgotten. I have afforded Estoran too many favours, and it is time he remembered his purpose here. His skill is with horses, so let him remain with them. If his desires overwhelm him he must find his contentment with the stable boys. Meanwhile, I agree. The weaker ones have their uses as you wisely point out. After all, the boy is not deformed. The woman, however, may serve a purpose by her death. If nothing else it will show Estoran the error of placing personal considerations above his duty to the blood."

We stayed there a while longer, watching in silence. I felt uncomfortable, being so close to my birthplace, and was then too young to imagine that it might contain anything more appealing than the unbroken misery that I had endured in the first years of my life.

I was lost in the distasteful memory when my father finally rose, and did not notice that he had moved until I heard him calling to me from a few yards along the pavement. I pulled myself back to the present and rushed to his side at once, on which he placed an arm around my shoulder and said with a smile, "When the time comes, I will make Estoran your guide to the delights of your mother's former home. By then his appetite will have grown enough for him to teach you all you need to know, and more."

The idea pleased him so much that he was still smiling to himself when we reached the fields beyond the south gate. To my relief there was no sign of Estoran, who must have been away hunting. At once one of the horse masters came up to us, and a long discussion ensued on the subject of the stock and the state of several new foals. My father examined them all carefully, asking my opinion now and then, after which we took refreshment in one of the houses overlooking the training fields.

Despite my love of the horses, which was one thing I knew I shared with my father, I could not quite pull myself away from my earlier reverie. The sections of a puzzle were beginning to fall into place, but still there were vital pieces missing, and I knew, to my frustration, that if I could only find them my chances of survival as well as my understanding would be greatly increased.

I became aware that my father had been watching me for some time, his face set like flint. I began to panic, realising that he had been following my every thought. His voice, when he spoke, was so quiet as to be hardly audible.

"We are more alike than you think, Rendail. In less than a year you will discover just how much you are your father's son. You are right – I will preserve your blood, for there can be none now to replace you. But take care that your cleverness does not make you wish you had never been born."

In answer I simply bowed my head. The room was deadly quiet, and I could feel his inner struggle with his temper, but at least he had confirmed what I had already concluded. There was something in my blood so valuable that he would never risk my death, despite his words of the morning. But more than that, I had recognised his greatest flaw, the thing that he denied even to himself. In all his life he had loved but one thing aside from the blood – his daughter, Mira, my mother. She had rejected him utterly, and had suffered and died for it. I understood in that moment that her death, my father's greatest error, had saved my life, but my heart did not soften towards her as a result. If anything, the knowledge made me angry that her hatred of him had made my early life so miserable.

Without thinking, I looked up at him and said, "It is my honour to serve you, Father."

I saw him relax, and after a pause he nodded and said, gently, "You must leave me now. I wish to ride alone. When I want you, I will call."

I got up obediently and went to the door. As I reached it, I heard him speak to my mind, the first time he or anyone had spoken to me with the silent voice.

"Have patience, Rendail. The gift will answer you before too long." I nodded, and made my way slowly back to the south gate.

CHAPTER 7

Time passed, the stream of days seeming to flow together, my father's influence dominating every aspect of my life regardless of whether or not he was actually present. Every aspect, that is, except one. Each morning when I woke, Ilvan was there, the fire lit, the morning meal set ready for me. Likewise, if I was out all day, I would return in the evening to find food ready and fresh water for me to bathe. He moved around the place like a ghost, invisible except when I required him, and then he would be at my side almost before the thought was in my head.

If I was fearful, which I admit I was at times, he brought me wine and calming herbs. On the occasions that my father's temper ran away with him and I came home bruised and bleeding, he was ready with his gift. It was as though in a way I had taken the place of his lost brother, for he could not have cared better for Castillan than he did for me. After the evening meal it was our habit to talk, as we had on that first night when my father gave him to me, and I asked him once how he could be content, stripped of the position that he once enjoyed, now no more than a servant. He shrugged and answered, "I am happy to serve you, Lord, for in doing so I serve the blood." Then, with a faint smile he added, rather insolently I thought, "Besides, I think I find my current position far more comfortable than my previous one." Raising my hand to the still tender bruise on my cheek, I had to admit he had a point, and found myself completely unable to be angry with him, much to my frustration.

The winter of my thirteenth year was a particularly harsh one. Game was scarce, and the hunters' boys were sent out, day after day, with picks and shovels to try to hack holes in the river ice. The task was a thankless one. In places the streams were frozen right down to the mud, and the catches so small it was hardly worth the effort. Every man in the settlement was diverted to the vital task of gathering enough food to keep us all from starving. Our best hunters ranged far beyond our usual territory, some gone for a full turn of the moon, returning with whatever they could find, even small birds.

Although Lord Corvan was counted among the best of our hunters, he did not accompany the main expeditions, preferring to oversee the labours of those closer to home. He and I went out daily, my father's presence spurring the groups at the river to greater efforts before we both set off to raid rookeries, dig out rabbit warrens and bring home whatever else we could find.

The gravity of the situation, however, did nothing to curb my father's volatile nature. One morning, we were preparing to go hunting for fish beneath the ice of the west stream that split from the main river on the far bank just below the pine forests. To say that Lord Corvan was in a foul temper was probably an understatement. He had mislaid his favourite hair clasp, an ancient and intricate silver circlet fashioned in the shape of two leaping fish. After much furore he was obliged to use another, equally beautiful clasp that took the form of a set of stag's antlers.

Half way down the pavement, however, he changed his mind, and ordered me back to his rooms to search for the leaping fish. I knew that the place had been turned upside down, and that I had little hope of finding it. I had no choice but to obey, knowing that at the very least my inevitable failure would result in my being beaten to within an inch of my life, if not beyond. After searching for as long as I dared, my father waiting impatiently by the south gate arch, I returned empty handed, my legs shaking with terror. I could feel the heat of his fury from two hundred paces away.

Then, as I approached, half praying that I might expire before I got there, I saw a small figure run up to him and bow. My father batted the annoyance away, but to my astonishment the boy didn't give up, but grabbed hold of my father's arm. It was then that I realised who it was. Kyrolan, the boy to whom I had once shown a kindness, was remonstrating with Lord Corvan on my behalf, trying vainly to offer me his protection. I stood still and watched, horrified, as my father reached out and closed his hand around Kyrolan's neck. A moment later my would be

70

protector was on the ground, his sightless eyes peering up at the icy sky.

My father turned and strode towards me purposefully, his unwavering gaze as cold as I had ever seen it. By the time he reached me I was trembling all over, my chest heaving with pure terror, and for one awful moment I thought I might bring up my breakfast all over his boots. I felt the shadow of his hand descend towards me and tensed, prepared for the inevitable. But he simply stroked my head gently. When I found the courage to look up I saw that he was smiling.

"It is no matter, Rendail," he said cheerfully. "This clasp will do well enough for today. Quickly now – I do not wish to miss the daylight." With that he turned and set off back down the pavement to the arch, his light footsteps barely audible on the cobbles.

But I speak as though there was no pleasure in my life then, and that would be misleading. Much as I feared my father and was wary of him, I craved his company. I had learned to be mindful in his presence and guard any thoughts that might displease him. To my surprise, I found that I was able to do this with an effort, perhaps because he judged any thoughts not immediately open to him to be unimportant. Sometimes he summoned me to attend him in his chamber and I fetched and carried for him, just as Ilvan did for me. Once or twice he even let me comb out his hair, which was glorious, and fasten it with slides. His power and his beauty captivated me, and I wanted nothing more than to be like him, to make him proud that he had chosen me as his heir.

When he went abroad in the settlement I walked with him while he explained the relationships of the various branches of the Family to the blood, what the gift brought to one man or another. Many times we sat on the wall of the compound, and it became clear that he knew every woman and every child, their names and their lineage. I wondered often how he was able to keep them all in his head. Occasionally he would go inside the compound and to my relief I was always left outside to wait. I was too young in any case – it would have been a terrible breach of protocol had I been allowed to accompany him.

The days that gave me the greatest happiness were those I spent riding. I had outgrown my pony by now, and he had gone to take his pleasure with the mares in the breeding fields. My new mount was a fine bay gelding one year old. My father had picked him for me as a newborn foal on the day that I had learned of his secret love for Mira. The first time we had gone to the stables after that I had been filled with anxiety, for my father, true to his word, had ended the life of the mother of Estoran's son and had forbidden my brother to enter the compound any more. However, when he saw us he was as deferential as ever both to my father and to me, showing no reaction at all to the slight. He brought our mounts to us promptly, having attended himself to their grooming and preparation.

As we rode away towards the river my father said quietly, "Do not be concerned about Estoran. He knows his place and will abide by the rule. His son also will be no threat to you. But the son of the son is another matter. When I am gone and you rule here, Rendail, you would do well not to turn your eye from Estoran's grandchildren."

On the days that I was not with my father it was my habit to ride and hunt alone. I was forbidden to stay away from the settlement overnight, so I made it my task to explore every inch of the land within half a day's ride of home. By the time the coming of the gift signalled the beginning of my adult life I knew every branch and blade of grass, every rabbit warren and rookery.

It was on such a day, as I was returning home from the hills on the other side of the valley, that I suddenly began to feel strange. My stomach gave a lurch, as though I had been thrown six feet up in the air, and at the same time my head began to swim so that I had to pull up my horse and sit still for several minutes. Dusk was not far away, but I knew it was still quite light enough to see. To my eyes the world had dimmed, so that I had to peer as if through a swirling fog to find my way. I sat on the horse, breathing deeply and trying to steady myself, but it was no good,

72

and in the end I struggled forward, wondering what could be wrong with me and getting quite frightened by the experience.

When I finally reached the stables I felt no better, and Estoran had to help me to dismount. He took me to his house and sat me in front of the fire, saying he would call for Ilvan to take me home. I managed to ask him what was making me feel so ill and he laughed.

"Nothing that a day or two under a blanket will not cure, young Lord," he said, although from his tone I did not feel reassured. "Then, when you rise, we will know what kind of princeling our father has sired."

By the time Ilvan arrived I was shivering all over as though I had a raging fever, and my sight was so dim that I was beginning to panic.

"Do not be afraid, Lord," he said gently. "You must walk now. Come, I will help you."

I struggled to my feet, and leaning on Ilvan managed to walk the seemingly endless distance to my house. There I collapsed in a heap on the rugs, convinced that at any moment I was going to breathe my last.

"What is happening to me?" I asked, when he came with a cool cloth for my forehead, and herbs for my stomach. "Am I dying? Why can't I see?" I lunged wildly with my arms through the fog, trying to find something to cling on to, and found his hand.

"Be still, Lord. There is nothing wrong. It is the beginning, that is all. First there is a fever and a blindness. It will last a few hours yet. Then you will sleep, and then the voices will come. There will be a lot of noise, but you must not heed it. When the gift awakens it is hard to control at first, and the stronger the gift, the greater the noise. But you will become accustomed to it and it will grow quieter in time. There will be other things, but there is no way of knowing what they will be. For each of us, the gift is different."

So, the end of my childhood was upon me. I had just passed my fourteenth birthday and was about to become a man.

And all I could think of to say, or rather scream, was, "I don't want it! I want it to stop – make it go away!"

How pathetic I must have sounded, and worse still, all I could think was how I wanted to curl up in my mother's arms – except that I had never really had a mother, which seemed to make it worse. But I had Ilvan. He held me tightly, bathing my face in cool water and stroking my head while I clung to him, moaning and shivering until at last, many hours later, the fever broke and I fell asleep, exhausted.

The respite did not last long. It must have been only two, maybe three hours later that I awoke to an even worse assault on my senses. My vision had returned – in fact, everything seemed brighter, sharper than before, but in my head raged a cacophony of voices so loud it made me want to beat my head on the floor to make it stop. Ilvan was curled up beside me, asleep, appearing not to hear anything at all. I tried to remind myself this was normal, that he had warned me of it, but the noise was so deafening it drove me to madness and I leaped up off the rugs with my hands pressed to my ears, as though it might make a difference. I screwed my eyes shut and realised that I was howling louder than a wolf, trying to drown out the intruding clamour with my own voice.

Then I heard a crash, followed by another and another, and opening my eyes saw a water jug fly past my head and smash itself against the wall, followed by several drinking cups and even the iron poker, which I had to duck to avoid. Ilvan was wide awake by this time and I saw him reach out to me, only to fall backwards as if he had been struck, hitting his head heavily on the floor. I dropped to my knees in the middle of the whirlwind in a total panic, unable to understand who was attacking me, or why. Then I heard one voice, raised fractionally above the others in a desperate appeal to what was left of my sanity.

"Stop, Lord. You must stop. You are too strong. Hear my voice. Concentrate only on my voice and the others will go quiet."

For a moment I didn't understand, but then the meaning of the words found their way through the din and I grasped at them

74

frantically, forcing myself to try to shut out everything else. Very slowly, everything went quiet. The voices were still there, but were gradually becoming no more than whispers, rustlings in the back of my mind. The room was eerily still, littered with broken pots and other assorted objects. The fire had gone out. Ilvan was still speaking to my mind, his voice soothing, reassuring, distracting me from the temptation to turn my thoughts back to the others that I was still hearing.

I looked across at him and saw that he was still lying on the ground where he had fallen, a trickle of blood running down his left cheek from an ugly gash on his temple. With a shock I realised that the wreckage that was my room was of my own making. It had been I who had flung Ilvan from me in my alarm, not some nameless attacker. I felt quite ashamed of my weakness, but then heard Ilvan speak aloud,

"Do not be concerned, Lord. It is like this for everyone." I looked across at him questioningly – neither of us had the strength to move. "Well," he said, seeing my expression, "it is not quite like this. Yours is the most powerful gift that I have ever seen. You must be very careful now, Lord, for your own safety – and, I think, everyone else's."

"How?" I asked. I was still overwhelmed, and thought that if it happened again I would lose control of myself completely. The voices had still not disappeared, and I was frightened that the noise would start to grow as soon as Ilvan stopped talking to me.

"The thoughts of the others will settle themselves of their own accord," he answered. "You will find it easier as you accustom yourself to their presence. It will be as though they do not exist. Then, you will be able to summon any one of the many, as you wish. We are all mindful of our own gift, and must treat it as we do our bodies and our speech in our dealings with others, otherwise we would all be blind with madness from it." I must have looked a little dubious, because he went on "If you listen, you will find that you can distinguish one from another, recognise each voice and know to whom it belongs. When the gift is new, it is as though you were inside the Dance, as the women are. I am told they hear all constantly, over great distances. But it is not so

75

with us. Once the first opening of the mind is over, we hear only what we wish to hear, or what is meant to be heard. It may take a little time in your case, for I think your awakening has roused the entire settlement from their rest."

I didn't know whether to be proud, or mortified. The idea that every man in the place had been forcibly subjected to the vision of me whimpering like a baby in Ilvan's arms made me cringe with embarrassment, but at the same time I felt an odd satisfaction that I had been able to do it. I was beginning to calm down now and sat back on my heels, breathing deeply to try to stop myself from trembling. Ilvan, too, had recovered a little and got unsteadily to his feet with the aim of trying to relight the fire.

"No, wait." I did not say the words aloud, but at once Ilvan stopped and turned to me, a surprised expression on his face. Without thinking, I had used my silent voice and it was clear that he had not expected it, at least not yet. I was no less taken aback, and just to make sure, formed the words, "Help me up – we will do it together."

His hidden voice came back to me.

"As you wish, Lord."

I was shaking with fatigue and still a little confused by the noises in my head, so was glad of his shoulder to lean on as I fought to keep my footing on a floor that seemed to shift like quicksand. We sat together in the hearth, he breaking kindling while I made a spark, and soon after we had a good fire going, which I realised I sorely needed, and he was busy heating water in which to steep his herbs.

After a while I lay down again on the rugs. I felt as weak as a kitten and was frightened that despite my exhaustion the voices would not let me sleep. I think there must have been a deal of mistle leaf in the drink that he gave me, because I found myself drifting into dreams, not caring what strange babblings were in my head. But just as I was on the edge of sleep, a sensation came over me as though I had been suddenly buried in thick honey, cloying and sweet, the smell of it in my nostrils, the taste in my throat. I felt a touch, like many hands brushing against my skin, feeling my whole body, and opened my eyes to see Ilvan

76

dozing several feet away beside the hearth. Then I heard the voice, soft, sweet, unmistakeable.

"Perfect, Rendail. You are perfect. You are the past and the future, the keeper of the blood." The silent laugh that came after rolled around my mind as I turned on my side and tumbled into a deep and silent sleep.

CHAPTER 8

For three more days I stayed in my room, for the most part curled helplessly in the rugs as wave after wave of bewildering visions crashed over me. Both my body and my mind were completely beyond my control, and after a day or so I realised that the speed with which my gift was developing was frightening even Ilvan. My eyes, reflected in a polished stone, were no longer blue, which was to be expected, but a deep, fathomless ink black, darker even than my father's. That in itself was extraordinary, as the change of the eyes is slow as a rule, sometimes taking more than a year to complete in the normal course of events.

I suppose I had always suspected that my gift would not be normal, but even so, I had not prepared myself for anything quite so dramatic. Blind terror gave way to violent rages, which in turn dissolved into sheer exhaustion upon which I slept for several hours, only to have the whole thing start all over again. I attacked Ilvan more than once, both with my hands and with my mind, and I think that by the end of the second day he had begun to fear for his own life as well as mine. He huddled in a corner, not wishing to leave me, yet helpless to intervene, until at last, when I fell asleep after a particularly violent episode, he resolved to seek help from the only person he knew who had the power to put a stop to my outbursts.

Lord Corvan arrived at my bedside in a frightful temper – not surprising, as he had been disturbed some three hours before dawn. I had just opened my eyes again, and on seeing his tall figure looming over me, I thought I must be in the grip of yet another terrifying hallucination. Then I caught sight of Ilvan, white faced and trembling by the door, and realised that for the first time, probably since he himself was a child, the head of the Family had been summoned to attend another. By the look of things he wasn't too pleased about it. A swift glance sent Ilvan scurrying out of the room like a frightened rabbit. The moment the door had closed my father turned on me in a fury, dragging me up off the rugs and slamming me painfully against the wall. But then, inexplicably, he dropped me as though I was a hot coal and took a step backwards.

I fell onto my knees, and looking up at him saw, to my astonishment, that his face had paled slightly, and he was staring at me uncertainly, his head slightly to one side. At the same time I felt, just for a second, his confusion, and beneath that, amazingly, a tiny ripple of fear. He moved away from me and stood staring into the fire. He was unsure, trying to decide what to do. I sat back on my heels, watching, fascinated. Finally, I heard him silently command Ilvan to fetch hot food for us both, then he turned to face me, his eyes full of gentleness now, all trace of his former anger gone.

Still I did not understand. The gift was too new, too startling for me to find my bearings, be aware of how greatly my position had changed – or rather strengthened, for I was still Corvan's son and heir and always had been. But now I was no longer the heir of his choosing. I was the heir by right – by the force of my own gift. He could not have taken that away from me even if he had wanted to, and therein lay the source of his quickly hidden fear. I was stronger now, and at the tender age of fourteen I had the power to hurt him if I so chose. But that realisation had not yet come to me, and the sudden delicacy in his attitude, the tenderness with which he approached me, was well beyond the ability of my vision fogged mind to grasp.

"Come," he said, crouching slowly beside me and holding out an arm carefully, so as not to startle me further. He might have been trying to tame a wild stallion – I had seen him make the same gesture many times to a frightened horse. I found myself nestling into him, my body relaxing at his touch. "Do not be afraid," he was saying. "Be still, let me come to you. Do not struggle, I can help you."

I tried to calm myself, to stop myself fighting against the images that were flooding into my mind, but it was no good. If anything they became more vivid, as if I was seeing and hearing every living creature in the settlement all at once, their thoughts a mad jumble that I just couldn't shut out. Then I became aware of the sweet scent, the same that had surrounded me on the first night of my ordeal, filling my nostrils, becoming so thick that it was impossible to concentrate on anything else. Once again, the air around me seemed to turn itself into something living, massaging my body with the strength of a thousand invisible fingers. I sank into the embrace and as I did so the visions began to recede, and the noise in my head fell, as it had before, to nothing more than a lulling whisper.

"I should have known. I should have come before." My father was using his silent voice, and to me it sounded so much more beautiful than when he spoke aloud. "You are glorious," he said, "the greatest thing I have ever made. The blood will live in you, and when we take back what is ours, your offspring shall rule all."

"What do you mean, Father?" I asked wearily, resting my head on his shoulder, speaking as he did, only with my mind. What he said made no sense to me at all. He sighed.

"All in good time, my son. First you must learn to be what you are. You are not a child any more Rendail, but a powerful creature, more powerful than any within the Family, or outside it. What the blood has given you is too great for you to comprehend or control, but you must not fear it. I will stay with you now, teach you how to make it yours, help you to use it as it should be used. When you have mastered your own mind, you will be master of all others."

As he conveyed all this to me he was stroking my head, his eyes bright with excitement as his mind surveyed the possibilities that his creation had opened up before him. But still behind it all lay the uncertainty. I could feel it as clearly as I felt his touch on my brow, and as I puzzled over it I realised that he did not know the extent to which I saw his thoughts. In all of us there is a place that we keep hidden, a veil behind which we place our most secret selves. He thought himself safe from scrutiny, but in silencing the chaos in my mind he had allowed my gift to range freely around his inmost thoughts, and I read them as clearly as if he was shouting them in my ear.

"Thank you, Father," was all I said, and at that moment Ilvan came with hot stew and bread, and I realised I had not eaten since the thing had started.

For almost a month after that I stayed in my father's house. At night I slept in his room, where he could exert his influence over me to provide me with much needed sleep. During the day he set about teaching me how to command my gift, and from dawn 'til dusk he gave me his full attention, except now and then when he was called to make important decisions. When that happened he did not send me away, but kept me closely by his side so that I would learn the reasoning on which his judgements were founded.

After a week or two I began to find my feet, so to speak, and my growing awareness of the power I possessed began to exhilarate me. I still broke things occasionally and when my temper was roused, which seemed to happen quite often, I was impossible. Strangely, my father did not seem to mind, and smiled delightedly at my rages, saying, "Do not be concerned. Those who hear you will fear your strength, and that is all to the good."

When young ones were brought to him, some of whom, I have to say, were older than I was, he showed me how to examine the nature of the gift in them, inviting me to pronounce my judgement on their fitness to contribute to the blood. Once, he was called to see a baby in the compound, and this time I went with him, my heart pounding with apprehension as we entered that dreaded place. I could feel the tension all around us as we walked across the courtyard, and with my new found skills I was able to sense the utter hatred of us in some of the women that we passed. They took no pains to hide it, and I felt my annoyance at their lack of restraint threaten to turn itself into direct anger. My father, however, seemed to find the whole thing amusing.

"They do not have our strength," he said, patting my shoulder. "At least, they do not unless we give it to them. Then, they become dangerous creatures, able to twist our minds, distract us from things of importance, make our strengths become weaknesses."

He stopped and turned to me. "Whether they hate us or fear us, it makes no difference. These creatures exist for one purpose, and one only – the furtherance of the blood. Never let yourself forget it, for if you do, they will take everything that you are and turn it against you."

I felt the knot of bitterness that rose in him as he spoke, and knew the reason for it. I resolved then and there that no woman would do to me what Mira had done to my father. I glared round the courtyard, letting a little of my anger float out towards the small gathering there, and saw the women shrink away from it.

"There," my father said, smiling. "They cannot harm you. And neither are any of them fit for blood such as yours. Sooner or later one will be born who is worthy of you, and you will take her to the exclusion of all others as I did with your mother. Until then, these here will be good practice."

I did not question his words, although I didn't understand them, and we proceeded together in silence to a room on one of the upper floors of the great compound building. There we found the child he had come to see – a grotesque thing with a twisted foot and a hunchback.

"It happens from time to time," he said, "and more often now, as the blood becomes stronger. It is important, therefore, to know from whence the issue came, so that further matings of this kind can be avoided." He handed the child to me, and as he instructed I stopped its heart cleanly with my gift, while its mother stood silently by.

So, my life continued. As soon as I had sufficient control over myself not to need my father's constant support I went back to sleep in my own house, where Ilvan was waiting to keep me fed and comfortable. There was a wariness about him now, and he treated me with less familiarity than he had before. As time passed I was given greater responsibility within the settlement and often took my father's place, especially in matters of the blood. At first I would take before him any decision I made, but he never contradicted me, and before long I was making judgements without consultation.

In fact, the thoughts of those I encountered told me that in some ways I was even more feared than my father, for although my temper was more predictable than his, my moods were less capricious. Often he would fly into a fit of passion, only to have it dissolve as he became distracted by some small thing or other. My own anger, on the other hand, never wavered once roused, and although I gave no outward sign of it, those around me knew that once my mind was set nothing would change it no matter they said or did.

No one was more aware of the heat of my slow burning anger than my brother Safim, the one who had so ill treated Kyrolan. Perhaps my feelings were spurred as much by guilt as by Safim's behaviour. Twice, I had asked my father to turn Kyrolan over to me as a servant, and it may be that my request was the cause of his death, especially if Lord Corvan suspected that I harboured any affection towards the boy. Whatever the case, in my own mind I determined that Safim would pay the price.

Safim was regarded by my father as of strong blood, even though he had sired several daughters, but no sons. It was also well known that his preference was for male bed partners, and he retained several young boys in his household as servants. I set about making it my business to observe them all, until I was able to pick out his favourites. At the same time, I made Safim aware of my dislike of him in subtle ways, catching his eye whenever I saw him on the pavements, ensuring I turned up wherever he happened to be. He started to feel uncomfortable in my presence, but believed himself high enough in my father's standing to be beyond my reach.

After a year or so, I managed to gain the confidence of his most regular bed partner, who was less than delighted at the honour done to him by Lord Corvan's third son. Eventually, after much encouragement and sympathy, he confided to me that Safim's pillow talk strayed way beyond the bounds of what was acceptable within the Rule. My brother was both arrogant and ambitious. He was also very stupid. In the throes of his passion, he whispered to his young lover of his hatred of me, and his contempt for Lord Corvan. He boasted of how, one day, he would gain the strength to overthrow our father, and described my fate in disturbing detail to the terrified boy.

A few nights later, forewarned by my informant, I contrived to walk with Lord Corvan past the door to Safim's house, just as the boy steered the talk to Safim's usual topic. My father caught the whispered conversation as I knew he would. Safim did not live to see the dawn. His last vision, I think, was of my face as I threw him a knowing smile, then left him to his fate, taking the boy down to the stables to start a new life as a groom.

Estoran in particular avoided me, now that I had the power to see his true thoughts. My father knew as well as I did that he hated us both, but me most of all, for I had by my very existence taken away both his position and his natural rights. But my father was also correct in his assessment of my eldest brother's character. No matter what his personal feelings he served the blood faithfully, and would not have risen up against us despite his obvious dissatisfaction. The child of the woman we had taken from him was by now some five years old and went everywhere with its father. That fact disturbed me, but I could not place a finger on the cause of my disquiet. Time would prove my concern well founded, but in those days I had other, more pressing matters to occupy my time.

I was fifteen years old, and had passed from infancy to manhood with barely a backward glance. I was tall, sleek and strong, and had the power to kill with a simple thought. With the exception of my father I commanded all around me, but yet again I was to face the trial of battle with my own body.

The awakening of my natural desires did not come gradually as they do with some of us, but all at once, in a sudden surge that left my mind reeling and my body aching with a need I could never have imagined. Strange as it may seem, I had no idea what to do about it despite being well versed in the theory, and for some reason could not bring myself to mention it to my father, although I'm sure he was well aware of my inner turmoil. I was constantly distracted by it, and at night could do nothing but toss and turn as though I had a fever. My temper fluctuated wildly, as it had when the gift had first come to me, and one or two of those who crossed my path unwittingly did not survive to tell the tale. My infrequent visits to the compound were dreaded even more than before, and most of those outside it simply tried to stay out of my way as much as possible.

Ilvan once more became my unwilling saviour. Night after night for weeks he watched in silence, until finally he could not endure my suffering any longer, and came to me.

"With your permission, Lord," he whispered, kneeling beside me, "I can help." I nodded, and lay back, helpless, while he used his hands to release the fire that was in me. For several minutes I lay completely spent, overcome with the enormity of it. I heard him rise, his quiet footsteps as he moved about the room, fetching water for me to wash, and something to quench my thirst.

When I opened my eyes it was to see a slight smile on his face as he came towards me, and for some reason the sight of it enraged me. My respite had only been temporary, and once again my limbs were on fire and the pounding in my head was driving me wild. When Ilvan realised what was in my mind he paled, and sinking to his knees whispered, "No, Lord. Please!"

But his pleas were in vain as I fell on him like a ravening wolf, and tearing off his clothes dragged him naked onto the rugs. Despite his being some five years older, he did not have my strength, and his struggles were to no avail. When I drove into him he cried out once, then lay still while I vented on him all my rage and passion until I was utterly exhausted.

When I came to myself I found I was shaking all over, and deathly cold. I wrapped a blanket around myself and stared, disbelieving, at my servant, who had not moved from where I had thrown him. I did not need my gift to tell me that his right wrist was broken and there was blood, too, running from the corner of his mouth. His face was wet with silent tears.

For a full minute I was transfixed with horror. I had never, since the coming of the gift, so lost control of myself, and I felt

85

remorse welling up in me until I thought I was going to choke. Frantically, I sent him signals that it was over, that he was safe, but when I reached out to tend to his wrist I felt him tense at my touch. I let my mind work the bone back into place, and caressed his shoulders gently. All the time, his eyes were on me, accusing, defeated. Then I went to the hearth to fetch the water and the drink that he had prepared for me, and washed him, then offered him the cup. He did not resist, and when he had finished I took him in my arms and rocked him to and fro like a baby, stroking his head and asking him over and over with my silent voice to forgive me.

It might have been minutes, or hours – I lost track – before at last I felt his tension dissolve and he relaxed against me, returning my embrace.

"There is nothing to forgive," I heard him whisper finally, speaking aloud. "I am here only to serve you, in whatever way you wish."

His words did not make me feel any better, but I could tell that there was something more he wanted to say.

"What is it?" I asked gently, feeling that I did not want to intrude upon his thoughts. He pushed me away from him a little so that I could see his face. His eyes filled once more with tears, but he did not let them fall.

"When Lord Corvan chose my brother," he said hesitantly, "he did so knowing how cruel it was that he had not chosen me. He knew that what was worse than death for Castillan was what I most wanted, and in that way he was able to torment us both."

For a moment I was lost for words. Such a thing had never occurred to me, but then, there was no reason why it should have done until now. I should explain that given the way that we lived, for one man to take another, out of necessity, was quite natural for us. Those lucky enough to be granted permission to mate were quite used to the advantages of both, while those who were not had to content themselves with but the one alternative. What rendered me speechless was the true extent of Ilvan's devotion, that he should freely offer himself after what I had just done to him, for in truth there was no guarantee that the madness would

86

not come upon me again. In fact it did, many times throughout my life, and I was later to discover that what triggered it more than anything else was the stirring of affection in me, the same curse that afflicted my father. I pulled Ilvan to me and held him. The desire that I felt was quite unlike that which had overwhelmed me earlier. For the first time, I caught a glimpse of something that went past the notion of simple need. I set it aside. In the world that I would one day inherit, there was no place for any consideration beyond the furtherance of the blood.

CHAPTER 9

The years passed in relative contentment. I had my position and my ever growing power, and as well as my father's favour by day I enjoyed the sweet caresses of my obedient servant and lover by night. As my father had promised, I was guided through the not so gentle art of taking a woman by my brother Estoran who, released into the compound after so many years of abstinence, went wild in his passion and taught me things I would hardly have believed possible had I not seen them with my own eyes. Of course I had the right to take any one of them I chose and exercised it to the full, although I was always careful that no living seed of mine should enter any of them. My blood was too precious to waste on siring offspring from such creatures, and besides, I was learning to silently question some aspects of the way my father went about things.

In the beginning, there had been a need for many births. In those days a man's strength had been measured by his ability to further the blood. But as the settlement grew its needs began to change. By the time I was born the community numbered more than two thousand, and would have been even greater had it not been for the practice of putting the weaker ones to death. I say weaker, but in my mind I already hesitated to use the term. For those in whom the blood produced deformities of one sort or another I saw the logic. However, I knew instinctively that the criteria by which Lord Corvan judged a person's strength were flawed. Blinded by his ambition, he selected those of the greatest power in the hope that one of them might exhibit the gift he so desperately sought, the ability to cross the Great Emptiness to the future.

It was an ambition I shared, for I knew the importance of it. When my father told me the full tale of Amala, my mother's sister, and what she had done, my stomach tightened, first with fury, and then, as I thought about it, with fear. What if the gift to walk in the future came first to her adopted tribe? Derlan's people hated us, and although, as yet, they could not match our collective strength, they were far from weak. There was no knowing what they might be capable of, were they to gain knowledge of events beyond our own time. The slightest diversion from the natural course of things might lead to disaster for us. The strength of the Family would be as nothing without the power to protect ourselves from our enemies' foreknowledge.

A group of our men kept watch constantly on Derlan's people, ready to strike the moment Amala's blood produced a female child – it was our firm belief that the ability lay only in the female line. So far there had been but a single male, and he was possessed of no gift that we did not already have. The longer we waited, the more complacent their tribe would become, although my father was constantly riddled with impatience at their apparent unwillingness to breed as frequently as we would have liked. But despite our shared hatred of those who had stolen from us, I found myself in fundamental disagreement with him on matters of the blood within the settlement.

Two things in particular caused me some concern. Firstly, those whom he considered of weaker blood were only seen to be so within the narrow confines of the settlement. In any other place they might have been looked on as immensely powerful. Their blood was needed, I reasoned, to provide the variety that might lead to even greater enhancements of the gift. Besides, they often had more subtle, hidden skills – greater sensitivity for example, such as was displayed by my brother Ilvan, depths of perception that were lost on my father.

Secondly, and more importantly, more than three centuries of my father's rule had inevitably led to a certain amount of envy and lust for power among some of the stronger males. It is true that he and I were still by far the most formidable Dancers living, but for how long I did not know, and some of the others were equally obsessed with the possible opportunities that control of Amala's gift might bring. My path was clear. If I was to rule effectively, I must take possession of that blood the moment it appeared, in order to prevent the Family from descending into violent chaos. Not to do so would mean not only the downfall of my people, but possibly of the wider world as well, so powerful had we become over the years.

My father was blind to the danger, believing himself invincible despite his great intelligence. I realised that in truth he took no account of events that might unfold beyond his lifetime. He still believed that he would live to see his dreams fulfilled. Of late he had grown more impatient, more capricious than ever, and on two or three occasions I had been forced to use my not inconsiderable powers of persuasion to deflect him from decisions that would have been disastrous in the long run.

I spent much time riding, alone or with Ilvan, for whom I had chosen a magnificent gelding almost the equal of my own. I stopped his protest by saying that as my servant it was his duty to accompany me whenever I wished it, and that no other mount would be able to keep up with mine. He acquiesced gracefully, as always, and I noted with great satisfaction the skill with which he could handle horses. As time went on I entrusted him more and more with my inner thoughts. The pact that I had made with him on that first night, that when alone we should treat each other as brothers, held true. His trust in me, and his candour, made him an invaluable advisor.

It was on one of these rides, far into the hills and woodland on the other side of the valley, that the day I had been prepared for from my birth finally arrived. I was just turned forty years old, fully grown and as dangerous a creature as anyone could wish to meet. The day was warm, with just a gentle breeze, and Ilvan and I had stopped to bathe in one of the clear icy streams that ran down the hillside. I was sitting naked in the sun combing out my hair, which reached almost to my waist by then and was as glossy black as my father's, when my mind was assaulted by the most terrible cry, a chilling scream that stopped my breath and made me jump to my feet in alarm. Ilvan, who was at the stream fetching water, heard it too and I saw him freeze, the bowl half dipped in the water. There was an unnatural silence, followed a few seconds later by another cry, then rapidly by another until the air was thick with the noise, and other sensations as well that only my gift could hear – anger, confusion, terror.

We were some five miles from the settlement as the crow flies, yet I knew from whence the tumult came, and who was the cause of it. There was only one other who could send such powerful thoughts over such a distance. Ilvan knew it too, and looked to me in panic. I came to life, started to throw on my clothes and tie back my hair, wordlessly commanding Ilvan to do the same. It took us more than an hour at full gallop to make the training fields, and in that time the clamour had reached such a pitch that I was hard put to see where I was going. My companion simply clung onto his horse, his eyes screwed shut against the din, hoping that his mount would follow mine.

My first thought was that my father was being attacked, that perhaps some of the more powerful males among us had decided to take their chance against him while I was away from home. But I knew deep down it could not be so. None had the strength to withstand him, I was sure of that. He would have defeated them in minutes. My thought was confirmed when I saw Estoran rushing towards us, his eyes as panic stricken as Ilvan's, his discomfort at the noise clear on his normally impassive face.

"You must stop it, Lord," he cried, not even waiting for me to dismount. "Three have tried, but never got past the doors. You are the only one he will listen to now. If you do not stop him, he will destroy us all before it is finished."

"Before what is finished?" I couldn't work out what he meant, and my mind was so reeling with the invasion that I could hardly think. Estoran could only shake his head, too overcome by the struggle with his own senses to say anything more. Ilvan, the weakest of the three of us, had gone completely white, and looked as though he might collapse at any moment. Nevertheless, I wanted him with me, so I grabbed him by the shirt and dragged him after me up the hill to the gate.

As we reached it he took me by the arm and begged me to stop. I did so, realising that I was completely out of breath, and turned to him. He looked dreadful, but I knew that he was trying to tell me something important. I dared not use my silent voice – it would have done no good anyway, so I waited impatiently for him to gather his strength enough to speak.

91

"Death," he managed to say eventually.

"What?" When I still couldn't fathom it, he simply looked at me, his eyes pleading with me to understand. Then I did, the realisation hitting me with ice cold clarity. What I was hearing was the voice of my father raging against the only thing over which he had no control – the time of his natural death. I motioned for Ilvan to stay where he was, and without another word turned in the direction of Lord Corvan's house and ran.

When I reached the doors they stood open, no sign of the guardians anywhere. I dashed in and up the stairs, and without waiting to be admitted burst into my father's room. The scene that met my eyes held me transfixed in the doorway. The room was in complete disarray, the floor littered with shards of broken pottery, the wooden table no more than a pile of splinters. The mats and rugs had been torn up and thrown about, and in the middle of it all my father crawled around on his hands and knees, by turns howling like a wounded animal and whimpering piteously like a baby. All trace of his former beauty seemed to have left him. His hair was hanging loose in knotted tangles about his face, his cheeks were sunken, his face pale, and as I watched I saw a dribble of saliva escape his lips and roll down his chin.

I felt both ashamed and disgusted. All trace of restraint was gone from him, and the fact that the whole settlement was witness to his weakness made me feel quite sick. He caught sight of me standing there, and before I could move lunged towards me, crying, "Out! Out – get out!" at the top of his lungs, at the same time sending a wave of fire from his mind that would have killed any other man instantly. But to me it was no more painful than the stroke of a lash, and ignoring it I took a step towards him, thinking to grab him, make him see some sense.

When he saw that he had had no effect on me his mood changed at once and he began to weep. He reached out for me, sobbing, "Help me. Help me, Rendail, my son," and then, in a terrifying high pitched scream that I was sure could be heard right down the pavement; "I don't want to die!"

I retreated a step, my whole being suddenly shuddering with anger and disgust. I thought of all those that he had sent into the void, so many of them, my mother included, meeting their fate with stoical acceptance. I thought of my brothers, Castillan and Kyrolan, and how much more courage they had displayed in the knowledge of their own deaths. Ilvan, my servant, he that my father had called an insult to his line, had risked his life many times in his sojourn with me, with never a thought for his own safety. And here was the most powerful man alive, the taker of life from so many others, grovelling on the mat in front of me begging for his own. My father had taught me well. His eyes met mine and I stared back coldly at the terror I saw there. I could not stand the sight of his weakness any longer. I reached out with my mind, and with no more thought than I would have given to a deformed newborn, I broke his neck.

An eerie silence followed. The air seemed still and heavy, and I felt the entire settlement stop, their minds turned towards me, filled with both apprehension and expectation. Shafts of sunlight streamed through the window, striking the crumpled body on the floor. I stepped over it, desperate for the feel of the breeze on my face, and looked out over the valley at the cool streams, glittering as they tumbled down the hillside on which Ilvan and I had rested so contentedly no more than two hours before.

I wondered idly whether I would ever know such peace again. I was the head of the Family now, and every step I took would be watched, every breath counted in a way that it had never been before. I heard a movement behind me and swung round to see Ilvan in the doorway, open mouthed, eyes wide with shock. When he saw me looking at him he drew himself up and bowed, then with an effort composed himself, awaiting my command.

"Get this place cleaned up!" I snapped, not trusting myself to say much else. He bowed again and took an apprehensive step towards my father's body. "No," I said, more gently this time. He stared at me, confused. "You are the personal servant of the head of this Family," I explained. "It is not your place to attend to such tasks. Fetch others to do it, then go and guard the doors until it is done. Let no one enter against your wishes."

"Yes, Lord." He rushed off at once, and without a backward glance I walked from the room, wanting only to be outside, where I hoped that the breeze would blow the last, awful memory of my father from my mind. I strode swiftly back to my own house, where I bathed, changed and arranged my hair properly, for there had been no time earlier. Now was the one time that I needed to look perfect.

When I was quite satisfied with my appearance I made my way slowly back to my father's rooms, or, more accurately, my rooms now. Ilvan waited obediently by the doors, and I beckoned for him to follow me inside. His place was immediately taken by two others, clearly on his instruction, and I acknowledged his forethought with a nod. All trace of the wreckage had been cleared away and new furnishings had appeared as if from nowhere, even down to the matting on the floor. Wine had been set on the table, and bread – it was as if the events of the last hours had never taken place.

I sat and poured myself wine, bidding Ilvan to do the same. He obeyed, and I sat watching him for some time, until finally he asked, "You require something of me, Lord?" I nodded, but did not speak. I was not sure what exactly I should say. "I am yours to command," he went on, my silence making him uncomfortable. "I did as you requested. Is there something more I should have done?"

"Your mother – does she still live?" The question clearly startled him, and his eyes narrowed slightly with apprehension.

"I believe so, Lord. I have not heard otherwise."

I drained my cup and rose.

"Then take me to her."

"My Lord?" Now he seemed really frightened, but nevertheless got to his feet at once, and I followed him down onto the pavement and into the courtyard of the compound. Here he seemed at a loss and stopped, searching his memory. He had not entered the place since the day he had left it, more than thirty years ago. Finally he made up his mind and entered the great building, turning to the left and ascending the first flight of stairs.

All around us I could feel the consternation of the women, most of whom had retreated to their rooms at our approach. He came to a halt outside a door and turned to me. I nodded, and he opened it and entered. My eyes fell on a most beautiful woman, dark haired and green eyed, the alarm clear in her face.

"Ilvan is your son?" I asked, although there was no need. I could see the likeness in the delicate lines of her face, the sweet, sensitive mouth.

"Yes, Lord," she replied, fearful, but firm. I nodded.

"What is your name?"

"Serenisse, Lord."

"Do not fear, Serenisse. Your son wishes to speak with you. I will return in one hour."

I left them, and seated myself on the edge of the stone well in the middle of the courtyard, watched from a distance by the scattering of women who had not shut themselves inside. The uneasiness that pervaded the whole settlement had not diminished. No one doubted my power. My right to rule had gone completely unchallenged, and only a fool would have questioned it. But my intentions were unclear, and it was that which was causing the disquiet. I allowed myself a faint smile, and settled myself to contemplating the glorious tints of red and gold that accompanied the setting of the sun.

When I returned precisely one hour later I found Ilvan and Serenisse deep in conversation. Ilvan rose and bowed as I entered, and although I saw his mother's brow furrow in agitation, there was no concern on the face of my servant, who knew my moods better than anyone. Rather, he was nonplussed, unable to fathom the reason for my unexpected generosity. I ignored him, however, and turned to Serenisse.

"My brother has told me that you have a great gift," I said, trying to make my voice as unthreatening as possible. "He has said that Lord Corvan chose you on account of it. Is that so?"

"Yes, Lord," she replied without hesitation, and then, after a pause, "He did me great honour."

Her thoughts belied her words, but I let it pass.

"Then you are well acquainted with all the women here, more so, perhaps, than most others?"

The question was unexpected, and I felt her fear give way to confusion.

"I see further than many, Lord, and often deeper, so it is said."

"Then," I went on, "aside from yourself, who of all the women here possesses the greatest gift in the Dance?"

Now she was flustered, and out of the corner of my eye I saw Ilvan shift uncomfortably on his feet. She could not refuse to answer, however, and after a long pause she said in a whisper, "Rysha, daughter of Morlain son of Sovan, Lord. Her gift equals mine, and she is as yet but twenty-five years old."

"Call her to me," I commanded, then sat and waited.

A few minutes later the door opened and the most exquisite waif of a creature appeared in the room. She was perfect. She was so tiny I thought I had only to let out my breath in her direction and she would fall. She was terrified of course, trembling all over, her eyes full of tears which by some miracle she prevented from spilling down her smooth pale cheeks. Her hair was black as ebony, her eyes the most startling blue I had ever seen, and despite her terror she held herself gracefully, her lineage unmistakable in her bearing, as though her body could not hide it, much as she tried. At the sight of her I almost forgot my purpose, and had to quickly quell my natural responses. When she spoke her voice, like running water, quavering in her fear, only served to increase her desirability.

"I am Rysha, my Lord. You desired my presence?"

Yes, I thought, and with every passing moment I desired it more. I curbed the impulse and simply nodded. Ilvan was as entranced as I was, standing behind me, eyes wide, so still I hardly heard him breathing.

"Tell me Rysha," I asked, without preamble, "have you been claimed by any man?"

Too terrified to speak, she shook her head, trapped by my gaze, unable to look away. With a sigh I reluctantly broke the spell she was unwittingly laying upon me.

"Fetch me a comb," I ordered, and at once Serenisse obeyed. I turned to Ilvan who, by the look on his face, must have thought I had completely lost my senses. "My father considered your blood to be of no value," I said, and as I spoke I combed out his hair, forming it carefully into the pattern that signalled his rank as the son of our former ruler. "I, on the other hand, judge it to be beyond price. As you were Lord Corvan's gift to me, so this woman is my gift to you. She is yours, to do with as you wish, for as long as you wish, to the exclusion of all others. You may enter this place freely, come and go whenever you wish, and sire what offspring you will from her, for the furtherance of the blood."

Already I was beginning to regret my decision, so beguiling was the vision that stood trembling before me. But I knew that if I had taken her I might well have forgotten myself and fathered a child, and the time was not yet right. To Ilvan I said curtly, "Attend me at noon tomorrow," and left the room before I could change my mind. So, my first decision as head of the Family was made, the first of many. In some ways, I reflected as I strolled slowly back to my new house, it may have been the easiest, and in others the hardest, for my body was still alight with desire for the girl that I had given away, and I had given her into the warm arms that would otherwise have been waiting in my room, ready to still my passion. Still, I thought, such a thing was simple to cure, and making up my mind I turned on my heel and walked swiftly back into the compound, where, willing or not, I had the choice of a hundred others to take into my embrace.

CHAPTER 10

Ilvan opened his mouth twice, then very wisely closed it again.

"You are here to do as I tell you," I continued, turning my back as my father used to do, and staring out of the window. I was more than a little annoyed, even though I had expected some protest on the part of my new second in command. "Until such time as I desire to sire my own issue, you are my heir, with the freedom and the responsibility that such a position entails. You will become used to it in time – after all, you have served me long enough. Is it too difficult for you to continue to fulfil your obligation?"

I knew what he was thinking. The effect of my choice on certain others within the settlement, and on Estoran's line in particular, would be profound. Estoran himself was not young, and held no expectations, but he had sired children of considerable power, who were about to be passed over in favour of one they considered weak and without merit. Nor was it an accident that I had chosen one of Morlain's daughters as bed partner for my servant. Sovan was dead, but those of his line were powerful and had the ear of many. To mix blood with that of my designated heir, even if the position was only temporary, would keep Morlain's faction docile, at least for a time.

The whispers of favouritism would soon be silenced. There were no real grounds for complaint – Ilvan was my brother after all, and powerful enough in his own way. Besides, it was not brute strength that I needed. I had enough of that of my own. Wisdom and good judgement were of far greater importance, together with the presence of an advisor whom I could trust implicitly to carry out my orders without hesitation, yet not be too afraid to speak his mind.

"You honour me, Lord," Ilvan finally whispered, although in his mind I still caught the shadow of doubt. I turned back to him, and for a moment admired his looks, dressed and presented now as befitted his rightful position. I had not noticed before how imposing he could be, his tall, lean figure filled with an elegance that had been hidden up to now, every inch of him shrouded in graceful stillness. No one could challenge him, I thought. His impassive gaze missed nothing. At times even I had to take care with my thoughts, although it was rare that I kept anything from him. He noticed what most others did not, and stored away information that to any other mind would seem unimportant. Such a skill was invaluable, in the right hands.

"The honour is mine," I said finally, then, "You are tired. I trust your evening was satisfactory?"

"Indeed, Lord," he replied, blushing slightly, "I found it most informative." Then, changing the subject quickly, he said, "Thorlan, son of Estoran wishes to see you. He is waiting outside."

"How long has he been there?"

"Since just after dawn, Lord. I believe he requires permission to mate."

"Then I should give him my full attention. Tell the doorkeeper to let him wait another hour, then admit him. There is a matter I should attend to first."

"Which is, my Lord?" He was already at my side, taking the wine cup from my hand and placing it gently on the table behind us.

My brother's son, the little child that I had once saved from my father's judgement of death, stood before me unblinking, awaiting my decision. He was just a little over thirty now, handsome and gifted enough, but there was something in his demeanour that I did not like. It was not that he was insufficiently respectful – on the contrary, he observed the correct protocols with ostentatious precision. His thoughts were bland, uninteresting even, and it was that which gave me pause for thought. For although his mind told me one story, in his eyes was quite another. Behind them lay a deep, smouldering passion, such that just a tiny breeze might set them ablaze. I could have searched his mind, as was my right, but something told me to draw back, to reveal nothing of myself to him. My instinct was to

99

deny his request, simply because I did not like his manner. But I had no sound reason for doing so. His blood was valuable and he was fit enough, a young stallion stamping in his impatience to be let loose with the mares. To refuse him would mean to alienate Estoran's brood still further.

Besides, when it came to those who might prove troublesome, I had learned two things. First, to create confusion was to maintain control. The years spent watching my father had shown me the effectiveness of unpredictability. Corvan's capriciousness, however, had been without motive, the product more of passion than of forethought. In some ways he had destroyed as much as he had created through his inability to master his own moods. I, on the other hand, for the most part at least, had no such difficulty, and found that the more uncertain people were of their standing with me, the less they felt inclined to cross me. There was nothing as important as the favour of the head of the Family, and as long as the promise of it existed the more dangerous ones among them would remain docile. It humoured me though, to push them to the edge, to see their discomfiture as I frustrated them one minute, rewarded them handsomely the next.

Secondly, no matter how desperate for power certain groups became, the rule was inviolate. None would dare to break it, even in the most extreme circumstances. It was the Rule, the complex hierarchical system by which we lived, mated and died, that prevented the settlement from descending into chaos. Each knew his place, and his place was determined by the blood. That was the one thing that could not be argued with. My ability to maintain order rested entirely on how vigorously I applied the rule, and it was clear to me that I must be seen to be both ruthless and without favour in my dealings with the blood.

My father had not been as vigilant as perhaps he should. In his eagerness to expand the changes in the gift he had allowed too many of the stronger males to mate freely with whomever they chose. That, I decided, would have to stop. All choices would be mine, and in that way our women would be protected, the bloodlines more closely controlled. Not everyone had my degree of restraint when it came to the siring of offspring, and indeed had been encouraged to produce as many young as possible, regardless of quality.

I sighed, and pulling myself out of my reverie turned back to the still faced young man whose frustration and impatience were roaring in my mind.

"You have my leave," I said, and saw him visibly relax.

"I am grateful, my Lord." He bowed, and took a step back as though the audience was over.

"When I have chosen a suitable mate, you will be informed," I continued smoothly, and had to prevent myself from laughing out loud as the jolt to his anticipations almost made him lose his footing. So, I thought, he had a particular female in mind, or perhaps he had expected to take his pick. "You have no objection, I trust?" I could not help but ask. His attitude irritated me beyond words, and I was not going to let him go without gaining the satisfaction of seeing him forced into a corner. At once he became nervous, flustered.

"I … No, Lord. How could I object? I am honoured." He hesitated. "If I might enquire, Lord, how long …"

"The honour is mine," I said firmly, cutting him off. "You will be informed."

I flicked my attention from him and called silently for Ilvan. To his credit, Thorlan had the presence of mind to bow before fleeing from the room as if he had been nipped by a hungry wolf. Before nightfall, the new stricture would be known throughout the entire settlement without my having to expend the slightest energy. Ilvan appeared in the doorway.

"Will you see Rysha tonight?" I asked.

"With your leave, Lord," he replied, "it was my intention."

"Good," I said, although a pang of jealousy pierced me briefly. "Ask her who she would choose as a suitable mate for Thorlan. I wish to reward him well for his patience."

Ilvan smiled.

"As I said from the beginning, Lord, you are wiser than your father ever was. She will be honoured to assist you."

The following morning I woke determined to correct yet another of my father's errors. Strange as it may seem, I had never spoken to his second son, my brother Rolan, who was also, I should remind you, my Uncle, a fact which disconcerted me somewhat. There had been no love lost between my father and his son, and Rolan had made it his task to deal with the short lived merchants in the closest towns, some of which were several days hard riding from our settlement. Consequently he rarely stayed at home, only returning now and then to collect our surplus horses which he exchanged for the finely woven cloths, metal ores and other things that we brought into the settlement from elsewhere. In fact, even when he came to the settlement he did not enter the gates, but camped across the valley, where all that he needed was fetched by his two servants, and they spoke to hardly anyone.

He possessed the rare ability to tolerate the undisciplined minds of the short lived people, the awful outpouring of emotional chaos that would have driven most of us to distraction. That was a useful gift in itself, but I had a suspicion that it might not be the only thing about him that was out of the ordinary. What puzzled me most was why my father had not insisted that Rolan exercise his right to mate. Surely, being the full brother of the two most prized women in the settlement, his blood must be invaluable, yet he had been pushed aside, his name never mentioned in all the years that I was growing up. There was a time when he had been seen about the place every so often, but not once since the death of my mother Mira, and I assumed that he bore no more love towards me than she had, I being my father's chosen successor.

Either by chance or design – I did not know which – he happened to be encamped outside the settlement in time to witness, as we all had, the unpleasant death of my father, and my subsequent rise to the leadership of the Family. That had been some three days ago, yet uncharacteristically he had made no move to be on his way. Taking the opportunity I summoned him, and he, with surprising alertness, acknowledged my command at once. In fact it was clear from his response that he had expected something of the sort, and had delayed his journey on account of it. I did not like to be second guessed, so as I waited impatiently for his arrival I found my intense curiosity doing battle with a certain amount of irritation.

I was leaning on the stone window sill staring out in the direction of the camp when I felt, rather than heard a slight movement in the room behind me. I turned, and with a shock found myself face to face with Rolan, who had clearly been standing watching me for some time. There was no sign of Ilvan anywhere. It crossed my mind briefly that my heir designate had come to harm at the hands of the visitor, but I dismissed the thought almost immediately and gathering my wits began to examine the man who had appeared, ghost-like and completely without warning, in my room.

He was unlike any Dancer I had ever seen. At first I could not put my finger on it – he was tall, muscular yet graceful, as so many of us are. He was handsome too, quite beautiful in fact, and I could see clearly certain characteristics that he shared with his sisters, the long, golden hair, the delicate curve of the mouth. I saw my father in him too, in the honeyed skin and fine slender fingers, attributes that we both shared.

He stood before me in an attitude of perfect calm, no trace of fear, not even the slightest apprehension. If anything, his expression as he studied me was one of appreciation, as though he saw something in me that I could not see myself, but did not wish to share the thought. His eyes were deeply expressive, almost sorrowful, and his lips curved upwards in an enigmatic smile.

It was only then that it struck me, with the force of a blow, that I could hear nothing of his thoughts beyond the tiniest of whispers, that he had crept up on me without my having felt his coming. Neither I, nor Ilvan, nor indeed anyone in the settlement had felt more than a ripple of his presence, as though his mind was the still surface of a pond disturbed only by the lightest of breezes. So that was his gift, I thought. It was a gift almost beyond price, and one that he was making no effort to hide from me, although, I reasoned, he must have kept it from my father.

For a long moment we stared at each other, then he bowed his head slightly and said, "Lord Rendail. I am honoured."

I nodded in response, but said nothing. The fact was, he held me speechless. Being able to see him only with my eyes, I had no basis on which to judge how I should proceed. Added to that, his expression unnerved me. There had been no trace of irony in his voice, and in his eyes there was a look almost of affection. I could feel myself weakening, and as usual I found my anger rising as I struggled to suppress my desire to return his sentiment. Furthermore, I had no idea how far he could see into my thoughts whilst concealing his own, and that made me angrier still.

He nodded slowly, still holding me in his gaze.

"I see nothing," he said, as if in answer to my unspoken question. "When my mind is silent, all others are closed to me. I will lift the veil if you wish."

I shook my head, trying to remain calm.

"Will you sit?" I asked, gesturing towards the table, on which was set wine and fruit.

"I am honoured," he replied, and we both sat. I poured him a cup of wine, which he accepted with a nod, taking a deep draught before setting the cup back on the table. His calm was as great as my agitation.

"You are not afraid of me?" I was not asking a question so much as stating a fact. He shrugged. "What is there to fear? If you wish to take my life, I cannot prevent you. Those I feared for are gone, save one, and that one is in no danger, at least not yet."

"What do you mean?" I snapped, furious at his measured tone, his openness, his quiet deference. "Who do you wish to protect, and for what reason?"

"You suffer from our father's affliction," he observed, deliberately not answering my question. "He too found it difficult to control his temper, as indeed did your mother. Mira did not treat you well. I am sorry."

"This is insufferable," I responded, quite incredulous. "I should strike you dead where you sit. First, however, perhaps you will extend the courtesy of answering my question."

"I beg your forgiveness, Lord," he replied, quite earnestly, "but I also crave your indulgence. If you will calm yourself I believe you will find a part of your gift that you did not know, and that its discovery will provide the answers you seek."

"I grow tired of your riddles," I said, but at the same time I made an effort to quell my anger, some instinct telling me that Rolan would not be taking such a risk unless it was to try to tell me something important. It was evident that he had no concern for himself, and that whatever he had to impart could therefore only be of value to me.

I forced myself into a state of calm, and in the silence that followed, began to hear, indistinctly at first, the whisper of a train of thought that I knew could only belong to him. I concentrated on it, and all at once it became so clear that I wondered why I had not heard it before. I could not penetrate the veil beyond those thoughts that were close to the surface of his mind, but nevertheless I could push it back a little way. That is what he had meant to show me, but I did not understand why, any more than I understood the reason for his wishing to reveal his gift to me.

As if in answer, I saw an image, one that he brought to the forefront of his mind for me to see. He was with Mira, not long after I was born. He had used his gift of silence to go to her, and further, to veil her mind as well, so that my father would not know of it. The guards that were always with us were outside the door – the result of his persuasiveness no doubt, which told me how powerful his gift must be. They were arguing in hushed tones, and it seemed I was the subject of the dispute. My mother had a knife in her hand, and clearly she had planned to kill me despite my father's many threats. But Rolan had prevented her. His hand was fast around her wrist so that she could not strike, his body firmly placed between us.

I heard my mother say, "How can I not hate him? He is his father's monster, destined only to bring more misery down on us all. Already Corvan has claimed him, body and soul. It is better we all die."

"Am I not also our father's son, and you his daughter?" Rolan answered. "He is a child, and as much of our blood as of

Corvan's. Who are you to say what will become of him? If you cannot love him Mira, then at least let him be and do not harm him. If he becomes as strong as his father believes, then perhaps he will not be so quick to blindly follow the path laid out for him."

I saw my mother's grip relax, and Rolan gently take the knife from her hand.

"I will not love him," she said. "I will not care for him, nor give him comfort, for his father has given me nothing but pain since the day I was born. But for your sake, because you ask it, I will not harm him. Corvan will never sire another child by me, and I only hope that he takes this one out of my sight before it dies of its own accord. After that, you may care for it as you wish."

Rolan nodded, and then he turned and gathered me briefly in his arms.

"Be strong, brother Rendail," he whispered, then, setting me down again, he left me there to remain chained to my mother until the day that her vow was fulfilled and my father released me.

"Why have you shown me this?" I was still puzzled. His answer had been most eloquent, but still it only served to raise more questions.

"To show you," he replied, "that I am not your enemy. You are my blood, perhaps more than any other of our father's sons. I do not wish you harm, although I doubt I would have the strength. You are certainly not in need of my protection. But I ask you to be wary, particularly of Morlain's sons, and Estoran's."

I sat back and at last took up my cup.

"I had already surmised as much," I said. "What surprises me is that you would concern yourself with my welfare. Perhaps you would be so good as to answer my other questions – your voice will do perfectly well. I do not think there is any further need for your dramatic demonstrations."

He smiled fleetingly, and bowed his head.

"It would be my honour, Lord. I wish only to serve you."

"Then," I said, sipping my wine, "tell me this. You have a very powerful gift, yet my father did not see fit to make use of it. How is it that you were able to hide it from him? I assume that to all others your mind is completely silent, as it was to me until you made me aware of my own capability just now. So, one way or the other, he could not have failed to see the value in your blood."

He laughed quietly and refilled his cup, quite at ease with me still.

"The answer is simple. Our father had the same gift. Like you, however, he was unaware of it. He caught the surface of my thoughts, and assumed that what he saw represented the entire extent of my gift. He saw me as weak, but not troublesome. If I stayed far enough away from him, and if his mind was not on me, I was more or less invisible to him. What cannot be seen is easy to forget, and so I was forgotten. To be out of Lord Corvan's mind was, to my way of thinking, a very fortunate state to be in."

I could hardly disagree with that statement.

"So because my father had that gift, you guessed that I might also?"

"More than a guess," he replied. "You have my blood in you, and I have the silent gift, which was given to me by our grandmother. But unlike Corvan, you not only have the ability to pierce the veil, but also to cover your own thoughts, at least in part, although you cannot make yourself completely invisible. You protect your mind instinctively, without realising it, and only one of my gift would recognise it."

It was only as he said this that I realised it was true, that there had been thoughts I had been able to keep secret even from my father. Up to now, however, I had explained it in terms of the sheer strength of my gift, and not as a subtle facet of it.

"I still do not understand," I said, "why you choose to reveal all this to me. Surely you must harbour some hatred towards me. After all, I was in part responsible for the death of your sister, and she was right to say that Corvan had claimed me from the moment of my birth. As long as I lead this Family, I shall apply the rule just as my father did, perhaps with even greater severity. To have such attachments goes against the Rule.

You know this, yet you have freely admitted it to me. Why then have you come here, knowing that you would be putting yourself in danger?"

"You forget, Lord," he replied evenly, "that it was you who summoned me."

He was right. I had completely forgotten. He went on, "As for my being in danger from you, if that is so, so be it. But you are wise enough to know that the Rule cannot command what is in a man's heart. I will commit no action against the rule, but my thoughts are my own and will remain so. If you will permit me, Lord, may I ask you a question?"

My brother was either outrageously foolhardy, or possessed of admirable courage and wisdom. He was driving me in circles and he knew it, but then, I was hardly more than a child in those days, albeit a very powerful one, and he was treating me to the benefit of some three hundred years or so of his experience. I nodded, wondering what on earth he might say next.

"Is it your intention to continue to pursue my sister's children?" he asked simply, and if his purpose was to throw me off my guard, for just a moment he succeeded. I was once again infuriated, but then with a great effort I controlled myself, realising that he had unwittingly given me the upper hand for the first time since his arrival in my rooms. With great deliberation I refilled my cup, and sipped my wine thoughtfully for a moment or two. Then, leaning back, I answered quite calmly, "I have a mind to hang you by your feet from the arch of the south gate. However, I may have a better use for you. Before I answer, I have a question of my own. Lord Corvan did not deny you permission to mate, yet you have never done so. That in itself I would interpret as an act against the Rule. What reason can you give me that would explain such a failure in your duty to the blood?"

At last he seemed wrong footed. With some reluctance, I thought, he replied,
"What need was there of my blood? My father never insisted, and it was for him to decide whether or not I was guilty of a sin of omission."

I smiled inwardly.

"Our father," I said, "was unaware of the nature of your gift. I am aware, and it is now for me to decide whether or not you should fulfil your obligation to the Rule."

He bowed his head in acknowledgement, but was clearly becoming a little uneasy. I continued, "Our former Lord believed that only those who displayed certain qualities of the gift were useful to the furtherance of the blood. Thus, he did not pursue the child, your namesake that Derlan defiled with his impurity. I, on the other hand, hold a different view. There may be treasures in the blood that hide themselves in one generation, only to become apparent in the next. All blood is therefore useful, and to ignore the possibility of a dormant gift is wasteful. It was agreed, many years before my birth, that no purpose would be served by the pursuit of their half breed males. But I am not sure that the decision was wise. Derlan's son has mated, and now there is another child. Perhaps there are attributes in him that we cannot see, and it would be better if he was where we could keep a better eye on his development."

Rolan shifted uncomfortably, his eyes fixed on his cup, his lips a thin line as he struggled to remain silent. With my new found gift I could feel the tension in the surface of his mind as he fought to keep his inner thoughts from spilling out to where I could see them. I let him mull over the possibilities for a while, then said quietly, "Perhaps we can make an agreement, you and I."

He looked up sharply, wary now, realising that he had, perhaps on account of my youth, underestimated me. I saw now what he had tried to do, and why. By revealing his gift to me he had thought to establish a trust between us, one by which he could begin to manipulate me, draw me closer to his way of thinking. He wished me to see him as a protector, as one concerned only with my welfare. But despite his apparent lack of interest in the hierarchy of the Family, he craved influence over the decision making process, his ultimate goal being, I had no doubt, to instigate fundamental changes in the Rule, perhaps try to do away with it altogether.

Not only was the idea heretical, it was sheer madness. The alternative to the Rule was chaos and death, not only within the settlement, but very possibly also outside it. He, in his naivety, for all his long years of life, did not see the inevitable outcomes, blinded as he was by his misguided empathy with his sisters. I waited patiently for him to come to terms with the turn our conversation had taken.

Finally he raised his eyes, which for the first time betrayed both anger and frustration, and whispered, "An agreement, Lord?"

I nodded.

"The females of Derlan's tribe are mine. That is inevitable. I can take no other course, and of that you are well aware. Only moments ago you warned me of the danger. Or would you rather I left them for the pack to dispose of? I think not – you know the likes of Thorlan and his kind as well as I do. But the boy I will let alone, despite it being against my better judgement. You have made it quite clear that you think I can force you to do nothing against your will. I beg to differ with you on that point. However, it would be less troublesome for both of us if we came to some amicable arrangement. Do you not agree?"

"And in exchange for this boy's freedom, what 'arrangement' must I make with you?"

He was cornered now, not having even considered that his behaviour might pose a threat to any but himself.

"I make no excessive demands," I replied reasonably. "I simply wish you to do more than take no action against the Rule. I wish you to act in accordance with it. Spawn a child, and I will be content."

For an instant he reacted with horror, then wisely hid the expression. I continued, "You know the value of your blood. If the offspring is female she will be well kept, and if it is male, it will grow under my protection. I ask nothing more of you. Surely you cannot find it that difficult a task?"

I knew full well that what I was demanding of him was possibly the worst thing he could contemplate. I was asking him to contribute his gift to the search for the ultimate prize – the

110

ability to cross the Great Emptiness to the future. In a way I sympathised with his dilemma, but it was necessary to demonstrate my authority, not only to him, but to the rest of the settlement. There was little he could say by way of objection. According to the Rule he was being extended an honour. Nevertheless, he took in a breath and muttered, "What if I refuse?"

"Then," I answered, "not only will I take the boy and kill its mother, I will find you a woman in any case, and each one you refuse I will kill also. The decision rests with you."

He nodded finally.

"I will do as you wish. After all, you have given me little choice."

He controlled his rage well, and his bitterness. I found myself wishing that our encounter had been a little more companionable. I both liked and admired him. Foolish he might have been, but there was no doubting his courage, nor his forthrightness. I sent out a call for Ilvan. As I waited, a sudden impulse took me, and I said quickly, "Be assured that when the time comes, Amala's blood will come to no harm with me. You have my word."

He rose and bowed his acknowledgement as Ilvan appeared in the doorway, clearly flustered at finding me with my guest. The slight smile that appeared fleetingly on Rolan's lips roused my temper again.

"Our brother has decided to remain with us for a while," I said pleasantly. "Escort him to my old rooms. They are pleasing enough. Then go to the compound and find him a girl – one that is good for breeding and has not yet been taken. But first, see that he is whipped for his insolence. It will serve to remind all of who is master here."

"It would be my pleasure, Lord," Ilvan responded, treating Rolan to a contemptuous stare. He was clearly more than a little piqued by his failure to detect my visitor's entrance.

At the door Rolan hesitated, then turned and with a deferential bow murmured, "Your generosity honours me, Lord."

111

The respectfulness in his voice was as clear as the disdain in his eyes. I inclined my head.

"I assure you," I said, "the honour is mine."

CHAPTER 11

It took Rolan an unconscionable time to fulfil his part of our bargain. It was not that he was guilty of dragging his feet, so to speak. He was as anxious to have the whole thing done with as I was, but I admit that after the first ten years I had begun to grow a little tired of his failures. I had been forced to dispatch three of his offspring, all quite visibly unfit to survive. That, in itself, was not of any great importance to me. What was of concern, however, was the dreadful example he made of himself every time the necessity arose. The more he snivelled over his dead brats, the more I felt inclined to prolong his effective incarceration.

Nevertheless, as time went on I began to think it might be better after all if I were to take notice of his constant pleading to either release him from the vow, or from life altogether. The latter course was one I hesitated to take. The settlement needed him in his former role of trader with the short lived. None had his skill, nor his experience. Generation upon generation of townsfolk had dealt with him, and I realised after only a short time that his contribution, if not to the blood, to our way of life, held an importance that I had not taken into account.

The short lived ones were wary enough of our kind as it was, and those tribes that chose to live openly among them had quite rightly done nothing to allay their fears and suspicions. The fragile trust that Rolan had forged with the other settlements kept us supplied with the things we needed, and none of his replacements had shown anything like his trading skill. Thus, I had little choice but to curse my rashness and my temper and give him back his freedom, on the understanding that he return at least four times a year to attempt a successful mating.

Yet another ten or so years were to pass before his efforts were rewarded, and then, to my surprise, he sired not one but two offspring, born from the same womb within minutes of each other. Such an event was almost unheard of among our kind, and had never occurred before within the Family. There was a male, the elder of the two, a fine, strong infant whom he named Amal, after his sister, which in the old tongue meant 'height' or 'summit', but also, I noted, 'enough'.

The second child, a female, was equally worthy of life, perfect in every way, but this one he would not name, and simply wept over it in a most pathetic fashion. When I took him to task over his reaction, he, as always, answered me openly and fearlessly, saying that he would rather have the child die nameless than have it treated by me as my father had treated his sisters. That, I could understand, but from a different point of view. The cruel life that my father had imposed upon Mira had been, to my mind, ill judged and unnecessary. It had served only to make her a danger to her own offspring – to me, in fact – and had ended in the waste of valuable blood.

I took Rolan aside and reminded him of the terms we had agreed upon – that should he perform his function successfully, I would undertake to see that no harm came to either of his children. Further, I said, for I felt him worthy, for all his faults, of my reassurance, I would ensure that the girl would not be ill treated, that I would not touch her, and that she would only be given to one whom I trusted to treat her with care. He accepted my word graciously, albeit reluctantly, but still refused to name her, and within hours of the births had left the boundaries of the settlement, never to set foot inside again.

As the task was then left to me, I called her Amora (meaning literally 'fleeting', or 'forgotten', but also, in some senses, 'untouched'). I hoped that the reference would not be lost on my brother and that he would be reassured by it. As I had promised, I charged one of the other women, one who had recently lost a child to my judgement, to help the young mother to feed and care for the new additions to the blood.

As I watched Rolan ride away leading a string of young horses behind him, I was surprised to feel a sharp pang of envy. He was freed from his burden, while the weight of mine would be on me until the day I died. Never in my life had I ridden more than a day's journey from my home, and that life had already

114

been longer than that of most short lived men. I was filled with a sudden yearning to see the world beyond the boundaries of our land with my own eyes rather than through the thoughts of others, and as the time went on the urge grew stronger, the thirst for knowledge almost unbearable. But I was chained to my place as surely as I had been chained to my mother, and could do nothing but wait, hoping that the opportunity would present itself to leave the leadership for a while in the hands of my servant and designated heir, Ilvan.

In the meantime, I found myself following the progress of Rolan's children with an interest which surprised me. I was not enamoured of young children, and while I saw it as a woman's duty to express concern, even affection towards her offspring, a similar response in a male was quite unacceptable, at least until the creatures were grown enough to leave the compound. From that point on, of course, a father became responsible for the conduct and education of his sons. Still, I was the head of the Family and could be seen to do as I pleased, within the Rule, and it pleased me to keep a watchful eye on the two outcomes of my bargain.

Some thirteen years passed reasonably uneventfully. Ilvan sired two sons and one daughter, all out of Rysha, and I'm glad to say that he took no interest in other women, as I needed him in my bed as much as I had ever done. Estoran's son Thorlan was less successful, much to his embarrassment, delivering to the Family but one daughter of inconsequential gift. Estoran himself came to the end of his life in the thirtieth year of my rule, taking his beloved horse and riding up into the hills on the far side of the valley. The animal returned riderless three days later and allowed no one near it, so, on my command and with much ceremony, it was sent the way of its master. Morlain had died some years before. His life had not been particularly long, but long enough to spawn some formidable children, as indeed had Estoran. Keeping them in check took a great deal of my time and energy, as I was particularly anxious that they all understood fully that the deaths of their fathers were not a signal for anarchy.

The squabbles over who should preside over Morlain's line came to a head when one of the younger sons took it upon himself to dispatch the eldest, not by legitimate use of his gift, but in a cowardly night time attack that left the unfortunate victim literally in pieces. Such behaviour might have gone unpunished in my father's time, but this was my time, and the act was an affront to the blood. The object of my displeasure, an unintelligent creature by the name of Keslar, seemed to think he had done nothing wrong. That is, he had the notion until he found himself chained by the wrists to the wall of his house, suspended some ten feet off the ground. He was allowed water, which the idiot accepted, thinking that the longer he stayed alive the more chance there was that I might change my mind.

His distasteful death had the required effect, and Morlain's brood quickly brought themselves to order. In fact I bypassed the first generation altogether, settling, strangely enough, on a son of Keslar's, Selim, who seemed, of them all, to have inherited the greatest portion of common sense. Luckily it was rarely necessary for me to emphasise my authority so dramatically, but as is the way with men, memories fade with the passage of time, and every so often I was obliged to remind the more forgetful members of the Family of the wisdom of adhering to the Rule.

Meanwhile, the children of Rolan were growing up. The gift came first to Amora, and it was clear from the beginning that it was formidable – greater, perhaps, than that possessed by Rysha, or even by Ilvan's mother Serenisse. Amal also showed signs of great strength and I had a suspicion that, like his father, he was possessed of the gift of silence. He did not display it to me however, and I let it be, knowing that if it was true it was best left alone. The Family would one day need someone to take Rolan's place and who better than his son, whose silent gift would make him an acceptable and worthy successor.

The pair were both in their mid twenties by now, and there had been no real trouble within the settlement since the episode with Keslar and the ordering of Morlain's dynasty. I rode, hunted, and took my pleasure with the women occasionally. I granted and refused requests for anything from the building of a new dwelling

116

to the taking of women. I judged the fitness of babies and the nature of the gift in the young ones. Many of the minor decisions I now left in Ilvan's hands, and it was rare that I was called upon to intervene. He had excellent judgement, and only those matters that concerned the blood were left to me alone. In short, I was bored. Not only that, my yearning to see the world beyond the valley had turned itself into a necessity, to my mind at least. My father had never concerned himself with the world outside, but for me, seeing with my mind's eye was not enough.

It was not as though we kept ourselves in complete isolation. Several of our men travelled far and wide, some trading as Rolan did, others keeping an eye on the development of the world outside. Added to that, of course, was a group of twenty of my most trusted servants who took it in turns, five at a time, to make the long journey to the south, where they kept a constant watch on the descendants of Derlan. Each year at midsummer a group returned, to be replaced by another.

The young child that I had vowed to let alone in return for Rolan's obedience was now of full breeding age, and had taken a mate, it seemed. Yet there was no sign of offspring, much to my annoyance and frustration. Clearly, I thought, their tribe placed little importance on the furtherance of their own blood. Instead, the boy and his woman had taken up the care of other peoples' children, many of whom were in no measurable way related to them. The idea was utterly mystifying to me – after all, to invest in one of unknown blood was, as far as we were concerned, a waste of energy.

I was intrigued, and determined that I would make the journey myself when the next group set out, an event that was due to occur at the next full turn of the moon. Meanwhile, I had another plan by which I hoped to extend my knowledge and relieve the tedium of my daily life. The sun was just setting, and finishing my wine I turned away from the window and made my way through the growing dusk to the compound.

Amora was not at all put out by my unexpected appearance, despite the late hour. It was a strange thing, but somehow I felt more at ease in her presence than with anyone but

117

my faithful Ilvan. Like him, she showed no fear of me, and trusted me completely, even though such an attitude was rash to say the least. She bowed, as was customary, offering a shy smile, which was not, and bade me be seated, offering me wine and bread. I made myself comfortable and sat watching her as she flitted about the room, tidying and making up the fire, apologising for her lack of readiness. Her innocence, her open manner, brought to me the closest thing I knew to contentment. It was as if she saw a part of me that no one else could see – least of all me.

I waited patiently until she was seated before me, giving me her full attention. Eventually, as I had said nothing, she asked, "Is there something I can do for you, Lord?"

I nodded, and as there was no point in hesitating, I answered simply, "I wish to see what it is that you see in the Dance. I wish to enter it, and see with my own eyes."

I might as well have said that the roof was about to fall in. She jumped up with a gasp, eyes wide with shock, and I thought for a moment she might fall down in a dead faint. She took some deep breaths however, and managed to control herself enough to sit down again, shaking her head and muttering, "No, impossible!" under her breath.

It struck me then that she might be afraid of what I might see in the minds of other women inside the compound. It was a reasonable enough assumption, as it would be easy for me to detect any violation of the Rule if I were to be presented with the inner feelings of the entire female population of the settlement. An unauthorised liaison or affection might be easy enough to ignore if it was not brought to my attention, but once I knew about it, the Rule would give me no option but to act.

"You misunderstand," I said quickly. "I have no wish to pry into the secrets of anyone here, male or female. What you see within the settlement does not concern me."

"Then what, Lord?" She was puzzled now, and, I realised, genuinely concerned. "It can't be done," she went on. "It is not possible for a man to see with the eyes of a woman. The gift does not allow it. You would be lost in the maze of the Dance, unable

118

to find your way. It is said that if a man enters, he can never leave, and his mind will be lost forever. Tell me what you want to know and I will look, and tell you what I see. I will show you everything. But please, Lord, do not ask me to take you to your death."

Her fear for me was touching, and everything she said was true. There were tales from the old times of men who had tried to follow the myriad delicate threads of the Dance, and whose minds had been emptied, shattered by the confusion of so many diverging paths all calling to them at once. I recalled the pain of the first days of the coming of my gift, and how I had been driven almost mad by the noise and chaos of what must have been only a pale reflection of the complexity of the true Dance. Yes, it was dangerous, but my mind was made up. She knew it as well as I, and fell silent, although she looked more frightened than if I had demanded to mate with her.

"How far can you take your mind?" I asked, trying to make my tone gentle, conversational. She shook her head again, considering, then said, "A long way, Lord. I do not know how far exactly. Is there something – someone, that you wish to see?"

I nodded. "You know who and what I wish to see. But perhaps we should not begin with so ambitious a journey. Listen, Amora. I believe that you are strong enough to guide me, to keep me safe within your Dance. I trust your skill and will be guided by your judgement. You will not fail me."

"If you command me, Lord," she replied uncertainly, "I must obey. But I beg you to reconsider. What if I am not strong enough? What if harm comes to you? I will be held responsible. Perhaps you or your heir will take vengeance on all of us, and the other women will suffer for my failure."

She was on her feet now, pacing up and down in agitation. She was right again, and I admit that I hadn't really thought about what might happen if things went wrong.

"The Lord Ilvan is aware of my intentions," I lied, "and has been given the proper instructions. There is no need for your concern."

119

At last she seemed mollified, and with a nod of resignation sank down opposite me.

"Good," I said. "Now, can you take me to where your father goes? I wish to see what kind of people he deals with in the world of the short lived. It is a long time since Lord Corvan held them under his influence, and I need to know more about how they live, what their intentions are towards us now."

All this, of course, I knew already. I felt it prudent to choose something simple, close at hand, something that Amora would feel was within her grasp. But aside from that I had another motive. Since the coming of the gift I had always been particularly sensitive to noise. It was my intention to deliver Rolan's son to him, and to accompany them both on their next trading expedition. But I knew myself well enough to know that I might well create havoc among the short lived, possessed as I was of such a volatile temper in the face of even the slightest irritation. Within the settlement I rarely felt the need to exercise undue caution, but the outside world was a different matter, and if I was to encounter outsiders I must learn to master the curse that my father had placed upon me. Within Amora's Dance I would place no one in danger except myself, and perhaps my young and innocent guide.

She looked up at me, and after a moment's consideration nodded her assent.

"Please forgive me, Lord, but I must ask you to follow my direction completely. Whatever I tell you to do, you must do, without hesitation."

"I agree," I said, trying to remain as patient as I could with her. She nodded again.

"It will take me a moment to find my way. When I am ready I will call to you. Only then may you enter, see what I see. But when I tell you to leave you must do it at once, no matter how much you wish not to. Please understand, Lord, that I only say this because it is necessary."

"I understand," I replied. "I am ready."

She closed her eyes, and I watched, fascinated, as her body gradually became still as stone, her breathing almost imperceptible. Time seemed to drag on interminably, the stillness grow heavier and heavier around me. As I waited, the feeling came on me that I was witnessing a thing that was not meant for my eyes, a secret place from which I, and all men, were excluded. No power, no confinement could ever still the Dance. In the heart of my own stronghold, where I controlled every living thing with the mere whisper of my presence, was something as far beyond my grasp as a creature like myself might have been from one of the short lived merchants of the town. How right my father had been, I thought, to be wary. In each one of these delicate vessels of the blood lay the power to confuse and bewilder, to take a man's mind from him and sap his strength completely, that is, if the man allowed it.

I was beginning to understand the enormity of what I had asked for, and to regret my rashness in believing that my own strength would protect me. But it was too late to have second thoughts, for at that moment I heard Amora's voice in my mind, calling me softly to come, to risk my sanity in the most dangerous place I could imagine myself to be. Looking back, I can only say how little imagination I truly had in those days, and that the pain of what I was about to experience paled into insignificance when set against what was to come later in my life.

I gathered myself, and sent my thought to join hers, carefully, in case the strength of my mind should overwhelm her. I need not have worried on that score. The moment I entered her thought I was swept away, as though the entire heart of me was being ripped out of my body and flung such a huge distance that for a second I was thrown into a panic, thinking that I would never be whole again. I was assaulted by myriad visions at once, each with its own sights, smells and sounds, some near, some far, all cascading over my senses with alarming speed and intensity. I felt as though I was drowning, and was about to cry out when I felt myself lifted up high above the whirling images, and pulled along, away from the noise and into a brief and blessed silence.

Unfortunately the state of calm did not last long. The vision of a huge settlement appeared before me – a great town filled with bustling activity, many times bigger than our own. It was teeming with short lived men, women and children, who rushed up and down the narrow earth streets, the wider main concourses packed with people and carts, all pressing against each other as they jostled through the crowds, making their way hither and thither like so many bees in a hive. The images were much brighter, more direct, than anything I had seen through the eyes of our traders. It was though I was actually there, suspended in mid air several hundred feet above the earth. Amora was casting her mind about, seeking out the threads of thought of individuals way down below. She seemed suddenly to decide, and we descended rapidly (at least that is the only manner in which I can describe the movement).

Almost immediately I was overcome with such a barrage of noise and uncontrolled emotion streaming from the inhabitants of the town that I began with all my strength to pull my mind away. But I was helpless, trapped inside her Dance, and the closer we got the more agonising it became until I was quite beside myself, unable to keep control of my own thoughts, lashing out wildly and incoherently with no other thought than that I wanted to be gone and back inside my own body. The more violent my struggles became, the worse it got, until the pain of their thoughts was quite unendurable. My body, in some other place, so far away that I had no sense of it at all, was, I somehow knew, suffering equally, and I became quite convinced that if I ever managed to return to it, it would be mangled out of all recognition.

We were right in the midst of the crowds now, and in a last supreme effort I flung Amora away from me, thinking that if I was released from her I might escape from the torture, somehow find my way back through the labyrinth to safety. What happened, though, was quite the opposite. I was stripped now of even her meagre protection, and in a flash the town had disappeared, leaving me descending with frightening speed into the terrible mass of thoughts, images and feelings that had assaulted me when I had first entered the confusion of the Dance. I was bereft of even the smallest foothold, being driven slowly mad by the deafening noise that tore at my mind, blinding my senses to everything but sheer terror.

All of a sudden I was struck by a phenomenal force, the shock of which made me cry out as my mind was hurled out into some cold, dark place, all the sounds cut off as though a door had been slammed behind me. A second later I felt a different pain, one that I vaguely recognised as coming from the flesh of my physical body, although I had no idea whether or not it was in the same place as before, or even whether my mind was back inside it. I was blind, deaf and deathly cold, and I don't think in all my life I had ever been in such torment. It felt as though all the skin was being torn from my bones, a sensation made worse by the fact that I could neither hear nor see. In my mind I curled myself into a tiny ball and gave myself up to my despair, shivering violently, moaning uncontrollably, hoping only that my life would soon end, and with it the terrible pain and helplessness.

At first I shrank away from the hand that grasped mine in the dark, its touch burning white hot, increasing the anguish that was spreading through every fibre of my being with alarming speed. I think I tried to protest, but in vain, and the touch moved to my head, the hands covering my ears and remaining locked there for what seemed an age. I began to hear a buzzing, as of many insects, getting louder and louder, denying all my efforts to shut it out, until finally I heard a voice, faint and far away, but a real voice, in the air and not in my mind.

"My Lord?" I had not the strength to answer, but tried to turn my head in the direction of the sound. "My Lord, can you hear me?"

I struggled to find my voice, but the effort made my head spin. I drew on what little reserves I had left, and finally managed to whisper, "I hear you." My mouth was so dry I could hardly form the words. I heard a long sigh of relief. I opened my mouth again.

"I can't see."

"Open your eyes," came the reply. "They are not damaged."

It took me a while to make the connection, to remember how to make my mind work my body, then I realised that my eyelids were screwed tight shut. With some difficulty I managed to send the commands that would open them, and when I did I was blinded again by the bright glare of torchlight. Slowly, I began to make out blurs of colour, hazy movement in front of me. I couldn't focus, and when my head was lifted the whole room seemed to lurch wildly, so much so that I felt quite sick. A cup of water was placed to my lips and I drank gratefully before allowing myself to sink back onto a cushion that had been placed behind my head. The buzzing in my ears was beginning to fade, and very slowly the fog cleared from my vision.

"What happened here, Lord?" Ilvan's face betrayed his confusion and concern.

"How badly am I hurt?" I asked. I had not dared to examine myself, as I was sure my body had been torn half to pieces. He shrugged, unsure how to answer.

"I don't understand, Lord. You are not hurt, except that your ears were burst open. I have never seen such a thing. They are healed now. That was all. There is nothing else that I can see."

I looked up at him for a moment in disbelief, then checked for myself, and found that what he said was true. Apart from my hearing, which was improving rapidly, I had not a scratch on me, much to my amazement. I let the fact sink in for a moment, then said, "Help me up."

I had to lean on him for a while to get my balance. Finally, everything stopped swaying and I looked about me, my eyes falling at once on a crumpled heap in the corner of the room. I took in my breath and looked questioningly at Ilvan, half dreading the answer I knew he would give. He shook his head.

"Every bone is shattered, Lord. She was dead when I entered the room." His incomprehension was complete. With another shake of the head, he asked again, "What happened here?"

CHAPTER 12

It was hard to decide which was worse, being subjected to Ilvan's recriminations or being left alone to try, unsuccessfully, to ward off my own. I was guilty of the worst stupidity, arrogance and wastefulness, and I couldn't deny it, no matter how hard I tried to justify my actions. It had been more than two days since my escapade and I was still in considerable pain, even though there was apparently nothing physically wrong with me. My heir was singularly unsympathetic, his ministrations as perfunctory as he could manage, although I couldn't fault the efficiency of his attentions. He was sulking, in part, because I had not confided in him. That was as well, I thought, as he had no right to expect to be apprised of every one of my intentions or decisions. Nevertheless, I missed his gentle comfort, and only had myself to blame for his coldness. I had been brought supper, but had no appetite for it, and contented myself with the wine jug, sipping morosely and hoping that the strong drink would provide some relief from my discomfort.

I must have fallen into a light doze, because the next thing I remember was being awakened by a soft movement somewhere in the room. At first I thought it must be Ilvan, come to check on the fire and refill the empty jug. I had taken far too much wine on an empty stomach and my defences were low, my mind sluggish. I opened my eyes just in time to see the flash of metal in the darkness right above me, and must have instinctively tried to roll aside, as the next thing I felt was a sickening pain in my shoulder which jolted me wide awake. I had no time to think, however, as already the blade was on its second downward arc. I grabbed wildly and by some good fortune caught the wrist of my attacker, then, launching myself up managed to throw him off balance, and landed heavily on top of him, pinning him to the floor. I twisted the arm until I heard the snap of bone, followed by the clatter of the knife spinning away into the darkness. The two of us lay there for a moment, breathing heavily. I needed light. Shifting my

125

position so that my knee was on the man's chest, I drew back my fist and struck a blow to his temple, hard enough to knock him cold for the minute or so I needed to gather myself and kindle a flame.

I knelt on the floor in the light of the torches. Blood was streaming from my injured shoulder, but I hardly noticed. My dilemma had just become even more impossible to solve. The Rule was clear. Violence against the head of the Family was the greatest of crimes – to even contemplate such an action was, theoretically, punishable by death. But this was far worse. My house had been violated, I had been injured. What choice did I have but to act in accordance with the Rule, and send the boy, who still lay unconscious before me, to a fate so terrible that even I had some difficulty imagining it? I wiped my hand across my forehead in exasperation, unable to think of any solution, wondering what I would have done if I had been in his place.

My reverie was interrupted by a low moan and I saw my assailant open his eyes and glance about the room, trying to remember where he was. Eventually his gaze rested on me, and immediately a fire kindled in his eyes that he could not control. With a swiftness that surprised me he tried to leap to his feet and launch himself towards me once again, hissing, "Murderer! Liar!" under his breath.

It was only then that he realised that his arm was broken, and giving a little yelp paused long enough for me to hit him hard in the chest with the palm of my hand. This sent him sprawling back onto the floor where he lay, helpless, glaring up at me with all the hatred he could muster.

For what seemed like several minutes we stared at each other. His eyes flitted from my face to my bleeding shoulder and back again several times, and gradually his animosity gave way to confusion. Finally he whispered, "Why am I still alive?"

I wasn't about to tell him the true reason, so I allowed myself the smallest flicker of a smile and answered, in a voice that I hoped he would find chilling enough, "Perhaps because I don't wish to deprive you of full knowledge of the consequences of your actions."

I saw the shadow of fear fleeting across his face, but he stuck his chin out gamely and said, "Do as you wish, Rendail. But it makes you no less a murderer, or a liar!"

I slapped his cheek, somewhat harder than I intended. "I thank you for your honesty. But if you wish to insult me, you would do well to remember your manners while you are doing it."

He lowered his eyes, and nodded grudgingly. "Forgive me, Lord." Then he raised them again and said, "But I won't take back my words."

"I should hope not," I replied. "I would be most disappointed to think that after coming so far, you had lost your resolve. But have you really thought things through? You accuse me of actions that you seem to wish me to repeat. You have certainly not considered the effect, whether you had been successful or not, on your father and on your line." I cocked my head, considering, then went on, "But perhaps he knows you are here. Perhaps he sent you, knowing that you would fail, and that I would be forced to break my word yet again. I have to say that if that is the case, I have underestimated him somewhat. It was a clever ploy, if a waste of his own blood."

My young assailant sat up, aghast, his eyes burning with outrage. "No, Lord. My father knows nothing of this. It was my idea – mine alone. No one knows I am here. My father is weak, a coward. He hides beyond the gates, afraid to enter. He leaves it to me to do to what he doesn't have the courage to do. He could never do such a thing, never!"

I slapped the boy again, sending him flat on his back, and he propped himself on the elbow of his good arm, glaring at me resentfully.

"You have a lot to learn," I said quietly. "No, your father could not have done such a thing – he doesn't have your stupidity. As for being a coward, if he desired to challenge me he would come in the daylight and look me in the eye, not creep into my chamber to kill me in my sleep. Courage takes many forms, but I have never known the term apply to an assassin that comes armed in the night. Your father is a brave man, and you would do well not to forget it."

He looked a little ashamed now, and I could see his anger slowly peeling away to reveal the grief that had driven him to his thoughtless and reckless action. He shook his head, and in a voice that mirrored his confusion he whispered, "You betrayed him. You killed my sister. Why? You gave your word. Why does he not avenge himself?"

I sighed and regarded him in silence for a moment. When he had calmed himself a little I said, "Your father once told me that I had the misfortune to inherit the affliction of my father's blood. It seems that you are equally cursed. Listen carefully to what I say. I never intended to harm Amora, nor to break my word. I regret her death, perhaps more than you know. Her blood was possibly the finest of all our women, and I would not knowingly have wasted it. I put myself in danger, and she gave her life to save mine. Now you wish to destroy what she died to preserve. You think that a fitting return for her sacrifice?"

I got up and cast around for a cloth to staunch my wound, which thankfully was beginning to bleed less heavily. At the same time I sent out a silent call to Ilvan for food and more wine. Deliberately, as I did so I turned my back on Amal, and was relieved to find that he made no attempt to renew his attack, but just sat himself up, watching. I sat down again, dabbing at my shoulder, and a moment later the door opened to admit my tense and tight lipped servant.

At the sight that greeted him, Ilvan made no comment – the look in his eyes was enough to quite adequately convey his feelings to both of us. I am sure that given the slightest sanction he would have torn Amal limb from limb on the spot, and at the sight of my wound took in his breath, laid down his tray and rushed off to get water and more cloths. Amal stayed still while Ilvan tended to me, after which I bade my servant take possession of what could have turned out to be a murder weapon, and sent him away again.

When we were once more alone, Amal spoke. "I think you misunderstand my sister's motives, Lord. She didn't sacrifice herself to save you. She was concerned only for the lives of the other women, and what danger to them might have resulted from your death. If I were to kill you, no blame would fall upon them, and your heir would take vengeance on me alone. I am ready to die, but I only wish that it could be with the satisfaction of knowing that you had preceded me."

It was a bold speech, but it was also a lie. The boy was terrified, and not without reason, but I suppose he knew as well as I did that he had nothing more to lose. The act was done, and no words could make the slightest difference to the slow and agonising death that awaited him.

"You should eat," I said, pushing the tray towards him. "You will need your strength."

I took some bread for myself, and poured the boy a cup of wine. It was strange, but the events of the last hour had somehow brought me back to life, and the ill effects I had suffered as a result of my intrusion into Amora's Dance were now rapidly dissipating. Amal stared at the food, pale faced, as if it might jump up at him. I could well imagine that his appetite had by now completely deserted him. Daylight was still some two or three hours away, so without a second thought I settled myself back on my rugs, and turning away from him let myself sink into a deep, untroubled sleep.

Dawn had just broken when I opened my eyes again. Amal had not moved, it seemed, but was still sitting where I had left him, staring blankly at the untouched food on the tray. The wine cup was, however, empty. I washed and groomed myself with particular care, breakfasting on the remains of the bread and fruit before turning my attention to my brother's unfortunate son. His untreated arm was by now quite swollen, and must have been causing him some pain, although he was doing his best to show no sign of it. The hours spent in silent contemplation of his fate had taken all the fight out of him, and he simply sat, defeated, staring straight ahead, his body tense with fear.

When I was ready I grabbed him by his injured arm and hauled him to his feet. He whimpered, but offered no resistance. Without a word I gestured for him to walk in front of me, and we

129

made our way out and down the staircase to the great reception hall below. There, Ilvan awaited us, and at my nod he pressed against a stone in the far wall opposite the door. It swung back to reveal a narrow hidden stairway leading downwards. I handed over my charge, who was becoming more frightened by the second, and watched as Ilvan pushed him roughly down the stairs into the darkness, the stone swinging shut behind them.

I couldn't help but praise my father's ingenuity as I strolled down the pavement in the early summer sunshine, making for the stables. Beneath his house a great system of passages had been carved out, a maze with many false turnings and hidden exits. The thing had taken more than two hundred years to devise, and was entirely secret. In around my thirtieth year he had shown me the structure, taught me which passage led to where, how to move the stones that blocked the routes to just about every corner of the settlement. One who knew the system could travel more or less anywhere without being seen, and so I could come and go as I pleased, leaving everyone with the belief that I was safely out of sight and mind within my own rooms. Ilvan was the only other living soul who knew of the existence of the maze – at least he had been until now. As I took my horse from the waiting groom I wondered briefly whether my present course of action might not be a mistake. Given the other decisions I had made recently it was not beyond the bounds of possibility, but only time would tell. A silent command sent my mount flying at a swift gallop, away from the woodland and across the peat marshes of the valley towards the barren crags to the north of the settlement.

I had been comfortably encamped for several hours when Ilvan finally appeared, dragging the unfortunate Amal behind him. The boy had been forced to walk the entire way, over quite rough terrain, under Ilvan's watchful eye, the latter on horseback, following just behind. He was deposited in front of me footsore and exhausted, nursing his broken arm, for which he had somehow managed to make himself a makeshift sling. I consulted swiftly with my servant, who confirmed that neither had been seen leaving the settlement, then bade him farewell, and watched as he rode away, leaving the two of us alone. My assailant was thoroughly chastened by this time. Frightened and confused, he huddled by the small fire not daring to say a word. He glanced at me once and I gave him the benefit of a grim smile, on which he shivered and looked away, but otherwise I ignored him completely and settled myself to wait until nightfall.

At precisely the hour agreed upon I heard the approach of a single rider, slow and cautious, coming up to the foot of the crag. The hooves fell silent and were replaced by soft footfalls. A moment later the tall figure of Rolan appeared in the firelight. I stayed where I was, seated, making no sudden movements. Amal, wrapped in his misery on the other side of the fire, didn't even look up. Rolan came to a halt, not looking at his son, his eyes fixed on me, waiting. I didn't return the look, but gestured towards the boy.

"Take him," I said after a short silence. "When you have tended to him, join me."

I sensed the curt nod in response, and watched as Rolan walked over to Amal. He took the boy by the hair and yanked his head up, his expression quite thunderous. Amal looked from his father to me and back again, completely uncomprehending. Rolan hauled him to his feet and they disappeared into the blackness, just out of earshot. A little while later my brother re-emerged, and sat opposite me. I finally met his eye, and allowed myself the luxury of acknowledging his silent accusation with a nod.

"He is young," I said quietly, "and impetuous. He acted without consideration, as young ones do. It is fortunate that he made use of his father's silent gift. I don't think I could have brought him here otherwise."

Rolan's eyes narrowed, and he thought on it for a while, then said, "You think you owe me a life. You wish to spare my son in payment of the debt. Did you really think that this gesture could do more than scrape the surface of your guilt? If you expect any measure of gratitude from me, then your journey has been wasted. What you have done cannot be undone, and I will take none of the weight of it from you. The life of Amal is a poor

131

exchange for my forgiveness. If that is your price, I will not pay it, so it is better you take him, and deal with him according to the Rule as you would any other of our people."

"As always," I replied, "you honour me with the truth. But you mistake me. I didn't turn aside the Rule from any sense of guilt, or to obtain your favour. I brought him here because I want you to understand that I would not knowingly break my word, and that I didn't intend to harm your daughter. Your son has been extremely foolish, but he is also brave and honourable. Had I been in his place, I can't say I wouldn't have acted as he did. As for Amora, I both admit and regret that my own foolishness was the cause of her death. I only ask that you keep watch over the boy, and keep him safe from his own passion until he is of an age to control it. You must make him understand that any further attempt on my life can only meet with failure, and I will be unable to protect him a second time."

My speech was met with a stony silence, but that was of no particular concern to me. I had said what I needed to say, and so I rose, and walked across to where my horse was tethered. Rolan followed, and as I was about to ride away he placed a hand on the rein to prevent me.

"Tell me, Rendail," he said, "what did you find, within the Dance? Was it worth my daughter's life?"

I let the lack of courtesy pass. After all, I had come to offer my brother the truth, and it was no less than he deserved.

"I found a forbidden place," I answered. "I found a loneliness in the midst of crowds, a power that I could not control. I saw what it might be like to die, blind, deaf and alone. If Amora had not used her last strength to thrust me out, I have no doubt I would have been lost forever. We can't go there, and it was foolish to try."

He looked closely into my eyes, as if trying to gauge my sincerity, then drew back with a slight smile.

"You need not fear that either Amal or I will ever seek to end your life. It is my greatest wish that you live a very long time, and I will make sure that he understands it."

"How so?" I asked, surprised.

He smiled again. "My daughter's death was not in vain. You will never be rid of the seed she has planted in you, and the longer you live, the more it will grow. You are fated to become all that you most despise, and death is as nothing in comparison to the suffering that awaits you in the centuries to come. I have never sought revenge, yet it is already mine. That is my daughter's gift to me, and I treasure it."

He turned, still smiling, and disappeared into the dark, leaving me quite alone. A moment later I heard the sound of his horse's hooves fading into the distance. With a shrug I turned my mount and headed south, back to where I knew my servant would be waiting with wine, food and whatever else I desired.

CHAPTER 13

Never become unwary, my father had once told me, for even those you trust will betray you. In some ways his wisdom was far greater than mine. Decades of power had made me complacent in a way that he would never have been. Even the episode with Amora, and after with Amal, had taught me nothing. The incident was no more than a ripple in the tide of my life, soon put out of mind as the business of dealing with the day to day affairs of my people took over my thoughts. In addition to that, I was still determined to fulfil my ambition to see more of the world, and so I began to leave Ilvan in charge of things while I went wandering about the countryside, studying the land and the people in it.

At first I went on only short journeys. I was careful to remain within earshot, so to speak, of the settlement, and stayed away no longer than three or four nights at a time. Once or twice I accompanied the traders on their routes to one town or another, but made sure that I kept my distance from Rolan and his son, who had remained together, dealing mainly in the trade of horses far to the north. It soon became apparent, however, that this plan of action was far from satisfactory. Any pretence of normality dissipated the moment I appeared, all my observations coloured by the obvious anxiety of my guides. Therefore I took to journeying alone, and as time went on my periods of absence grew longer, sometimes two or three turns of the moon.

I rarely entered the towns and settlements. The clamour of the short lived was still painful to me and I did not trust myself not to lash out at some noisy innocent if my irritation overcame me. If, out of necessity, I was forced to engage in some transaction, I would wait until the quietest part of the night and then haul a sleepy merchant from his bed to see to my needs. It amused me to see how their gruff demeanour changed instantly into an obsequious eagerness once they realised what kind of a creature I was.

The further I went, the more I encountered, from a distance, others of our kind, mingling freely with the short lived, not in secret, but displaying their gift quite openly. For the most part their skills were feeble, inconsequential when compared to those of even our weakest ones, and it was clear that I must keep myself at quite a distance to avoid being recognised for what I was. These people seemed to have no regard at all for the protocols that governed the control of the gift. Men and women mixed together as though they were equals. Their true thoughts were emblazoned on the forefronts of their minds with no heed to who might be listening. They mated at random, even, on occasion and to my complete disgust, with the short lived ones, siring half breed young that were neither one thing nor the other. Even these weak ones, I thought, were of the blood, and it was their duty, whether they realised it or not, to act in accordance with the Rule.

When I discussed my observations with Ilvan, he agreed that it was indeed a strange way to behave. It was not true of all, however, as he reminded me. Derlan's family was one of the oldest, perhaps even as old as ours, and they also regarded the inferior mixing of the blood as unacceptable. At least it appeared so from their behaviour, much to my relief.

At last, I felt that I was ready to see for myself. It was a risky venture, but one that had obsessed me for several years, and which had driven me to the disastrous encounter with Amora. One of the consequences of that had been to make me shy away from any further ill conceived adventures, but now, two years later, I thought myself much better prepared, both in body and mind, to make the journey. Ilvan, too, was now well versed in the art of command and entirely capable of maintaining control over the settlement while I was away. He expressed some apprehension when I told him that I might be gone for as much as half a year, but my mind was made up, and three days later I set off on the long and arduous journey to the far south, to see and feel with my own eyes and mind the nature of our sworn enemy, the keepers of Amala's stolen blood.

It was late autumn and already the first frosts had visited the valleys inside our borders. You might think it the worst possible time to make a journey of any sort, as indeed it was, but I had not chosen to leave near the onset of winter entirely by accident. Since my father's death there had really been nothing to challenge me. I had taken power, and exercised it with what amounted to little effort. The force of my will lay heavily over my people, and it had been a long time since any had dared to contradict me, at least openly. Now and then someone might be foolish enough to go against the Rule, but such matters were summarily dealt with, without argument or hindrance. If I truly wished to test my strength I needed an opponent worthy of my gift, and what better than the force of nature at its most bitter, most unforgiving season.

I aimed to travel by the hardest route of all, over the high peaks that ran for many miles right down to the milder climate far to the south. Even there I would find myself with a formidable distance to cover if I wanted to reach the place where Derlan's tribe had made its home, in the fruitful valleys close to the western sea. Here, the people fed off fat tender sheep that grazed on the perpetually green hillsides, and hunted more for amusement than from necessity. We kept no more than a very few cattle to provide us with milk, and had not the terrain to provide us with the abundance enjoyed by Derlan's people. The harshness of our land was, I suppose, reflected in our lives and in our thoughts, and we prided ourselves on our skill in the hunt, our endurance of the cold.

I will not describe all that befell me on that journey. It was long, much longer than I intended. I fought with biting winds on the high, bleak moors, with cold and heavy snowfalls. I bathed in snow and drank from icy streams, going for many days without fire, surviving on roots that I dug from the frozen ground and ate raw. Had it not been for the occasional fox, scurrying across the peaks trying to find shelter, I would have believed myself the only living creature left on earth. I discovered caves and hollows along the route, and stored away their whereabouts in my memory so that I would be able to find them again if there was ever need. If I found a good place I would stay for several days, warming myself, allowing my horse to rest. I gloried in the hardship and the solitude. For once, I found myself truly knowing what it was to be alive, to be at one with all things, my gift inconsequential in the face of the deepening winter. When I finally descended into the valleys at the southern tip of the range the season was turning, and the smaller hills and meadows were swathed in no more than a fine coverlet of frost that melted away in the midday sun.

I moved on at a leisurely pace, drinking in the sights and smells of the unfamiliar countryside. Wild game was plentiful, and everywhere there was colour, even the pink and white of early blossoms on the trees, their sweet scents filling the air. At home the snow was still lying thick on the pavements and would remain for perhaps another month. I was entranced by the beauty of the land, its softness, the way the grass yielded under my horse's hooves. But I knew that I did not and would never belong there, nor would ever be tempted to stay.

At last I came to what I knew were the outer borders of the lands of Derlan's tribe. It was a little bleaker here, the green landscape broken here and there by outcrops of white rock, the hillsides dotted with coarse scrub. The peaks were nothing like as commanding as those I had crossed on my journey, but nevertheless the summits of some were still capped with snow, and the winds were a little more chill. I went forward cautiously now, not wishing to come upon any other Dancer by accident. My gift was too powerful to hide, and any encounter might send word back to the ones I sought, to warn them of the presence of one of Corvan's people. It took several days to traverse the distance from the border to the main settlement. I stayed well outside the mass of dwellings that I found nestling in a wide valley between the range of high hills and the sea.

For several days I watched, tentatively searching with my mind for the presence of others of my kind. There were several dotted about this settlement, mingled with the usual din of their short lived neighbours. But unlike those I had come across in other places, these were the sensations of a clan of impressive power. In their dealings with the short lived they were courteous and gentle, but at the same time they held themselves aloof from the common crowd, conducting themselves with the propriety and restraint that I would have expected from the old blood.

My comrades, the servants that watched over the future vessels of the blood, were many miles away, keeping their constant vigil over the young one and his mate as I had commanded them. But he was not the object of my curiosity. It was the father, Amala's child, my cousin, who consumed my interest. He had been named, curiously enough, after Rolan, my brother and our common uncle, and I wished to feel for myself what blood had passed into him, what gifts his offspring might be capable of in the years to come. The time was fast approaching when I would need to sire my own sons, and if it was to be with a daughter of his line I had to satisfy myself of the worthiness of her blood. That is, I thought bitterly, if the wretched creature's child ever saw fit to spawn.

Finally, one evening after dark, I decided to risk moving just a little closer, and made my way on foot through the woods that lay beyond the fields at the western edge of the town. The year was still young, and the population all happy to be closing their shutters and stoking their fires almost before dusk had fallen. I made my way unhindered to the woodland edge and looked out across the fields. Nothing was stirring, and my mind told me that no watchers guarded the approaches to the houses. For perhaps an hour I wrestled with my curiosity and then, making up my mind, I skirted the tall hedges that marked off one field from another, until I found myself just some twenty paces from a low stone wall, beyond which lay a green lawn leading up to a large, somewhat ornate stone building.

The owner of this house, I judged, must have been of high standing, as the ownership of land such as this, kept only for pleasure and adorned with all manner of beautiful plants, was everywhere a rarity. I was about to move a little closer when I heard the soft click of a door opening and footsteps coming round the side of the house, in my direction. I quickly concealed myself behind the last section of hedging, which was tall enough to allow me to stand unseen, and observed the figure that strolled across the lawn towards the stone wall.

As the man reached the wall and came to a halt the clouds parted, letting the bright light of the moon shine full upon his face. It was all I could do not to gasp with amazement. I froze, hardly able to believe that he could be unaware of my presence just a matter of feet away from him. But he was – he simply stood, gazing out over the fields, lost in some pleasant reverie, a slight smile playing on his lips. I had no doubt that I was looking at Rolan, son of Derlan and Amala.

The resemblance to his namesake was striking. He had the same sensitive face, the same honeyed skin that his grandfather Corvan had given him. There was but one difference, and it was striking. Whereas my brother had inherited his mother's straight, golden hair, this one possessed a head of the most extraordinary dark curls that tumbled around his face and down his back as though they had a life all their own. It was the mark of Derlan, visible proof of the taint that had been placed upon our blood, yet in its way, I had to admit, a handsome defect. It was then that I realised why it was that he had no idea I was there. His name and his looks were not the only things taken from my brother. Both of them, it was clear, possessed the gift of silence and both, when their minds were veiled, could not sense the thoughts of others.

I pondered on this for a moment, then decided to take just one more risk. With an effort I was able to reach through my brother's veil a little way. Did I have the same skill in reading my cousin's silent thoughts? I composed myself, and sent out the tiniest sliver of enquiry. My answer came in the form of a jolt to my senses as my own force was reflected back at me, rather like a ray of sunlight bouncing off the surface of a lake. Rolan, however, did not move or make any sign that he had noticed anything untoward. I tried again, a little stronger this time, and again, the strength of my own thought came back to me. But this time another impression accompanied my effort. I saw no glimpse of what was in his mind, but beneath the shell which protected his thoughts I sensed his power, and knew instinctively that there were few who could match it. Estoran might have rivalled it once, or Selim, Morlain's grandson. Whatever mixing there had been of the blood, the gift had not weakened because of it. I knew now what I had come so far to discover. If this man's son was as strong as the father, then any female born of the line would be beyond price.

At that moment, I heard the door open again, and a woman came out to join Rolan. She was small, beautiful and clearly of pure blood, her blonde hair sparkling in the moonlight. He turned to her and with a welcoming smile enveloped her in his arms. She was his mate, clearly, and one to whom he was completely in thrall. Suddenly she broke off his embrace and peered fearfully into the darkness. She could sense something, but did not know quite what. This, I thought, might be dangerous. If she persuaded her mate to lift his veil of silence I would be revealed in an instant, and all our careful years of watching might come to nothing. I stayed as still and quiet as I could, battening down my thoughts with all the strength I could muster.

"What is it?" I heard him say.

"I thought I could hear something," she replied, unsure. "Come, it's cold, and I want you beside me. There is something unhealthy about the air tonight – I can feel it."

He laughed, and putting his arm around her waist turned back to the house. Together they went inside, murmuring to each other, he reassuring her, teasing her gently about her unease. I heard the door close behind them and heaved a sigh of relief. I had taken a great risk, but now I knew what I had come to learn. I smiled to myself as I made my way back to the woodland, where my horse was ready. Without waiting for the dawn, I rode away from the town, and started on the long journey back to the home that was waiting to welcome the first female descendant of Amala.

CHAPTER 14

There was no urgency in my journey home. I had satisfied my curiosity, and knew that to remain so close to Derlan's tribe for any length of time would have been a mistake. So, having seen I withdrew, resisting the temptation to join the ever watchful guards and glimpse the child, Devren, and his mate. However, my thirst for knowledge of the world was as unquenchable as ever and I travelled many miles out of my way to see one sight or another before resuming my leisurely course northward.

By the time I reached the borders of our territory almost three quarters of a year had passed, and a warm summer was drawing lazily to its end, the leaves just beginning to turn to the reds and golds of early autumn. As soon as I crossed into our lands I felt the familiar buzz of thoughts from the settlement, which was still several hours ride away through the pine forests. Of course, although I could distinguish even individual voices, I remained invisible to them, none having my gift to range so far. It was mid evening, so I stopped and made camp in a small clearing, intending to ride the final distance at first light.

I had eaten, and was sitting comfortably with my back against a tree, letting the fragrance of my own land wash over me, when something made me uneasy. There was no danger at hand – that I knew for certain, but something, I knew not what, was amiss. I suppose the best way I can describe the feeling was the sensation of running a finger across a finely woven fabric and coming across a thread in the weave slightly coarser than the others. All in the settlement appeared as it should be. Nothing had changed in the demeanour of my people. The whole place was shrouded in the calm quietness of evening. No attempt had been made to challenge my rule in my absence – I would have perceived that at once. And yet something gnawed at my mind, an almost imperceptible flaw in the essence of things, a faintly troubling doubt that I couldn't name. Instinctively, I searched for Ilvan. At first, his weaker gift made him indistinguishable from

141

the murmurings of many others, but I knew his mind better than any, and after a while I caught the familiar shape of his thoughts as he moved silently down the darkened pavement towards the house that we shared.

He was unusually pensive, it seemed to me – guarded, even a little furtive. It was unlike him, and at first I thought that perhaps he was feeling the same unexplained apprehension as myself. But he didn't appear to think himself in any immediate danger from anyone else in the place. He moved with his customary confident ease, surveying his surroundings with an air of lordly superiority, just as I would have expected from my heir and principal steward. What, then, was the cause of his disquiet?

When he reached the hall he gave the instruction to the doorkeepers to close the doors and allow no one to enter. Then, taking a torch from the wall he moved to the secret entrance of the underground maze, and to my astonishment pushed the stone that revealed the opening and disappeared into the blackness beyond. I was nonplussed. It was not as though he wasn't entitled to make use of the system – I had shown him how to navigate it in case there was ever a need. But what reason was there now for secrecy? There was no threat that I could discern, and apart from the vague apprehension that emanated from him there was no sign of real fear, no urgency in his movements.

I was sitting upright now, tense with concentration, my mind following his every move. He was walking swiftly, confidently, as though the path he was taking was a matter of habit, the illumination of the torch hardly necessary. He turned this way and that, sure footed in the near darkness, until finally he ascended a steep stair cut into the rock and reaching up pushed against the ceiling to reveal an opening in the stone above his head.

I knew the place. He nimbly hauled himself up and replaced the stone slab in the floor of the room. The fit was perfect, so that once the stone was in place the secret passageway below it was quite invisible. The room was one of the largest in the central compound with a doorway leading straight out into the courtyard. It was variously used as a meeting place among the women during the day, and at night occasionally a man would take a woman there, especially if there were children in her own room and a little extra privacy was required. Ilvan, of course, had the right to enter the compound whenever he chose, take whatever woman he wished within reason, so why he should make so clandestine an entrance was beyond my comprehension.

The room was completely dark, and even though he left his small torch burning in a sconce on the wall the light from it was too weak to make out much detail. I heard a rustle in the corner of the room, and a moment later a woman emerged into the glow, her shadowy figure hardly visible in the dimness. I knew at once, simply from the way she moved, that it was Rysha. The two stared at each other for a moment, and then she rushed into Ilvan's arms, and he returned her embrace with an almost desperate passion. Then his mind opened. He could not prevent it, and although I knew that no one else could feel it except me, the force of its contents hit me like a tidal wave, and I found I was on my feet, disbelieving, shaking with rage and dread.

It was not possible, I kept telling myself. What I was witnessing could simply not be true. I was too far away to be certain. I was misinterpreting the outpouring from his heart. But my own heart was telling me a different story, and what I was seeing was a fact. There was no argument that could convince me otherwise, and it was not for want of searching for some other explanation. Here was the cause of his furtiveness, his apprehension. Everything fell into place with the weight of a great boulder crushing my mind. I wanted to turn away, take my thoughts from his, but I couldn't, and remained frozen, horrified and sickened at what I witnessed, the two of them clinging to each other, their thoughts mingling together, revealing the true extent of their violation of the Rule.

Since the very beginning the joining of a man and a woman in this way had been forbidden. It had been my father's first and most inviolable law, and so it remained, the keystone of the furtherance of the blood. There had been a time once, long ago, when the choice of a mate had been free to both men and women, and the bond for life, signified by the exchange of tokens, and more importantly, by the exchange of thoughts. Once done, the joining of minds was irreversible, the woman able to see much through the eyes of her mate, the man falling under her spell for the rest of his life, perhaps, even, beyond.

Such a situation was, of course, completely unacceptable, for two reasons. First, the prime duty of any man was to mate solely to further the blood. A woman as an object of affection detracted from the true purpose of the act. To desire the female body signified good health. To desire her mind was dangerous and worked against the Rule. Second, as my father had pointed out, and indeed as I had found to my cost, the minds of women were not as weak as their bodies. Like wild horses they must be contained, subdued, else they might trample the very heart of the Family, bring it crashing down about our ears. They rejected the tenets of the Rule as a natural state. They had always refused to honour it, and the very existence of the compound was a testament to their resistance. Few accepted us willingly, and those that did we naturally suspected of some deviousness, some plan to make our desire an entrapment. Thus, it was not surprising that the penalties for pursuing an unwarranted affection were, of all our laws, the most harsh, harsher even than the fate that Amal might have faced for his unsuccessful attempt to rid the Family of its head.

I was blinded by fury, hardly able to think, torn by a jealousy that left me cold, trembling with the enormity of it all. Why? The question circled my head like a carrion bird hovering over a dying stag. Ilvan, my faithful servant, to whom I had given the woman as a gift, standing now, betraying his honour and mine with every fibre of his being, courting death with every whisper of his thought, every movement of his hand. He would not be able to hide it forever. A stray thought, the forgetfulness of passion would give away his secret, showing the entire settlement my lack of wisdom in my choice of heir, my weakness at not knowing of his treachery and acting on it.

Even worse, it might be believed that I had known and done nothing. There were those who watched constantly, waiting to expose any mistake, any weakness that they could pounce upon and use to wrest my position from me. If that happened, as I have said before, the entire future of the Family and the greater world might be at risk. So I told myself, and it was true beyond doubt. Ilvan knew it too, yet here he was, the one person to whom I had given my complete trust, taunting me with his deceit, seeming to care not at all about the consequences of his vile indulgence. All thought of sleep left me, and as if in the grip of a dream I kicked earth over the fire, and mounting my horse began to ride slowly homeward.

Just after dawn I found myself looking out across the valley, the settlement spread out below me, the stone buildings gleaming in the early morning sun. Everyone was by now aware of my presence. I had not the skill of Rolan or Amal, and inevitably the power of my gift had announced my arrival while I was still many miles away. The rage inside me had not abated, but I hid it carefully, not wanting to give any sign to Ilvan that there was anything out of the ordinary. A part of me still harboured the faint hope that I had been mistaken, that there was another explanation for what I had seen. I had to be sure, and the path that led to certainty required that he should have no hint of my suspicion.

Two hours later I entered my rooms to find him, as always, waiting for me, his glow of pleasure at my return once more giving me cause for doubt. There was food and drink, and hot water for me to wash away the stains of travel. I let him bathe me, and afterwards lay still while his sensuous fingers rubbed scented oil into my skin. As he rose to fetch me clean clothing I grabbed him by the hand and pulled him down beside me. He made no protest, but wrapped himself around me, kissing my neck and shoulders with as much gentle passion as he had ever shown.

It was the last time we lay together, and knowing it was the last I took him with such care and tenderness that he lost himself completely, shuddering with pleasure at my every touch. When the moment came he could not contain his thoughts, and unheeding he opened his mind to me as I knew he would. The confirmation of his guilt flared as bright as a hundred torches in my head, and he was completely unaware of it. It was only for a second, but it was enough. That part of his thought that he shared with Rysha nestled deep within him, but not so deep that he could keep it hidden from me. There were others, I knew, who would pry the secret from him eventually. The signs were unmistakeable for any who wished to look, and he had neither the gift nor the artfulness to dissemble forever. I bit back my fury and tried to imagine that this moment might last forever, that I could halt time, and see him always in my mind as beautiful as he was now.

He was lying on his back, his eyes closed, the sunlight playing on his glistening golden skin. I propped myself on one elbow and smoothed the hair from his face, then bent my head and kissed him lightly on the lips. He opened his eyes and turned to me lazily, reaching out a hand to stroke my cheek. I took him in my arms, and holding him tightly to me whispered softly in his ear, "How long?"

"My Lord?"

His voice was puzzled, filled with false innocence. I could hardly speak. Pushing him gently away so that I could see his face, I repeated, "How long? How long since you betrayed me?"

Trapped under my gaze, I saw the light of fear come into his eyes, the colour drain from him. For a long moment the lie hovered on his lips, then receded unspoken as he realised the futility of it. Finally he nodded, and replied, struggling to keep his voice steady, "Just half a year, Lord. No more, I swear it."

The words tore into me, the finality of his confession freezing my heart, transforming my anger suddenly into an icy calm. I reached over just once more, and gave him one last kiss, then rose and began to dress myself, at the same time calling with my mind for Selim, son of Keslar, and Thorlan, son of Estoran, probably the two most despicable creatures that the settlement had ever seen fit to produce. An unsavoury nature was not the only thing the pair had in common. In addition to my power and position, there was one further object of their lust, and that, at least, they would at last see satisfied.

Still naked on the rugs, Ilvan watched my every movement silently, not daring to move or speak. I didn't look at him, but gave my full attention to my preparations, making sure that I

146

looked quite perfect by the time Selim and Thorlan arrived at my door. They entered uncertainly. Apart from the customary petitions to mate, I had kept them fairly at arms length, and this was the first time they had ever been in my presence at my request. The sight of Ilvan made them even more confused, and they looked from one to the other apprehensively as I greeted them courteously, asked after their children.

Both had recently been delivered of sons, powerful little beasts, I could tell, and every bit as unpleasant as their fathers. Thalis, Thorlan's child, was but two years old and his father's pride. The mother had died giving birth to it, luckily, I thought, for her. Selim's boy, Karim, had already taken on his father's sharp, unwelcoming features. Of the two, Karim would grow to be by far the most dangerous. The men of Morlain's line were both powerful and cunning. Thalis would be equally strong, but it was already clear that he had inherited both his father's handsome looks and his tendency towards stupidity.

Within minutes I had both men fairly at their ease, and then, making sure there was plenty of wine on the table, I said, "There is a matter that I must attend to. However, you would honour me by remaining here as my guests." I gestured towards Ilvan, who, becoming aware of what was in my mind, was frozen with horror, his eyes pleading with me, but to no avail. "A gift," I said. "Do as you will, but I want him alive. When you have tired of him, summon his sons, but do not touch them, or let them speak to their father. I will return three hours before sunset."

I had reached the door when Ilvan finally found his voice and cried out in desperation, "Please, Lord! Not Rysha! Not my children!"

I didn't look back or even pause as I closed the door on his pleas, and summoning two of my servants to follow, I made my way purposefully towards the compound.

Rysha was waiting for me, not cowering in some corner as I had expected, but in the middle of the room facing the door, her tiny hands clutching a reasonably heavy length of firewood. As I set foot inside she flew at me with astonishing speed and strength, born, I knew, of her terror and fury at Ilvan's suffering. I could close my mind to it with relative ease, but she, being joined with him, could not, and the enforced sharing of his pain at the hands of Selim and Thorlan washed through her, driving her almost to madness. Soon, I thought grimly, Ilvan would learn equally that the sharing of minds could be a thing of little joy.

She was disarmed, of course, before she got within six paces of me, and stood there struggling wildly, held in the iron grip of my servants, screaming as many curses as she could think of at me. I remained quite still, my eyes boring into her, until at last her cries became weaker and she slumped to her knees, exhausted. I had thought to give her to my servants, but watching her I remembered what an exquisite creature she was, even now with her hair tumbled over her dirt and tear stained face, her dress torn almost to nothing in her struggle.

At the sight of her all the rage that had been dammed up inside me spilled out and I fell on her in a frenzy, taking her again and again with a savagery that mirrored my anguish at their betrayal. When my anger was finally spent I staggered to my feet, leaving her barely conscious.

Before I left her I ordered her bound, so that she could not harm herself, and crouching down again murmured, "Before I take your life, you will see your lover and his children die. You will see the price that my brother will pay for what you have done to him, and it will be a warning to all women here who would seek to persuade a man to violate the Rule."

I returned to my rooms to find that my brother's tormentors had been no more gentle than I had been with Rysha. He lay in a dishevelled heap, his hair tangled and matted, the rugs beneath him stained with his blood. His nose was broken, his face bruised and swollen, yet he was still beautiful, and I struggled vainly to make myself believe that he was not. The dark eyes that stared out at me conveyed both pain and innocence, but way beneath that, for me alone, in the face of the Rule that he had already broken, he gave me his affection.

I ordered Thorlan and Selim to wait outside. As I had commanded them, they had summoned Ilvan's three sons, and they stood silently in a corner of the room, by now fully aware of the reason for their presence. I studied them for a moment. All were fine, well gifted, as handsome as their father was. Suddenly I heard Ilvan's silent voice, weak, pleading with me.

"For the sake of the love I bear you, I beg you, spare my children."

I turned slowly to face him and said, deliberately speaking aloud, "For the sons of Corvan, to love is to act against the Rule. You condemn yourself with every word you speak." I paused, then went on, "My father spoke truly. You are an insult to my line. But today I am feeling generous. One of your sons may live, and it is for you to decide which it shall be."

I saw the cruelty of the words cut into him, and very slowly, his eyes clouding with pain, he pushed himself up onto his knees.

"I beg you, Lord. Do not do this."

"Choose," I said, "and choose quickly. I am fast running out of patience."

A stillness seemed to come over him and he bowed his head, then, raising his eyes to mine he said, steadily and with great deliberation, "Then I choose the one that is not yet born. The one who will never know its father, even though its father will see it grow."

I stared at him in disbelief, wondering if his ordeal had not sent him mad. It took a moment for the realisation to come to me and when it did, it sent my mind reeling. He had seen what I had done to Rysha, naturally, but what he had also seen, what I had failed to see, was that in my fury I had forgotten myself and fathered a child. There was no doubt. My spawn was in her, and I could do nothing to change it. Whether a final act of love or last challenge I did not know. He could have remained silent, saved one of his own offspring, and left me to dispose of the woman and the life within her. His faithfulness, even in the midst of his betrayal, was moving, and also, I acknowledged, an act of great honour to the blood.

To the astonishment of his sons, who had no idea of the true meaning of their father's words, I stepped back and bowed to him formally.

"Ilvan, son of Corvan, I am honoured. Your choice is accepted."

He nodded, but said nothing, still staring at me, waiting, posing the unspoken question. Was I no better than my father, or did I also have the courage to act with honour? I turned once more to the three young men, who stood meekly awaiting my judgement. The youngest had begun to weep, more for his father's shame, I thought, than for himself. I took a breath, and kept my gaze on them as I spoke to Ilvan.

"These three are no longer your sons. They are as you once were, no more than the servants of the blood. They have no standing here, and unless I say otherwise, they will not mate. This one," I indicated the boy who was still tearfully staring at his father, "I shall take as my servant. The others will go to the two who wait outside. You will command them to remain silent about all that they have seen and heard here, and to obey that command until death."

There was a short silence, then Ilvan replied, "It is done, Lord. I am grateful."

I nodded, and continued, "The one that you have chosen shall be your heir, and carry the name of your line in accordance with the Rule. Tell the woman this. Tell her that if she seeks to harm herself or her unborn child, the lives of these three will be forfeit. When the child is born she may do as she wishes."

"She understands," came the whispered reply.

I called Selim and Thorlan back into the room, and with a strict instruction that their new charges should remain alive and suffer no permanent harm, I sent them both home, delighted, no doubt, to have fresh objects for their spiteful desires.

The sun was getting low, the day drawing at last to its inevitable end. There was but one task left to perform, and I turned to the white faced boy, who was pressed so tightly against the wall that I think he was sure that with just a little more effort he could melt into it.

"You belong to me now," I said, making sure that my voice was sharp enough to command his attention.

He looked at me distractedly. He was little over fifteen years old, his gift still new and raw, and he was completely unable to understand precisely what had happened, or why. I remembered how, at that age, I had adored my father, how I had followed behind him proudly, hanging on his every word.

"Do you understand?" I asked, and the boy jumped and nodded his head. "Then listen carefully," I went on. "It is your task now to prepare this creature for death. You are to cut off his hair, and see that he is dressed."

I took out my long curved knife and held it out to the boy. Hesitantly he took it, walked across to Ilvan and knelt beside him. He was weeping afresh, and tried three times to make the first cut, but each time failed, letting his arm fall helplessly. Finally he let the knife drop onto the rug and flung his arms around his father's neck, sobbing. All the while Ilvan had kept his eyes on me, and seeing my look harden he slowly bent and took the knife himself, placing it back in the boys hand.

I heard him whisper, "Orlim, Lord Rendail is your master now. You must do as he commands." At the same time he took the boy's hand, and guiding it carefully helped him in his task, holding out his long locks to make them easier to cut.

The sight would have moved the heart of any other man, but not mine. For the good of the Family there was but one course, and having no choice but to take it what room was there for question? My complacency had almost led to disaster; the death of my heir would correct the error, and serve as a timely reminder of the supremacy of the Rule. At last, they were ready. Ilvan could hardly stand, but refused Orlim's help and struggled to his feet, his quiet dignity making him more radiant than ever, despite his injured face, his roughly shorn head. I stood in silence as he was taken away, to be left deep in the woodland hung from the bough of a tree, a living feast for the passing wolves.

The weather was still warm, and the wildlife plentiful. For three days I remained in my room, eating nothing, drinking only wine, allowing no one to enter. On the third night of my silent vigil the wolves came at last, catching the scent of his blood, sensing his growing weakness. His mind no longer had the

151

strength to keep them at bay. There were three of them, first circling, suspicious, then still, the leader making ready for the kill. As it sprang Ilvan let forth a piteous cry, just a single word – he called my name.

In the weeks and months that followed, my already formidable reputation for intolerance reached new heights. I became colder, more cruel, more fearsome than ever before. The death of Ilvan had shocked the entire settlement. Even Selim and Thorlan were unusually subdued, careful in their excesses, although I noted that they had taken me quite literally with regard to Ilvan's former sons, leaving them constantly suffering from ill use, but healthy enough, and alive. I had at first regretted my generosity in allowing them to live, thinking it might be seen as a sign of weakness. But as time went by I came to realise that their current state was as salutary a lesson as I could have provided, one which made a far more lasting impression on the population at large.

The boy, Orlim, was a different matter. He had his father's look and manner, and although he tried his utmost to do as his sire had commanded him and obey my every instruction, I could not bear the sight of him. Each time I looked on him I saw my faithful lover, the man on whom I would have bestowed all my love, if I had but known what love was and how to give it. Three times I resolved to do away with the child, and three times I could not bring myself to do it. In the end I sent him to the stables to work as a groom, but on the stipulation that he never attended me, and that he should be kept out of sight whenever I was with the horses. The only wrong the boy had done was to have loved his father, and to be unable to keep the accusation out of his eye when he looked at me. And, of course, to have his father's face.

It had begun. I did not know it, but it was the beginning of Rolan's long awaited revenge. The first of many arrows had hit its mark, and I was bound tight, as helpless as my heir had been, the wolves circling, waiting for the first sign of weakness, the first faltering of my resolve. Unlike Ilvan, however, my mind was closed to any suffering, as it had been since my birth, and the wound was locked so deep within me that I was not yet aware of the hurt.

Exactly three quarters of a year after the death of her mate, I was informed that Rysha had produced a son. As with all newborns I was required to pronounce on its fitness, and so, somewhat reluctantly, I found myself once more face to face with the cause of Ilvan's downfall, the unwilling mother of my child. The infant was eight days old, sleeping at its mother's breast, and a tremor of recollection passed through me when I saw that she held it with its head turned away, refusing to look at it.

I ordered everyone away, and once alone she turned on me and hissed, "Will you not take your monster away from me? I have borne it because I swore to the one I love that I would do so. I have done what I promised to do. Will you keep your word also, and release me?"

I went to her and lifted the child into my arms. The movement woke it, and as I turned my back on her and walked with it to the window it wriggled against me, its tiny fingers entangling themselves in my hair. It was a beautiful child, its soft skin the colour of my own, its eyes the same deep blue that mine had once been. Rysha had served me well, I thought. I turned to her and gave a slight bow.

"You are released," I said, and with a breath of my thought sent her to join her former lover.

I held the child to me for a long time, staring at it in wonder. I could not take my eyes off its feet, its hands, its wide, trusting eyes looking up at me, the delicate curve of its mouth. It was as though I had never seen a newborn infant before. I suppose I had not – not with the eyes of a father. This was my first, my oldest son, and he would grow never knowing his father's name. He was hungry, and offered me a slight protest which, when I did not provide him with milk, became more insistent. I called for my servants and one of the women to come, and handed him to her, saying firmly so that it would be understood, "This child is of more value than any other in this settlement. He will be kept well, and you are to see that he is treated with honour."

The woman nodded, and asked tentatively, "Has he been named, Lord?"

"His name," I replied, "is Sevrian. Sevrian, son of Ilvan, son of Corvan."

CHAPTER 15

The passage of the years did nothing to soften me. If anything I grew more inflexible as time went by. If I had a weakness, looking back, it was for the boy, Sevrian. Although he had lost his mother I took pains to ensure that he was well cared for, and gave him, eventually, to Ilvan's mother, Serenisse, who showered him with affection, thinking him to be her grandchild. I found myself looking for him whenever I entered the compound, and after a while he got used to my watching him and began to return my stares with open curiosity.

He was a quiet child, but quick witted and strong – a natural leader among his peers, deferential and obedient in the company of his elders. When he reached the age of ten I had him removed from the compound and placed him in the care of one of my servants, in the rooms that my father had given to me as a boy. The gift, when it came to him, was a powerful one, and that, together with his tendency to silence, made him a perfect servant to tend me in my rooms. Therefore it was not thought strange when, at the age of twenty, he was commanded to take up residence on the upper floor of my house. Once there he took up the task of caring for my personal needs just has Ilvan had once done, but with one exception. Since the death of Ilvan I had shared my bed with no one, and so things remained.

As time went on, however, I found myself seeking out his company in the evenings, and before long I was confiding in him more and more, just as I had in my former heir. Despite his youth he had already developed excellent judgement, and was starting to become an invaluable advisor, as forthright and as fearless as Ilvan had been.

In terms of strength there were only two others to match him, and they were Thorlan's child, Thalis, and Karim, the son of Selim. As I predicted, Thalis grew to have as uncomely a nature as his father. He was a mean spirited, petulant creature, whose lust for power dominated his every action. He was also both a coward and a bully. I saw him often, goading the younger, weaker boys, but only when he was either close to his father, or with his friend and protector, Karim.

Karim was a different beast altogether. He was by far the more powerful of the two, and equally as ambitious. Already, at just twenty-four, he was showing signs of becoming the most formidable leader that Morlain's line had ever seen. Unlike most of his forebears, Karim was possessed of a keen intelligence. He also had an unsettling ability to engender loyalty and obedience among his growing band of followers, which for the most part comprised the discontented youth of his own and Estoran's bloodlines.

My father would simply have rid the settlement of Karim, but that, I reasoned, in the present climate, would be a mistake. The seed of knowledge of the future was coveted by all, and there were many who had privately begun to question the right of Corvan's heirs to claim exclusive possession of the precious blood of Amala's descendants. While none would dare stand alone against me, it might be different if there were a hundred.

Powerful as I was, the outcome of such a confrontation was not certain. It would certainly be disastrous for the settlement – a rebellion would inevitably lead to bloodshed, and the physically weaker ones would not survive. Unfortunately, they tended to be the ones with the less obvious gifts, and the least likely to carry the deformities of mind and body that plagued our people, so their blood was invaluable to our future. Karim and Thalis cared nothing for the Family. Their only goal was to persuade others that they should be the ones to inherit the prize.

Also, Karim's cunning made him a difficult target. He conducted himself with great care, presenting himself always as a vociferous proponent of the Rule. Unlike my father, I was seen as a man who never acted on a whim. Karim's blood was valuable and I had no reason to kill him. To do so would make me look weak. Moreover, his followers would be driven underground, be made so much more difficult to identify and keep under my watchful eye. So, I decided, I would play their game, for now, and wait.

I needed to keep a close watch on Karim, and decided that the best way to keep control of the situation was to have the highest ranking member of his coterie right under my nose. To have Karim himself too close would have been dangerous, not to say exhausting. Being of Morlain's line, he was technically of lower rank than Thalis, my brother's grandson. Therefore, with Sevrian's full agreement, I brought Thalis within my inner circle, appointing him joint advisor with my son. Of course, this meant that Sevrian was able to keep track of his and Karim's every move without suspicion. I, in my turn, could learn, through Thalis, every intimate detail of the workings of Karim's mind, and so predict his actions at any given moment.

For all his power, Thalis was man of very little wit, and easily manipulated. Naturally, he was delighted at his elevation, for to have the ear of the head of the Family was a great honour, and increased his standing with Karim's group most favourably. At times I felt almost sorry for him, trapped as he was between two dangerous and unforgiving masters. At all times, though, I remained on my guard, careful to feed Thalis only that which I wanted him to know, an indirect reminder to Karim that any challenge to my authority would be unwise.

It was in the spring of Sevrian's thirtieth year that the long awaited news finally arrived. The line of Derlan had at last produced a female child, the daughter of Devren and his mate, Mirielle. A buzz of excitement ran through the settlement, and immediately I dispatched a group of twenty riders. Tempted as I was to accompany them I knew that it would have been a mistake, given the consequence of my former absence. There was also the matter of Karim to consider, and I didn't trust him further than I could stretch my arm. Therefore, I sent Sevrian to oversee the others, charging him with the task of recovering the prize without, in so far as was possible, doing any damage to those I had sworn to let alone, namely Rolan, my brother's namesake, and the son, Devren. I further stipulated, for the safety of the child, that no action be taken until she was able to do without her mother's milk. The journey was a long one, and something of a risk for one so young and vulnerable.

The baby was some three months old when at last an opportunity presented itself and it was taken from its grandmother's arms as they sat in the garden on a sultry night in high summer. The household was asleep, and Sevrian had hoped to accomplish the mission without bloodshed. Sadly, both he and I had underestimated the courage of Rolan's mate, who resisted with such strength that there was no choice but to silence her. Added to that, Devren, the father of the child, displayed a gift of astonishing power, managing to kill three of his attackers and leaving Sevrian little choice but to retaliate. Happily I heard later that he had survived, thanks to the skill of his father in healing, but the woman, Alisse, did not, largely due to Rolan's choice to save his son rather than his mate. The incident was regrettable, but unavoidable, and besides, the loss of a female of inconsequential blood was, to our way of thinking, a small matter.

It was a great relief to me when, some four months after they had set out, Sevrian placed the child, Sherenne, safely in my arms. She was a pretty little thing even then, blue eyed and golden haired, so very like her great grandmother Amala. The question of what to do with her until she was of an age to provide me with offspring was one I had given a great deal of thought. I did not want her imprisoned as my mother had been. Such a course might endanger any children I might sire by her, if, through hatred of her captors, she turned against her own young. However, neither could she go unwatched. In her blood lay the continuation of my line and my power, and there were those who might harm her to prevent the joining of her blood with mine.

She needed a protector whom she could trust, and so some weeks previously I had sent a rider northwards to bring home the one person I knew would lay down his life for his distant cousin. Amal stood next to me now, his face expressionless, although the surface ripple of his thought oozed disapproval. He had grown well over the years. He still disliked me intensely, which was quite understandable, but at least had become wise enough not to translate his thoughts into violent and futile demonstrations. Having satisfied myself as to the child's fitness I handed her over to her new guardian, who took her into the compound, the place

158

that was to be her home for the rest of her life, however long that might be. That task accomplished, I turned my mind to other matters, and put the question of my future issue out of my mind.

The years drifted by without real incident. Immediately he was of age, Thalis petitioned to mate, and I granted his wish, only to be forced to revoke his right within a year after it became apparent that his tendency to violence was too costly to the females of the Family. He was wasteful and profligate, and harboured an unhealthy preference for the youngest of our women, some less than twenty years old – far too young to be mated safely. I needed to keep him close enough to control, so when I found him visiting a young girl without my permission I simply had him flogged, and forbade his entry to the compound until he should decide to temper his desires somewhat.

Glad to be able to retain his position, and indeed his life, he accepted my judgement gracefully, albeit with a certain amount of cowardice. But as I impressed upon him, such an offence in any other would have resulted in more than just a little pain and the need to take advantage of a male servant or two. Sevrian, however, presented a different problem. He, too, was old enough to mate, but my blood was in him, and I was concerned over the nature of any possible offspring he might sire. I took him aside and quietly suggested that the rivalry between the two of them might tempt Thalis to harm his children if he were to mate now. Better, I said, to wait until Thalis had been given the opportunity to fail to produce worthwhile offspring. Luckily, Sevrian saw the wisdom of my advice, and reluctantly agreed to stifle his natural inclinations, at least for the moment.

Although Karim had been granted access to a woman of my choosing two years before, he had not yet sired young, and for that I was grateful. He seemed strangely unconcerned with the process of breeding, preferring the company of his young male servants. A dislike of female company was not uncommon, and I made no effort to force him to fulfil his duty to the blood. The longer he remained childless, the better it suited me.

It was at around this time that Amal was delivered of his first son. The boy, Estil, was a weak and ungainly creature, having few of the handsome qualities of his father and grandfather. Still, by some chance, he was possessed of the same uncommon gift of silence as his sires. His gift, however, was fairly weak, and I could break through it with an effort. He and Sherenne often played together as children, so I heard, under Amal's watchful eye. But as soon as he was old enough I was relieved to be able to remove him from the compound, where his influence could have no effect on the future mother of my children. Clearly he was of his father's mind when it came to his opinion of me, and it didn't take him long to be embraced by the followers of Karim, perhaps the only man that Amal hated more than he hated me. I let it go however. Best, I thought, that all the rats shared the same nest – it made it simpler to keep my eye on their activities.

They were strong, this little band of rebels, growing in power with every year that passed. They had, however, one weakness, and that I was able to exploit to the full. The ringleaders, Thalis and Karim, lived, as we all did, by the Rule. As long as my own actions were seen to be governed by it, many of their followers would not countenance any move against me or my leadership.

Their eyes were on me every minute of every day, and I could not afford to be anything but ruthless in my dealings with the blood. If they hoped to find a weakness, they were disappointed. In fact, I set Thalis the task of dealing with any violation that came to my attention, a responsibility that he grasped with more than adequate enthusiasm as I knew he would. He was a vicious little creature, and while I engendered fear in my people without effort or intent, it seemed that the torment of others was the focus of his satisfaction in life, a skill which he spent most of his time honing to perfection.

I was tempted to intervene, on many occasions, in Thalis's little displays of spite. I rarely did, however. It suited me to have it known that I took any violation of the Rule, however small, as an affront to the Family and the blood. After all, if minor matters were dealt with severely, it could only give pause for thought to those who wished to join with Karim. But once or twice he went too far and I was forced to rein him in.

On one occasion I caught him down at the river with a young boy, no more than twelve, I guessed. The unfortunate youth was in the process of being tied in a sack, his ankles weighted down by stones. I recognised him as the son of one of the stable hands, of no great consequence, but not without value. He had been out of the compound just a day or two, and had obviously tried to sneak back there to see his mother. It happened frequently among the weaker boys, and normally a beating and a night without food were enough to put an end to it. For some reason, though, Thalis had taken a dislike to the boy, and certainly, death by drowning in a freezing river was inappropriate, considering the crime.

When he saw me, Thalis became clearly uncomfortable, and tried to tell me some story about his victim trying to enter the house of one of the young girls in the compound. On hearing this, the boy almost fainted with fright. I doubted very much whether he even understood the nature of the accusation against him. I admit I almost laughed at the idea. Then, it struck me that it was far more likely that Thalis had tried to force his attentions on the youth, who had probably stood up to his tormentor and refused, and thus sealed his fate. The boy immediately went up in my estimation. I gave Thalis a lecture on the waste of young blood, then took the lad away with me and gave him to Sevrian as a servant. I was smiling to myself all the way back to my house, which frightened the boy even more. If Thalis wanted him, I thought, he could have the pleasure of seeing him every day, firmly out of reach and under Sevrian's protection.

I was comfortable, if not entirely content. I spent much time with my horses, training the young ones, riding a great deal, although I could not afford to venture any distance. To maintain control I was needed at home, and always, at the back of my mind, was a concern for the safety of the child of Derlan's blood. When I needed it I had Sevrian for company. He possessed a stillness that often reminded me of Ilvan, so much so that at times I was almost convinced that he might be my former lover's child after all. Indeed, the resemblance was noted upon by others, which was all to the good in many ways. But I only had to look at him, feel his gift, to know that he was mine.

The more he grew, the stronger the bond between us became. Once or twice it even crossed my mind to tell him the truth, but always I resisted it, thinking that the time was not yet right. Perhaps I should have spoken – it is hard to say, but knowing now what came after, I think that my decision was a good one. What Thalis might have done had he been aware of Sevrian's true blood I can only guess, but I believe it might have precipitated an action for which neither I, nor the Family as a whole, was yet prepared.

It was soon to become a secondary issue, however. I had somewhat lost track of the passage of time, and so I was surprised when, one evening as we sat together, Sevrian said quietly, "You know, Lord, that Sherenne has just passed her thirtieth year?"

I had to admit that I had no idea. It seemed only a short space of time since my party of raiders had placed her tiny body in my arms. Seeing my look of surprise, Sevrian gave a brief smile, and murmured coyly, "I think that the time has come, Lord, for you to provide this Family with its long awaited heir."

CHAPTER 16

After some deliberation I decided that the large room that had once been the secret meeting place of Ilvan and Rysha should be given to Sherenne. It was one of the biggest and brightest in the compound, and the woman with whom I was to sire my offspring was entitled, I thought, to some indication of her status. In addition to that, of course, was the secret tunnel underneath, by which I would be able to enter unobserved if necessary. I gave her a cycle of the moon to make herself comfortable there, and then, one fine summer evening, I strolled confidently across the courtyard to claim my prize.

I was curious, naturally. I had purposefully avoided her as she was growing up, and apart from reports from Amal and Sevrian, that she was pretty, well bred and with a fine gift, I knew little of her, and only vaguely remembered what she looked like. It was of little importance. It was her blood that I required not her looks, although if she happened also to be desirable it might make the process a more pleasurable one. Amal had been instructed to make her ready to receive me so that my arrival would not be too much of a shock for either of us, so without hesitating I pushed open her door and strode inside, letting it swing gently closed behind me.

I took two paces inside and stopped. She was standing in the middle of the room, arms folded, feet firmly planted on the stones, her face set in an attitude of reproach. It was the kind of posture I had sometimes seen in a woman when confronting an errant child. It was not at all what I had expected. As we stared at each other in silence, I began to notice certain things about her – her total fearlessness, her determination, but most of all her overwhelming beauty. Her eyes were the deepest blue I had ever seen, her hair as warm and yellow as the sun, and slightly curled, so that it fell about her face in the most desirable way. She was as delicate as a flower, yet within the exquisite body I could sense the strength, the immovability of a mountain as her eyes sparkled

163

out at me like two flaming stars, daring me to come closer. I stayed still, drinking in the look of her, not wanting to dissolve the pleasure of the picture she presented to me.

Finally she tossed her head, which made her hair glint delightfully in the evening sunlight pouring through the window, and said, "So, child stealer, you have decided to come at last to see the proceeds of your thievery. I hope that it was worth the effort."

I had not been spoken to in so insolent a manner for a very long time, and I have to say it surprised me that the little swell of anger that I felt lasted no more than a heartbeat. I continued to hold her gaze and replied smoothly, "Indeed, at first sight it appears that my effort was not in vain. However, I can make no definite pronouncement until I have made a closer examination."

I took a couple of paces forward, so that I was no more than a foot away from her, but she did not back away. Instead, with a speed and strength that astonished me she swung back her arm and slapped my face as hard as she could. For several seconds I was stunned. I think the last time anyone, male or female, had actually struck me in such a way was when, as a small child, I had annoyed my father. I was enraged, but for some reason I was rooted to the spot. My cheek was burning, but quite apart from that, desire was flaming up in me like a summer brush fire. I wanted to grab her, to take her as I would take any other woman in the compound. But she was not any other woman, and some force, perhaps the silent strength of her will, held me back, prevented me from acting as I had always done.

Not knowing what else to do I returned the favour, being careful not to strike her too hard in case I damaged her. She swayed, but did not falter and, glaring at me, said haughtily, "I see that you are not only a thief, you are also a man of little honour. To threaten someone of your own size might present too much of a challenge for you. Now, having demonstrated your courage and your fine manners, perhaps you would care to leave. I have much to do and you are taking up my valuable time."

I was incensed. Her behaviour was quite outrageous, and I had finally had enough of it. I grabbed her by the hair and pulled

164

her to me. A second later I found myself on my knees, a sudden, violent pain shooting though my whole body, so agonising that I felt quite sick. It took a moment to register that the woman had applied her foot to my most tender parts with sufficient force to take my breath away. There I was, on my knees, struggling to catch my breath, while she calmly turned her back and began to busy herself washing roots in preparation for the evening meal.

In my whole life I had never felt such humiliation, to be brought down by a single blow from a woman who then proceeded to behave as though I simply wasn't there. After a moment or two I was able to get to my feet, shaking with fury. She must have heard my movement, but still did not turn round. I could feel my self control beginning to slip away, and with a supreme effort I turned and walked out of the room, slamming the door behind me.

The next few days I spent pacing up and down my rooms like a caged wolf, stricken in turns by fury and desire. Even Sevrian had the sense to stay well away from me, for I took out my temper on every living thing that I caught sight of, human or not. Eventually I came to the conclusion that I could not spend the rest of the year in such a manner, and that I had to settle things before someone died as a result of my mood. I steeled myself, and taking a deep breath strode purposefully into the compound. Without waiting I burst into her room with a terrific crash.

She had her back to me, heating water on the fire, and at first didn't even turn her head, but carefully continued to select herbs to steep in the water. I opened my mouth, but was completely at a loss for words, and stayed frozen, my frustration practically driving me to distraction. At last she got up, and with another of those delightful little tosses of the head turned to face me, a look of mild enquiry on her face. Her cheek was still bruised, I noted, from the blow I had dealt her, but she seemed not to notice.

The whole situation was completely unbearable. Finally, unable to contain myself, I demanded, "What is the matter? Have I not given you every comfort here? Have I not commanded that you be well cared for? You have been let alone, given the best that any woman can expect here. What more should I have done?"

She gave a little incredulous laugh and walked right up to me, hands on hips, eyes glittering contemptuously. I was so startled that I almost took a pace backwards.

"Well cared for, you say? Let alone? What you mean to say is that you stole me, you imprisoned me here, and then you ignored me until such time as you wanted to take notice of me. And you think that you have extended me a courtesy? You want me to be grateful? I am sorry to disappoint you."

She sniffed, and continued to glare.

"It was your great grandfather who was the thief," I protested. "It was he who stole from us. I have simply taken back what is mine and there is no wrong in that. It was my duty to the blood to retrieve you and I have done so. And as it is done, and cannot be changed, I see no reason why you should not accept it. You are of this Family now, and as such you also have a duty to the blood."

"I have a duty to nothing," she replied, "except to myself. You expect to come here and take what you want. You don't even ask my permission to enter, and you have no regard whatever for my wishes. Come, then. You are the most powerful man alive, so it is said. Do what you came for and get out of my sight. Show me beyond doubt that you are no more than a common thief without manners or honour. Otherwise, leave me alone and take your dubious pleasure elsewhere."

As she said this, she gave me a sharp push towards the door. It was intolerable. I remained motionless for all of a minute, glaring at her, holding my breath. Then I turned on my heel and walked out, closing the door behind me. Once on the other side I stopped, my head in my hands through sheer frustration. Then I gathered myself and swung round with the intention of storming back inside. But the door might as well have had a hundred chains holding it shut against me. I let my hand drop from the catch, and for some reason that I have never to this day been able

166

to fathom, I leaned against the frame and rapped on the door three times with my knuckles.

I heard footsteps, and the door opened a crack. Fighting to keep my voice calm, I said, "This is quite unforgivable. You have done nothing but insult me, despite the fact that I have treated you better even than I treat my horses."

The door opened a little wider, enough so that I could see her face glowering at me through the gap. "Then I suggest," she said coolly, "that you go and mate with your horse." The door slammed firmly shut an inch from my nose and I was left, utterly defeated, on the other side.

I didn't sleep at all that night, nor indeed the next. Every time I closed my eyes her face was in front of me, her wide blue eyes laughing at me, her golden hair tumbling down behind her shoulders. My mind was in turmoil, and my stomach seemed to want to follow suit. I tried to put her out of my thoughts, concentrate on other matters, but it did no good. I was stinging with humiliation, totally ashamed that I had allowed her to get the better of me, not just once now, but twice.

I had to regain control, I decided. She needed to be put in her place, shown in no uncertain terms that I was master of my own domain, that she was no more than a vessel for the furtherance of the blood and must live according to the Rule. I was prepared now, and would take her whether she wanted it or not. Perhaps then the churning in my stomach would stop, and my life might regain a little normality. I waited until dusk, then set off once again, determined that this time I would fulfil my obligation to the Rule, even if I had to beat her senseless to do it.

The resolve with which I set off lasted only until I came once more to her door. Then, with a suddenness that terrified me, all my strength of will seemed to leave me and my heart started to pound so hard in my chest that I thought for a moment that I would stop breathing altogether. I almost turned and went back the way I had come. How could I possibly be frightened by a mere woman? Yet I was – in fact I was almost sick with fear, or at least that is how it felt to me. I paced up and down in front of the door for perhaps five minutes, and then, hardly knowing what

I was doing, I stopped and tapped very gently, thinking that I probably looked as foolish as I felt.

The door opened, wide this time, my antagonist planted firmly in my path, her eyebrows raised questioningly. I took half a step back, and before I knew what I was doing had asked, very softly, almost pleading with her, "What is it that you want from me?"

She put her head on one side as if deciding whether or not she should take my question seriously. Then she nodded, and replied gravely, "What I want is what I know you cannot give me. You do not have the power. Now please go away."

Her answer confused me even more. My heart was heaving in my chest so hard I was beginning to feel dizzy.

"May I have your permission to enter?" I asked, hardly believing what I was saying. She took in a breath and drew herself up in suspicion. I held up my hands. "I wish only to talk. Nothing more, you have my word."

She considered again, and finally gave a curt nod and stood aside. As I walked in ahead of her, I noticed for the first time how comfortable the room seemed. The place was filled with soft brightly coloured hangings and mats. The small summer fire in the hearth let out a gentle glow, and the scent of sweet herbs lingered in the air. She gestured for me to sit and followed me, making sure that she was well out of my reach.

"What did you mean?" I asked, when it became clear that she was not going to speak first. "What is it that I cannot give you? I hold the power in this place. There is nothing that I can't do if I so choose."

"That is not true," she answered. "I want my freedom. You know as well as I do that you can't grant it even if you wished to, and you do not wish it."

"And why could I not grant it if I wished to?" I responded, intrigued. She rose and went over to the fire, returning a moment later with two cups of warm wine, one of which she offered to me. I took it from her outstretched hand and for a brief moment our fingers touched. I felt as though I had been stung. She drew away quickly and sat down again.

168

"You are but one among many thieves," she said. "Perhaps you are the strongest, the most cunning, but you are still just one of many. If you had not come for me, then it would have been another. If you released me now I would simply be taken by one you judge to be inferior. You pretend that you have kept me here for my protection, given me things for my comfort. But I am not deluded. You desire only my blood, and you would do anything to prevent it going to another."

I opened my mouth to reply, but she silenced me with a wave of her hand. "Please do not insult me with lies. I don't wish to hear your reasons, for even if you believe them yourself, I do not. Now, I have given you my answer, and in return, I have a question for you, if you will hear it."

I took a sip of my wine, and with a nod gestured for her to continue.

"Tonight, you came here with the intention of forcing your way into both my home and my bed. Yet you did not. Why?"

Again I was at a loss, for I did not entirely know myself. I thought for a moment, then answered slowly, "You are right. It was my intention. But when I came to your door I found that I could not. What you have said is true. Even before you were born it was your fate to come here, to bear my children, for the furtherance of the blood. There are those here who would take you from me, for the same reason. Until tonight perhaps I would have been no better than the others, although I might have been more gentle than one or two who spring to mind. But I ask you to believe me now when I say that I wish you no harm, that I have always sought to protect you, and will continue to do so for as long as I live."

"You wish me no harm?" She turned her head delicately to indicate the bruise that still lingered on her cheek.

I shrugged. "May I remind you that it was you who hit me first?"

"You deserved it," she said pointedly. But before I could respond she continued, "That is not the point, however. You have still not answered my question."

She was right, and in truth I had no idea how to answer her, for I did not know myself.

"You accuse me of being a thief," I replied after a pause. "I will not argue the point. Whatever the case you now belong to me, and it is my right to do with you as I wish." She began to bridle, but it was my turn to cut her short. "However, when I came to you tonight I felt something that I don't understand. I have desired women, and have always taken what I want from them regardless of whether or not they were of the same mind. That is how things are here, as you must know. As we sit here my body cries out for you with such insistence that I can hardly think. Were you any other woman we would not be quietly and politely drinking wine. But you are not any other woman, and even though every inch of me is on fire for want of you, I am paralysed, I can't act. You don't leave my thoughts, whether I am awake or asleep. Since I first saw you I have been driven to distraction by you. But I can't touch you – at least, I can't unless you permit it. I want …"

I stopped, hardly believing what I was saying. She was staring at me, her eyes wide with astonishment, her hands gripping tightly to the rim of her cup. Finally I threw all caution away. I had come too far to stop now.

"I want you to desire me. I want you to come to me because it is your wish. I do not want you to bear my children and loathe the sight of them, as my mother loathed her offspring. I do not …" I paused again, horrified at my own words. "I do not want you to hate me, despite what you think I have done."

There followed a silence, in which a wisp of straw falling to the stones might have sounded like a clap of thunder. She didn't take her eyes off me, and I returned the gaze, waiting for the startled look to turn to contempt, or even worse, to pity. But it did not. Rather a warmth kindled behind her eyes, and she seemed to be thinking deeply.

At last she shifted slightly and said, "I am tired. If you would be kind enough, I wish to be left alone."

She didn't say it angrily, which was possibly a step in the right direction, I thought, but despite her look there was no warmth in her voice – more a cool distraction. I rose, wondering how I was going to manage to leave the room with my sanity intact.

I placed the cup gently on the table, and unable to keep silent I said, "Before I leave, perhaps you would permit me ...?"

I gestured towards her bruised face. She hesitated, then gave a slight nod, unsure. Very slowly I reached out, and she did not pull away. I stroked her face carefully, taking away the hurt, and marvelled at how it was that I was able to stop myself from breaking the word I had just given. But I tore myself away and walked swiftly to the door. As I reached it I heard her voice again.

"I need time – to consider. Will you return tomorrow? Just after dusk? And I thank you ... for your courtesy."

I did not dare turn round, but walked out into the night, quietly closing the door behind me.

CHAPTER 17

The next evening I returned as she had requested. When I arrived in the compound I saw that her door was open, held back by a carefully shaped and polished stone. Small dishes of perfumed oil had been placed around the threshold, beneath which candles burned, filling the air with a sweet scent to keep the night insects away. Dusk was just beginning to fall, and I could see movement within as Sherenne lit small torches, their welcoming glow spilling out onto the stones of the courtyard. I stopped, taking in the scene from a distance. The feeling that it aroused in me was quite unlike anything I had experienced before.

The entire settlement was built around function. We lived simply, with few possessions, and in general the look of our dwellings reflected the austerity of our lives. The houses and rooms of both men and women were kept scrupulously clean, with few furnishings or decorations. I suppose that there was a certain beauty in that, reflecting the barren grandeur of the land around us. But here was a different kind of beauty, one that contained warmth and colour, a bringing together of unnecessary things to make something that suddenly seemed to be very necessary indeed.

Until now I had thought my own rooms luxuriously comfortable, and so they were in comparison to most. But they were not comforting, not in the way that this relatively small space had become, with its bright hangings and soft, warm lights. The feeling that welled up in me now was neither fear nor anger, nor even pleasure at the sight. I was overtaken for the first time in my life by a terrible yearning, an emptiness that reached right down into my bones, making my throat tight, my stomach churn. I so longed to be comforted, as Ilvan had once been my comfort in the old days, long ago.

As I thought his name a deep pain shot through me and I felt a sharp stinging behind my eyes. In my entire life I had never cried and I did not then, but the effort of controlling myself was so great it made my head spin. I closed my eyes and turned away, gasping for breath. It was as my father had told me, I thought. Women were dangerous creatures, and if I was not careful this one would tear out my very soul, rob me of my reason. Was that, I asked myself, the fate that had befallen Ilvan? If so, then nothing could have saved him, but perhaps I could have held him, told him that it was not my choice, given him, at the very end, the knowledge that I was with him, that I had heard his last cry. After all, it had not been Rysha's name that he called, but mine.

I was in such a confusion that my thoughts made no sense to me. I looked back at the inviting light that shone from Sherenne's room. As I watched, I saw her cross to the fire, and for a second the light caught her face, her hair shimmering in the flicker of the torches. How beautiful she was, and how remote. Without knowing it she was showing me a place where I had never been, perhaps to which I could never go, and I was shattered by it.

"Do not hate me," I whispered to myself, and turning on my heel strode away in the direction of the stables.

I rode as if all the wild wolves in the country were at my heels. It was several hours before I reined in my horse, the beast and I both shaking with exhaustion, a cold sweat on my brow. It was the dead of night, but there was still a faint light in the sky as there always is in high summer. I could hear the bubbling of a small stream tumbling from the high crags and made my way towards it, desperate for the feel of the icy water on my skin. It was madness, I thought. What did I think I was doing? I dismounted and plunged my face into the stream, hoping that it might bring me back to myself. My hair was tumbling down in unkempt tangles, and despite the cool of the night my shirt was sticking to my skin. I tore it off and flung it away, then sat down next to the stream, dripping wet and chilled to the bone.

I have no idea how long I sat there. I was so absorbed that I did not hear the footsteps coming up behind me. Even when I felt something, a rug I think, being placed around my shoulders I did not look up. I was still soaking wet and shivering violently, in the grip, so I learned later, of a deadly chill. I vaguely remember the hazy vision of a hand reaching up to my forehead, and a sudden tiredness, so that I couldn't keep my eyes open. Then, a sleep so deep that for the first time since I had lain eyes on Sherenne I did not dream.

When I opened my eyes I couldn't remember where I was or how I had got there. It was dusk again, the sun dipping low behind the crag. I shot up, startled, only to fall to my knees as my legs gave way under me. I felt as weak as a newborn and was consumed by the most terrible thirst. Straight away I felt a strong arm around my shoulder and a cup was placed to my lips. It was filled with warm water mixed with honey, and I gulped it down as if I was frightened it might be snatched out of my hand. As soon as I had finished it was refilled, and I must have drunk at least six cups full before I finally slowed down and allowed myself to be pushed gently back so that I was sitting with my back leaning on a rock.

A fire had been lit and I lay back for a while, exhausted again, bathing in the warmth and sipping the sweet liquid. It didn't occur to me to wonder who it was that provided for me so diligently, placing a blanket carefully behind my head, covering my body with furs to keep me warm. My saviour had not spoken, and to focus my eyes would have taken too much effort. As I slipped once more into oblivion, the last sensation I had was of the cup being lifted from my hand as I let it drop.

The next time I awoke my vision was sharp, my head clear. I was still hardly strong enough to lift my head, but as I was propped up against the rock I could look around easily enough without moving. It was still dark, the fire well tended, and my nostrils caught the scent of cooking meat from a metal pot that sat in the embers. There was a movement in the shadows, and a moment later my benefactor appeared in front of me carrying a skin filled with water. If I had been standing I think I would have fallen with the shock. It was none other than my brother, Rolan.

With hardly a pause he nodded briefly, and going to the fire filled a wooden bowl with broth from the pot and brought it to me. Without a word I took it from him, feeling ravenous. There were strong herbs and chunks of deer meat in it, and I wolfed it

174

down, paying no heed to politeness, I felt so hungry. When I had finished I felt stronger, and realising that my manners had left something to be desired, I nodded my thanks – I still felt too frail to speak. He took the bowl away and came back with more honey water and a cloth with which to wipe my hands and face.

The questions were beginning to teem in my mind. Where was I? How long had I been here, and why was he there? As if sensing my disquiet he sat down beside me, but he didn't drop his guard so that I could communicate with my silent voice. He simply began to speak quietly, knowing the questions that burned in my mind.

"Three days ago I came upon you by chance, on the edge of the brook just to the south of here. You were in a delirium, close to death. By my reckoning you must have been there at least four, maybe five days before I found you. It was lucky for you that it is the warm season, and luckier still that I came this way. Normally at this time I travel much further to the north. Until yesterday I didn't think that you would live, but then the fever broke and you were able to drink. You will be weak for a time yet. In two, maybe three days you will be strong enough to travel. In the morning I must go back to my work. I will leave you food, water and wood to keep the fire. Do not exert yourself until you are well rested, otherwise the fever might return."

I was confused. At that moment I didn't even remember the ride, or anything much beyond my standing in the courtyard watching the light inside Sherenne's room.

"I can't remember," I whispered finally, the effort of speech making me short of breath.

He shrugged and said, "It was clear that you had ridden hard for some miles. You were hot and tired. You stopped and drank cold water, then sat still in the cold air. By the end of the night you were sunk in the fever. I don't understand why – you as well as anybody should know the dangers of cold water and chill air after such a ride. At least your horse had more sense. I found him just a few paces away, waiting."

"I must have lost my senses," I admitted. I was beginning to feel a little stronger, and he filled my cup for me again.

175

I heard him laugh. "I would say that you are beginning to find them. The result, in either case, is often the same."

"What do you mean?" I asked, drinking slowly. Normally such a conversation would have annoyed me, but for some reason I felt more fearful than angry.

He looked at me thoughtfully, as if trying to decide how much he should say. Finally he said, "Forgive me, brother, but in your fever you talked a great deal, to yourself rather than to me. I believe that your words came from your inner mind, and revealed much that you would keep hidden, even perhaps from yourself."

"And you did not use your gift to help me, even though you thought I might die? That I can understand, but what I can't fathom is why you remained here. You have no love for me. Surely you could have simply left nature to take its course."

"I assure you," Rolan replied, "the thought crossed my mind more than once. But although I couldn't bring myself to heal you, no more could I let you die. Then, when I heard you cry out with such pain the name of our brother, whom you sent to his death, I knew that you suffered for a reason. I knew that if you survived you would wake to a different future, to a knowledge that you might have gained many years ago, had my sister not denied it to you."

He settled himself more comfortably in front of me, a sad smile on his face, and went on, "For many years, as you know well, I blamed you for the death of my daughter. But now I see that the fault was not entirely yours. We all share the horror that our father brought upon us, and we are all equally responsible for the tragedy that is our people. I am no exception. It was I who helped Amala to escape. I took her from the compound under the veil of my silence, set her upon a horse and let her loose to ride into the arms of Derlan. She was my sister and I loved her. I didn't think that my action would so fuel our father's madness, place an entire tribe of innocents in danger of his retribution.

"Had I not acted as I did, Mira would have remained the sweet and gentle child that I knew, and you might have known her love, and so have been capable of it yourself. I understand now what I didn't before – that you have never had any choice

176

but to act as you have done. As head of our Family you have curbed the worst excesses of Corvan's legacy to his people, and you have kept Sherenne from harm in as much as your power allowed.

"It is a hard road that you travel, brother, and now it will be harder still. As I foretold, your worst suffering is just beginning. But I no longer desire revenge as I once did. You didn't ask for the life that you were given, and the burden you carry would have crushed me long ago."

I was speechless. Of course, it should have occurred to me before that Rolan had somehow been instrumental in Amala's escape. How else could she have reached the edge of the settlement undetected? My father hadn't known of my brother's gift, but even so, it must have taken a great deal of courage to risk moving through the entire place with a woman in tow. I felt a new admiration for him and, strangely, an understanding as well.

Before I could stop it the thought came to me that if any man were to try to touch Sherenne, I would happily tear him limb from limb – not because she was my property, but because it would be against her wish. Was the future of the Family really worth the misery that I had caused both to her and to her people?

Only then did I realise that I had been gone from the settlement for several days. I had simply disappeared, leaving her alone there, and no one knew where I was or why I had gone. What if Karim or Thalis took it upon themselves to take advantage of my absence? What of Sevrian, my son? I began to panic and tried to get up, but my legs were not yet strong enough to hold me and I fell back, helpless.

"I must get back," I said anxiously. "I will be missed. Perhaps some of those who would take power think that I am dead."

"Have no fear," he replied. "Amal has sent word to your son. Sevrian is strong enough and wise enough to control your kingdom until you return. You should place greater faith in him. After all, he is your blood."

177

"You know that Sevrian is my son?" I was aghast. "No one knew of it, except those that are gone. How could you have learned of it? It's impossible!"

He laughed again. "My dear brother, you told me yourself, in the midst of your fever. How you must have loved Ilvan, to give him such a precious gift. Several times in your sleep you wept, and called our dead brother's name. Over and over again you asked his forgiveness, and told him that you had kept your word, that your first child would never know his father. Listen, Rendail. You have heard of the gift of memory?"

I nodded. I knew that such a thing existed, although I had never met a man who possessed it, and I myself had no such skill.

Rolan placed a hand on my arm. "I have that gift. I share it with my sisters. You don't have it, but your descendants will."

"My descendants?" My mind was in a turmoil, hearing one revelation after another.

"My life is almost over," Rolan continued, "but before you die you will see our lines come together. The child of your child, and the child of my child – they will join, and their issue will be far greater in power than either of us imagine.

"Our great grandson came to me from a far distant future, and told me many things. Most of what I know I can't tell you, but this much he asked me to say. His words were; 'Our fate rests with you. If our Family is to survive, it will do so only by your strength and your sacrifice. You are destined to lose all that is most dear to you, but you must trust in those you love. The way is long and dark, and filled with pain. But if you stand firm and keep your faith, then all that is taken from you will return, and at the end you will see your dreams fulfilled.

" 'The gift to cross the Great Emptiness will come again, and there will be a great struggle. You must take Sherenne and keep her safe. Let yourself be guided by her and don't be afraid. When the time comes, your actions will determine the fate of both present and future. If you fail us, then all will be lost both within the Family and outside it.'

"I can't tell you any more. But I will say that when our great grandson spoke of you, he did so with reverence, and told me that they all, in that far time, remember you with both honour and love."

There was a long silence. Eventually I asked uncertainly, "What is his name, this child who came to you, this leader of our people from the far future? He must be powerful indeed, to make such a journey, and his need to speak with you must have been very great for him to even attempt it."

"His name will be Daniel," Rolan answered. "You will not live to see him born. And yes, he is a most powerful creature, yet he does not lead the Family. He left that task to another of your line. It was on account of this other that he came to speak with me. I can't say more, except that it concerned the struggle that I spoke of, and the influence of your blood. You will learn the rest in time. But this much I will say. You were right, that day, the first time that we met. I sought then to exert my influence over you, to lead you into a path that I know now would have been disastrous for all of us. You were too clever for me then, and it is just as well, for Amal might never have been born otherwise, and without him there would be no Daniel.

"I grieve for my daughter still, but she has also played her part, and her fate was inevitable. Through her you saw the Dance, within which is the seed of the love of all things. Once swallowed that seed can't die, and after a long time buried it has begun to grow. I don't know what caused its awakening, only that you refused to accept it, and that is what gave you the sickness. Perhaps you can't weep now for all that is past – you will in time. But you must embrace your new knowledge in the present and let it lead you wherever it wishes to go, if you are to save yourself and our people. Now, I must go. I doubt we shall meet again. Remember what I have said, my young brother, and when the time is darkest, don't let your despair sway you from your course."

He got up, and making sure that I had wood, food and water close at hand, walked off into the dawn.

"Wait," I murmured, but he did not heed me, and I heard him mount his horse and ride away. I settled back, exhausted again, and closed my eyes, but before I could drift into sleep there came into my mind a silent voice.

"Farewell, brother Rendail. My hope goes with you. Watch over my son."

For the first time, Rolan had lifted the veil that cloaked his thoughts, and with the voice I felt the strength and beauty of his gift. I framed my answer in my own thoughts.

"You honour me, brother Rolan." Then he was gone, as if a candle had been suddenly snuffed out. I never saw him again.

CHAPTER 18

It was two more days before I was well enough to ride. My brother had left me well supplied however, and I was able to simply eat, sleep and regain my strength. I set off an hour before dawn on the third day since Rolan's departure, travelling a little more slowly this time, and before long was surprised at how far I had actually come on the frenzied ride that had almost cost me my life. It was late afternoon when I finally came to the settlement and handed my weary mount to one of the grooms. The man was about to lead the horse away when I called him back.

"You know Orlim, the young groom?"

"Yes, Lord, of course."

"Does he fare well here? Does his skill with the horses satisfy his masters?"

"Oh yes, Lord," the groom replied. "It is often said that he might become a master himself, were he granted the opportunity. He is called on often to help with the training of the young ones. However, as you commanded, Lord, he remains with the stable hands."

I nodded thoughtfully. "Take word to him that I wish him to attend me tomorrow, at noon," I said, and without waiting for the groom to respond, strode away up the path to the south gate.

In my rooms I bathed slowly, changed my clothes and sent for food, although I did not feel particularly hungry. Sevrian was in his own rooms above, and I felt his surprise at not being sent for the moment I returned. I let my thoughts reassure him, conveying my intention to fulfil my desire for female company, a notion that he accepted without question. I was brought cheese, cold meat and bread, which I wrapped in a cloth, and taking the bundle in one hand I made my way into the compound and across the courtyard.

As on the night that I had left, Sherenne's door was propped open, the same soft, warm light spilling out onto the

181

stones. My heart was pounding once again, but this time I did not run from it. There was no escape, I knew that now, and besides, something in my mind told me that I no longer wished to flee, even though I was facing a danger far greater than any I had seen before. I walked quietly up to the open door and tapped lightly with my fingers. She came up to me at once, and I thought I caught a slight hint of concern on her face as her blue eyes looked up at me.

"Amal told me you had gone away," she said. "I trust your journey was a pleasant one."

I almost laughed. "Thank you for your concern. It was not an easy expedition, and I have to say I'm relieved to be home. I am also glad to see you well. I hope that you were well cared for in my absence."

"I need no one to care for me," she replied in a disdainful tone, but seeing the sincerity of my expression her voice softened a little as she added, "Nevertheless, I thank you for the thought."

She had not stepped aside to let me in, and I offered her the bundle.

"Would you care to dine with me tonight? As you see, I have brought food. I don't wish to make myself a burden to you."

She bridled again. "You think me incapable of providing sufficient hospitality for such a great Lord? Your manners may have improved a little, but they still appear to leave a lot to be desired."

It seemed that every conversation I had with this woman drove me to complete exasperation.

"What is it that you want of me?" I demanded, my voice shaking with sheer frustration. "Tell me what it is and I will do it. Tell me what you want and I will provide it. It seems that nothing I do can please you, and I begin to wonder whether it is worth the effort."

She considered a moment, then blushed slightly and lowered her head.

"Forgive me. I see that you are trying your best. Perhaps I was a little hasty." At last she stood aside to let me enter, and as if demonstrating her confidence in my intent, closed the door behind us.

I placed my offering on the low table and moved a little closer to the fire, where it was brighter and she could see me clearly. As I did so I heard her give a little gasp.

"You have become so thin!" she exclaimed, and something in me rejoiced at the concern in her voice.

I turned to her and gave a little smile. "As I have said, it was a hard journey."

"And you have not eaten since you returned? Come, you must sit, now, and take some food."

I didn't argue. I suddenly felt ravenous, and she quickly unwrapped the cloth as though she thought I might expire at any minute, setting a jug of wine and a cup beside it. I sat, but did not touch the food.

"What is it?" she asked, her anxiety making my heart dance in my chest. "Why don't you eat?"

"I will eat," I replied, "when you have brought another cup, and are seated also. I asked you to dine with me, not to stand watching me as if you were a servant."

She hesitated, but realising that I was not going to take a bite until she had joined me she sighed, and fetching a second cup sat down opposite me. I divided all that I had brought into two and pushed half towards her, then filled both cups with wine. Only when she had taken a mouthful did I follow suit, and we ate together in silence. I could see that she was not really hungry, that she joined me only so that I would take some nourishment.

Every so often she glanced up at me, only to blush as she found me staring at her. I was trying not to, but I simply couldn't take my eyes off her. In the entire world I don't think I had ever seen anything more beautiful. If only, I thought, she could look at me and see anything beyond the cruel, tyrannical ruler that she believed me to be. But why should she? After all, that is exactly what I was, whether I had justification for my actions or not.

My hunger satisfied, I set the rest of the food aside and poured myself more wine. Hers remained untouched. For the last half hour neither of us had spoken, and I felt that if I didn't say something we would still be sitting in silence at dawn the next morning. But whatever I said she seemed to take amiss, and I was becoming quite desperate. Finally, I threw all caution to the wind.

"I don't know what to do," I confessed. "I know that you don't want me here, but I can't stay away. If I could take you from this room, place you on a horse as my brother Rolan did with his sister and watch you ride away, I would do it. But I can't. I want to make you happy, but I can't do that either. The Family awaits an heir. They watch, and wait for you to bear my child. But I can't touch you."

I paused, and when she did not move nor change her expression, I shot to my feet and in utter despair cried out, "What must I do?"

She jumped, but said nothing, simply continuing to stare at me coldly with those beautiful blue eyes. I shook my head and, turning away, walked to the door. My hand was on the latch when I heard her soft voice behind me.

"Wait."

I froze. A moment later I felt a light touch on my shoulder, the sensation setting my whole body on fire. I closed my eyes and leaned my forehead on the door, struggling for control.

"Please," I begged in a whisper, "tell me what I must do."

She took my hand and gently pushed it away from the latch. I felt her fingers on my cheek, and had I not been leaning on the door I think I would have fallen. I couldn't open my eyes, or move a muscle. The blood was coursing through my veins, and I was so terrified that I might hurt her. I knew many ways to take a woman, but none of them gentle, none of them with any thought but for my own passion.

With a little shock I realised that she was taking the slides from my hair, combing out the twists so that it fell loose down my back. Then the soft pressure was on my arm, turning me to face her, and I felt my shirt fall from my shoulders, followed by the touch of her lips on my naked chest. I think a little cry escaped me. I was locked there, unable to move of my own volition, afraid to reach out and touch her, or even to look at her.

"Open your eyes," she whispered, and I obeyed. "Come with me."

She took my hand and led me away from the door into the cool darkness beyond the firelight, pulled me down onto the rugs. I lay helpless as she undressed me, and only realised when I felt her, warm beside me, that she was naked too. Under her wordless direction I slowly moved my fingers over every inch of her glorious skin, my heart leaping as she responded to my touch. I followed the path of my fingers with my lips, suckling like an infant at her breast, brushing her lips tenderly with mine. I forgot my own need completely, so absorbed was I in the task of pleasing her.

When she pushed my hand away I almost cried out in protest, but she silenced me with a finger on the lips, and raising herself up slightly began to kiss and stroke me all over until I thought I would go mad with the pleasure of it.

She kissed me and pulled me closer, her hand stroking my head, guiding my mouth once more to her breast. I recognised the fire rising in me, but with it came a sensation that I had never felt before. It was more from my mind than from my body, a feeling that was overwhelming me as much as any height of physical passion could do. I had a terrible urge to share it with her, and at the same time a fear that she might reject such an invasion of her thoughts.

I reached out tentatively with my silent voice – no words, just the feeling, hoping that she would understand my need to share it. Immediately her mind flew open in a blaze of warmth to draw me in, sending the same sensation back to me, but from her own thoughts. She let me enter her then, body and mind together, and for the first time I knew what it was to be a Dancer, to mate as a Dancer should.

It seemed to last forever, and when it was over I found myself clutching her to me, my head resting on her shoulder, the tears coursing down my cheeks. I thought that I might weep until I died, and wondered how anyone could endure, at the same time, such terrible pain and such perfect joy. She held me, rocking me to and fro as if I were an infant, stroking my hair, kissing my tear

185

stained face. We were still locked together in a silent embrace when the first light of dawn came in through the window.

Throughout the whole night neither of us had spoken a word. At last she gently prised herself free, and fetching water and cloths proceeded to wash me all over. I made no protest, still revelling in her closeness, not wanting her to move even an inch away from me. When she had finished I took the cloth from her and bathed her in my turn, while she combed out my hair. Then she brought bread and honey and fresh water and we breakfasted together, still curled on the rugs, not speaking. When we had finished eating she further amused herself by taking the honey jar and, to my consternation, pouring the sticky liquid over my chest. I had no time to protest, however, as she then set about licking it off again, her eyes sparkling with amusement.

My eyes were being opened to one revelation after another. I had never before seen the act of mating as a humorous matter, any more than I could have described it as a sorrowful one. Yet for the first time in my life I had knowingly shed tears, and now, to my astonishment, I found myself laughing as I pulled her down on top of me, making her as sticky as I was. So, my journey of discovery went on, until we both fell back exhausted again, and slept in each other's arms until almost noon.

Only when I woke did my thoughts start to turn back to the world outside. I had been away for many days and had not spoken to a soul aside from Sherenne, nor even thought to make my presence known, except to Sevrian. The previous day seemed a lifetime ago now, and with a shock I realised that I had summoned Orlim to attend me, and had forgotten all about it.

I leapt up and set about hunting for my clothes, which were strewn all over the place. Immediately Sherenne got up, and motioning for me to calm myself helped me to dress and arranged my hair perfectly, slipping the slides neatly into place. She looked me up and down, then confirmed with a nod that I looked tidy enough to leave with some dignity intact. As I reached the door I turned, hardly daring to ask the question. She put a finger to her lips and smiled, then nodded again before gesturing that I should be on my way. I responded with a quick bow of the head and strode purposefully out into the bright sunlight, back into my former self.

Sevrian was waiting for me at the doors to my house and greeted me with a deferential bow. "Your presence honours us, Lord. I am glad to see you well. I trust your journey was satisfactory?"

I nodded in acknowledgement, beckoning for him to follow me. I swept past the figure of Orlim, who was waiting in the reception hall, and leapt up the stairs two at a time, Sevrian hard on my heels. Once inside my own room I sighed audibly and turned to my advisor.

"All has been well in my absence?"

Sevrian nodded. "I can report nothing out of the ordinary, my Lord. There has been one birth, a normal, healthy child, a female. Thalis took it upon himself to go out hunting the day after your departure, taking Amal's boy, Estil, with him. It is my belief that he wanted to follow you to see where you had gone, and what your purpose might be. However, Amal returned unexpectedly and came to see me. He conveyed your wish that no one should venture more than a day's ride from the settlement until your return. As an extra precaution he expressed a desire to join his son in the hunt, and so Thalis spent a day riding in the southern woodland, and got no further."

I got the distinct impression that the episode had caused Sevrian more than a little enjoyment, although, as ever, his expression remained unreadable. I couldn't help but allow myself a little smile at the vision of Thalis's frustration, and at the same time sent my grateful thanks to Rolan for his foresight.

"I want you to arrange for wine to be brought, then bring Orlim to me," I said. With a bow, Sevrian left at once. A few moments later a jug of wine appeared, followed by Orlim, who stood in the doorway, nervous and a little uncertain, Sevrian just behind him.

"Come," I said at once, not waiting for Orlim to speak. "Sit, and take wine with me."

From the look on Orlim's face I might as well have asked him to hurl himself from a roof, and I saw Sevrian's eyebrows

187

rise slightly in surprise. I signalled silently that the latter should remain and received a stiff nod in response.

"You honour me, Lord," Ilvan's youngest son managed to stutter, but stayed frozen in the doorway.

"Then be so good as to honour me by sitting down," I answered curtly, at which he bowed and hurriedly seated himself. Sevrian poured out three cups of wine and arranged himself comfortably at one end of the table, while I took the other, leaving Orlim between us. I suppose, given his knowledge of me he had every reason to be apprehensive, and he sat clutching his cup as though it were his anchor, his eyes firmly on the floor.

"You have grown well," I commented. How like his father he was to look at. It still pained me to see the resemblance, the elegant frame, the soft, almost feminine features, the long, curled eyelashes. He bowed his head again.

"You ..."

"Yes, I know – I honour you. Now, there are several matters on which I would like your opinion, that is, if you can allow yourself to progress beyond the usual courtesies."

"I am ... Yes, Lord, of course, if I can be of value."

"That I will judge in due course," I replied, and proceeded to question him thoroughly for an hour or more on the subject of our stock of horses, his opinions on breeding and the development of the stables, which lines should be trained and which kept for trade, and so on. After a while he relaxed, becoming more animated as he spoke of what he knew best, and I found that the groom had spoken truly. Orlim's knowledge was both extensive and valuable. He had an instinctive feel for the animals in a way which many, even among the horse masters, did not.

I brought him to a halt finally and said, "I wish you to take personal charge of the selection of my own horses. I require a line that is both strong and receptive, yet of superior intelligence. Use your own judgement in the selections for breeding, and keep me informed of all issue so that I may choose for myself which I will decide to train. Those you select will be kept exclusively for my use, and you alone will be responsible for their care and exercise.

Naturally you will be given accommodation befitting your rank, and will be answerable only to me. I trust this arrangement pleases you?"

Orlim was gaping at me, unable to believe his ears. It took him a moment to realise that I had finished speaking, and was waiting for some response.

"Yes, Lord," he managed to stammer at last, "I am honoured."

"Good," I said. "Sevrian will ensure that you have all you need. I will follow your progress with interest."

Sevrian rose, and seeing that the audience was over Orlim followed suit, still a little stunned by the sudden change in his fortunes, and, I suspected, unsure of whether the change was for the better. Despite his nervousness the elegance of his bow and the grace with which he held himself reminded me once more of his father, so that I was obliged to turn away for fear that my expression might betray me.

When he had gone, I turned to Sevrian. "It is in my mind to reinstate Orlim to your line. What is your opinion?"

My advisor pondered for a moment or two, then answered, "For myself, I would welcome it, Lord. He is of good blood, and valuable. And after all, he is my older brother. But I do not think it is wise. In the current climate you should not be seen to reverse what was a legitimate decision. The sons of Ilvan are removed from their line according to the Rule. Until it is changed, the Rule may not be disregarded – at least, that is what some others here believe."

"According to the Rule," I said pointedly, "all the sons of Ilvan should have joined their father in the void. Yet they all live, and you have your elevated position here, and retain the name of your line."

"As was agreed at the time of your judgement, Lord."

Sevrian's poise was unshakeable, and I allowed myself the indulgence of a little pride in his self containment, together with a pang of regret that I could not tell him so as a father. He was quite right, however, on all points.

"You advise well, Sevrian," I said with a faint smile. "Where is Thalis now?"

"Hunting," he replied, with an almost imperceptible expression of distaste. "If allowed his pleasures I find his presence a little less burdensome."

He met my gaze levelly, and despite the impropriety of the remark I could not bring myself to take him to task on the point. The absence of Thalis from within the gates was a state that most found quite desirable. We moved swiftly on to other matters, and the afternoon turned to evening almost before I was aware of it. And with the setting of the sun came once more the turmoil that I had managed to hold at bay for as long as there was still light in the sky.

CHAPTER 19

I waited until it was quite dark before tracing the now familiar path across the courtyard. The evening was cooler and the door was closed, but as I approached it swung silently open for me. She was as radiant, I as helpless as ever. I could hardly believe what was in my mind to do, yet I could do nothing to stop myself from taking a course that was utterly forbidden according to the Rule. I kissed her softly, and took one of the small torches from its sconce in the wall. I handed it to her and placed a finger on my lips. She nodded, her face alive with puzzlement and curiosity. Taking my knife I eased the heavy flagstone that concealed the hidden passageway up out of its socket, grasped it and slid it away.

Sherenne's hand flew to her mouth, but she kept silent as I lifted her up and gently lowered her down into the blackness, letting her feet find the first narrow step cut into the stone. I leapt lightly down behind, and taking her by the hand led her down the steps and through the labyrinth, the little torch that she carried casting almost no light on the path ahead. She trod in my footsteps without hesitation, trusting me completely, until eventually we came to the large central chamber, crossed it, and began to ascend the steep winding stairway that emerged behind the wall of the reception hall of my house.

There, I doused the torch, leaving us for a moment in complete blackness, and applied a slight pressure to the concealing stone. It swung back, and as we walked out into the silent hall I could feel her shaking, her fear as much for me as for herself. I picked her up and swiftly carried her up to my private room, closing and bolting the door behind us.

When I set her down she went straight over to the window. The distant crags loomed black against the pale night sky, while down below us the constantly burning watch fires beyond the gates lit the ground with an orange glow. I brought her wine and we stood together in silence, neither of us wanting to think beyond the moment. I couldn't remember when we had last spoken to each other – it might have been a century ago.

Finally she turned to me, and whispered, "You should not have brought me here. You are in danger now."

Well, that was a fact I couldn't argue with, yet my heart filled with joy that she was concerned only for me. Then it struck me that my foolishness might lead her to a fate much worse than any that could befall me, were we discovered, and I suddenly felt ashamed of my self indulgence. This was madness, I thought, yet I couldn't stop it, could do nothing about it, and here she was, a woman in a forbidden place, the two of us courting ruin and death with every breath that we took.

I kissed her. "I wanted you to see," I said lamely. "I wanted you to know this place outside your prison, to know that it is my prison too, and that neither of us can be free."

She held me close for a moment, then let her eyes rove around the room, taking in the austere, unadorned walls, the plain low table surrounded by woven mats, the neat pile of furs in the corner on which I slept and which were the only thing in the room with any softness. She nodded, reached up and stroked my cheek.

"Why did you take such a risk?"

I hesitated a moment, then answered, "Because I need you to understand what I am. You see me as a cruel, monstrous creature, and it's true. I am the essence of the Rule, and therefore I am, of everyone here, the most subject to it. This place contains a dangerous people, and I am the most dangerous of them all. Were I less powerful, less ruthless, the danger would spread outside this settlement, and would bring disaster on us all."

Rather than be startled by my admission she walked over to the table and sat on one of the mats, holding out her hand for me to join her. I obeyed meekly, and she took my hand in both of hers.

"Tell me everything," she said simply, and so I did.

I told her of my mother and father, of the burden that had been placed on me by Corvan's madness. "The power to see beyond the Great Emptiness consumed him," I said, "and when it appeared and was taken from him the obsession grew with every passing year. He was determined that the gift to cross the divide between present and future be returned to him, and that the power should rest with him and his heirs alone. He didn't consider that he had unleashed a force that even we might not be able to contain – only that the power to control the future might now rest in the hands of others. When he died, the threat that issued from within our own blood became clear. Corvan was not alone in his obsession, and there are those here – Thalis, Karim and their followers, who would possess that gift and turn it against their own kin in their lust for power."

I went on to tell her of the dangers that beset the Family, that forced me to perpetuate the commonplace horrors that controlled the direction of the gift. I told her what I was even though she knew already – that I was a murderer of children, that, for the good of the people, I imposed the harshest penalties on any who violated even the slightest injunction of the Rule.

"And you must know," I told her finally, "that the madness is in me no less than it was in my father. The strength that the blood gives to me contains the taint that was in him. All who live here fear my anger, and it is that which gives me the strength to maintain the Rule. But you, it seems, have no fear. Rather, for the first time since I was a child it is I who am afraid. I have sworn to protect you with my life from any who would harm you, but I can't protect you from myself and the madness that is in me. I know now that I loved Ilvan, my brother, but it didn't save him from death when he betrayed me and went against the Rule. Now, my love for you makes me as guilty as he was, and by my actions I have condemned us both.

"How can I impose a law that I myself have now broken? You have taken from me that which gives me strength and left me as helpless as a child before the coming of the gift. I can no longer do the things that I must do, knowing that my every act causes your hatred of me to grow. Yet if I do not keep the Rule, how many others, both here and in the world outside, will suffer? I beg you to help me now, for I don't know what to do."

I fell silent. I could hardly believe that I had made such a speech and knew it must have sounded to her as though I had lost my mind. She stared at me for a moment, then took my face in both her hands and kissed my lips softly. She nestled into me, her arms around my waist, and we held each other close for what seemed an age before at last she spoke.

"You must not bring me here again," she said, no room for argument in her tone. "You must keep the love you have for me buried deep in some secret place within you, a place that only you and I can see. For the good of all you must rule these people and show no sign of weakness. And though I will hate what you do, yet I will still love you, and even in the darkest times you must not forget it. You are the head of this Family and it is your task to guard the gift of the future. If you should fail and let it fall into the hands of one like Thalis, then we are all lost. Therefore, my love, you must be strong and ruthless in your dealings with the blood, in order to safeguard both my people and yours, and to preserve the lives of our children."

I sighed, squeezing her even closer to me, letting my chin rest lightly on the top of her head. "And when the madness takes me, as it has always done, and I hurt you, as I hurt all things that touch my heart, what then? Will you not hate me when that time comes, loathe my presence as all here do, find my touch unbearable?"

She pushed me away from her and took my face in her hands again, holding me with her gaze. "When that time comes, I will fear the madness," she answered, "but I will not fear you, nor love you less. You must be what you are, for there is no one to take your place, at least not until you have sired a son who will inherit your strength, perhaps be even stronger. Until then, is there no one here that you can trust?"

The question took me by surprise, as I admit I had not really thought about it. Ilvan's betrayal had served to strengthen my resolve to trust no one with my inner thoughts to the same degree as I once had with my brother. However, on reflection I realised that I had, more than once, been at the mercy of Rolan, who had had more reason than most to see my downfall. Yet he had remained silent, protecting me from my own folly. But Rolan was dead and his son, although under the protection of the vow I had made to his father, bore little love for me. I shook my head.

"No one," I said. Then, after a pause I admitted, more to myself than to her, "No one but you."

How I needed her. I needed her touch, her closeness, her understanding. Even Ilvan had not awakened such yearning in me, such desire for an end to my isolation. Rolan was right, I thought. For me, true suffering was only just beginning.

So once again, on that second night I took her, there in that forbidden place. Once again I wept at the unfamiliar joy she brought to me, and I lay like a child in her arms, wishing that our bodies could remain entangled forever. I begged her, through my tears, not to place her trust in me. I told her what had happened to Amora, whose innocence had led her to her death, and of Ilvan, and how no grief of mine could atone for what I had done to him. But she stroked back my hair and held me fast under her unflinching gaze, a frown on her beautiful brow.

"You cannot command me, Lord," she said, "so do not try, unless you wish me to disobey you. I have said, I belong to no one but myself, and I give you both my love and my trust because it is my choice. No Rule of yours can prevent it, just as no Rule can take your love away from me."

I lowered my eyes, defeated by her, and sank again into her embrace. This time, at her bidding, I let loose my living seed into her, and together we felt the moment of conception rush over us like a warm tide.

We must have slept, for when I opened my eyes the pale light of dawn was in the sky and I could hear movement on the pavement down below. I shot upright, alert for the slightest movement nearby, and felt Sherenne's hand, trembling, on my shoulder. I turned to her, but did not need to gesture for silence. She simply nodded, understanding at once the grave danger in which my stupidity of the previous night had placed us.

I dressed quickly and was about to concentrate my mind on the route back to the hidden door in the chamber below when I caught the thoughts of Sevrian turning towards me, followed a moment later by the sound of his footstep coming down from the

195

upper floor towards my room. He would not enter without permission of course, but nevertheless I froze. Sherenne, watching me, also stood motionless, her eyes wide with panic. Sevrian had perhaps the most powerful gift in the whole settlement next to mine, and it was inconceivable that he would not sense the presence of Sherenne in my room. Was this the price of my foolish action – that I must be forced to kill my own son to preserve my position and my lover's life? I waited, despairing, for the footsteps to reach the door, willing Sevrian to walk on, to be on some other errand, even though I knew it was a vain hope, that it was me he sought.

He was close now, just a few strides away, and with a dry mouth I prepared myself to strike. But before he reached the door I heard his silent voice, calm, businesslike, cutting through my rising tension.

"The way is clear," I heard him say. "You must go quickly. A boy was found in the compound in the night with one of the women, against the Rule. Thalis believes you to be there and has gone to seek your judgement. You must go now, or he will find the room empty and guess that you are both here. I will keep the doors closed until you are gone."

All this he conveyed to me without slackening his pace, and I heard him go past the door and down the stairs, coming to a halt at the outer doors. For a second I was so startled I couldn't move and then, shaking myself awake I grabbed Sherenne by the hand and we flew out of the room and down into the reception hall. Sevrian had his back to us just inside the doors, making sure that the guards outside made no attempt to open them. I gave him no more than a quick glance before opening the hidden door, and streaked down into the underground maze pulling Sherenne behind me. I sensed him closing the entrance behind us and we ran through the pitch darkness, back up the steps on the other side, hauling ourselves up into the room in the compound gasping for breath.

I had no sooner replaced the big flagstone in the floor and checked my clothing for dust and dirt than there came a light tap at the door. Sherenne had dived under a blanket, and lay there

196

motionless as if asleep. I opened the door slowly, setting my expression to one of cold annoyance.

Thalis bowed. "My Lord, I hope you will forgive the intrusion ..."

"I do not," I responded in the quietest, most threatening tone I could manage. "I hope, for your sake, that you have a very good reason for this inexcusable display of ill manners."

"Forgive me, my Lord," he replied, taking an involuntary step back and bowing again, "but a grave matter has come to my attention, and I was of the opinion that you should be informed immediately. As you know, I will take no action without your permission."

He was quite correct in that, but even so I had the impression that nothing was so urgent that it could not have waited until I was out of the compound. He had quite clearly sought to gain some advantage from disturbing me, and it was only with an effort that I managed to keep my temper in check enough not to strike him. For a second I wondered at the coincidence of his appearance at that precise moment, but I quickly reassured myself that both I and Sevrian would have detected any suspicion he might have.

I could see that he was beginning to regret his rashness but he stood his ground – he could do little else, as two of his servants stood a few paces away, watching nervously.

"Be swift then," I said, letting my displeasure bore into him until he paled slightly, much to my satisfaction. I saw him glance behind me at Sherenne, who was sitting up now, still swathed in the blanket. Clearly he felt that his errand could not be discussed in front of a woman and so, with a faint smile I opened the door wide and leaned against it, adding to his discomfort.

"As you wish, Lord," he said finally through gritted teeth, and gestured to his two servants, who immediately went off, returning a moment later dragging a youth of about twenty or so, and a young girl.

"Your point?" I asked tersely, when, after a pause for effect, Thalis offered no further explanation.

My advisor swallowed hard and, clearing his throat, said, affecting an air of outrage, "This creature," – here he indicated the boy with an extravagant flourish – "has taken this girl, in defiance of the Rule."

I shrugged. "What of it? Such things happen. You have authority to deal with these matters. Why else do you hold your position here?"

Thalis bowed again.

"Indeed, Lord. But this case is more serious than I thought at first. He has caused her to conceive. Given that there is now a child involved I judged it best to seek your opinion."

I could not argue with that. "How long have you known this?" I asked, still more concerned with the attitude of Thalis than with the boy, who knelt, shaking, on the stones of the courtyard where the two servants had thrown him. The girl stood weeping some distance off, not daring to move.

"My servant found him leaving the girl's room just before dawn," Thalis replied.

I concentrated my mind for a moment on the girl, making sure, then said, "The child within her has been growing for almost two turns of the moon. And you discovered it this morning?"

I looked at her again. She was no more than a child, perhaps eighteen years old, blonde haired and tiny even for one of our women, which made her look even younger than she was. Just the type of girl that would appeal to my joint second in command, whose activities, you will remember, I had severely curtailed some time before. I laughed inwardly as the scenario became clear, and had to acknowledge the cleverness of the plan. Not clever enough, however, as Thalis was beginning to realise. The girl's belly had not yet begun to swell visibly, and so he had counted on my not giving my attention to the state of her unborn child – his child, there was no doubt.

He didn't answer my question, knowing that to do so would make him guilty of either direct disobedience or a gross failure in his duty, being, as he was, in charge of the prevention of such occurrences. He had hoped to disturb me at my pleasure and so find me distracted enough to take little heed of the circumstances. That I was not was now causing him a great deal of discomfort, which he was barely managing to hide.

I began to calculate quickly. To expose Thalis would give me the perfect opportunity to rid the settlement of his presence. That, however, might be a mistake, considering the alternatives, namely Karim, or possibly Estil. Karim was prone to fits of heedless violence, much less controllable than Thalis. He was also sharper of wit, and at any hint of weakness in me, was quite capable of starting some ill judged insurrection that although doomed to failure would nevertheless turn the entire settlement into a bloodbath. Such a course would neither serve the blood, nor would it keep Sherenne and the gift she harboured safe.

Estil was also a dangerous antagonist, having inherited to some degree the gift of silence from his father. His mind was much less readable, and that made him unpredictable. Thalis might be cunning and highly intelligent, but I knew him well enough to make his moves obvious, even though he didn't realise it. So, while Thalis would not escape my anger altogether, no purpose would be served either by his death or his exclusion from my inner circle.

As for the decision that faced me concerning the young pair that had been brought before me, the solution was much less apparent. Both were clearly innocent, the boy in particular, but it was plain that he had already been warned quite effectively against making any kind of protest to the contrary. As I searched my mind for an appropriate course of action, I suddenly heard Sherenne's silent voice in my head.

"You cannot allow the birth of the child. You know that Thalis must never sire fit offspring."

I glanced back at her, veiling my surprise. She had not moved, nor did she give any sign, and was staring past me at Thalis, her eyes flashing with pure hatred. I turned back to my advisor.

"Bring the boy to me," I commanded, and at a gesture from Thalis a servant hauled him across the courtyard and deposited him in front of me, where he knelt despairingly, his eyes on my boots.

"You are responsible for the woman's condition?" I asked, and he responded with a nod, not daring to look at me in case I should see the lie. "Get up and present yourself properly," I ordered, and he obeyed at once, bowing tentatively and trying to brush the dust from his knees at the same time.

I caught him by the chin and forced his head up. "I congratulate you," I said with an appreciative nod. "You must be talented indeed to have evaded the eye of Thalis for so long. Either that," and here I rested my eye on the latter, who was starting to look even more uncomfortable, "or the head of my guard has been very remiss in his duty, and that is quite unthinkable. I believe, Thalis, that you could learn a great deal from this boy. He has clearly outwitted you on several occasions, despite your skill and diligence. It is therefore my decision that for a period of two cycles of the moon he is to accompany you wherever you go, and aid you in your duties to the blood. Perhaps then you will learn to deal with such matters without the need to disturb me with requests for judgement after the event."

Thalis almost lost his composure. However, my pleasure at the sight did not last long, as there was still the question of the pregnant girl to resolve. Thalis was well aware of my feelings on the usefulness of fit young ones and, sanctioned or not, had counted on my sparing the girl at least until the child should be born. But the Rule was clear, and I had once again stretched it as far as I could in favour of the boy. Not that it would help him. My guess was that he would barely see out the last day of his service, given the risk he posed to Thalis. Nevertheless, I could not be seen to show such leniency twice. I beckoned to the two servants, who came up to me at once.

"The girl is yours until sunset," I said. "After that, if she is still alive, kill her."

Thalis opened his mouth, then thought better of it. "The matter is settled. Now, I suggest you leave before I begin to grow impatient. Enough time has been wasted already."

The assembled company bowed, and had it not been for the look of plain terror on the face of the youth I would have been far more gratified by the frustration and humiliation I had managed to visit on my reprehensible underling. As it was, I closed the door firmly without another word, and with a long sigh leaned my head against it, my eyes closed.

I heard Sherenne come up behind me, and felt her place her hand lightly on my arm.

"You see?" I whispered, despairing again. "You see what I must do? They have done nothing against the Rule, yet still I condemn them, because I have no choice. Do you still say that you can bear to touch me, that you do not hate me for what I have done to two innocent children?"

She pulled on my shoulder but I could not turn to face her, so she slid her arms around my waist, her head resting on my back.

"You did not condemn them," she said firmly. "It was Thalis who came into the compound, who acted against your order and forced the girl into his bed. It was he who fathered a child against the Rule and sought to keep it from you. You can't allow him to produce an heir. It would strengthen him, give him a power he must not have. He used the boy and he will kill him. His death is not on your conscience. But there is something you can do. Watch for the time, and when it comes do not let him die a cruel death. You have the power to release him into the void and rob Thalis of his pleasure. The girl too – you have only to reach out with your mind to end her suffering, and no one would know it but you and I."

I slid my hands over hers, and after a moment nodded. "It is done. What do they say, the other women, in the Dance?"

"That you are evil – a monster. They grieve for Cassia and her child. It is natural that they should."

"Yes," I agreed, "it is natural. But if you see their Dance, do they not see your mind? Can you be a part of it, and not reveal all that you know?"

She smiled. "I can remain hidden. It is a part of my gift."

I spun round in surprise. "You have the gift of silence?" Then I laughed. "Of course – both Rolan my brother, and Rolan your grandfather were possessed of it, so I suppose there is every reason why you should also. But your thoughts are not invisible to me. How is it that I can hear them, when those in the Dance cannot?"

"Because my gift differs from that of my father and grandfather, and of Amal. I can choose who sees my thoughts and who doesn't. This morning, when Sevrian came past the door, he guessed that I was there from what was in your mind, but he didn't know. He couldn't see me. Also, I can make some of my thoughts visible while veiling others, just as you can. So, my gift of silence is not readily detected. You see most things, yet you were not aware of it."

I hugged her close, and kissed her. "That you trust me with this secret," I murmured, "does me great honour."

I would have happily remained in her embrace for the rest of the morning, but her words had reminded me that there was yet one more difficulty to resolve. We might still be in danger, she and I. She knew it too and stepped gently away, kissing me lightly on the cheek to see me on my way.

Sevrian was waiting calmly, as always, on my return. A stranger might have thought that in my absence he simply came to a halt, remaining motionless wherever I left him. Appearances, however, were deceptive. He had already dealt with several matters since dawn, including a trip down to the stables to oversee the progress of Orlim, who was preparing a group of new foals for my inspection later in the day. It was a not inconsiderable walk, and dusty on a hot day, yet he looked cool, unflustered, for all the world as though he had just taken a leisurely bath. He bowed with the usual deference as I entered, and followed me up the stairs.

"I believe you were wise to let it pass, Lord," he commented, after I had explained the events of the morning. "The safer Thalis believes he is, the less dangerous he becomes. I don't think that Karim knows the child was his, and he cannot risk a disclosure. Nevertheless, his behaviour was unforgivable, and it is a pity that you didn't have him flogged again, if only on account of his apparent negligence."

"It crossed my mind," I replied testily, "and I'm still tempted, were it not for the fact that the man made such an infernal noise over it the last time."

The corner of Sevrian's mouth twitched slightly with amusement, but he quickly settled himself as I said, with a sigh, "It's a pity about the boy, as his involvement was simply ill chance. He is safe for the moment, although two months in the company of Thalis might change his view of the attractiveness of life. As things stand, Thalis will make sure he does not live a day beyond that time, but I can think of no reason to make myself overly concerned with the boy's welfare. After all, in the eyes of the settlement, he is guilty of the worst act against the Rule."

I poured wine, and as I handed a cup to Sevrian noted that he made no comment, but took a sip, his brow furrowing slightly.

"You have something to say?" I asked, when after a long pause he still did not speak. He raised his eyes slowly and acknowledged the question with an inclination of the head.

"The boy's name is Nyran, Lord. I do not believe he was selected by chance."

I stared for a moment, then all fell into place. "He is your bed partner?"

Again Sevrian gave a slight nod, a rare glimpse of sadness in his expression.

"For almost three years now," he answered. "I suppose it was too much to hope for that Thalis was not aware of it."

I was about to comment that I had known nothing of it, but then, the means by which Sevrian satisfied his needs was none of my concern. I could imagine though that the discovery must have filled Thalis with malicious glee – he hated Sevrian every bit as much as he hated me, and saw him as a much more vulnerable target.

"And does Nyran please you, Sevrian? Does he perform his duties well?"

Sevrian sighed. "I find him most valuable, Lord. He will be difficult to replace."

"Then I have a reason to give him back his life. If you are prepared to accept him I will inform Thalis that he is to be given

203

over to you as your house servant, undamaged, at the end of two months. He will naturally be forbidden the right to mate, or to enter the compound. Also, his position must not be seen to be too comfortable. While I can make some suggestion of his innocence as far as the girl is concerned, still he was inside the compound without leave, which in itself is a serious matter. The decision rests with you."

Sevrian bowed. "You honour me, Lord. I am grateful."

"It is settled, then. I will speak to Thalis tomorrow. I have endured his presence quite enough for one day."

The matter that concerned me most still remained between us. It was not so much a case of whether Sevrian might speak of what he knew, more one of whether, under extreme circumstances, he would be able to keep his mind silent. Therein lay the basis of my lack of trust, and to a degree I found myself with the same dilemma that Thalis faced over the unfortunate Nyran. Sevrian was waiting quietly, sensing my unease, but saying nothing. There was only one way to be certain. I walked across to the window and leaned on the sill, looking out across the valley.

For a moment I hesitated, then, without warning, unleashed my power in a controlled assault that sent Sevrian crashing backwards into the wall. He crumpled to the floor with a gasp and I pinned him there, paralysed, letting my gift work into him until he was in such pain that his thoughts became wild, incoherent. When he was at the very limit of his endurance I bore relentlessly into his mind, tearing violently through every thought, every memory, every secret notion harboured in the darkest places. There were things he could not hide. His attachment to the boy, Nyran, was easy to pry from him, as was his hatred of Thalis, his contempt for Rolan's son, Amal. But of what I sought there was nothing, not even the tiniest whisper, and finally, with a shock I found myself repelled, as though I had run headlong into a stone wall.

I drew back, then pushed with renewed strength against the barrier, increasing the pressure until the effort of holding it against me forced an anguished cry from him. But he did not give way. Rather, in desperation he pulled back the veil a little, revealing a single, wordless expression – that of his unshakeable devotion to me. Beyond that he would yield nothing. The secret of my love for Sherenne was buried where no one, not even I, could touch it. If I could not prise it from him, no one could. All of a sudden Sherenne's question came back to me: 'Is there no one you can trust?'

"Only you," I whispered to myself. "You, and my firstborn son."

I released him suddenly and he fell back, breathing heavily, a sheen of sweat on his forehead. I realised that I too was gasping for breath. If I had continued I might have killed him. How strong he was, how like me in so many ways. I began to wonder why I had ever doubted him. I poured another cup of wine, and kneeling beside him lifted his head, helped him to drink.

"Forgive me," I said softly. "I had to be sure."

"I understand, Lord," he replied, his voice still a little ragged. "You must keep her safe. It is my honour to serve you."

I remained silent for a while, stroking his brow, refilling his cup, until he was strong enough to sit up, and then we sat together side by side, our backs against the wall.

"Tomorrow," I said finally, "I will speak to Thalis. I will not allow Nyran to die."

CHAPTER 20

It was generally considered inappropriate for a man to visit a woman if she was with child, and so for several months I was obliged to make use of the secret passageway that ran below the settlement to make my agonisingly brief visits to Sherenne. We spent the time together curled up in each other's arms, my hand pressed wonderingly against her swelling belly, feeling the life of our daughter growing within her. The process was a revelation to me. I had, up to now, had no idea of the trials that beset a woman during pregnancy, and I was overtaken by the enormity of it all, dazzled by her ability to take it in her stride as though it was the most natural thing in the world, which of course it was.

Considering the Family's obsession with the blood and with offspring, I can forgive a certain amount of laughter at my ignorance. After all, I was the leader of the people, and my everyday decisions most often centred around the subject of the Family's young. But this was my child, the first child to be conceived of my will with the woman that I loved, and that being so, things took on an altogether different light.

When I was out of my rooms in the dead of night, Sevrian diligently guarded both my house and the one I had gifted to him, next door to my own. No one was allowed in or out, regardless of the urgency of their errand. His own servants were habitually forbidden to leave their rooms between the hours of midnight and dawn unless directly instructed, so the restriction did not appear unusual. If a nocturnal event occurred requiring immediate attention, the settlement became used to its being dealt with by Sevrian. The rules of his own household were, more often than not, enforced by young Nyran, who was shamelessly devoted to his master, both in bed and out of it.

On hearing the news that Nyran was to be spared, and further, left untouched, Thalis had barely contained his fury. His anger had, of course, been coloured more than a little by trepidation, knowing that the main party to his offence would

206

remain a threat indefinitely. Worse, he now lived in some fear that an accident might befall the boy for which he might be blamed, so he was forced to take steps to ensure the continuing safety of the lover of his most hated rival. The situation was, for me and for Sevrian, a most gratifying one, but perhaps sweetest of all for Nyran, who flaunted himself in front of Thalis at every opportunity, a behaviour we did nothing to restrain.

What good days they were, in that brief time before my daughter's birth. Sherenne seemed to become more beautiful with every passing day. Her hair grew thick and shone like silk; her eyes brimmed with contentment and expectation. As she grew larger I did not dare to mate with her, despite her constant assurances that she was not as delicate as she looked. She teased me unmercifully for my over protectiveness, whilst at the same time relieving me of my frustration in the most inventive ways.

Occasionally I was compelled, at her insistence, to seek my pleasure elsewhere in the compound. It would have looked odd if I hadn't, as she rightly pointed out. These public visits I made reluctantly and without any enthusiasm, but at least the women that I chose were lucky, as my lack of interest meant that they were not inconvenienced for long. As the time went on, however, and the birth drew nearer, I saw a change come over Sherenne. It was slow at first, almost imperceptible. She grew quieter, smiled less, and spent most of our time together clinging fast to me, even weeping now and then for no reason that I could see. When I asked her what was wrong she could not, or would not say, but begged me to hold her, talk to her, so that she could listen to my voice. When I pressed her, she said only that after the child was born things might not be as they were, and continued to fret despite my reassurances. I know now, of course, what ailed her, why she refused to tell me, but at the time I simply put it down to her condition, perhaps to her fear of the birth itself, and concern for our child.

At last, one mild spring night, it began. I had not long left her when I sensed the commotion in the courtyard, and Sevrian took a message to say that women had been seen going into Sherenne's room armed with blankets, water and cloths. He stayed with me in my rooms, bidding Nyran to attend us with food and drink, and tried unsuccessfully to calm me down a little as I paced the floor as if determined to wear a hole in the stones. I was told afterwards that for a first birth the process was unusually quick, but to me it seemed endless. When, finally, a servant sent word that I had a new daughter, and that the mother was well, I almost collapsed from a combination of exhaustion and relief.

My next thought was that it would be eight days before I would see either – an unbearable amount of time. By tradition, a woman's confinement extended for a period beyond the birth. It had always been so, even before my father had made the Family what it was, and it was inconceivable that any man should intrude upon that time. Even he had not done so. Therefore I comforted myself that woman and child were in good health, and with gritted teeth set myself to wait impatiently for the days to crawl by until the time that I could see them.

On the seventh day, in the morning, a man came running to the doors, white faced and trembling from head to foot. Sevrian could get no sense out of him, and eventually, as he refused to speak to anyone but me, he was brought up to my rooms, where he still refused to open his mouth until Sevrian had left us alone.

As the door closed behind him he fell to his knees, terrified, and whispered, "My Lord, the child is dead."

For a moment I stared at him, uncomprehending, but the look on his face told me that I had not misheard. My vision suddenly dulled, and the world went strangely silent. For some reason I remembered how, many years ago in my childhood, everything around me had stopped, just like this, and in a panic I had asked my father if I was still alive. I had seen a momentary fear in his eyes, and then he had pulled me to the ground. Seconds later, for the first and only time in my experience, the earth had begun to shake. It had lasted only a moment, but in that moment I had been sure that the world was ending, and that when I opened my eyes everything I knew would be gone. The same dread came over me now, but instead of the ground beginning to heave I felt a rage the like of which I had never experienced before beginning to flood through me. The madness was taking me as it must so often have taken my father, spreading like a fire and tearing away all capacity for rational thought.

Kicking aside the hapless messenger I flew down the stairs, only to find my way blocked by Sevrian, who was pleading with me to slow down and gather myself before going outside. I had one hand on the door, preparing to wrench it open, when his voice cut through the turmoil, saying urgently, "Walk, Lord. You must not be seen to run."

With an effort I mastered myself and came to a halt, wiping away a bead of sweat that trickled down the side of my face. Then, drawing myself up I flung open the doors and forced myself to walk steadily, almost casually, out onto the pavement. The fury that was erupting in me made my body so numb that I could hardly feel myself moving, and everyone I passed drew back instinctively, not daring to look at me in case they should inadvertently catch my eye. I strode through the compound gates, and without stopping crashed through the door into Sherenne's room. She was there, alone, sitting in the middle of the floor, a tiny bundle clutched to her breast, her eyes locked on mine. There was no fear there – just the most terrible sorrow, but somehow something in me told me that things were not as they seemed to be.

I took a deep breath, and without a word walked up to her and took the bundle from her arms. I felt the limp little body, unnaturally heavy and still, and steeling myself I pushed aside the wrap that covered its face with the edge of my finger. For a moment I was frozen, staring with disbelief at the little strands of black hair on the top of its head, the line of the mouth, the tiny upturned nose. Then it struck me with the force of an icy winter blast – this was not my child!

Now it was clear. The strangeness of Sherenne's gaze, the unfamiliar atmosphere – her sorrow was indeed for the loss of her child, but not through death. She had used her gift to take my daughter from me, to hide her where I would not find her, and she had done it before I had even had the chance to look on what had become the most precious thing in my life. The weeping, the silences as the birth drew near – now I understood. She had planned it from the beginning, and I had been an unsuspecting fool.

I remember, vaguely, crouching down to place the body carefully on the ground. I remember drawing myself up, turning to look on the woman who still sat, calm and sad, on the stones, not meeting my eye, waiting for the storm to break. To my shame, to this day I remember nothing else, until I found myself back in my own room, the mist clearing from my vision to reveal the flecks of blood on my hands and on my shirt. Was this what had overcome Corvan, that day that my mother had spat in his face and he, in return, had cut her throat, spattering me with her blood? Was it my fate also, to destroy all the things that I loved? From the look of me there was no doubt that I had killed her.

The door opened quietly and Sevrian entered to find me whispering to myself over and over again, "Please, let me not be like my father."

"My Lord?" Sevrian reached out tentatively and I backed away, shrugging him off roughly. He tried again. "My Lord, listen to me. She is not dead. You did not kill her."

I shook my head. "Not possible," I muttered, turning away as he tried to get in front of me, make me look at him. "Look at me, Sevrian. This is her blood. Do not lie to me. She …" I could hardly bring myself to speak. "She has taken my child – she has taken my daughter and now she is dead."

I must have sounded as though I had lost my reason completely. Sevrian took me by the shoulders and halted my feverish pacing.

"No, Lord. I beg you to listen to me. She is alive, but will not remain so unless someone goes to her. My Lord, will you let me go?"

I tried to move but he held me fast. I was exhausted. He gripped my shoulders more tightly, and asked again, "My Lord, do I have your permission?"

The urgency in his voice somehow brought me back to myself, and I gave a curt nod. Without further ado he rushed from the room, not even pausing to close the door behind him. I sank to the floor, too weak to stay on my feet, but as I did so I sent out a plea to him with my silent voice. "Save her."

Immediately his answer came back, "Be still. I will try."

It was some hours before I heard Sevrian's measured tread on the stair. I waited quietly, not daring to ask the question, and he settled himself beside me setting down a large jug containing, of all things, hot milk and honey.

"What is this?" I asked, incredulous. "You think I am a child now, that I need such comforts?"

"Forgive me, Lord," he replied gravely, "but I am a little fatigued, and felt the need of something with a little more substance than wine. Of course, you are welcome to share it with me."

I laughed in spite of myself. "I would be honoured, Sevrian."

I knew from his demeanour that all had gone well, and so we drifted back into silence, concentrating on nothing more than the sweet taste of the milk. When the jug was empty Sevrian pushed it aside with his foot, and without turning to me murmured, "She wants to see you."

"What?"

I had thought of nothing in the past hours but the notion that were she to survive, I would never set eyes on her again, and all the joy that she had brought to me would be gone forever. I still couldn't understand why she had lied to me, how she had hoped to convince me with such an obvious deception. All my anger had dissipated, leaving in its place a dull ache that left no room for anything but the most complete despair.

Sevrian's voice broke through the fog. "Will you permit me, Lord, to speak freely?"

I nodded. If he had offered to take my life at that moment, I would not have refused him.

"I saw her mind," he said quietly, weighing his words carefully. "You understand, I could not avoid it if I was to help her." I nodded again, and he went on, "She has the gift of memory. She has seen the life she might have had, through the eyes of her dead grandmother. She wanted that life for her daughter – your daughter. As the time drew near the thought that her child would be imprisoned as she was became unbearable to her, much as she loves you, and so she decided to save the child from it, even at the expense of her own life."

I was about to ask why she had lied to me, why she had not trusted me, when Sevrian gestured for me to keep silent. "I said, at the expense of her own life, but not of yours. You cannot be guilty of a crime of which you know nothing. She lied to protect you, and for that reason alone. If she thinks you know the truth she will be consumed with fear for you. As long as she believes that you are ignorant, she will think you safe. That is all that matters to her now. Her gift of silence is greater than yours, and she was unsure of your power to hide what must remain hidden. Perhaps she could have trusted in your strength, but in her mind the risk was too great. If you still desire her happiness, then I advise that you never reveal to her what you know. As it is, she has her life, you have yours, and your daughter is safe. You will have other children, males, future keepers of the blood. Perhaps you may even surpass your father, and sire young who give you the gift he craved. But for now, Lord, you should go to her. She is waiting."

I retraced my steps down the pavement and across the courtyard in a daze. When I reached the door I tapped gingerly, and at once it was opened, by a woman that I recognised as one of Ilvan's daughters. She bowed and walked past me, leaving me standing on the threshold. I took a step inside, and stopped. The dead baby was still on the floor, and had been placed under a blanket in the corner furthest from the window. Sherenne lay still on the sleeping rugs, pale, but awake, watching me.

I opened my mouth, but could find nothing adequate to say, so simply dropped to my knees beside her and taking her hand kissed it gently. She tried to reach up to stroke my cheek, but she was still healing, and the effort was hurting her. How could she still love me, I thought, now, after all that she had seen, after what I had done? I could not bear to meet her eye, but lay down beside her and took her carefully in my arms, hoping that she would not try to exert herself further. I felt the tension leave her, and with a sigh she pressed herself against me, resting her head in the crook of my arm.

"Now I can sleep," she whispered, and before I could reply, I heard her breathing become soft and regular, and looking down saw that she had closed her eyes at last.

CHAPTER 21

"I must know," I said, combing out my hair a little more vigorously than was necessary. "I will not harm her, how could I? She is my daughter. I won't even let her see me, or speak to her. But I must know where she is and be sure that she is well. Surely you understand that?"

Sevrian's brow furrowed. "Yes, Lord, I understand of course. But it is not wise. Suppose you are followed? Suppose she has an image of you, and recognises you? That is not impossible, given her mother's gift. It is too dangerous. If such a thing were to reach the ears of Karim or Thalis, then what would you do? Besides, even though there are only two towns that Sherenne could have reached in a single night, still it would be like seeking out a single horse hair in a stable. The short lived settlements are large, and they sire many children in a given year. You might be searching for a season and be no wiser."

I had to admit that what he said was no more than good sense, and sat down heavily, letting out a long sigh. I had no doubt that my frustration could be felt a days ride away, although luckily the reason for it remained firmly within my own thoughts.

"I have an idea," Sevrian said suddenly, making my spirits rise in hope.

"Then would you do me the honour of sharing it?" I said irritably, when he showed no sign of continuing, but stared thoughtfully out of the window, stroking his chin with his forefinger.

"Forgive me, Lord," he said, turning to me with a slight bow. "I was simply turning it over in my mind. Amal takes Estil with him often when he visits the towns to make trade. Until last year Estil showed little interest. It is quite a recent development."

"I remember," I replied. "I gave my consent the season before last. But I don't see how that helps me. Neither Amal nor his brat are to be trusted. Estil is Karim's creature, and I often wonder at the reason for his new found enthusiasm."

"That is precisely why it helps you, Lord. It is no secret that you dislike him and don't trust his motives. Therefore it would not seem unreasonable for me to accompany them on their next journey, and the one after that – in fact on every journey until you are satisfied that Estil abides by the Rule when he is out of sight. Besides, I have a mind, with your permission of course, Lord, to make a closer study of those with whom we share the world. It is a gap in my knowledge that I would have filled, in case it should prove useful in the future."

Once again I was impressed by my son's ability to remain level headed where I could not. For the first time in many months I felt optimistic.

"You have my permission of course," I said with a smile. "When do they make the next trip?"

"In three days, Lord," my advisor replied. "They will be gone some twenty days, and visit both places. She will be – let me see – some six years old, will she not?"

"Six years and five days," I said wistfully, at which Sevrian nodded knowingly. Every year at about this time my mood darkened. I can't deny that I found it difficult, the pretence of grieving with Sherenne for a child that I knew was still alive. But had she known that I was a party to her secret she would have fretted, so I resigned myself to silence just as she did, and we made our pretences together.

Amal accepted Sevrian's presence without argument. He might have disliked me, but I had the feeling that perhaps he disliked his son more, and trusted him even less. Amal's gift of silence did not give him the ability to see into Estil's thoughts any more than I could, and his utter hatred of Thalis knew no bounds. To see his son falling under the spell of the one man in the settlement that he despised more than me must have caused him a great deal of disquiet. Therefore he grudgingly welcomed Sevrian's watchful eye, and the two set off pleasantly engaged in polite conversation, Estil following on a little way behind.

I watched them go from the furthest of the grazing meadows until they were no more than specks on the edge of the valley. Then, to take my mind off things, I went in search of

215

Orlim to discuss plans for the selection of next year's breeding stock. I found him out in the fields, checking the state of two pregnant mares. Immediately he came running up to me, anxious to be of service just as his father had always been. Thankfully he had grown in confidence a little, and I even caught a slight hint of pride as he gave me a tour of my private herd, pointing out the virtues of one beast or another.

Suddenly, before I could stop myself, I said, "You remind me very much of your father."

He came to a halt, looking a little shaken, and regarded me suspiciously before drawing himself up and answering stiffly, "I have no father, my Lord."

He could be forgiven, I suppose, for thinking the comment a test of some sort. I continued my examination of the next horse, so that he was obliged to keep pace with me.

"That is true," I agreed. "Nevertheless, you had one once, and the man that I remember would have thought well of his son."

Orlim hesitated, blushing a little, then gave a slight, elegant bow. "You honour me, Lord, as always."

"You have skill, Orlim, and a good skill should be honoured. Now, there is something that I wish to know, and I want you to answer me truthfully and not be afraid. Will you do that?"

"Of course, Lord. What is it you wish to know?"

"Against my command, you went to your father, the day that he died. Is that not so?"

I felt him grow tense, and continued my idle inspection of the horse. There was a short silence, and then I heard him say, softly but firmly, "Yes, Lord."

"You spoke with him. I want you to tell me what passed between you. All of it. I could search your memory if I wished, but I have said that you need not fear if you answer me with the truth. Perhaps you would like to sit?"

I didn't wait for an answer, but strode to the foot of the meadow, and sat cross legged on the ground beneath one of the

216

tall firs that formed the boundary. Orlim followed and seated himself a pace or two away, facing me.

"I was young then," he began tentatively, "not long in the gift. Forgive me, Lord, but I was filled with hatred of you, and wished that it was you tied there in the darkness waiting for death. But then, I began to think, when you gave my father the chance to save one of his sons, why did he not choose me? Why did he choose one he did not know, who had not yet been born? I was only a child, and consumed by anger that he had dismissed me so easily. Each night, after dark, I crept away and kept watch. The wolves would not come for him if I was there to protect him. I thought that perhaps when you saw that they would not touch him you would see it as a sign and release him. Then I could ask him myself why I had not been chosen."

Orlim paused, and glanced at me uncomfortably. He must have known that by his actions he had prolonged his father's suffering, and the thought clearly haunted him.

"And did you," I pressed him gently, "discover why it was that you had not been chosen?"

He nodded, and went on, "I kept myself well hidden, hoping that he wouldn't know I was there, but on the third night he called to me with his silent voice, ordering me to come out from my hiding place and speak with him. 'Why do you keep me from peace?' he asked. 'You have disobeyed the command I gave you, and brought dishonour to my line. Would you also have me starve to death here? Our Lord will not release me, he can't. The crime of which I am guilty is too great. The Rule may not be set aside, and the judgement must be accepted. At least you could grant me a death less painful than this. If you wish to help me, then tell your companion to strike cleanly, so that my life is gone before his pack begins its feast.'

"I felt ashamed, then, but still I had to know, and I found myself shouting at him, 'Why, Father? You told me that you loved me more than the others, and yet when you had the chance you chose another, and would have let me die.'

"He looked down at me and smiled. 'Yet you are alive, are you not? And your brothers also?' My confusion must have

217

shown on my face, because he went on, 'Listen to me, Orlim. What I tell you now I say only because you are the finest, most gifted and most loved of all my children. But you must never speak of it to anyone unless Lord Rendail commands you. Before I go on, you need to understand that the knowledge may cost you your life, and it is for you to say whether or not you wish to hear it.'

"Of course I wanted to hear, and told him so. 'Very well,' he said. 'I have made a bargain with Lord Rendail. He knows that the life I chose is not my issue, but his. In return for the life of his son, he has granted me the lives of mine. If I had chosen you, you would perhaps be safe for a while, but not for ever, and your brothers would have gone into the void three days ago. But you are now under the protection of Lord Rendail, and you will not be harmed for as long as he lives.

" 'You need have no fear that he will not honour his word. He has given it, and will not break it. I, for my part, have sworn that the sire of the child shall never be known, and it is now for you to ensure that my word is as good as his. His son will have my name, while you have none, but it is a small price to pay for your survival, and perhaps, one day, you will see that my decision was wise. Meanwhile, give Lord Rendail no cause to regret his generosity, and remember that no matter what you are in the eyes of the world, in your heart you will always be my son. Now, you must leave me. I am tired, and I wish this to end. Call your dark friend, and tell him I will not fight him if he will grant my wish. Then go back to your master, and do not speak to me again.'

"I did as he asked and called to the wolf. But it didn't come to me. It went straight to my father, and standing up on its hind legs, its forepaws on his shoulders, it looked him in the eye. Then it dropped to the ground, and turning to me bared its teeth and let out a menacing growl. I understood, and with a last bow to my father I left them there together. That was the last time I saw him, and as I reached the gate I heard the wolf howl, summoning its pack to feast on the kill."

Orlim fell silent, and I stared at him, stunned. "You walk with wolves?" It was the most unimaginable thing I had ever heard.

He nodded, turning his head away as if ashamed of his admission. "It is my only gift, it seems – to reach other animals with my thoughts. It is as though they are attracted to me in some way. I felt it first with the horses, when you sent me to the stables as a child. Then, I would often sneak out into the woods after dark, and although I could feel the wolves around me, I knew that they would never do me harm.

"There was one in particular, a great male, leader of its pack, that would come out into the open when I stopped to rest. At first it wouldn't venture too close, but as time went on it began to draw a little nearer, and eventually it would come right up to me and let me stroke its fur. We formed a bond, the wolf and I, and to my surprise, when it became old and died, its successor carried on the habit. So did the one after that and the one after that, and now the latest of the unbroken line walks beside me whenever I am out after dark."

It took me a while to absorb this revelation. Orlim's uncanny skill with the horses was explained, at least, but the gift to tame a wolf was almost beyond my comprehension. I changed the subject.

"Aside from your father, and our brother Rolan, both of whom are now dead," I said, "you are the only other who knows that Sevrian is my son. Something tells me that despite your manner, you did not keep silent out of fear."

"I do as my father commanded me, Lord," he answered simply, then added, "and as you would command me." He looked flustered, then said suddenly, "Sevrian is a great man. I am glad that others think of him as my brother. I think my father would be proud too, that in the eyes of the world his name is carried by one worthy of it."

I could not help but laugh. "Meaning that you are not? Did your father not tell you that you were the finest, the most gifted and most loved of all his children?"

"He did, Lord, but I don't understand why he should say so. My gift is of little value, and I have no courage. Surely he only said those things to comfort me."

I stared at him, astounded. Perhaps, long ago, Castillan might have said the same things of himself.

"You believe that?" I asked, with a smile. "Your skill with horses surpasses even that of my brother Estoran in the old days. You speak with all manner of beasts, a thing that no other can do. You walk with wolves, Orlim, the one creature that we all fear, for our gift gives us no defence against them. As for courage, it is easy for one to be brave who feels no fear. And as if it were not enough, you honour me not only with your skill, but with your loyalty. Your father didn't say those things for your comfort. He simply spoke the truth. What's more, I share his view. Were it not for the Rule, I would give you back your name and your line, but that you know I can't do, any more than I could have prevented your father's death. However, there are other things that I can do. I can continue to keep you under my protection, in fulfilment of my promise to your father. I make the promise now, again, to you. And when the time comes, and it is safe, you shall have your own line, and sire offspring that will carry your name. You have my word on it."

To my surprise, Orlim got to his feet, looking rather affronted. "Please forgive me, Lord," he said stiffly, "but it is not necessary for you to buy my silence with favours. It is an honour for me to be of service to you. I require nothing else."

"And you must forgive me," I countered sharply. "It was not my intention to insult you, nor to offer any undeserved favour. I do only what is right, according to the Rule. You have my decision, and you will abide by it, whether or not it pleases you."

He stepped back, nervous again, and bowed. "You honour me, Lord. I will, of course, do as you command in all things."

"Good. Then for the moment, I require your opinion on the fitness of the mare in the third meadow, if you will walk with me."

We passed the next hour deep in conversation on Orlim's favourite topic, his eyes shining with enthusiasm as he demonstrated his unrivalled understanding of the animals in his care. I myself was not without considerable skill, an acknowledged horse master, but I could not match him. He smiled with delight when I asked him if it might be possible to teach me to communicate better with my horses, and I finally left him, having made an arrangement to come to the meadows each day to spend two hours or so in his company, learning to embrace the minds of the beasts.

CHAPTER 22

As the weeks went by I grew to look forward to my daily sessions out in the fields with Orlim. Each afternoon, two hours before sunset, I found him waiting for me, and with infinite patience he trained me as he would a young foal, guiding me through the art of fashioning my gift to the shape that a horse might understand. It was quite a different thing from my own form of mastery of the animals, as I soon realised. Before, I had controlled them utterly, bending them to the force of my will so that every silent command was instantly obeyed. However, I now learned for the first time how to bond with another creature as an equal, and I found the freedom it gave me quite exhilarating.

I visited Sherenne most evenings, sometimes openly, but most often in secret, and she laughed with delight at my obvious enthusiasm as I replayed for her each triumph and each failure. Sevrian had made two fruitless journeys to the short lived settlements and was now away for the third time, so my time with Orlim proved a good distraction and helped, to everyone's relief, to steady my mood.

The year was turning, the air becoming cooler, and Sevrian was not expected back for several days. For the first time the young gelding with which I was working came galloping up to me before I called, shaking its head and twitching its tail at the pleasure of my arrival. I stroked its neck, savouring my new found capacity for unreserved trust, thinking how simple it was to place my faith in a creature with four legs while struggling so with those who had only two. Orlim caught my mood and I saw him smile as the horse nudged my shoulder, giving me a clear invitation to ride. I jumped up, needing no saddle or rein, and together Orlim and I rode out into the valley, letting the animals guide us along the path of a stream.

"Do you still walk out at night?" I asked as we dismounted to let the horses drink.

"Quite often, Lord," he replied, splashing his face with the icy water. "Especially when there is no cloud, and the moon is out."

"Then will you take me? Only, of course, if you would not find my presence disturbing."

By now I had the utmost respect for Orlim's gift, and could appreciate very well that there was a delicate balance to preserve in his dealings with creatures as dangerous and unpredictable as wolves. He paused for a moment, regarding me thoughtfully, then nodded.

"It would be my honour, Lord. Tonight, if you wish. The weather is still fine, and the night will be clear."

So, some three hours after sunset I found myself walking beside Orlim down past the meadows and out into the pine woods that bordered the south of the settlement. It was a place where no one ventured after dark without a strong horse, and never stopped without lighting a good fire. It astounded me that for so many years he had come here, alone and on foot.

However the world had been created, and for whatever reason, it was a fact that each creature had its natural foe. For the Dancer it was the wolf that reminded us of the foolishness of claiming absolute power. However great the gift, the wolf could not be harmed by it. The best we could do was hold them at bay for a time, but we could not destroy them unless it be with knife or spear. They, in their turn, had learned to come in threes and fours, never alone, unless the victim was a child with no gift to delay the inevitable defeat. Even setting my gift aside I was immensely strong, a good hunter, but even so I felt a shade of apprehension as I walked beside my companion into the darkness beneath the trees. He, on the other hand, strolled as calmly as if he was in a sunlit meadow at midday, his eyes gleaming with pleasure at the taste of the autumn night air.

The first rustle in the undergrowth sent an involuntary shiver down my spine, but Orlim merely smiled, and placed a hand gently on my arm. I came to a halt, my every sense alert. We stood in a small clearing, just enough of a break in the canopy to allow the faint light of the moon to penetrate to the forest floor.

I could see no more than three paces in any direction, and trying not to betray my growing sense of unease, I followed my companion's lead and stood quietly, waiting. We were surrounded now, the sounds of the creatures moving towards us through the undergrowth coming from every direction.

There were four, perhaps five of them circling the clearing. I could hear their eager breaths, imagine the sharp fangs, the pink tongues lolling over jaws strong enough to break a man's spine in one bite. I had a sudden notion that Orlim had brought me here so that he might avenge his father and treat me to a similar death, and was on the verge of panic when, without warning, a great grey head appeared out of the gloom and an enormous wolf walked straight up to us, eyes glittering in the moonlight. I stayed stock still, not daring to move a muscle, watching in amazement as it looked from one to the other of us, then padded up to Orlim and nuzzled against him affectionately. Orlim's response was to reach out and bury his hand in the great beast's fur, as if it was no more dangerous than a young pony already trained to the rein. I could see its white fangs glinting as it raised it head, pressing its muzzle into Orlim's chest.

The greeting over it turned to me, and to my surprise began to snuffle around my ankle, pulling gently but insistently at the top of my boot. Somehow knowing what was wanted I sat down and pulled the boot off, revealing the faint, almost invisible remains of the scar that ran from my ankle right up to my hip. Which of this beast's ancestors, I wondered, had given me this scar at the cost of its life, so many years ago? It sniffed curiously at the old wound and then, unbelievably, I felt the roughness of its tongue rasping against my leg. I looked up at Orlim, who from his expression was as intrigued as I was, although he seemed a great deal less nervous. The wolf stopped licking me and lifted its head, nudging my hand with its nose. Mesmerised, I began to run my hand through its fur just as I had seen Orlim do, and as I did so the others, who had been hanging back under the trees, came forward to join us. There were five altogether, muscular, powerful and well fed, milling about us as we sat there, sniffing and licking our hands and faces as if we were young cubs that needed to be washed.

For perhaps half an hour they remained with us, and then I heard a howling in the distance, perhaps a mile away, and as quickly and silently as they had appeared, the wolves were gone.

"One of their comrades has killed," Orlim said quietly. "We shall not see them again tonight." I absently reached for my boot, still too entranced to speak. "They know your scent now," he went on. "If you are ever alone here they will not harm you, neither these nor their kin." I saw him smile to himself in the gloom. "Sometimes I have the impression that despite our years they think of us as their young ones, foolishly wandering in the dark and in need of protection. Once, one of them even brought me a portion of the kill, just as a mother would take food to her cub. They have accepted you into their tribe, and their rule is every bit as strong, and much more ancient than ours."

The idea that I was now, in some sense, a child of wolves left me speechless, and we had been walking for some time back towards the settlement before I found my voice.

"Tonight," I said, finally finding my tongue, "I have been accorded a great honour. You have given me a great gift, and I don't know how to thank you for it."

"No thanks are necessary, Lord," he replied with a small bow, "but if it is your wish, you may grant me the favour of allowing a question."

I stopped and turned to him. "On this night," I said, "and on no other, you may ask the question, and I will answer if I can. But once spoken, all that is said must be forgotten."

He nodded, and taking in a breath, said, "Did you truly love my father as he said? And if so, is what he also said true, that you could have taken no other course?"

Even though I had expected the question, still it took me a moment to find the words to give voice to what I had for so long guarded deep within me.

"Yes," I said at last, "I loved him with all my heart, although at the time I did not know it, and in my heart I will grieve for him and honour him always. And yes, it is true; I could

225

take no other course. My duty, and your father's duty to our people and to all others outweighed all friendship and all love, as it still does. That is the burden that our father laid upon us, and I cannot set it down, unless all that Ilvan suffered is to be for nothing. You have my answer, and I will not speak of it again."

"You honour me, Lord," he whispered, to which I replied, bowing as a servant would to a master, "The honour is mine, son of Ilvan, and that at least remains to be my comfort. Tell me, shall I place you in charge of all my horse masters?"

"Oh no, Lord," he replied at once. "I beg you not to do such a thing!"

He looked so stricken with nervousness that I could not help but laugh.

"Then I would not dream of it. But at least allow me to make you a gift of one of my horses – whichever one you choose – after all, if it were not for your talent I would not possess such a fine herd."

"Again, you honour me, Lord," he said shyly, "and I am happy to accept your gift. If it pleases you, I will take the bay mare, the one in foal that we saw this afternoon."

I laughed again, this time at his shrewdness, and nodded my assent. I could not very well take back the offer, despite the fact that the mare was one of my favourites.

I walked back up the path from the stables in reflective mood. There were, it seemed, those within the settlement determined to relieve me of my isolation, whether I wanted it or not. I was fast coming to the conclusion that my father might have been wrong about a great many more things than I ever realised. The manipulation of the gift was one thing – it was already done, and the danger that his obsession had placed us in could not be undone. But what creature, I thought, could live without friendship, without affection? Surely these were the very things that bound us together, made a people strong. Even the sharp fanged, relentless wolves of the forest treated their mates and their cubs with care and tenderness. But was it not also true that they weeded out the weaker ones, left the unfit to fend for themselves against the constantly watchful birds of prey, the ravages of the winter weather? I was still lost in thought, brooding over the implications of my responsibilities to the blood, when I reached my door and almost bumped into Sevrian.

He hid his concerned look much faster than I was able to conceal my surprise at his unexpected return, and bowed calmly. "It pleases me to see you well, Lord," he murmured, with characteristic understatement.

"I didn't expect you for at least another three days," I replied as he followed me up the stairs. "There is nothing wrong, I hope?"

"Indeed not, Lord. In fact, the very opposite."

I waited until the door of my room was safely closed, then spun round eagerly to face him. "You have found her?"

He nodded. "There is no doubt. I first saw her yesterday, and rode through the night to bring the news. She is your child. It is unmistakeable, for one who knows how to look."

"Tell me. Tell me everything!"

Sevrian was tired, I could see, but knew there was no hope of my allowing him to rest before I had the whole story, so he sat, resigned, and I called for a servant to bring a large jug of his favourite restorative, hot milk with honey.

"I found her by chance," he said, leaning back and filling his cup, "in a small village just to the north of the town that lies at the bend in the river. It is Amal's custom to sit with the traders in the town square after all business is concluded. It is where they all gather after dusk to exchange wild stories and take strong drink. I admit that at first I found the process a little uncomfortable, but watching Amal I soon began to see the advantage of it. It seems that much store is placed by the short lived in idle chatter – in fact they see it as the foundation of good trade. Estil, I have to say, does not have his father's skill. It would be disastrous for us if he were ever to be let loose in these places alone."

He paused, shaking his head, and stared thoughtfully into his cup.

"Never mind that," I snapped. "Get on with it! How did you find her? When did you see her?"

He pulled himself out of his reverie with a start.

"Forgive me, Lord – of course. We were in the square, Amal and I. The night was closing in, and we had been listening to some interminable story, about a giant fish, I think. As the gathering began to break up, one of the men came up to us and offered food and a room for the night. I was surprised. Generally, the short lived like to keep us at arm's length. Amal explained that occasionally one was a little braver, or more curious, than the rest, but he would never accept such an offer. It was obvious that both he and Estil held the local townspeople in contempt. I had no such reservations, however, and accepted the man's hospitality gladly – if only to spend a while away from the company of Estil, who was beginning to get on my nerves.

"My host was one of the more successful merchants, but even so, his small house in the centre of the town was cramped and dark, compared with our own dwellings. His five young children crowded round me as soon as we arrived – I don't think they had ever seen one of our kind before. It was all very undisciplined, but once I got used to it I admit I began to enjoy myself. His woman prepared a meal for us, and ..."

"Never mind all that, Sevrian," I hissed, feeling that if he didn't get to the point I might throw him out of the window. Sevrian, seeing my look, bowed his head and coughed.

"My apologies, Lord. After dinner, when the youngsters had gone to bed, my host and I began to talk. He was most interested in learning more of our beliefs, and was quite shocked when I told him that our people have faith in nothing beyond what we can divine using our own senses. I did ask him, however, to give examples of experiences that might have led him to think otherwise. He warmed to the subject at once – invisible creatures do seem to be a popular topic of conversation.

"He started to tell me about his cousin's daughter, who had fallen sick shortly after her birth. For five days the parents had waited for her to die. On the sixth day however, just before dawn, they heard the baby crying and rushed into the room to find it kicking and screaming lustily for milk. It was, he said, a miracle, for only the gods could have saved her and made her so

228

well in the space of a single night. Since that day, he said, the girl has grown to be one of the strongest, most healthy that anyone has ever seen. She never fell prey to any of the normal childhood illnesses and now, at just over six years old, she is the prettiest, the most adventurous child in the village, and all the local people look on her as blessed by the gods.

"Of course, by this time I had become most interested in what he had to say, and expressed my desire to see for myself the result of this so called divine intervention. He gave me directions to a farmhouse some way out of town, and I set off there just before dawn.

"I arrived mid morning, and was washing the dust off myself in a nearby stream when I sensed that someone was watching me. I didn't look round straight away, but dried myself and combed out my hair in a leisurely fashion, then dressed carefully before turning to greet my observer. I knew at once that I had not made a mistake. There she was, standing quite still a few paces away from me, staring at me with open fascination as children do, her head on one side."

"What does she look like?" I asked eagerly, unable to stop myself from interrupting him.

"Very fine, Lord," he replied with a smile. "She has your look about her, there is no doubt of that. Her hair is so black that it shines almost blue, and falls long and straight as yours does. She has your colouring – a little darker than most short lived people, as though she has lived her life out in the sun. Her eyes, though, are a deep green, not blue like her mother's, and they are full of excitement. They belong to a child who loves life. Do you wish to see? I can show you now, if you wish."

I shook my head. "Not yet, Sevrian. Tell me, did you speak to her? What is it like for her, living with these short lived people? Do they care for her well?"

"Yes, Lord, I spoke to her. When she saw that I had finished my preparations, she came a pace or two closer – she had no fear of me at all – and asked, 'Have you come to see my father?'

" 'No,' I said, 'although if he has a little milk to spare, I would be grateful. I have a long way to ride before sunset, and I used the last of my supply yesterday.'

She considered me carefully, then nodded. 'If you come to the house, I'm sure mother will give you some.' She fell in beside me and we began to walk together across the fields towards the house. After a while she remarked, 'My father thinks that people like you are spirits, sent from the Gods. But I don't think he is right.'

" 'Oh?' I said, trying not to laugh at her seriousness. It seemed so incongruous in such a young one, to see her face set so gravely, her brow furrowing in deep thought. 'Tell me then, do you know where I am from?'

" 'Of course,' she replied without hesitation. 'You are one of the other people, the ones that live in the old town a long way off across the valley. All the men there have black eyes, like yours, and talk to each other without moving their lips. Can you do that too?'

"I had to smile at this. 'Sometimes,' I answered. 'But we don't talk like that all the time, only when we don't want others to hear us.'

"She pondered this, then said, 'Your Lord sent you here, and his name is Rendail. So God can't have sent you. Does my father think that Lord Rendail is God?'

"This time I could not help but laugh, although a part of me wondered how she could know so much. 'I am sure he thinks no such thing,' I replied. By this time we were strolling together alongside a fence that had been constructed round a small field, in which some captive hens scratched at the grass. 'I have to collect eggs,' she announced suddenly. 'Will you help me?'

"So, for the next quarter of an hour or so we scoured the clumps of long grass and rummaged in the little wooden shelter at the top end of the field, until we had gathered a good dozen or so between us. 'I have to do this every morning,' she said, pouting a little. 'I don't think it's fair that I should do it all the time. Father says it's not work for men. Do your women have to collect eggs and sticks too?'

230

"The question gave me pause for thought. Eventually I shook my head and said, 'No. Where we live, we don't keep fowl for eggs. The men collect them sometimes when they are hunting, and bring home wild birds for meat.'

"I did not add that neither did our women walk on grass, nor see anything of the world outside. She eyed me carefully, then declared, 'When I grow up I will go and see what the world is like. I might come and see where you live. I will be older then, and you might not recognise me. My name is Maylie. Will you remember, so that you know who it is when I visit you?'

" 'My name is Sevrian,' I replied, and bowed to her quite seriously, which made her laugh. 'I will certainly remember you, Maylie, and I am honoured that you would want to visit me. But we are generally not a very friendly people, and do not accept strangers. There are far better places in the world to visit.'

"Her face fell, and I thought she might cry if I didn't say something, so I went on, 'However, if I come to this village again I will certainly come to see you and your family. I would like us to be friends, and I will think of you when I have gone.'

"She brightened up at once, and together we took the eggs in to her mother. I stayed with them until just before the noon meal, then rode back to Amal and told him that there were matters requiring my attention at home. He was happy enough with my reasoning and so I set off and rode here as fast as I could, knowing that you would want to be informed without delay."

I was quiet for a long time. Sherenne had been right. Our daughter walked on grass, laughed, rode ponies – things that our women could never do. She had a family who loved her, a mother and father who lived together in the same house, who watched over her, thinking her a gift from their gods. What would happen, I thought, when she grew and the gift came to her? Surely then she would find other women of her kind in the Dance, learn the truth of her real family, what kind of man her father was. She would hate me, certainly, and I would not, could not disillusion her, much as it would break my heart. She must never come here if she was to remain free, and I must never reveal to her that I knew of her existence.

I almost wished I had not asked Sevrian to find her, but at the same time I was desperate to see the images he held of her in his thoughts.

"Maylie," I whispered, turning over the sound of the name in my mind. "It's a beautiful name. Show her to me, Sevrian."

He obeyed at once, and the vision of her flooded into me. It was as he had said. She was pretty, dark haired, with the most penetrating green eyes. He was right too that there was no doubt that my blood was in her. She had my look, in the shape of her face, the colour of her skin. I could hardly bear it. I wanted so much to reach out and touch her, take my most precious creation into my arms and hold her, talk to her, tell her who I was, and that she never need be afraid of me. But I couldn't, and it struck me then that were she here, in the compound with her mother, things would be no different. I would still be denied those simple demonstrations, the hugs, the kisses, the things that men in other places did without thinking every day.

"Stop!" I said, unable to keep the pain out of my voice.

The image faded immediately, and Sevrian reached out, uncharacteristically, and placed a hand on my shoulder. I felt ashamed of my weakness, but could not shrug it away. 'How much more?' I wondered. First Ilvan, the pain of his death made sharper by the monstrous bargain that he had made for the lives of his children, that I should keep from my first, my beloved son the true knowledge of his blood. Then Sherenne, who had almost died as a result of my madness. Now our child, in whose mind I would be forever reviled. Whether or not Rolan had regretted the curse he had placed on me, it made no difference. Already his words were coming true, and death was as nothing to the suffering that I was being forced to endure.

I was beginning to despair, but the memory of our last conversation somehow filtered through into my thoughts. The voice from the far future had sent me the message. Stay firm. Do not waver, and all that you have lost will come back to you. This was no superstition, but a message born from foreknowledge, and

I clung to it like a drowning man, fighting the urge to disgrace myself completely and weep in front of Sevrian. As if sensing my struggle he let his hand drop, and said, "There is something else, Lord."

I forced my mind to block out my growing turmoil and turned to him. "Something else?"

He nodded, and hesitated as if unsure how to find the right words. What more could there be? Had he not given me enough cause for regret already? Unable to speak, I steeled myself and waited for him to go on.

"She has the gift," he said. I stared at him in disbelief. Had he lost his mind? "I know," he said gravely. "It is impossible. She is but six years old. But she has the gift nonetheless. And what is more, she knows enough to keep it hidden. When she spoke of our people her knowledge had not come from those with whom she lives. She sees this place in her mind. She simply does not understand from whence that knowledge comes. Also, she is some distance away from us. Were she closer, she would see a great deal more. She has not yet entered the true Dance, but it will not be long, and then she will see all. Truly, Lord, the joining of your blood with that of the female of Derlan's tribe will have far reaching effects. Who knows what your future sons will do?"

At first I could not answer. The implications were almost too great to contemplate. How long had the gift been with her? Since her birth, for all we knew. And if one female had developed the gift while still a child, could there have been others? In women there was no changing of the eyes to signal the moment, and it was only at the changing of the body that any heed was paid to the nature of their abilities. Was it just the presence of Derlan's blood, or had the settlement produced such women before, little children prying into our thoughts as they played, unheeded, outside the compound gates?

"This must never be known," I said softly, to which Sevrian nodded and replied, "I agree, Lord. Who knows what Karim would do, if he believed that any of the women might be possessed of such a gift? If there have been others, then the secret has been closely guarded, and I see no reason to reveal its existence now. It would only create difficulties. Your daughter is safe and hidden, and all else is of no importance."

I sighed and got up.

"Will you go to her, Sevrian? Every year, at this time, will you go to her and make sure that she is well? It is a great deal to handle for one so small, and she may need the help of one of us as time goes by."

"It would be my honour, Lord," he answered, rising and bowing before leaving me to go to his well earned rest.

And so, at the end of every summer I saw him ride away to visit Maylie's family, to return some days later with news of how strong and how well my child was growing. At least that was how it was for some nine years, and in the tenth he came to me with the message that Maylie was gone. No, she was not dead, the father had said. On the morning of her fifteenth birthday she had taken a blanket and a horse, and with a brief farewell to the people she had known as her family she had ridden away, they knew not where.

The parents were grief stricken, but had not been able to persuade her to stay, and knew, they said, that it was her intention never to return. What cause could she have, they asked, to go? Had they not loved her, cared for her, given her all she could have asked for? They did not understand, but I, wrapped in my own grief, understood only too well. My daughter had finally entered the Dance, and there she had learned the truth. She had seen the Family, heard the tale of the blood, and through the Dance she had finally seen the monster that was her father. As I stood at the window looking out over the valley, I sent out a silent plea, hoping that she had ridden far away, to some place where she might find contentment, and never have to think of me, or see my face, even in her dreams.

CHAPTER 23

It would be easy for me to say that I ceased to be concerned with the whereabouts of my daughter, but it would be a lie. Seldom did a day go by that my thoughts didn't turn to her, and almost every evening, as night fell, I offered up a silent prayer for her safety and her happiness. For perhaps the first time in my life I set aside the importance of the value of the blood. Hers was precious indeed, but it did not even enter my head to take it into account. I could have sent Sevrian, or even Orlim, whom I had learned to trust equally, to seek her out, keep watch over her, but I did not. Sensing one of the Family near might have frightened her, and I did not want her to think herself pursued.

Although we never spoke of it, I somehow knew that Sherenne was of the same mind and had hidden herself from Maylie. I had still given no sign to her that I knew of my daughter's existence, and had no intention of ever doing so in case it should upset her. As time went on the burden, although not lessened, became a little easier to bear, and I was kept busy enough dealing with matters within the settlement to prevent me from brooding on it too much. At around this time Thalis, having been finally let loose once more in the compound, produced his first child. The infant lived no more than the customary eight days, after which I pronounced it unfit, much to Thalis's dismay and everyone else's relief.

The episode deflated my son's rival somewhat, so I judged it a good time to suggest to Sevrian that now was the moment to show his mettle, so to speak, and demonstrate his superiority in matters of the blood. His response was simply to murmur, "As you wish, Lord. I await your choice," as though I had asked no more of him than to take a pleasant ride through the valley on a warm afternoon.

After careful thought I chose a pretty young girl who, although exhibiting no gift out of the ordinary, was a gentle and perceptive creature, much beloved of Sherenne. It would comfort my chosen mate, I thought, to know that her friend was under the protection of my joint heir and advisor. I knew well that Sherenne hated the custom dictating that I alone decide who should lie with whom. She reminded me of it forcefully and quite often. But aside from her chiding she understood the necessity, and reluctantly admitted to me that given the circumstances there was little choice left to me but to intervene in the direction of the furtherance of the blood. Thankfully she did not protest my choice on this occasion, as she knew Sevrian to be careful and not unkind in his dealings with women. Sevrian, for his part, also seemed not displeased, although of course he would never have shown any sign of dissent.

Our brief and companionable discussion on the subject over, I lay contentedly in Sherenne's arms, idly stroking her breast, when she rolled over suddenly and said, "Sevrian may soon have a son. Is it not time that you also secured your line?"

The question took me by surprise, and my apprehension must have shown in my face, because she went on, "We cannot live in fear of the past forever. We must put it behind us. It is your duty to sire an heir and the Family expects it. Have they not waited long enough?"

She was right, of course, and as always I could not refuse her, even though I thought to myself that I could not endure the loss of another child. So, my heart thumping in trepidation, I did as she bade me, and fell back on the rugs not daring to ask of the gift whether the spark inside her was male or female.

I felt almost dizzy with joy and relief when I heard her whisper in my ear, "Do not be afraid, Lord. Our son will be strong, and he will live." I wrapped my arms around her and held her to me all night long.

The next morning the steady drizzle that followed the rising of the mist in the valley did nothing to dampen my cheerful mood. I wanted air, a little solitude, and a touch of my favourite pastime, hunting rabbits. I set off in high spirits, and by noon had nine healthy specimens strung from my saddle, a feat of which I was almost childishly proud, considering that I had made no use of my bow or knife, but had relied simply on the delicacy of my horsemanship and the speed of my hand. It was still raining, and I was debating whether or not to seek shelter for an hour or so to take a noon meal of the bread and cheese that I had stowed in my pack, when I caught sight of a small wisp of smoke ahead. It was perhaps a mile away down the valley, barely discernable against the grey, overcast sky.

None of my people were near – most were working in and around the settlement, out of the damp. I was intrigued, and a little annoyed to think that anyone not of the Family would dare to encroach on our hunting grounds. What was more, I should have been able to sense the intruder, even at this distance, but I could not. Was there one among us harbouring a gift of silence about which I knew nothing? I didn't think so. Whoever it was, the more I pondered the question the more irritated I became, not least because the harmony of my thoughts had been disturbed, so I set off at a brisk canter along the line of the river towards the smoke.

As I drew closer I could clearly see the flame of a small fire, protected from the drizzle by the overhanging branches of two large firs. They had, in fact, been skilfully lashed together to provide a crude but effective shelter. I slowed my horse to a walk and approached warily. There was still no sign of the owner of the camp, and what was slightly worrying was that neither had any presence revealed itself to my mind. I was some hundred paces away when a man suddenly emerged from behind one of the trees carrying sticks with which, I assumed, to replenish his fire.

I could see at once that he was not one of us. He looked ancient, streaks of grey running through his long, earth coloured hair, which not only covered his head, but quite a portion of his face as well. So, I thought, he is no Dancer, for no Dancer that I ever heard of was capable of growing hair on his face. That was something that was only ever seen in short lived men. Yet if he was one of the short lived, why could my mind not hear him? A half breed of some kind perhaps? Surely that was impossible.

Unconsciously I had brought my horse to a halt, some fifty paces from him. At first he did not seem to have noticed me, for he laid down his sticks carefully, then picked out a few good sized ones, which he used to build up the fire. I watched, open mouthed, as the flames shot up a little higher and he rubbed his hands together happily, declaring, "There. Much better!" At the same moment he turned in my direction and shouted, waving his arm, "Come. Aren't you getting a little wet, out in the rain like that? It's not good for you, you know, not unless you keep moving. You can sit here for a while, if you want to get dry, although I doubt it would do much good as you will only get wet again going home. This rain will last all day, take my word for it, and probably the best part of the night as well."

I was speechless. Who on earth was this man, and did he have any idea who he was talking to? I could feel myself becoming quite furious. He was paying attention now to a little metal bowl that he had left out to collect rain water. It was more than half full, and into it he threw a handful of what looked like some sort of coarse grain from a bag he had dangling from his waist. Then he set the bowl carefully on the fire.

I walked the horse forward until I was just on the edge of the shelter, and looking down on him, in the coldest tone I could manage I demanded, "Do you know who I am?"

"No idea," he replied without looking at me, intent on stirring the contents of his bowl with a stick.

I wanted to explode, but controlled myself with an effort and said, raising my voice, "I rule these lands, and all the people on them. You would do well to remember that, old man."

His response was to throw back his head and laugh so loudly that I was convinced I was in the company of a madman. By now I had decided that however long he had lived up to now, he was not going to live much longer. Finally he looked up at me, still chuckling and wiping tears from his eyes, and said, "How like the young! They think they know it all! Perhaps you could explain how you come to rule the land? Do you say to this tree 'come' and to that blade of grass 'go'? The land, boy, is ruled by no one. And as for the people on it, I am on it, and you don't rule me."

He said this in a half amused, half reproachful tone, as if he was explaining a simple point to a dull witted child. It was clear that not only did he not know who I was, he was quite unaware of what I was, and of how dangerous his situation had become. Meaning to enlighten him, I used my gift to give him a sharp push, which would have flattened even Sevrian.

To my surprise, the man did not seem to feel it, but turned back to his bowl and clicked his tongue reprovingly, muttering, "So impolite too. Can't you see my lunch is burning?"

Unable to help myself despite my fury, I peered at the horrible grey sticky mess in the bowl. It looked quite disgusting and completely inedible.

"How very fortunate," I retorted. "You mean to tell me that you actually intend to eat that?"

He grunted. "Most certainly, if you stop distracting me with your childish games. At least I won't have to share it with you, which I suppose is some compensation for having to put up with your infernal cheek."

He wrapped a cloth around his hands and picked the bowl out of the fire, then without another word sat down and started to blow on it to cool it down. Enough, I decided, and sent the bowl flying out of his hands and into the trunk of a nearby tree, the dismal contents depositing itself in a slimy heap on the grass. At last I had his full attention. He drew himself up and glared at me.

"You think you are clever, boy? Perhaps it is time someone taught you a little respect for your elders."

I wanted to knock him down again, but before I could gather my thoughts I found myself unseated and flat on my back on the ground some six paces behind my horse. I tried to send out a bolt that would have broken every bone in his body, but instead was suddenly overwhelmed by a searing flame of agony that ripped through me, leaving me gasping for breath. My own attack had been turned back on me and, furthermore, I was pinned down, unable to move even a finger, watching helplessly as he rooted through my pack and pulled out the bread and cheese that I had stowed there.

"A poor exchange," the man said with a shrug, "but I suppose it will do at a pinch." He sat down again beneath his shelter and proceeded to demolish what was to have been my noon meal.

The more I struggled to get up, the less I was able to move. I had never felt so undignified.

"Let me up!" I shouted finally, to which he replied, his mouth full of my cheese, "What? And let you disturb my lunch again? I would thank you to keep quiet while I eat, and then, perhaps, I will think about it."

There was no point arguing, so I was forced to lie still, the persistent rain stinging my eyes and trickling into my nose, until he finally brushed away the crumbs and stretched, sighing with satisfaction.

"Now will you let me up?" I demanded, seething with frustration.

"Why should I?" he replied with a sniff. "You haven't asked properly. Besides, I think it would do you good to stay where you are for a while and let the rain cool your temper." He got up and slung a small net over his shoulder. "A good day for fishing," he remarked. "Don't worry. I'll be back in a few hours. You might be a little more sociable by then."

He made to stroll off towards the river.

"Wait!" I cried, thinking that in a few hours I might have caught my death of cold. "Don't leave me here. Let me up. Please!"

"Aha!" He turned round, his eyes as sharp as an eagle's. "So you have been properly brought up. I was beginning to wonder. And what if I do? Will you try to attack me again? It won't do you any good, you know. I can put you back where you are before you can blink."

I did not doubt it. "No," I replied at once. "I won't, I swear it. And I ask you to forgive my temper. But please, just let me up. If you leave me here for hours I might die of a chill."

He gave a derisory little snort. "I doubt that very much. However, you seem to have lost a little of your arrogance. I hope you have learned a lesson, boy."

"I am not a boy," I muttered under my breath, and saw him raise his eyebrows threateningly. Nevertheless, to my relief I found that I could move again. I was so stiff that I could hardly raise my head, and my joints were still painful from the jolt that I had inadvertently given myself.

I sat up gingerly and was rubbing my ankles to get some life back into them when I heard him snap impatiently, "Hurry up. I don't have all day you know," on which he set off at a brisk pace, considering his apparent age, leaving me to struggle to my feet and hobble along behind him until I got the feeling back in my legs. I followed him down to the river, where he thrust the net into my hands and shooed me into the water.

For the next hour he sat on the bank, sheltered under his cloak, shouting directions as I waded about feeling utterly ridiculous on top of being cold, wet, cross and tired. Finally I threw his useless net onto the bank and set about catching fish using my own method, until I had half a dozen large specimens piled on the grass.

"Better than nothing," was his comment as I finally protested that I was too weary to go on, and that what was more I had taken no food since the very early morning and was genuinely starting to feel quite weak. "No stamina, you young ones," he commented cheerfully, which was all very well for him to say, I thought, considering that he had done nothing but sit, and had eaten all my food.

Back at the camp I was set to work reviving the fire and gutting the fish. Four of them he wrapped in leaves and laid inside his travelling bag. The remaining two he spitted and set to cook on the fire.

"I take it you have no objection to sharing my supper?" he asked, and hastily reassuring him that I had none at all, I peeled off my wet clothes, wrung out the water and set them in the branches to dry a little while I ate. By now my anger had given way to keen curiosity. If the man had set out to instil a healthy respect for his powers, whatever they were, he had succeeded. I had the impression that I wouldn't be allowed to leave until it pleased him, but that idea was furthest from my mind. He was

241

rummaging in his bag again, and with a triumphant flourish pulled out a skin flask and a tiny wooden cup.

"Here," he said, pouring a few drops of dirty brown liquid into the cup and handing it to me, "this should make you feel better."

I wasn't aware that I needed to feel better about anything. I wasn't too cold despite the fact I was naked, and the cooked fish had given me back my energy. Nevertheless, I thought it best to humour him, and sniffed dubiously at the contents of the cup. It smelt as bad as his bowl of mashed grain had looked earlier.

"Come on," he urged. "No need to be so fussy. Get it down in one go. That's the best way." I closed my eyes, and taking a deep breath tossed the whole lot to the back of my throat and swallowed hard. A second later my throat was burning, my eyes were watering, and I was in a panic trying to gulp in some cold air.

"What have you given me?" I asked, between splutters. "Have you poisoned me?"

"Don't be so silly," he replied huffily. "Just sit still and stop gasping. You'll be all right in a minute."

I tried to calm down, and felt the burning in my throat start to recede, to be followed by a not unpleasant tingling sensation that spread through my whole body. I suddenly felt incredibly warm, and strong enough to fell a full grown stag with one hand.

"See?" he said, with a chuckle. "No patience, that's your trouble. I told you it would do you good."

I had to agree that however foul the stuff tasted, the effect was marvellous. I nodded. "Thank you. I am honoured. But if it is not an intrusion, may I ask you who you are? I've never met anyone like you before."

"No, I very much doubt you have," he replied, "and no, I don't suppose it is an unreasonable question. But surely, as you are the guest here – uninvited I might add – it is for you to introduce yourself first. I have to say I didn't think much of your earlier description of yourself. Far too cocky if you ask me."

I resisted the urge to remark that I hadn't asked him and had no intention doing so. I got the feeling I might find myself

242

flat on my back again. Instead, I stood up and bowed formally, feeling a little awkward as I still wasn't wearing any clothes, and said, "I am Rendail, son of Corvan. I am honoured to meet you."

"So you should be," was his reply, which from my point of view was by far the rudest response that either of us had made all day. But then I saw his eyes mist over and his brow furrow, as if he was struggling to remember something. He peered at me intensely for some minutes, and then his eyes lit up and with a loud exclamation he jabbed his finger at me and declared, "Of course! I thought you looked familiar. Corvan's son, eh? Well, well. He thought far too much of himself too. Nasty little devil he was as I remember. I had to knock him down more than once. He soon learned to stay out of my way, I can tell you."

He wrinkled his nose in distaste and took a huge swallow of the foul liquid, straight from the flask.

"You knew my father?" I could hardly believe it, and stared at my strange acquaintance with new found wonder.

"Oh yes," he replied. "And your grandfather. He was quite a pleasant chap – can't remember his name now. And your great grandfather. I was related to him, but I can't remember how. I can't remember a lot of things. It's age you know. The longer you live, the more things you forget it seems. But none of it is important when it comes down to it. Not like teeth. Now teeth are important. Memory is nothing, but toothache, now that's another thing altogether."

"What?" My mind was reeling. This man knew my great grandfather? Then how old was he? No wonder he referred to me as a boy. To him I must, for all my years, seem nothing more than a child. He had encountered my father, yet my father had never spoken of it, and apparently Corvan had been no more successful against him than I had been. And here he was, complaining of toothache, as though everything else was of no importance. But he was speaking again.

"What was his name, now? It is on the tip of my tongue. Corvan's father – I do remember that he dined with me not long before he died, and told me of his worries. We ate fowl. That I do recall. Wild hens that his mate brought to us. Now she was a beautiful woman, kind, gentle as a lamb. It upset her, all the arguments between father and son. Yes, it was a bad time, so sad for everyone. Lena, her name was. But as for him – remind me – if you say it I will know at once."

I didn't know what to say. For me, as for all of us, it was as though nothing had existed before the settlement that my father had founded. So my grandmother's name had been Lena. She had been beautiful, and kind, and joined with my grandfather, clearly, given the way the man spoke of her. But of them and their lives I knew nothing. I had never even considered the fact that I must have had a grandfather, let alone what he might have been called.

"I'm sorry," I said finally. "My father never spoke of him."

He sighed, and shook his head. "I suppose I am not surprised. Too ashamed, most likely, after what he did."

I hardly dared to ask. "What did he do?"

"Why, he killed them of course. Didn't you know that? Crept up on them as they slept and murdered them in their bed, vile creature that he was. He was hardly full grown at the time, but then, it was typical of him – took his first life before he took his first woman, and things didn't get any better after that."

"Why? Why did he kill them?"

He stared at me coldly, but then his face softened, and he reached over and patted my knee, rather patronisingly I thought.

"You really don't know, do you?" I shook my head, and he pursed his lips for a moment, considering. "Ah well," he said at last, "I suppose you are entitled. And now that I look at you, it all starts to come back to me. You're not such a bad boy, for all your attitude. I can see a touch of Lena in you, despite your father's best efforts." He pulled my clothes out of the tree and tossed them to me. "Here. If you're going to stay for a while you had better get yourself dressed. You'll be more comfortable."

They were not completely dry, but quite adequate, and when I was presentable once more he made me take another swallow from the flask. I didn't fight the sensation this time, letting the liquid work on my senses, heightening my awareness, while at the same time making me as warm and comfortable as if I was wrapped in thick rugs.

"He was a monster," the old man said, "even when he was a child. Long before he came into his power people were afraid of him. If he had any affection in him at all, it was for his mother. Lena was such a sweet thing. Strange that I remember her name, and not your grandfather's, but I suppose, of the two, she was the most unforgettable. Never have I seen a pair more devoted to each other as Lena and her mate. It was a harmonious house, and I am one who likes harmony, so whenever I passed by I would visit them, and they would treat me as their honoured guest.

"I travelled a lot in those days, you see. I still do. I don't like to be in one place for too long. It doesn't do to be too comfortable. Nowadays I don't go as far, at least not beyond the borders of this island, but then I went across the great seas, saw the most magnificent places, and didn't return for years on end. Yet no matter how long had passed they always remembered me and were pleased to hear my stories in exchange for a warm bed and good food.

"They had four sons altogether. The eldest was a fine boy, always polite to me as I recall, strong and handsome too. The middle sons were all right I suppose, weak willed, easily led, but in those days there was no harm in them. I will never forget, though, the first time I laid eyes on young Corvan.

"He must have been somewhere around six years old when I came back after many years away. He opened the door when I knocked, and as soon as he saw me he jumped back from the door with such a look on his face, as though I was something less than a man. I think he must have mistaken me for one of the short lived ones. I looked old even then, you see, and had my long beard and grey in my hair, although not as much as now, of course. Anyway, without taking his eyes off me he started to scream for his mother, jumping up and down like a wild thing, and spitting at me in between his wailing and stamping. I don't think I had ever seen as undisciplined a child in my entire life. Poor Lena came rushing up to see what was the matter, and at once the boy clutched at her skirts, sobbing that he was frightened of me, and at the same time glaring at me with a hatred I could hardly imagine in such a small child, whenever his mother wasn't looking.

"Lena set herself to comforting the child, eventually shooing him off to find his father. As soon as he had gone she embraced me warmly and pulled me inside, clearly embarrassed by her son's woeful performance. As we waited in the kitchen, she confided to me that since he had started to walk he had been no end of trouble. In the last year, she said, he had attacked his father twice with a knife over the most trivial restrictions, and that nothing his father said or did seemed to have the slightest effect on his behaviour. On the other hand, the boy rarely disobeyed his mother, and had an almost fanatical attachment to her, which of course served to annoy the father still more.

"The boy made a perfect wretch of himself all through the evening meal. I could see that both parents were quite exhausted. I know it is the custom of your kind not to use what you call your gift with the little ones – at least it was in those days, but I felt that in this case an exception might be made. I restrained myself, however, out of courtesy to my hosts, and after dinner felt that a little night air might calm me down.

"I had been outside no more than a minute when I felt something whiz past my ear. A second later a large stone struck the back of my head, and I turned to see the boy standing there, smirking at me as if he was daring me to do something about it. Well, for all that I respected his parents I couldn't restrain myself any longer, and knocked him right off his feet, just as I did with you this afternoon. I pinned him down and took a stick to him, and believe me I was hard pressed not to thrash him half to death.

"He was nothing if not a coward, your father. But I don't think it was the pain that frightened him. You see, he knew, even then, that one day he would be much more powerful than his father. He knew that once he had grown there would be none of your kind able to restrain him. He was clever, and ambitious. He could wait, and one day he would be free to torment whomever he chose. But as soon as I revealed myself to him he knew that he would never match my strength. What he didn't know, of course, was that I could no more use that strength to kill than I could fly.

246

Nor was I the slightest bit interested in using my power to control others. It is just the way I am – the way we are. We like to stay hidden, away from people, and prefer the open country to towns and cities, although we do visit such places now and then."

"We? You mean there are more of you?" The thought of more of these strange creatures wandering about the countryside was quite unsettling.

"Oh, don't worry," he said with a laugh. "I doubt you will ever see another of my kind. I've only ever seen three others in the entire world, and perhaps that is all that there are. We don't exactly keep in touch, you know. But that's beside the point. Your father, as I said, was by no means stupid. As soon as he realised that I was not exactly what I seemed, he quickly deduced that I must be of a great age to look as old as I did. He was subdued, yes, and wary, but even as he lay there glaring with resentment I saw the flame of envy come to life in his eyes. Immortality, that's what he wanted. The one thing that frightened him more than anything else was the idea of death. Even though, being what he was, he would live for centuries, it would never be enough.

"He never told his father or his mother what had passed between us. I stayed for several days, and they both marvelled at the sudden change that had come over their son. He was quiet, retiring, clinging like a limpet to his mother whenever I was in the room, but by the same token he never took his eyes off me, his lust for my power oozing out of his mind, unseen by his parents but as clear as day to me.

"I went on my way a few days later, and I didn't return for perhaps another ten years. I often wondered how he had turned out, and one look at Lena's face when I saw her again was enough to tell me that time had done nothing to soften his nature. Aside from her eldest son, Corvan's brothers were now completely under his spell, following him everywhere, and together the three of them terrorised everybody within a weeks ride of their home.

"He hated the short lived in particular. My guess is that they reminded him of the thing he feared most. He couldn't stand to see any weakness, any infirmity, and to him the process of ageing and death was an abomination. The sight of imperfection sent him into a blind rage, and despite his fear of death he seemed to take delight in bringing it to others. Perhaps it gave him some control – he might not be able to give himself life, but he could take from others what they had."

He paused, and I could not help but see once again the terrible image of my father, crawling on the floor, crying like a baby and begging me to save him from death. I became aware of the old man's keen eyes on me, and looked up. He nodded, as if he knew what I was thinking, and went on with his story.

"Even in those days he was obsessed with what he called 'the blood'. Lena told me that all through the years since he last saw me he had constantly asked questions. How come I was so old? How long had I been alive? Was I immortal? Now, I had long since forgotten of course, but I was of the line of your grandfather's grandfather. Somehow I had been born different, and as I said, I am not the only one. It is a rare thing, to be sure, but every now and then there pops up one like me. Young Corvan had come to learn of it, and that's where he got the idea, that if he could make the blood pure enough, then he could make a race of people who would live forever.

"It's preposterous of course. Nobody can do that. And if anybody knew what it was like, toothache, pains in your knees, bad eyesight, you know the sort of thing – well, you don't, but you can imagine I expect. How lucky you young people are, to be able to live your whole lives at the height of your strength. It's not my fault I was born the way I am. I had nothing to do with it, and believe me, boy, if I had been given the choice I would have said keep it and have done."

He grunted, then cackled to himself quietly. "But then, it's no good grumbling about things we can't change, is it?"

I shook my head in emphatic agreement.

"Well," he said, settling down again, "Lena and I were talking, and who should walk in but the little devil himself. I say little – he had grown a bit, and I guessed that his power had come to him, his 'gift' as you say, no more than a year before. I had to admit that he was a fine specimen. At sixteen he was taller than his father, and stronger. As for his looks, he was stunning. I had never seen one so beautiful to look at, and he was graceful too. But the eyes …" He shook his head sadly. "One look in the eyes and I saw the tragedy at once. I have never seen anything so entirely evil as that boy's eyes. There was not an ounce of feeling in them, except for one thing – hunger. He had an insatiable desire for power, for control. I could quite imagine the rages that overtook him whenever he didn't get what he wanted, no matter how trivial. But I expect you know that as well as I do."

"Yes, I know," I said, the memories coming thick and fast as I remembered all the things my father had done, and all that he had taught me to do, to be, for the good of the Family and the furtherance of the blood. The sky was darkening now. It was getting late, and the rain still fell steadily outside our little shelter. The old man stopped talking and put a bowl of water on the fire to boil. Suddenly, the blood was not the only meaning that had been given to my life.

CHAPTER 24

"So there we were," the old man said, shaking his head, "standing in his mother's kitchen, face to face for the first time since I had given him a taste of his own medicine, so to speak, all those years ago. My back wasn't so bent then, but even so he was the taller by a good foot or more. Yet he bowed to me deferentially and gave me a greeting in a voice so sweet it made me shudder, and I am not a man to be easily put out, especially by a wilful child, as he most certainly still was."

The man stopped and handed me a cup of hot water containing just a splash of the stuff from the flask. I needed no encouragement to drink, as despite the mild but damp weather I was beginning to feel cold again, although the chill had nothing to do with the night air.

When we had both refreshed ourselves, he went on, "It was only then that I witnessed the full extent of his monstrosity. Without taking his eyes off me he reached out and grabbed his mother by the throat and pulled her to him. Then, with a smile that almost made my blood freeze, he kissed her on the mouth. It was a long, passionate, terrible kiss, and at the same time his hand was on her breast, fondling her as if she were a street girl, every movement exaggerated for my benefit. She could do nothing to stop him, and I saw her body tense in revulsion at his vileness.

All of a sudden he released her and turned to me, the smile still on his face.

'Behold my mother,' he said, stroking her cheek tenderly as she stood, trembling, ready to weep. 'Is she not the most beautiful thing on earth. Every son should love his mother, is that not so?' He began to laugh quietly, and still laughing he bowed to me, then turned and left the room.

"Poor Lena. I held her while she wept, and she told me how he sought to take his father's place, of his envy and his rage when he saw his parents together, and of the constant battles between father and son. She begged me to stay, for it was clear to

250

her that if the boy had respect for anyone it was for me, despite what I had just witnessed. If I was there, she said, at least he might curb himself in his dealings with his father.

"I agreed, and stayed more than two turns of the moon. When it became clear that it was not my intention to leave, Corvan's behaviour softened a little as he tried to ingratiate himself with me, to learn whether or not I might have any secrets that might be of use to him. Of course I had none, and eventually he realised that I was not going to put him on the road to immortality no matter how long he waited. But at least he was still wary of me, and held himself in check as far as his behaviour towards his father was concerned.

"The night before I left, Lena, her mate and I dined together. Corvan and his brothers were out, creating some mischief or other I am sure, in the country round about. After the meal Lena asked me to walk with her outside. There was something she needed to say to me, I could tell, that she couldn't say in front of her man. When we were far enough away from the house she turned to me, and told me that she was expecting another child, that it was due to be born near the end of the year. At first I couldn't understand why such happy news would cause her so much distress, but then of course it all became clear. It was Corvan's child. The boy had threatened to kill his father unless Lena did exactly as he wished. Such wickedness in one so young! The father had no idea of course, and thought the child was his own.

"I was incensed. I was all for going off and hunting the boy down, but she begged me not to. He was young, she said. He might grow out of it. Grow out of it indeed! The blindness of a mother! But deep down she knew that he was evil through and through, and that my intervention would only serve to tell him that she had confided in me. She knew that when it came down to it I wouldn't kill him. It was not in my nature, not then, not now.

"It was all my fault I suppose. Me and my precious principles. But how could I know what he would do? I should have. Well, the truth is I didn't, and that's that. Too late to do anything about it now. Too late."

He shook his head again, clicking his tongue and staring morosely into the fire. Then he laughed and said, "But then, I expect you are quite happy that I let him alone. As I said, you're not a bad boy when all's said and done. A bit headstrong perhaps, but you can't help that. You didn't choose your father after all. Poor lad. I wouldn't like to have been in your shoes, not for all the fish in the river. A bad business to be sure, but how was I to know? I never thought he would take it so far. But he did, and that's that."

The man seemed to lose himself in his thoughts, and I was about to remind him that he had not yet come to the point of his story when he shook himself, and continued, "The day after the child was born he killed them both. He couldn't bear it, seeing his father claim the child that was his. Neither could he abide the thought, insane as he was, that any man should be higher in his mother's affections than he was. So he waited until they were both asleep, and cut first his father's throat, then his mother's, and took the baby, a little girl, from the crib. He summoned his brothers, who by this time were mated and had children of their own, and together they rode away to found a new world, a new society based on your father's madness.

"When morning came it was Lena's eldest son who found the bodies, and immediately he rode after Corvan, with nothing but murder in his heart. He found them, and he died. For a long time they wandered, causing mayhem wherever they went, killing and stealing whatever they wanted, while Corvan sought out the perfect place to start his dynasty, to begin his experiments with the blood. Eventually he came here to this isolated place, and I suppose the rest you know, or at least as much of it as is important. Here they stayed and here you are, you and the rest of the brood, the twisted legacy that your father has left to us, may we all be preserved."

"What happened to the girl? What happened to my sister, Corvan's daughter?" As soon as I spoke, I wished I hadn't asked.

"What do you think, boy?" he snapped, his sidelong glance full of derision. "Your sister? Surely you mean your aunt, or even

252

perhaps your great grandmother! It was never a part of your father's plan to dilute the blood."

He must have seen my pained expression, because he sighed and carried on more softly, "He had killed his mother, the one object of his desire, the one thing in his life that he considered pure. The next best thing, for him, was his daughter, and she became the matriarch of your line, the one who gave him his first son, and another daughter. From that time on he never sired a child that was not from one of his own issue. He boasted of it to me the last time we met. Oh yes, we did meet again, don't look so surprised. It was not far from here, believe it or not. He was out hunting alone, just as you were today. I felt him coming long before he saw me, and stepped out in front of his horse as he rode past. It reared up and he fell right off into a bog. It took me quite some time to stop laughing, that I do remember, and of course he was furious.

"As soon as he saw who it was, though, he changed his manner at once, and became full of false politeness, thinking he could lull me into complacency. He still hoped I had some secret to offer him, I think. He wasn't getting any younger, he said, and the nightmares that had pursued him all his life were getting worse as time went on. His greatest terror was nipping at his heels and the thought of it drove him mad.

"At first he begged me to help him, to tell him how to find a way to extend his life, but when it became clear to him that I couldn't unravel any mysteries, that I was as in the dark as anyone else, he turned on me like the madman he was. He tried the same tricks you did, and of course he only ended up hurting himself. You at least had enough sense to only try it once. He came at me again and again, until I was genuinely worried that he might kill himself. I suppose I should have let him, but as I said, hindsight is a wonderful thing.

"At last I had to put a stop to it and knocked him over. I didn't harm him, you understand. I just made sure he couldn't move or hurt himself. Then I left him to come to his senses. I reckoned that a night stuck in the woods might help him get things into perspective. There were wolves about, you see, and I thought the idea that his life might not last as long as he anticipated might do him good. They would never have touched him – I made sure of that. But they came up to him and had a good sniff – must have frightened him out of his wits."

The old man giggled at the memory, while I simply stared at him, trying unsuccessfully to visualise my father pinned to the ground in the dark in the middle of a wood being sniffed at by wolves.

"By morning I was long gone," he continued, "and I imagine your father was fairly stiff by the time he found he could move again. Not too pleased either I shouldn't think. Clearly, as you claim now to be in charge of things, he never found what he was looking for. I only hope you have more sense than to travel his road, because I can tell you now boy, it will do you no good."

At a loss for words I sat with my head in my hands, the stark truth of my existence, of what my father had created, pressing down on me like a cold stone. I had always known it, but for the first time I was forced to see clearly what we were. I, my brothers, the entire people over which I ruled were no more than the product of one man's madness. There was no higher purpose. We were an aberration, an abomination, a thing that should never have been, born of my father's fear, brought to life by the suffering of others. But the fact was, here we were, and nothing could be done about it now. As the man had said, hindsight was a wonderful thing. I felt a hand on my shoulder and looked up to see him gazing at me, his eyes filled with concern.

"What is it, boy? He's gone now isn't he? Gone to the place he spent his entire life trying to avoid. He failed and the world is free of him. If the short lived ones are right – I'm sure they're not mind you – but if they were, and there was such a thing as payment after death for things done in life, then Corvan would be in a pit of eternal fire by now. It almost makes me want to believe in such things as gods. But we, at least, don't have to worry about it any more."

I shook my head slowly. I felt empty, and when I spoke my voice sounded flat, without meaning.

"You have no idea do you?" I said, staring blankly into the flames. "You really have no idea what my father has done. He failed to find eternal life, that is true. But he found something much more dangerous, something that could yet destroy us all."

The old man listened quietly as I told him of the Rule of the Blood, of how powerful we had become, and of how my father's madness had in some measure entered all of us. I told him of the gift to see the future, to cross the Great Emptiness, and how it had been discovered, lost, and recovered from Derlan's tribe through my taking of Sherenne. Finally I told him of those who lusted after that gift, and how it had fallen to me to be its unwilling guardian.

He was silent for a long time after I had finished, his eyes screwed shut and his chin on his hands. When at long last he opened his eyes again it was to look at me with such intensity that it gave me quite a start.

"Poor boy," he said, his voice edged with compassion. "You've pretty much got your hands full haven't you? Such a weight you have to carry. I can see how you would be a little short tempered with strangers. Things will likely not be right for a long time yet – no, not for a long time. But time, boy, is something I've seen a fair bit of, as you can imagine, and it has a habit of righting itself eventually if people have enough patience. Tell me, have you ever seen the sea?"

I confessed that I hadn't, except from a great distance, the time that I went to the south to spy on Derlan's son.

"Then you must go," he said. "Go to the edge of the sea and find a stretch of sand. Pick up a pebble and wait until the tide turns and the sea goes back. Then take your pebble and roll it on the wet sand. The more you roll the pebble, the larger it becomes, and if you had the strength you could turn the entire stretch into a giant ball of sand, all sticking to your tiny stone. In your hand, boy, you have a pebble, and already it begins to roll. You may not live to see it come to rest – that may be many generations hence. But you have set things in motion, and time will take care of things, as it always does."

"But what do I do now?" I asked. "How will I know which direction is the right one, which way I should turn?"

He laughed, but not unkindly. "Your father did something he would have thought unforgivable," he replied. "He sired a child with a heart, and worse still he chose that child to be his heir. Stupid of him, but it shows that he wasn't infallible doesn't it? Learn to read your heart, boy. Use it as your weapon and your guide. You have already done so several times, from what you tell me, even though you don't realise it. You have great power and a clever mind too. Use them all together and they will not fail you. But perhaps I can help a little. After all, if I had acted as I should have all that time ago, your situation might be rather different. Actually you wouldn't have a situation at all, as you might never have been born, so in a sense it could be said that your existence is my fault."

Before I could object he had reached into his bag again and brought out a leather pouch, which he tossed to me. I opened it, and found that it contained a fine red powder which I did not recognise.

"It's what makes the fire water," he said, in answer to my questioning look. "Don't worry, I can get more. There is enough in that pouch to last for many years, possibly more than you will live, as you only need to add a tiny pinch to a jug of water. Use it only when you need it, to give you strength."

I thanked him graciously for his gift.

"There is something else," he said after a pause. "I can help to make things less burdensome for you, but to do that I will need to touch you. There is no other way I'm afraid, inconvenient though it is."

Intrigued, I agreed, and he knelt in front of me, indicating that I should sit back and try to relax myself.

"Might hurt a bit," he warned, and before I could prepare myself I felt his hand clamped to the top of my head and heard him muttering some incantation under his breath. What began as a faint burning sensation grew and grew until I felt that a hole was being drilled into the top of my skull, and it was all I could do not to scream out loud. Shortly after that, everything went black, and the next thing I remembered was lying curled up by the fire, warm and content, filled with an indescribable feeling of calm. The pain was gone, and I somehow felt lighter, more at ease with myself than I had ever been in my life.

"What was it?" I murmured, turning lazily to face him, feeling no inclination at all to get up.

"A little trick I picked up on my travels," he said with a tired smile. He looked quite exhausted. "The man who taught it to me called it the 'dream voice'. The effect is rather like sucking poison from a wound, but the poison, in this case, is the burden that a man places on his mind. Guilt, loss, rejection – you know, all those sorts of things that a man carries around with him for no reason, clouding his judgement, cluttering his thoughts. Those things are not gone – just made more bearable I suppose. All I did was take the responsibility for actions you could do nothing about, and just like removing a poison I sucked it in, and spat it out. It's a dangerous thing, mind you, and perhaps if I had known just how much of it there was in you I wouldn't have bothered. But there we are, it's done now, and I expect you feel better for it."

I had to agree that the effect was extraordinary. I thanked him once more.

"The man who taught the skill to me is gone now," he said, "and I suppose I am not getting any younger. It's a useful thing, and it would be a shame if the one secret I have to give died with me. I think you are worthy of it, boy. Much more than your father ever was. It wouldn't have interested him in any case. If you like, I will show you how it's done – it might come in handy – you never know."

So, I stayed with him for most of the night, and he taught me the secret of the dream voice, a gift which, like the others he gave me, has proved invaluable over the years.

It was getting on towards dawn when I finally left him, a different man from the one who had ridden up to his camp the day before. I had gone no more than a hundred paces from the camp when I realised that he had never told me his name, nor whether or not we would meet again. I turned to call out to him,

257

but all that was left of his camp was a tiny wisp of smoke from the dying fire. Of the man there was no sign. Had it not been for the small pouch of powder in my pack and the peace that I felt in my heart, I would have thought the whole thing a dream brought on by fever. I offered a silent wish for his safekeeping, and set off back towards the settlement hoping that one day, before I died, I would see him again, if only to tell him that the rolling pebble was beginning to gather grains of sand.

CHAPTER 25

I never did go to the sea. I always intended to make the journey one day, but one thing led to another, as things do, and I never quite managed to find the right opportunity. My life was no less difficult than it had been before. If anything, things grew harder as time went on. But somehow I felt better equipped to deal with the trials that faced me every day. My mind was clearer, my purpose well defined, and if anything my new knowledge served to make me even stronger, more powerful than I had been before. I accepted the inevitability of loss, of suffering, and knowing there was more pain to come in my life I held my head up to meet it, comforted by the conviction that my actions were right and for the greater good.

The Family was not entirely evil, that I believed without doubt. Even one as powerful, as mad as my father could not have made it so. There were those among us who deserved to live as normal men, who were capable of a vision beyond the blood, and one day, I promised silently, they would be set free. Of course, if I had known just how bitterly fate would deal with me in the years that were to follow I might have fallen to my knees then and there, and begged all who would listen to release me from it. I look back now and give thanks for my ignorance, for although my resolve was to be tested to the limit more than once, I kept my footing as the blows rained down on me and did not falter.

She knew at once of course. The light, she said, shone about my face as I greeted her that night, a light for her eyes only, the one person from whom I could not hide my heart. I did not simply tell her what had passed, I showed her, crime though it was for a man to so give his thoughts to a woman. When I had finished and she knew all I had to tell, her face was grave, filled with concern for me.

"You must tell all this to Sevrian," she said at once. "You know that he will follow wherever you lead, willingly, for he is of the same mind. You have no need to convince him. You cannot achieve this by yourself, however powerful you are. Even the head of the Family needs a guardian sometimes." She sighed with frustration. "If I were a man, I would stand beside you, fight with you for what is right. But I can do nothing locked away in this place, unable even to see the world beyond the gates."

"And if I were a woman," I countered, "I would be able to stay here in this room forever and never leave your side. But for once I am glad that you are here, for it means that you are safe and protected, and I do not have to constantly worry about you. Besides, in a short while you will be too large to fight, and you will not be able to stand for more than an hour at a time."

Her hand moved unconsciously to her belly, and with a smile she acquiesced.

"I suppose my task is great enough. There is nothing more important than the protection of your heir, my Lord."

As always, she used my title almost as a reproach, and in response I grabbed her and held her to me fast, so that she could not free herself however much she wriggled in my arms.

"How can you treat me so?" I complained. "If you cannot show me the proper respect I shall have to do something about it."

"Go on then," she replied fearlessly, tossing her head in the way that always made my stomach leap, her teasing eyes full of irresistible challenge.

It was dawn before I knew it, and reluctantly I made my way from the compound back to my rooms, where Sevrian was waiting. There, I did as Sherenne had advised, and sat with him the whole morning telling him of my experience, and outlining my intentions. He listened without interrupting, his expression thoughtful, then turned to me with a frown.

"Even before you met this man, Lord, you had begun to change the manner in which selections are made. You pronounced the child of Thalis unfit, and your decision was not questioned, not even by Thalis himself. In the lifetime of your rule, you have spared many of lesser power that your father would have deemed without use. Is that not so?"

260

I could not deny it, but the fact that Sevrian was aware of it was disconcerting. "You knew that there was no flaw in Thalis's son?"

He nodded. "I deduced it, but only because you show me the workings of your mind more clearly than you do to any other man. No one else would think to question your judgement on these issues. However, if you are seen to make too many such decisions against his followers, there will be suspicion. And forgive me, Lord, we are not strong enough to risk an open conflict. We, and a very few who are of our mind might survive it, but those whom you wish to save would not. It is a matter of fact that those whose feet are on the path of madness are, by their very nature, the stronger ones. To preserve the good we must think of a way to safeguard the weak, and that will not be easy, nor will it be quick. We are talking of years, not of days, of slow and careful selection that will build us an army capable of bringing us to our goal."

Sevrian was quite right, and listening to his measured analysis I blessed Sherenne for persuading me to confide in him. I did not know then that the years of which we spoke would become centuries, and that there would be times when I doubted I would live to see my people freed. But for the moment I was content enough that our way ahead was clear, and all that afternoon we spent discussing the inhabitants of the settlement, their lines, their offspring and their allegiances.

The Family now numbered just over eleven hundred full grown, and of those, three hundred or so stood behind Thalis and Karim. Most of our adversaries were descended from the two most powerful lines, those of Morlain and Estoran. It soon became clear that the task before us was formidable. It was true that none living possessed the power to challenge me or Sevrian, but a victory that left only the two of us standing would be hollow indeed. The confidence of the multitude would stretch only so far, and a minority of two was, by anybody's standards, a poor wager.

I had, however, certain advantages. I was the embodiment of the Rule, and the Rule was above question. My leadership, therefore, went unchallenged even by the strongest of my opposition. Secondly, and more importantly, both Karim and Thalis were afraid of me. They were not strong enough to challenge me alone, at least not yet, and without such a challenge their followers would not move against me. If they were ever stupid enough to take the risk they would lose, and so destroy all they were attempting to create. So, my initial instinct held true. To keep Thalis close to me, constantly remind both he and Karim of my superior power, and place them in such a position that any rebellion would be seen as an unjust treason against the head of the Family was the best thing I could possibly do.

It was early evening by the time I emerged from my interview with Sevrian and walked down to the stables to perform my final task of the day. I had already settled the matter with Sherenne the previous night, and all that remained was for me to persuade my reluctant master of horse to accept my proposal. As I anticipated, Orlim was at first bashful, then, as the idea sank in, fearful. I did my best to reassure him that the girl Sherenne had chosen was both attractive and suitable, but it did little to bolster his confidence and finally he stammered, as he always did when he was nervous, "I understand the honour, Lord. But what if I do not perform to your expectations? What if my offspring are not worthy of the blood? I don't think I could bear it, knowing that my weaknesses were paid for by the lives of my children."

Now, that was a novel way of looking at things, and one that up to now I had never considered. I thought for a moment, and then said, "Even Lord Corvan sired offspring that he did not consider worthy to survive. Even the strongest of us must take that risk. But if it helps, I will tell you now that no child of yours will ever be considered unworthy of the blood, unless it comes into the world so twisted that it cannot live. Your gift is a hidden one, and it will be passed to your children without doubt, so I can be clear on that point. You have no need to fear that any judgement of mine will go against them."

With that he was somewhat mollified, and finally gave his agreement, not that, having been commanded, he had much choice in any case.

I left him and strolled back to the compound to spend the evening with Sherenne, comforted by the knowledge that there were now at least three lines in which I could place my faith. The line of Ilvan was assured, Sevrian preparing to take delivery of his first son. The newly created line of Orlim would soon follow, and although I did not know it at the time, a small but vital part would one day be played by his youngest son. As for the line of Rendail, it was about to receive its long awaited heir. In a few short months, I thought as I took Sherenne in my arms and kissed the place where the life grew within her, I would at last hold in my arms a son that I could lift up before the world and acknowledge as my own.

CHAPTER 26

The night before my son was born, I did a thing that a century before I would have thought impossible. Head of the Family or not, it made no difference to the fact that from the moment the birth began I would be forbidden entry to Sherenne's room until my son was eight days old. I longed to be with her, to share the moment, perhaps even to share her pain, lessen it if I could. People might be forgiven for forgetting, understandably I suppose, that my gift was of healing as well as of destruction, and I was as formidable at one as I was at the other.

There was only one way that I could think of to be close to her when my child was born, and so I found myself, with my heart in a tangle, on my knees begging her to join with me. Too terrified to speak, she took hold of me and clapped her hand over my mouth, shaking her head furiously until I silently gave my assurance that I would not mention it aloud again if she took her hand away. Then she threw her arms around me and wept, pleading with me not to have such dangerous thoughts, not to put myself and our child at such risk. She became so agitated that I began to worry for the baby, and holding her close stroked her head and whispered reassurances in her ear until finally, to my relief, she calmed down.

"How else can I be close to you?" I asked her, letting her feel my desperation. "You know that I love you, more than my life. How can I be parted from you at the very moment that I should be by your side? I can't endure it. I want to burn down this entire place, so that only you and I exist and the curse of my father will no longer come between us."

"Hush, now," she said, talking to me as if I were a child. "You can't do any such thing and you know it. Were it not for the danger you know I would do as you ask without hesitation. But the world needs you as much as I do, and until it is safe we must both be patient. Think what would happen if we were discovered. Already you take risks, and the task ahead is difficult enough.

Think what would happen to our son, to the future of all who depend on you. You know that I would give my life for you, but I will not allow you to throw yours away for no purpose."

Everything she said was no more or less than good sense, but she could see from my expression that I was far from mollified. She showered me with kisses, and I lay still obediently while she rubbed my back and shoulders to ease my tension. Still I was not comforted.

"How can I wait eight days to see my son?" I asked her. She must have known what an agony it would be for me, after the events following Maylie's birth.

She thought for a while, then sat up suddenly, the look in her eyes bringing me fresh hope.

"There is a chance," she said, trying to measure her excitement with caution, knowing that my mood was such that I would cling to the faintest of possibilities.

"What is it?" I asked, unable to keep the eagerness out of my voice.

"When he is born," she said, "two women will stay. It is the custom. No men may enter, but that does not mean that you cannot place a servant outside the door, for my protection, if you will. Given that this is your heir, no one would question it, even though it is unusual."

I shrugged. "How does that help? Surely it only means that you will be more closely watched."

She smiled. "When all is done, and the women are satisfied that the child is in good health, I will demand to be left alone to sleep. They won't argue. The man you place outside will see them leave and inform you. Then you will be able to come to me – not for long, for I doubt I will be left alone for any length of time, but it is better than nothing. I will not make the request until evening, so that you can come by the secret way without being missed."

The idea was simple, but perfect. I knew at once who to choose as my messenger.

"I will send Nyran," I said, kissing her so hard that she fell over backwards. "He will pass the word to Sevrian, and I will be with you before you have taken a single breath."

At noon the next day the trial of the birth began. To demonstrate my lack of concern I went down into the fields to pass the time training horses with Orlim. He could see my distraction, but made no reference to it, other than to skilfully warn me whenever another of the horse masters passed by. Once, I caught sight of Thalis watching us from the arch of the south gate, but thankfully he did not start down the path, and after a few minutes he was gone about his duties elsewhere in the settlement. Nyran was in his place outside Sherenne's door, and I could do nothing now but wait, as the afternoon wore on into evening and dusk fell, so that I had no choice but to help Orlim brush down the horses and send them to their rest.

It was close to midnight when finally word was sent that my son had been delivered. The birth had been difficult, and much as I was desperate to know that my beloved Sherenne was well, I could not ask. It was not good protocol to be concerned for a woman, only for her issue, the contribution to the blood. That, I was assured, was a large, healthy specimen, already suckling well, with the makings of a fine heir, worthy of his line. I dismissed the messenger courteously and sat alone in my room for another three hours before Sevrian finally appeared, signalling with a silent nod that the way was clear. My mouth was dry as I raced through the dark underground passage, overcome with a sudden foreboding that things were not as they should be, that I must get to the room as soon as I could.

The moment I sprang up from the passageway and set eyes on Sherenne I knew that my fear was not unfounded. She was ashen grey, her eyes rimmed with red, her breathing coming in short, painful gasps. When she heard me she turned her head and tried to smile, but the effort of even such a small movement was too much for her. Without so much as a glance at the tiny bundle that lay sleeping at her side I scooped her up, cradling her head in my arm, searching with my other hand for the source of the hurt.

To my amazement I could find nothing vital amiss. The immense effort of the last twelve hours had simply exhausted her, and all I could discover was a small tear in her flesh, the result, clearly, of the baby's size. Nevertheless, ignoring her feeble protests I frantically set to work, not stopping even when I knew she was mended and a little colour began to return to her cheeks. Finally I felt her hand close over mine, pulling it away, and I held her, stroking her face, letting her kiss my fingers. I felt utterly drained.

For a while we remained silent, and then I heard her whisper, her voice still weak, "That was foolish. Now they will know."

At that moment I was so relieved that I didn't care if the whole world knew. I laid her head back gently on the folded rugs and kissed her, and at last turned my attention to the object of my visit, the creature that had cost Sherenne such pain and effort. I lifted the bundle and carefully parted the blanket that covered its face. To my surprise, the child was not sleeping, but staring up at me, its wide eyes the most brilliant shade of blue. Its mouth was set in a thin little line below a perfect, slightly turned up nose, the fine wisps of golden hair on its head highlighted against the pale honeyed skin. It was the largest baby I had ever seen, and without doubt the most beautiful, the very image of its mother aside from the colour of its skin. I watched, mesmerised, as it wriggled an arm free of the wrappings and reaching up grasped my finger with a strength I would not have believed possible in a newborn.

I tore my eyes away to find Sherenne watching me, smiling, looking stronger now, her face less pale.

"He is beautiful," I murmured, looking from one to the other, amazed at the likeness between them. His tiny brow seemed to furrow as he saw us looking at each other and he began to grumble quietly, tugging on my finger insistently until I laid him at Sherenne's side. He fastened himself to her breast at once and began to suck fiercely, and although she said nothing I could see that the baby was hurting her. After a while he stopped sucking and began to complain again, kicking in frustration.

"I don't have enough milk for him," she said weakly as I took him back into my arms, trying to quieten him with my finger. She was exhausted, and needed to sleep, but I was of no use to the baby, who was beginning to protest more loudly, his cries so shrill that I began to worry that someone might come to see what was the matter.

"I will get help," I said, "a woman who has milk. I will send the mother of Sevrian's child. The boy is almost three months old, taking solid food, and you and she are close. I will order it – she cannot refuse."

"You will do no such thing," she declared, pushing herself up on one elbow before I could stop her. "I will take nothing that is not freely offered. More importantly, you are not supposed to be here. It will be hard enough to explain my sudden recovery, without you rushing around intimidating people. It is no wonder that men are forbidden to see their children until the mothers are sufficiently rested."

She fell back again, breathing hard. Thankfully our son had stopped his wailing and was snuggling down into my chest, his ear pressed to my heart as if the slow rhythm soothed him. I stroked her forehead gently.

"I will do nothing that you don't wish me to do," I promised, kissing her. "You must rest and get well, and not worry. Perhaps when you are not so weak you will be able to feed him better. But meanwhile I will speak to Sevrian. He will ask his woman to help, I am sure. I will demand nothing, I swear it. At least, I will not as long as you lie quiet and do not tire yourself." I slid down beside her, the baby between us. "I must name him. Now that I see him it is harder than I thought, choosing a name for one so great and so beautiful. He is favoured with your face, your eyes. I have no words to thank you for the gift you have given me."

Her hand found mine and we lay gazing for what seemed an eternity at the bright blue eyes that looked up at us, full of curiosity, the little mouth firmly closed as if concentrating, trying to define what kind of creatures we were. Everything around us was forgotten, until suddenly two sharp taps on the door brought us back to ourselves. I squeezed Sherenne's hand quickly, and gave my son a fleeting kiss before quietly slipping from the rugs and back to the passageway. The child at once began to wriggle as if sensing my departure, and started to complain angrily, turning away from its mother, its hands making tiny fists. There was something disquieting about its display of fury, but I could do nothing for the present. In just a few moments the door would open and the women would return. Nevertheless I paused at the entrance to the underground tunnel and whispered, "His name is Malim." I saw her nod, smiling.

"Why do you name him so?" she whispered back. "Does it have a meaning?"

I nodded. "In the old times, it meant 'favoured one'."

I heard a hand on the latch outside, and in the next breath was in the darkness below the settlement, the stone slab firmly in place above my head.

"I am told the child is uncommonly large and strong," Sevrian commented as we made our way down the pavement. "They say that any woman would find him difficult to handle alone. It takes three women to keep him fed, and he seldom sleeps, so it is said."

It was the eighth day, and I was on my way to make my first open visit, ostensibly to see my son for the first time. I had not returned since the first night, so had no need to feign my excitement, nor my apprehension. As we entered the compound I saw my other advisor, Thalis, waiting patiently in the courtyard, together with Karim, Estil and Amal. They were present at my invitation. Any judgement I made must be seen to be fair, and in accordance with the Rule. Unlike my father's children, the fitness of my own offspring would be placed beyond question.

I gave them no more than a cursory nod as I passed, keeping all expression from my face as I threw open the door and without pausing marched imperiously into the room. The four women surrounding Sherenne stood aside, their eyes respectfully lowered, and for a moment there was complete stillness as the two of us stared at each other, playing the game perfectly for our sharp eyed audience. She was standing, holding the baby in her arms, still tired I could see, but with a flush of health on her cheek, her eyes clear and bright. Without a word she gave me a perfect bow, and walking up to me placed the child in my arms. As I took him I let my finger brush her hand, the gesture hidden by the baby's wraps.

Physically, he was perfect. I carefully peeled away the blankets until he was completely naked and held him up, examining every finger, every toe, testing sight and hearing, the straightness of his back, the flexibility of the joints. I could hardly believe I was doing this to my own child, but according to the Rule I had no choice. He was flawless. Even his skin was clear, almost luminous, no sign of a blemish anywhere. I lightly pressed a fingernail into the sole of his foot, and at once he kicked out at me, his face puckering angrily just as it had on the first night when I had left him with his mother. So, I thought, he was not only handsome, but wilful and strong minded. I allowed myself the faintest of smiles, and thought I sensed Sherenne relax just a little in response.

I had one more task to perform, and settled him comfortably into the crook of my arm. To probe the mind of an infant is not an easy thing. Too much strength may damage it, too little might miss the tell tale signs of the germ of the gift. Even in a newborn it is present – undeveloped certainly, and invisible to most, but there nonetheless, and a great deal can be seen by one who knows how to look. I had been trained in the art by my father as a boy, and had since combed the minds of countless young ones, seeking out the strengths and weaknesses of each. Usually they found it uncomfortable, and I wondered for a moment what my son's reaction would be to the brief violation.

I closed my eyes and steadied my breathing, letting the rise and fall of my chest lull him gently as he lay against me. Then, very carefully, I sent out the most delicate pinprick of my thought to seek out the tiny seed within him. It did not take me long to find it, and when I did the icy shaft that shot through my heart almost made me sway on my feet. In the same instant the child let out a furious cry, and I felt a sharp pain as its fingers twined themselves in my hair and tugged down hard. I opened my eyes and found myself staring into the contorted face, the blue eyes gazing coldly up at me. A second later the mouth curled upwards in a smile, as if challenging me to act on what I had seen. I looked up at Sherenne, saw the anxiety burning in her, then back at our son, who still gazed up, wide eyed, at me.

For all of a minute the battle raged inside me, knowing that I was not wrong, yet praying that my judgement might have failed me. I know now what I should have done, but I had neither the strength nor the courage to do it. There is no reasoning with love, and I loved my child as I loved the woman who had given him to me. So, without a word I passed the baby first to Sevrian, then in turn to the others, feeling Sherenne recoil as Thalis took the infant into his arms, examined him closely, then handed him back to me with a murmur of congratulation. It was done. In the eyes of the Family my son was declared fit, and the five witnesses, having given their acknowledgement, filed away, satisfied.

I was now once more free to come and go as I wished, and it was quite acceptable now for me to remain alone with my child and its mother. As soon as I closed the door Sherenne rushed up to me.

"What is it? What is wrong?"

I hesitated just a fraction too long before answering, trying to be reassuring,

"Nothing. You saw – Malim has been accepted. Be still."

I handed him to her and turned to leave, but she caught my arm, her anxious look cutting into me, almost causing me to drop my guard. But it was my turn to have secrets, at least for now, and I met her eye calmly, even forcing a slight smile.

"I said, be still. I am a little tired, that is all. Rest now. I will return later."

She shook her head and was about to argue, but I placed a finger on her lips and kissed her cheek, then left quickly before she could challenge me again.

Sevrian knew better than to say a word. We sat together, the empty wine jug between us. It had been refilled four times, and now neither of us had the energy to call for more. It was almost too dark to see across the room.

"Thalis knows," I said finally, breaking the silence. "I saw it in his eyes. He looked into my child – my child Sevrian! How dare he pass judgement on my son, put his filthy hands on him. I shall take out his eyes and cut off his hands. Then let him pronounce on his own fitness."

I stared out at the stars, which seemed to be moving a little more erratically than usual. Sevrian heaved himself to his feet and busied himself with the complicated task of lighting a taper from the one small candle that burned on the table.

"You invited him, Lord," he commented, sinking back onto his knees, resting his head on the table, his nose barely an inch from the flame.

"So I did," I acknowledged, finding myself fascinated by his struggle to hold the taper steady and lower it to its intended destination. Eventually he gave up, and propping his arm up on his elbow decided to move the candle instead. It didn't seem to make the task any easier.

"I have an idea," I offered. He paused in his efforts and looked up at me.

"You want to cut off his feet?"

"How would he walk without feet? I need him to walk. I just do not want him to see."

Sevrian shrugged, and went back to his task.

"My idea," I went on, "is that you hold the taper, and I will hold the candle."

"An excellent idea, Lord," he responded. So I slid across to him, and took up the candle.

After a while I began to realise why Sevrian had found the procedure so difficult. I was beginning to feel rather cold, and eventually I set the candle down again with a sigh.

"I have another idea."

"My Lord?"

"Call Nyran. He is well versed in these menial tasks. He will light the taper, and bring us more wine."

"I would not have thought of that," he replied, and at once tried to send out a silent command, but found the effort of concentration too much. He staggered to his feet, and throwing the door wide yelled at the top of his lungs before slamming it shut again with an emphatic nod of the head.

"He is coming, Lord," he announced, then flopped down again, and we both lapsed into silence. A minute or so later there was a light tap at the door, and a confused Nyran entered, with a bow. He looked from one to the other of us, nonplussed.

"You require something, my Lords?"

"Indeed," Sevrian replied, trying to sit up straight. "I require you to light this taper, and Lord Rendail requires you to bring him Lord Thalis's feet. Then we both require more wine."

Nyran went quite pale, his mouth opening in horror.

"I said that I did not want his feet," I interjected testily. "I want his eyes." Nyran became even more horrified.

"Forgive me, Lord, but I do not think that Lord Thalis would give them to me."

I glared at the boy for a moment, but then all of a sudden, for no reason that I could fathom, I started to laugh. This seemed to terrify Nyran even more, and he looked back to Sevrian for help.

"Lord Rendail is quite right," the latter said, nodding gravely. "I forgot. He only requires the eyes. If he wants feet, I expect yours will do. But first, be good enough to light the taper, as I requested."

"Yes, Lord, at once." Nyran carefully took it from Sevrian's hand and did as he had been bidden, then stood up, holding the lighted stem. "What do you wish me to do with it?" he asked innocently, at which we both exploded again into laughter, much to his consternation.

"Light the fire!" we both said at once, collapsing in helpless mirth, and he obeyed as if a pack of wolves were behind him.

"Now wine, and food," I ordered, taking hold of myself long enough to speak.

Nyran bowed. "And the eyes?" he asked anxiously.

273

Sevrian and I looked at each other.

"Never mind those," I said, forcing my voice to remain even. "I will get them myself in the morning."

Nyran disappeared at once, and the door had hardly closed behind him before hilarity overtook us once more.

It was a measure of Nyran's concern that when he returned he brought with him bowls of hot stew as well as cheese, meat and bread, and left a full jug of wine with clear reluctance.

"He is a good boy," Sevrian murmured contentedly, nibbling on the last of the bread, and pouring more wine. "Beautiful too – quite magnificent. I think we frightened him. I will go to him later, reassure him. That is, unless you would like to borrow him. I would be happy to lend him to you, although I would prefer he was not damaged."

"I am honoured," I replied, taking another large swallow from my cup, and amusing myself by idly aiming for the candle with my knife. "He is certainly an attractive boy, although I suppose he has become rather attached to you by now. Besides, Sherenne might not approve. I don't want her to be angry with me."

"Then don't tell her," Sevrian said flatly, trying to pick up breadcrumbs between his toes.

"I tell her everything," I replied, then suddenly began to feel a little maudlin, and added, "but that is not true. I did not tell her about Malim. I should have told her. I was weak, Sevrian, feeble. I rule this place and can't do the simplest thing. My son is tainted and I could not act. What have I done?"

I threw the knife forcefully, missing Sevrian's big toe by a hair's breadth, and feeling furious with myself. My companion did not even blink, and wriggled his narrowly intact big toe thoughtfully.

"If you feel so strongly about it," he advised, "then perhaps you should do something."

"What should I do?" I countered aggressively. "It is my blood that has done this. Should I cut his throat in front of her? Should I explain that I have made her give birth to a monster? It's my fault. I am to blame. I should not have agreed. I sire dead babies and monsters, and I am not capable of anything else."

I stood up, a little too quickly, and fell down again, which made me even more angry. I tried again, and swaying on my feet took my knife and drew it across my palm. I could see the blood welling up from the wound, beginning to drip on the mats, but strangely felt no pain at all. I tried again, another cut that crisscrossed the first, and stared at the evidence of the injury, willing myself to feel the pain, but without success. I thrust my hand under Sevrian's nose.

"This is what is wrong," I declared. "The stuff that is in my veins is spoiled, useless. And now it is in him. Well, not for long. I will see to it. He is evil. Evil and unfit. I will see to it, him and me together, and then there will be no more of it. No – him first, and then me. I will show her what I am, what we all are. Then she will not deny it, and when Thalis tries to take her she will kill him too. Then it will be finished."

I was waving my arm about, spattering blood everywhere, but didn't care. I closed my eyes, concentrating, trying to isolate the tiny spark that was my precious son's life. I couldn't do it. The wine had made my gift hazy, without direction, and the more I tried, the more my fury grew at my failure. I had no choice. I would have to go into the compound and face the evil that I had created and, I vaguely realised, strike him down in front of the woman who had borne him out of love for me. I swayed on my feet, and without waiting for Sevrian to comment I stormed out, slamming the door, my knife in one hand, the other dripping blood as I went.

I staggered down the pavement and into the compound. Luckily it was very late, and nobody witnessed the head of the Family in such a pitiful state of intoxication. Not that I would have noticed – my eyes were bright with fury and determination. It was all I could do to put one foot in front of the other, and the only thing that kept me on my feet was the notion that I could end it all, now, while I had the courage to do it.

Sherenne must have heard my unsteady footfalls as I made my way across the courtyard, because when I crashed in through

275

her door she was wide awake, staring at me in terror. Her eyes travelled at once to my wounded hand, which must have looked dreadful, then to the knife, and she covered her mouth, trying to ward off a scream. In a quick, frantic movement she grabbed the baby and held it to her breast, scrambling to her feet and backing away from me.

"Put it down," I hissed, lurching towards her, brandishing the knife.

"No!" she screamed, holding it even closer. "Get away from us. You are not yourself. Leave him! Get out!"

Tears were coursing down her cheeks and she had backed right into the far corner of the room. There was nowhere else for her to go. I bore down on her, beside myself with fury, and grabbed at the bundle in her arms, tried to pry it from her. There was a noise coming from it, and I realised dully that the baby was screaming as well. It didn't matter. She clung on with a ferocious tenacity, refusing to give the baby up until I curled my injured hand into a fist and struck her in the face so savagely that she fell as if her legs had been cut from under her, the blood spurting from my wounds all over her, the baby and the floor. She fell silent, but the child continued to wail as I grasped it and threw it down onto the sleeping rugs.

I raised my arm, the knife hovering above its throat. I thrust downwards with all my strength, but as I did so felt a great weight pulling me backwards. Sherenne had dragged herself to me and had caught me with both hands by the wrist, wrenching my arm back with all her might. I half turned, furious, and heaved my elbow back into her stomach, causing her to fall again. I took hold of the child by the back of the neck. The blankets fell away to reveal its face, the blue eyes filled with terror as I pressed my blade to its tender throat. I hesitated, shifting my grip on the haft of the knife, and as I did so heard a tremendous crash. A second later my vision started to blur and a dull sensation began to spread out from somewhere on the left side of my head. I watched my fingers open involuntarily, the knife slip onto the rugs. Then, the floor was coming up to meet me, and everything was black.

CHAPTER 27

The early sunlight streaming through the window sent a cruel stab of pain through my head as soon as I opened my eyes. I closed them again and tried to shift my body round, away from the light. At once there was pain from several other directions, and it took me a minute to realise that it moved with me, was a part of me, inescapable wherever I put myself. I took a deep breath and forced my eyes open again, gritting my teeth. I was sprawled on the floor, my cheek pressed against the cold stone. My head felt like lead, and after several unsuccessful attempts to lift it I contented myself with a study of the tiny grains in the stone slab an inch in front of my nose. Everything else was a blur. The only thing that my mind seemed to understand was the pain, which became more overwhelming with every second that passed.

A few more minutes went by and my awareness began to sharpen a little, despite my fervent desire for a return to unconsciousness. I could now isolate the main causes of my discomfort, which seemed to be the left side of my head and my right hand. Gingerly I lifted my good hand to feel the spot, and my fingers made contact with a lump the size of a hen's egg on my left temple. Even the light touch was enough to bring on an explosion of pain, and when I held my fingers in front of my eyes I could see they were coated in blood.

My right arm was stretched out in front of me, and slowly I made another attempt to move my head. This time it worked, and my eyes travelled along the arm to the hand, which I saw was crudely wrapped with bloodstained cloths. At the same instant I heard a faint rustle from somewhere beyond my hand, and let my eyes move on until they found the source of the noise.

Sherenne was huddled in the corner of the room, her eyes fixed on me, our baby firmly clasped to her chest. She was trembling uncontrollably, her face bloody and distorted, and as our eyes met I saw her shrink away, pressing her back into the wall, clutching Malim tighter as if her arms could protect him

277

from me. I was horrified. I tried to speak but my mouth felt as though it was full of sand. Using every ounce of effort I tried to sit up, and as I did so I saw her shrink even further back, the tears starting again in her eyes, shaking her head between her sobs.

In all the years I had known and loved her I had never seen her look at me with such an expression, and the sight of it made me want to die. I wanted to tell her, beg her not to be afraid of me, but no words came. I had to get out of the room, and despite my pounding head I tried to struggle to my feet. At the third attempt I managed it, and as I stood, swaying, trying to steady myself enough to walk I saw her drop to the ground, curling herself up into a ball of abject terror, turning away from me so that her body was between me and the bundle in her arms.

It was unbearable. I staggered to the door and somehow made my way into the courtyard, closing the door behind me. One or two women were about, and at the sight of me they fled in consternation. I can't remember whether anyone else was witness to my slow walk back to my own rooms. All I know is that the moment the door was safely shut I collapsed onto my rugs and wept until I was so exhausted that sleep took me, and did not open my eyes until it was quite dark again.

When I woke I did not feel a great deal better. My vision was a little clearer, but the pain in my head was, if anything, worse, and my hand was throbbing insistently, any attempt to move my fingers sending an agonising spasm through my whole arm. I rolled over painfully to find Sevrian sitting patiently beside the rugs. Nyran stood uneasily behind him, and seeing me awake Sevrian gestured to him curtly. At once a bowl of hot water, soap and cloths was placed at my side, and Sevrian lifted my head, offering a cup of warm milk which I drank down gratefully. He gestured for Nyran to wait outside, then cleaned and healed my head wound, which was quite a task, as apparently, he told me as he worked, my skull had been fractured.

"How?" I asked weakly. My memory was hazy. I remembered only the noise, a dizziness, and falling down.

"She hit you," he answered quietly, "with an iron pot. It is extraordinary, the strength a woman will find when she is protecting her child. With a broken cheekbone too. Quite incredible."

"She is hurt?" My last vision of her rushed back into my mind and I frantically tried to struggle up. "Has anyone seen to her? I must go to her."

Even without Sevrian holding me down it was clear that I would not be going anywhere, at least for an hour or two. He shook his head, trying to keep me calm.

"I went there this morning, Lord. To find out what occurred. But I did nothing. You were unconscious, and so I had no instruction."

"Then I must go," I said again, desperately. "Help me up at once. I must go now."

He shook his head again slowly, still preventing me from trying to get up.

"My Lord," he said, holding my head to keep it still, "you must listen to me. She has told me – requested me – to ask that you do not go there any more. She knows that you have the right, that she cannot prevent you. But all the same she begs you to stay away. Do you understand, Lord? Forgive me, but to go to her would not be wise."

I fell back, utterly crushed. Sevrian turned his attention to my hand, carefully removing the blood caked wrappings.

"She did that," I whispered, taking hold of his hand and pushing it away. "She bound my hand. She did it out of love. She doesn't mean it, Sevrian. She will see me. She just needs a little time, that's all."

"As you say, Lord," he replied. "Perhaps just a little time. You must rest, and let me tend to you. The wounds are deep and must be cleaned."

I looked down at my hand. The two cuts were indeed deep, almost down to the bone, still weeping a little blood. I marvelled that I had felt nothing in the midst of my madness, and felt somehow comforted by the pain that I suffered now. It was as though by enduring it I might offer some faint reparation to Sherenne, some proof that I was once again myself and the moment of danger was past. For the moment *was* past. I had failed in my duty to the blood, failed to do what I had sworn to do, to remove the threat that hung over our future.

I had tried. But even a gallon of strong wine to bring on the madness, to dull my senses enough to carry out the task, had met with failure. I would never have the courage to make another attempt. How much greater would have been the pain of my shattered heart if I had awoken to the knowledge that my son was dead? It was enough that I saw the terrible fear on the face of the woman I loved each time I closed my eyes.

"Leave it," I ordered Sevrian.

"Please, my Lord," he began to protest, but I cut him short.

"Go to her first. Make sure that she is comfortable and take away her pain. Tell her that I will not come, not unless she allows it. Tell her she is safe, and tell her …"

"My Lord?"

"Ask her to forgive me."

He nodded, knowing that he could not argue with me, and left me alone. I lay back, and closing my eyes deliberately squeezed the fingers of my injured hand into the palm, until pain drove all other thoughts out of my head.

"She is well?" I asked, when Sevrian returned. He nodded.

"Well enough, Lord. I have mended the bones, and she is resting now. The child is unhurt, and I have sent one of the women to help her."

I sighed with relief. "And you have told her that I am recovered? She has forgiven me?" His brow furrowed, and he hesitated. "Well?" I demanded, my pulse quickening anxiously.

"My Lord, I am sorry. She acknowledges your message, but she begs that you do not go to see her. If you care for her, she said, you will do as she asks, and leave her alone. Those were her words."

"For how long?" I asked, my stomach beginning to feel as though I had swallowed a bar of iron. "How long must I wait? I can bear it if I know. What did she say?"

"Forgive me, Lord," Sevrian replied evenly. "Sherenne said to me that she never wishes to see you again. Now, will you please let me see to your hand?"

I felt suddenly dizzy. Never? Did she not understand what I had tried to do, why I had acted as I did? Surely, given time she would come to see that I had no choice but to protect the blood, protect her from the monster that lay at her side, who would grow to place us all in danger. How innocent he appeared, my newborn son, with his bright blue eyes and golden hair. And how I loved him. I could not deny it, any more than I could deny what my blood had produced. If only he did not look quite so much like his mother. I turned to Sevrian, my mouth set in an expression of determination, a feeling of sickness in my stomach.

"It is too soon. She will change her mind. You will see."

Sevrian raised an eyebrow. "Assuredly, Lord. Now, please, your hand."

"Tend it as the short lived people do," I said. "Clean it, bind it and leave it. Then leave me alone. Do not come again until I call."

"As you wish, Lord." He was clearly unhappy, but did as I ordered, and reluctantly left me to my misery.

By noon the following day I was fighting a raging fever. How was it, I thought, that the short lived were able to survive anything worse than a grazed knee? It was becoming rapidly apparent that even if I lived through the infection I would lose the use of my hand, if not my arm, which was swelling alarmingly. Yet I did not call Sevrian. Life was suddenly meaningless to me, and my only remaining ambition was to end it in as painful a manner as possible in the hope that my conscience might be eased before I died.

I found myself talking to my dead brother, Rolan, protesting my weakness, admitting my failures, pathetically explaining how none of it was my fault. In my mind I confused images of Sherenne with those of my mother, imagined the chain that had once been round my ankle to be now fastened to my right arm, the metal biting into my flesh. When I fell into an uneasy sleep it was Sherenne that I saw at the other end of the chain, her face filled with hatred and contempt. In her hand was my knife, raised, ready to sever my arm above the shackle and so release herself from me forever.

The afternoon wore on, and still I had not died. I floated in and out of consciousness, by turns cursing the strength of the Dancer's constitution, and, when I drifted into brief moments of painlessness, praising the beauty of my demonstration of justice, one that Sherenne, for all her heartlessness, would be unable to ignore.

I had no idea of the time, only that it was night when I heard the door open quietly and soft footfalls coming up to where I lay. I opened my eyes, expecting to see Sevrian, but realised, through my fogged vision, that it was his servant Nyran that stood beside me. I had not the strength left to react, even with anger, to his intrusion. I tried to convey a warning stare, but he ignored it, and calmly set about unwrapping the bandages.

I tried feebly to order him to leave me, but in response he simply shook his head and whispered, "I cannot, Lord. I am commanded to tend to you. Forgive me, Lord, but you must not die. It cannot be permitted."

I tried to protest, order him away, but I was too weak.

"I command here," was all I managed to say. "Who dares to go against my wish?"

He bowed his head but did not reply, and carried on quietly, his brow knotted in intense concentration as he worked on the wounds, drawing out the poison in me and with it my hope of peace. When he had finished, he drew back and knelt on the mats a little distance away, waiting. His life was over and he knew it. He had courage, I thought, as I lay still, feeling the strength slowly starting to return to my body, the power of the gift rising back to my mind. There was no justification for his disobedience that I could think of. I turned my head and watched him through half closed eyes. He was calm, resigned, showing no sign of fear, but deep in his mind I sensed his regret at the shortness of his life, that he had not mated, that he would be parted from his lord and lover, Sevrian.

The boy shamed me. If he could overcome his fear of death, could I not overcome my fear of life? If I died, what outcome could there be but a bloodbath as Karim or Thalis sought to take my place? Sevrian would fight, and die, and

282

without me to protect her, what would become of Sherenne? It mattered not that she had rejected me – it would not save her from being condemned to a life with Karim and his followers. And what of Malim? He would grow under the tutelage of Thalis, be his perfect pupil until his gift outgrew his master's, and the Family came under the yoke of a man of greater cruelty, greater madness than my father had ever shown.

No, I thought. If that is our fate, so be it, but I will fight it. I will not leave those I love to face their future alone. I am the head of the Family – I am the Rule, and the Rule will be maintained, no matter what the desolation of my soul.

Nyran did not stir as I finally sat up and stretched myself, shaking out my hair and flexing my shoulders to get rid of the stiffness. He still knelt like a statue on the mats, his head bowed, eyes closed, mind resting in an attitude of perfect stillness. When I sent out a gentle prod he did not flinch, but raised his head and met my eye steadily, with total acceptance.

"Go to your master, Nyran," I said, deliberately keeping my voice soft. "Beg his indulgence for a little longer. I require water to bathe, and food and drink. You will help me, if he will be so good as to release you."

He got up at once and bowed, leaving without a word. A little while later he returned and helped me to undress, and bathed me gently, after which I lay down – I was still feeling very weak – and he massaged my aching muscles, rubbing in fragrant oils. He had brought herb infusions, bread and honey, and once I was clean I satisfied my hunger and thirst while he waited, at my direction, in a corner of the room, once more kneeling, his eyes lowered respectfully.

When I had finished I gestured for him to come and comb out my hair. Once engaged in the task, without turning to him, I asked, "Who commanded you to come to me?" The comb was suddenly still. "Come," I urged gently, "you would not sacrifice your life unless ordered to do so. Tell me on whose instruction you came to me, and I will let you live."

I felt his hand shake slightly as the comb resumed its course.

"Forgive me, Lord, I cannot say."

The voice was no more than a whisper, but firm. I waited until the task was finished and I was properly presented, then turned to him and said, "Go to Sevrian. Tell him I require his presence, and bring him here."

"I do not know, Lord." Sevrian's look of surprise made his answer irrelevant. Nyran's face was impassive, steadfastly determined to give nothing away. He avoided his master's eye carefully, keeping his steady, open gaze on me, as if willing me to understand his reticence, and to accept Sevrian's innocence. The boy was prepared to die to protect the one who had sent him, and I could not help but admire him for it. What was more, had it not been for his actions my attack of self pity would have brought the settlement into even greater risk of disaster, and it seemed unfair that he should be punished for my stupidity. I didn't want to make matters worse by probing his mind, so racked my brains for the answer, holding him with my eyes all the while in case he should falter.

Sevrian was angry, that was clear enough, and I could sympathise with him, at the same time hoping that he would not deal with his servant too harshly. I thought a while longer, then said, "As I recall, Sevrian, you offered me the use of the boy. With your permission I would like to take advantage of your generosity."

I felt another little ripple of surprise. "Of course, Lord. I would be honoured. Please make use of him in any way you wish."

Nyran did not turn a hair, but continued to keep his eyes on me.

"Then I would like him to come to me on every alternate evening. I have need of a servant to help me to bathe."

"As you wish, Lord," Sevrian replied, although a little grudgingly I thought. "Will you require him tonight?"

I answered with a slight nod, then, to the amazement of both of them, dismissed them without any further discussion. My decision was made. If I could not have Sherenne, then I would have no other woman. Like my father, my heir was born, and I had no more need to mate. And like my father, I would once again seek my comfort elsewhere.

CHAPTER 28

How do I best describe the period of my life that followed? At times I was overwhelmed by utter despair, at others I simply felt a dull blankness that hardened my heart to all suffering, whether my own or that of others. That first day I stayed in my room, curled on the wide window ledge, my head resting on the bars, letting the cold breeze stroke my face, thinking of nothing. The gift seemed to course in me with renewed strength, as though it were a blade tempered in the forge of my near death. A butterfly perched itself on my knee, and for an hour I stayed motionless, watching it bask in the sunlight, feeling a pang of sorrow when it flew away.

That is where Nyran found me as dusk fell, staring out at the flickering flames of the watch fires on the settlement's Northern boundary. Without a word I let him lead me away to the rugs, drowsed as his expert fingers teased the tension from my shoulders, then worked gently on my backbone until I felt the stiffness recede. When he was done I lifted an arm and stroked his cheek, then bade him return to his master, reassuring him that he had done nothing wrong, that he had given me all that I required, at least for now.

The following day I didn't go out, nor the day after that. It was not until Thalis appeared at my door on the morning of the fourth day, requesting, of all things, my judgement on a new child, that I was obliged to make an appearance in the settlement. As soon as I stepped over the threshold the sunlight hit my face like a splash of cold water, and suddenly everything came into a focus so sharp it made me stop dead. I saw Thalis start in surprise, and turned to him questioningly. He had gone a little pale, and as my eyes rested on him he bowed his head at once, fidgeting nervously. It was unlike him. Normally, unless directly confronted, he displayed what amounted to a swaggering confidence in my presence, mainly for the benefit of his troupe of followers.

I idly asked myself the reason for his uncharacteristic behaviour, and to my amazement he bowed again, and mumbled, "Forgive me, Lord. I am ready to continue."

It took me a moment to realise what had happened. I had no sooner thought of the question than it had been projected into his mind, without my even intending it. I looked around me. There were several men out on the pavement, engaged in one activity or another, but all of them had stopped and were staring at me apprehensively. Confused, I tried to clamp down on my thoughts, wondering just how much they could see.

A second later Sevrian came out of the doorway to join Thalis.

"Please give me a moment," I said, and drew him to one side as Thalis bowed yet again and settled himself to wait.

"What's happening?" I demanded anxiously as soon as we were out of earshot. Even Sevrian was looking nervous.

After a little consideration he replied with a frown, "I am not certain how, Lord, but it appears that your gift has undergone some kind of transformation, or rather, it might be more accurate to say an extension. We feel your presence in a way that we could not before. The air in the entire valley is heavy with it. You send out your commands without thinking about it, and it is as though you had spoken aloud. Your moods are felt more keenly, and over a greater distance. I don't know why this is so, only that it began just over three days ago. If you want my advice, Lord, you should be careful, at least until you have discovered the extent of your increased power, and how to adequately control it."

I nodded, thinking that it was lucky for me that I had in my company at least one man in whom I could place my complete trust. At once Sevrian bowed, and murmured, "You do me great honour, Lord," and at the same time raised an eyebrow, a fleeting smile on his lips.

"How much can you hear?" I asked, beginning to panic. Was my entire mind now an open page, my secrets clear for everyone to read?

"Do not fear, Lord," he replied, attempting reassurance. "Although your unspoken words can be heard clearly by those

287

meant to receive them, the rest of your mind is, if anything, more closed. I find it difficult to explain. You are more visible, yet more invisible at the same time. It is as though you no longer need to direct your commands through conscious effort. A hidden part of your mind is doing it for you, acting before you have even formed the words. Yet that same part also acts to make your mind completely unreadable, much more so than before. The entire settlement senses your power as a great weight upon them, but they don't know its meaning, nor its purpose."

He paused and scratched his head.

"Whatever has happened, Lord," he concluded, "it is most impressive. However, I would urge you to be careful what thoughts you direct towards Thalis."

I stood for a moment, mulling over the new development, careful not to direct my thoughts towards anyone in particular. I motioned for Sevrian to rejoin Thalis, and with my back turned to both of them, closed my eyes, searching the barrier that lay between my own private thoughts and my public ones. There was indeed something subtly different about it, as if the line was sharper, more defined, in keeping with my new perception of the world. I needed time to accustom myself to my changed situation. However, for now, as Sevrian had said, I must act with care.

I swung round decisively and signalled to Thalis that I was ready. He set off at once towards the compound, and as we neared the gates I tried unsuccessfully to quell the faint hope that was beginning to rise in me. The door to Sherenne's room was firmly closed. I pushed the bitter disappointment to the back of my mind and quickly strode past. I had thought that the judging of a young one might prove difficult, but in the event I went through the proper motions with hardly a thought. The child, a boy, was unexceptional, an average specimen, certainly not without use to the blood, but of no great lineage, so neither was he a threat. The whole thing was over in minutes, and without a word I made my way gratefully back towards my rooms.

I couldn't help but glance once more in the direction of Sherenne's room as I passed, but it remained closed, and, I had no doubt, bolted on the inside. For some reason I found that thought unbearable, and so I gave a command to Thalis as we strode out of the compound to ensure that all internal bolts on the doors to the women's rooms were immediately removed.

"Including the room of the mother of the heir, Lord?" he asked pointedly. I stopped in my tracks and fixed him with a stare until he became quite uncomfortable.

"That room in particular," I finally said, my voice a whisper. "You have my permission to begin."

"Yes, Lord. At once," he replied, and scurried away, thankful to be left once more to his own devices. Perhaps, I reasoned, the sight of Thalis inside her sanctuary, removing the flimsy protection at my request, might give her pause for thought. If she wished to dictate terms to me, then I had a few of my own that might make her life, such as it was, a little less comfortable. Nevertheless, before I could stop myself I had sent out an involuntary plea using my new found skill.

"Speak to me." There was no reply. I saw that Sevrian was looking at me, frowning slightly, and I realised that I had been standing quite still, staring at the closed door, for more than a minute. I breathed in deeply, and briskly went on my way.

Day followed interminable day. The new sharpness of my mind was balanced by the numbness of my heart. I carried out my duties for the most part without thinking, longing only for the brief hours of sleep, hoping that the nightmares that too often robbed me of even that brief respite would stay away. After dark I would find myself wandering, coming to a halt outside the compound gates, peering through the bars as though I were the one imprisoned. Once, in the summer, I came there to find her door open, and caught a brief glimpse of her as she knelt on the stone and lifted Malim above her head, a part of some game or other. She caught sight of me watching them, and softly, without haste, she put the baby down and gently closed the door.

He was growing – growing into something both beautiful and terrible. The eyes were hers, the mouth, the golden locks. But what lay behind the eyes was something that would have frozen her blood, had she been able to see it. And the mouth, when it curled up into a smile, was as cold as the winter snow. Once or twice, in the height of the summer, they sat in the courtyard with the other women and children, feeling safe, I suppose, surrounded by the crowd. She did not see me as I walked past – at least I don't think so – and once I paused and met my son's eye for a brief second. He pointed and smiled, although she did not notice it, and the face that I saw in him was no longer hers, it was my father's.

Each evening Nyran came to me. I learned later that it was at his own request, not Sevrian's. The boy was shamelessly devoted to both of us, and I can't deny that I found his tender ministrations comforting, his well practiced fingers kneading life back into my unfeeling flesh, bringing me precious moments of much needed peace. Always, when my nightly massage was over, he would kneel quietly, waiting, until I sent him away or Sevrian called for him. I knew why he waited, and finally, feeling the need to somehow reward him for his patience, I invited him to stay.

Some hours later when Sevrian came in search of him, he found him curled up sleeping at my side. I slipped silently up off the rugs, and for an hour or more Sevrian and I sat together sipping wine, transfixed by his beauty, his childlike trusting innocence as he lay in blissful sleep, the only sound the gentle rhythm of his breathing.

Between them, Sevrian and Nyran kept me from the emptiness that threatened constantly to engulf me, but I think it was the gift of Orlim that turned me from complete despair. Whenever the moon was bright enough to see I walked alone in the forests to the south of the training fields. Always, on the path to the south gate I would pause at the compound and silently repeat my plea, "Speak to me." But all that came back to me was the echo of my own thoughts. It had become a habit that I couldn't break, and I no longer expected or even hoped for a response. After a moment I would continue on my way, seeking solace in the gentle greetings, the soft rustlings of the wolves as they walked beside me under the shelter of the trees.

The days turned into months, then years. On the surface, life within the settlement went on as it always had, and my people quickly grew accustomed to my new found strength. As I studied the change in my gift, it became apparent that I could do certain things that had not previously been possible. I could probe the minds of others in much greater depth before they became aware of it, perhaps because the sheer weight of my presence masked all else. At the same time there was something finer, more delicate in the responsiveness of the gift, rather, I suppose, like changing a plodding pony for a lean, graceful horse for hunting.

Most interestingly of all, I could immobilise a man completely with but a thought, without causing him the slightest damage. I puzzled over it for a while, and my mind drifted often back to my encounter with the old man out in the valley. He had been possessed of that same gift, and I wondered idly whether perhaps he had been somehow responsible for the change. But I had never seen any sign of him since, and so could not ask him.

The seventh year of my exile from the place I most yearned to be was beginning to draw to an uneventful close. Sevrian's first child was now eight years old and he visited the boy often, keeping a close eye on his progress as the time of the coming of the gift drew nearer. At least that was his reasoning, although it would be some years yet before the boy became a man. Orlim, too, had been delivered of a fine son, five years old. His worries, as I had promised him, had been quite unfounded, for even without my undertaking to spare his offspring his child would have had nothing to fear.

As for my own son, my little sweet faced monster, I had not seen him for more than five years. I went into the compound only when I could not avoid it, and didn't search, neither for him nor his mother, on my infrequent visits. It was not that the pain of my loss had lessened with the passing of time. I had simply learned that it was a little easier to bear if I closed my eyes to it. Nevertheless, I still called out to her at night, unable to sleep until the ritual was completed, warding off the silence with gentle kisses for my docile servant Nyran.

Sometimes, during the winter months, rather than call the boy from the warmth of my bed, Sevrian joined us. At these times Nyran seemed most content, snuggled up between us like a child

291

between two doting parents. It was hard now to say to whom he belonged. It was simply accepted that we shared him equally. He treated us as though we spoke with one voice, the command of one always echoing the desire of the other. In the case of a contradiction, I made clear that he should always defer first to Sevrian, but I don't think that we ever placed him in such a position that he was forced to make the choice.

The end of the year was not far away, and it was bitterly cold. Nyran had bathed and anointed me with oil as he usually did, and was performing the same service for Sevrian before fetching us the evening meal. I sat, half naked by the fire, staring into the flames, absently sending out my habitual unanswered message, my mind half on the stock of new foals I had inspected that afternoon. I was about to lean forward to pour myself warm wine from the jug on the hearth when I heard a soft whisper in my thought, so faint that I could hardly make out the words. Even so, the source was undeniable; a tiny voice, weak, barely present.

"Help me!"

I sat bolt upright, so suddenly that both Sevrian and Nyran, who had been talking together quietly, fell silent, watching me. Without turning I gestured for them to be still, and concentrating hard tried to follow the thread of the voice back to its origin. There was nothing. I redoubled my efforts, to no avail, and was beginning to think that I had suffered from some sort of hallucination when suddenly it came again, this time bursting into my consciousness in a deafening cry of desperation.

"Help me!"

Then all went abruptly silent, the thread collapsing as it had done before. I leapt up, kicking over the wine jug in my haste, and bolted for the door, leaving Sevrian and Nyran staring after me, bemused.

I don't think I had ever run so fast. I dashed down the frozen pavement in bare feet, naked to the waist, knocking over two startled men hauling firewood as I rounded the corner and sped down the east side to the compound gates. Ice tore the skin off my feet as I ran, but I didn't even notice. When I arrived at Sherenne's door I hurled myself through it, almost taking it off its hinges, and slid, panting, to the rugs where she lay, frighteningly still, her eyes closed. All the torches had been doused and the room was in complete darkness. Neither was a fire lit, and when I touched her arm it was deathly cold and limp.

"Why is there no light?" I shouted, lifting her lifeless body in my arms, trying to work out what was wrong. At the same time I sent out an urgent call for Sevrian to come, bring hot water, torches and the pouch containing the red powder that I kept in my pack. "Why is there no light?" I asked again, "Why is a fire not lit? What is going on here?"

"I don't want light," a child's voice replied from somewhere behind me. "I told her, I don't want light. If it's light I have to look at her. The fire makes light and that is why there is no fire."

The voice was petulant, determined, chillingly cold. I heard my son stamp his foot angrily.

"What have you done?" I demanded, too busy trying to find Sherenne's heartbeat to turn round.

"She tried to light a fire," Malim said accusingly. "I told her not to and she was going to anyway. So I stopped her. She should do as I say. She wouldn't ignore my father like she ignores me. He would tell her. Half breeds have to stay in the dark where nobody can see them, everybody knows that. They have to be got rid of, like vermin. That's what my father says, so that's what I've done. When he comes to see me he'll be pleased, you'll see. And there's no point pretending that you did it, because he'll know it was me. I'm the heir to this whole place, I'll be in charge of it one day, and I'll make them all live in the dark, so that we don't have to look at them."

Thankfully, at that moment Sevrian arrived, carrying a large jug of hot water and the pouch. Nyran came in behind him with two torches, and at last I could see. Malim sat glowering in a corner, a look of pure satisfaction on his face. Sherenne had been struck on the head more than once, and her body was so pale that I almost cried out in panic. I couldn't find a pulse anywhere. Frantically, I emptied some of the powder into a cup of hot water and tried to force the liquid between her teeth.

For an age nothing happened, and I thought that perhaps I had come too late, but at long last I saw her chest rise and she took in a breath, followed by another and then another, a steady beat returning to her wrist.

Malim seemed to realise what I was doing and jumped up in a fury, shouting, "She's a half breed! She should die! Wait 'til my father hears about this!"

I couldn't bear to look at him, and turned to Sevrian. "Take this creature out of my sight. Put him in the cellar under your house. I will deal with him later."

Sevrian at once took hold of the brat and dragged him away, the boy screaming threats and kicking at Sevrian's ankles as he went. Nyran, meanwhile, had lit a fire and set more water on it to warm, after which he bowed and left the two of us alone.

Thankfully Malim, for all his claims, had not the strength of a grown man, and the blows Sherenne had suffered had caused far less damage than I had feared. The greater danger had been the cold, and having tended to her bruises I wrapped her warmly in the rugs, not too close to the fire, and sat beside her, unmoving, hour after hour, watching the colour slowly return to her cheeks. I must have dozed for a while, because I opened my eyes as the thin light of dawn was coming through the window, and looked across to find her staring at me.

"Forgive me," I said, unable to meet her eye. "I will leave." I got up, wincing as my grazed feet made contact with the stone.

"You are hurt," she whispered, weak with fatigue still.

"It's nothing," I replied, the sound of her voice making me shiver uncontrollably.

She spoke again. "And you are cold."

I shook my head, hardly trusting myself to answer.

"No," I whispered finally, trying to will myself to walk towards the door. I could not move. I was rooted to the spot, completely unable to make my body obey my commands. I could feel her intense gaze studying me, but I still could't look at her.

"You knew that this would happen?" Her voice was full of sorrow.

294

I could not speak. I simply nodded, standing trembling by the rugs, the tears rolling down my cheeks, wishing with my entire soul that I could make myself walk away before she told me to leave. I heard a faint movement, felt a light touch on my arm, and a second later her fingers had entwined themselves in mine. My legs could no longer hold me up, and I sank to my knees, pressing her tiny, cold hand against my cheek.

"Forgive me," I begged, clutching her hand tightly in both of mine. "I can't go. I can't leave you. You must order me away, tell me that you do not want me here, tell me that you no longer love me as you once did. I will do whatever you command, but I must hear it from your own lips. I can bear the silence no longer. I am lost without you. Order, and I will obey, but I beg you, do not punish me any more with your silence. I can't endure it."

My heart sank as she pulled her hand away, but a moment later I felt her touch on my cheek, a light pressure turning my head to face her. Our eyes met and I saw the tears sparkling on her face.

"How can I order you to leave?" she asked. "How can I say I do not love you? Both would be lies. I love you more now than I ever did. The years have been a torment to me. But what could I do? How could I choose between you and our son? Should I have stood by while you murdered our child? And what of you? What if you had done what you intended? Would you have lived with yourself, knowing that you had killed your own child, your heir, that you loved? I couldn't bear the thought of your suffering, and I turned you away thinking that rejection would be the lesser pain.

"Perhaps I was wrong. He is a monster, Rendail, and you knew it even then, when he was but a week old. So often I think that he doesn't deserve life, nor a father of such strength and beauty. But he is still only a child. He can be trained, drawn away from the taint that is in his heart. You can do it, I know you can. You are his father – he will respect you, obey you. You will teach him goodness, set him on the right path. If I have caused you pain, then avenge yourself on me, but promise me that you will not hurt Malim. He doesn't know what he is doing. He is so very young, and he will grow out of it in time, if you show him the right way."

Yes, I thought, he is young, as young as my father was when his mother uttered the very same words, only to find herself violated, murdered, her mate dead and her child despoiled.

"I promise," I found myself saying. "I won't harm him, and I will try to make him the heir that he should be. Out of love for you I will do it. But he will not come here again. He will stay outside the compound, where he can't hurt you or threaten you any more. He will find me a little harder to bully, and somewhat easier to annoy, I have no doubt. Now, I have given you my word, will you not do something for me? I ask – no, I beg you, on my knees as you see me now, to join with me as I asked you to do, all that time ago before our son was born. I know I am not worthy of it, but I will try to be as you want me to be. I will care for Malim, I will do whatever you wish. Only join with me, so that I will always know that you are safe, and never be parted from you, even when I can't be with you. I beg you, don't refuse me. If I have to be without you any longer I shall die. I would rather admit my fault to the whole settlement, and let Thalis have me strung from the arch of the east gate and flogged to death."

There was a short silence, and then she answered, "You do not have to bargain for my love. You have it always. Besides," she smiled, and my world was once again filled with light, "much as you deserve it, I would not give Thalis the satisfaction. You are trembling. Come to me and get warm, that is, if you can bear to leave your handsome lover for a while."

"You know about Nyran?" I was horrified.

"Of course," she said, laughing. "Who do you think sent him to you, the night that you were so determined to kill yourself? You couldn't come here, and I didn't want you to be alone. So I asked Sevrian to share him with you. I knew that you couldn't trust anyone else. Nyran is a sweet, gentle creature, and I am glad that you were not angry with him, that you accepted him and let him help you. He has helped you, has he not?"

For a moment I was speechless. "So that is why he would not tell me who sent him," I breathed, understanding at last.

She nodded.

"Of course. You see? Your army grows, and there are many who love you, more than you realise. You must be good to Nyran. He is precious, and will serve you well."

"It seems he has already served me better than I have any right to expect," I said, suddenly feeling that words were quite inadequate to express my love for any of them, my three devoted protectors, who seemed to have spent an extraordinary amount of energy saving me from myself. I dived under the rugs next to her, and taking her in my arms nestled against her, drinking in her warmth, her touch, the scent of her, all the things I had thought I would never have again. We lay for hours, quite still, and then, in answer to my silent question she gave a little nod, and our minds reached out to each other, our thoughts mingling, locking together as one. The Rule was broken, and in the breaking of it I was finally made whole.

CHAPTER 29

"What do you wish done with him?" Sevrian asked as we guided our horses down to the river.

I sniffed. "He likes the dark it seems. Let him stay there. You have fed him I suppose?"

"Yes, Lord, just bread and water as you ordered. But he can't stay there forever. You must decide what to do."

Malim had been in the cellar for three days. The truth was that despite my promise to Sherenne, I didn't trust myself not to tear him limb from limb the moment I saw him. I could feel her as I rode out across the valley, the gentle stream of her thoughts providing a lilting undercurrent to my own. I formed images of the country, the trees, the river, and held them for her to see, treasuring her delight in the things that I took for granted every day. When I thought of what I had almost lost, thanks to my child, my anger almost overflowed, but I had promised, and so I would try, even though I knew my efforts would most likely be in vain.

"I will leave him one more night," I said decisively. "In the morning we shall see whether or not a little time for thought has been of benefit. Meanwhile, I have something far more important to see to."

"You still mean to follow your plan? It is not without risk. But I approve, and so, I think, will Nyran."

"Then it's settled," I said, as we dismounted to let the horses drink. "Now, I wish to give my full attention to the fish, and show Sherenne how the creatures move before I take one home for her to cook."

Nyran looked from one to the other of us in amazement. I still hadn't told him the purpose of my plan, only that I wished him to see the passages below the house. That they existed at all had been a complete surprise to him, but when I informed him that I wished to actually show them to him, he was rendered completely speechless. With Sevrian keeping watch I led him down the narrow steps, through the central chamber and up again on the other side. Quietly removing the stone slab I pulled myself up into Sherenne's room, and taking his hand helped him to join me.

He stood at my side, open mouthed, as Sherenne took his hand and kissed his cheek, inviting him to sit. I left it to Sherenne to explain, while I stood a little way back in the shadows, wondering if, after all, my idea had been a good one.

"We have no words," she said, "to thank you for what you have done for us."

He glanced at me nervously, clearly unsure of the correct way to respond, and to whom. Finally he chose the path of safety, and looking at me bowed and said, "I am honoured, Lord."

"We can't repay you openly," she continued, "for Lord Rendail's judgement must remain against you, and this compound is closed to you, for your own protection."

He nodded. "I understand. There is no need …" but she cut him short.

"Lord Rendail requires you to mate. He wishes you to know what it is like to be with a woman. He has asked me to select one for you, one who is willing and who has agreed, and whom we can trust. You do not have to accept the gift. No one orders you to do this. If you refuse, no harm will come to you, or to the girl. Lord Rendail will take you back, and will think no less of you. Do you wish to stay, or go?"

I didn't think that Nyran could look any more surprised than he did already, but I was mistaken. His eyes widened alarmingly, and he blushed furiously, which made him look even more attractive, if that was possible. Finally he stammered, "Will you …will Lord Rendail require to stay?"

The question was so innocently posed that I could not help but laugh.

"Of course not," I said, as Sherenne covered her mouth, trying to remain serious. "We will leave, and you will have the use of this room until dawn. Then we will return, and I will take you back."

He thought for a moment, curiosity, excitement and nervousness all clearly fighting for supremacy, and eventually turned to me, his eyes shining, and said, "I am grateful, Lord. I will stay."

"Good," I said, still smiling. "Wait here, and when we are gone Sherenne will call the girl. You will not be interrupted, so you have no need to fear."

I lowered Sherenne down into the tunnel, and was about to disappear myself when I heard him whisper anxiously, "My Lord?"

"What is it?"

"I don't know what I am supposed to do."

I tried to stop myself from laughing again, and said, I hope reassuringly, "Do not concern yourself, Nyran. I am sure that you will think of something. If you need help, ask the girl. She will be happy to guide you."

"Yes, Lord," he answered uncertainly. Then I left him, and Sherenne and I made our way to the large central chamber of the maze, where I had lit a good fire and stored our supper.

Just before dawn I delivered Nyran back to his room. As we walked, I made a gentle enquiry as to the progress of his evening, but all he could do in answer to my question was offer a dreamy nod of appreciation. Clearly the girl had captivated him, and it made me happy to think that my gift had been received so well.

"So you would not object to a second visit?" I asked casually, at which he shook his head, then stopped short with a gasp. "What is it?" I asked. He was looking quite distressed.

"Forgive me, Lord," he answered, "but I became so involved that I forgot to ask her name. If I visit again she will think me uncaring, not to know such a simple thing."

"My dear Nyran," I said, hardly able to match his seriousness, "I can see that you did indeed involve yourself in quite the proper manner. But have no fear. Her name is Syrah, and I am sure she found your attentions most caring." His face became flushed at once, and avoiding my eye he walked on in silence, although I saw his mouth silently forming the word as he went.

Once back in the reception hall I bade him go to Sevrian to request that Malim be brought to me straight after breakfast. The boy, I told him, was to be neither bathed nor groomed, but presented just as he was so that I could see for myself his reaction to his brief imprisonment.

As it was, my first impression of my young heir was that I could not see very much at all. He had been left adequate water, but had made not the slightest attempt to keep himself clean. His face was all but invisible beneath the grime, his golden hair a dirty brown, coated in dust and pieces of twig. The rest of him was no better. The only things that shone were his eyes, brilliant blue orbs glaring out from beneath the layers of dirt. As Sevrian thrust him through my doorway I could see them first narrow in puzzlement, then widen as the realisation came to him that the man he had so insulted four nights before was none other than the powerful father that he claimed to so admire.

I had been not much older than Malim was now when I had first entered my father's rooms, and I remembered how terrifying I had found the experience. This child, however, although apprehensive, was to my mind not half frightened enough, considering my obvious displeasure at his recent behaviour. He was also completely lacking in manners, and simply stood glaring at me resentfully until Sevrian cuffed his ear sharply, on which he muttered under his breath, "You honour me, Lord," and sniffed loudly, wiping his nose on his grubby sleeve.

I stared at him for a moment longer, then took a step forward, which made him cringe slightly, although he did not actually step backwards.

"I have promised your mother that I will not harm you," I said quietly, and saw his mouth twitch in a grin. "However," I continued, "you should know that I feel under very little obligation to keep my promise, and Lord Sevrian here is under no obligation at all." The grin disappeared, and his eyes moved to the floor. He sniffed again and shuffled his feet. "If you wish to remain my heir," I said, "then you will begin to behave like one. Get undressed."

"Why?" he asked suspiciously, and immediately Sevrian cuffed him again, a little harder than before.

"Because it is my command," I replied, "and because if you do not obey me, Lord Sevrian, who is under no obligation, will beat you until you do. You will also obey Lord Sevrian, and Nyran, and all other servants that you meet in this household. You will continue to do so until I am satisfied that you merit any but the lowest position here. Do I make myself clear?"

He nodded sullenly, then, feeling Sevrian move behind him he said quickly,
"Yes, Lord," although with no enthusiasm.

"Now, get undressed," I repeated, "and fold your clothes."

Reluctantly he did as he was told, and when he was entirely naked I gestured towards a large tub of cold water in the corner of the room.

"Now get yourself properly clean. Today, Lord Sevrian will help you. Tomorrow you will be expected to wash and groom yourself, so you must pay attention to what he tells you."

Clearly things were not working out as he had anticipated, and he glanced over at the tub, then back at me, but didn't move. At a nod from me, Sevrian picked him up and deposited him with a splash into the water, which was cold enough to make him yelp.

"I forgot to add," I went on frostily, "that I expect my instructions to be obeyed without hesitation. I will return in one hour. You will be presentable, and ready to perform whatever tasks I may require of you."

The look on his face told me that he was not enamoured of the idea of being left alone with Sevrian, nor of being expected to do any kind of work. Life, I thought as I strolled out to begin the business of the day, can be most surprising for all of us.

When I returned, exactly one hour later, I found Malim scrubbed and dressed, thanks to Sevrian's enthusiastic assistance. The experience had clearly not been an enjoyable one, as he stood sniffing back tears as Sevrian briskly tugged a comb through his tangled locks, then fastened them tightly in place with slides.

"That's better," I commented as he was pushed forward for my inspection. "The first thing you must learn is that the son of a ruler does not snivel. It is unbecoming. You are not in the women's compound now." I got the distinct impression that he wished he was, for all his talk. "Secondly, when any lord enters a room, you bow. Then you remain silent until you are addressed. If you are spoken to, you reply politely and bow again. If you are not spoken to, you remain silent until you are. Do I make myself clear?"

"Yes, Lord," he replied sulkily, and when he did not bow, Sevrian gave a little encouragement by applying a downward force to the boy's ear.

"Good," I said. "For the rest of the day you will assist the servants in whatever way they wish. You are forbidden to leave this house unless you are accompanied by one of them as part of your work. Lord Sevrian will give me a full report of your conduct this evening. I expect to be informed that you have performed your duties well. Do you understand?"

"Yes, Lord," he said again, and this time made a half hearted attempt at a bow. Sevrian took in his breath, but I gestured for him to let it pass. I called for Nyran, who took charge of Malim and ushered him out.

I heaved a huge sigh of relief and turned to Sevrian. "I don't think I have ever expended so much effort on simply doing nothing," I said, leaning back against the window sill.

"Indeed, Lord," he replied. "Your self control was admirable. He is a most unpleasant little beast, with appalling manners. However, it might please you to learn that he refused breakfast this morning. He seemed to think that plain bread was inadequate for the son of a Lord."

I laughed out loud. "Then, if you will, inform the servants that he is not to eat until nightfall, after he has personally served me with my evening meal. Oh, and have him bathe again before he attends me. He needs the practice."

Sevrian smiled. "As you wish, Lord. But it is a little harsh, at his age. The boy needs energy. He has eaten little for four days, albeit from his own choice. I think his stay in the cellar affected him more than he would like to admit."

I sighed again. "Yes, Sevrian, he is a child, but this child almost killed my mate, and that is something I cannot take lightly. No doubt if Corvan still lived he would have praised the brat. After all, my own first encounter with my father ended in my being responsible for the death of one of my brothers. But I am not Corvan, and I will not teach my son Corvan's lessons. He should think himself fortunate that I possess a little more restraint. He will learn obedience and patience. Meanwhile you have my permission to take whatever steps you feel necessary to remind him of his situation."

I was beginning to become irritable, so I dismissed Sevrian with a wave of the hand, and decided that the best way to turn my mind to other matters was to join one of the frequent hunting parties that, by tradition, went out after deer at this time of year. Thus, I spent a pleasant afternoon with a small group of young, relatively inexperienced hunters, who were delighted to take advantage of my skill and experience, returning with three good sized animals to add to the winter store.

I listened attentively to Sevrian's report as Nyran rubbed oil into my back. Apparently my son's approach to effort was little better than his manner when dealing with people. He had soon learned, however, of the inadvisability of giving his masters the slightest cause for annoyance. Sevrian's eyes twinkled playfully as he predicted that I might find Malim somewhat less intolerable than he had been at breakfast. A minute or two later the object of our conversation appeared, struggling under the weight of a heavy tray carrying my evening meal of roasted meat, fish, bread and wine. I gestured for him to put it down on the table, and he obeyed immediately, eyeing Sevrian nervously. The latter raised an eyebrow, mainly for my benefit, and left, followed shortly after by Nyran. Malim tried to follow, but to his dismay I set him to wait in the corner, where he stood in a state of abject misery while I ate a leisurely supper.

The boy was dreadfully hungry, and out of the corner of my eye I saw him biting his lip, his gaze locked onto my plate. At least, I thought, he has learned something. I paused, and taking a long draught of wine beckoned him to come and sit opposite me. I tore off a chunk of bread and placed it between us.

"You must be hungry. I hear you have worked hard today."

He nodded miserably, then remembered some manners and said, "Yes, Lord," staring at the bread hopefully. I pushed it an inch towards him with my finger, and he made a grab for it, but not fast enough. I covered it with my hand.

"Ah, but I forgot. You do not care for bread. Unless, of course, I have been misinformed?"

I saw his chest begin to heave, but to give the boy credit, following my words of the morning, he didn't cry. He sat for a moment wrestling with himself, then looked up at me, his wide blue eyes filled with tears, and said in desperation, "I like bread."

It was the first sign of openness I had seen in him, and despite myself I was moved by it. As Sherenne had said, he was only a child. Perhaps, after all, he could learn.

"Well then," I said, a little more warmly, "it appears I was misinformed."

I watched as he fell on the bread ravenously. Tomorrow, I thought, I would make a start on his table manners. But the boy had received enough education for one day, and there was a serious matter that needed to be addressed before I finally allowed him to go to his bed. I gave him some water, and pushed my plate across the table. He accepted the remains of my supper gratefully, and made an earnest but not very practiced attempt to clean his hands and face when he had finished. He looked to me, hoping for some faint sign of praise for his efforts, but I was not yet ready to be generous.

"I think it is time that you explained to me why you wished to destroy one of my most treasured possessions," I said at last, measuring my words carefully. He fidgeted uncomfortably, but made no reply. "Well?" I demanded. "Has Lord Sevrian not explained to you that the head of the Family should not be kept waiting? Or do you not listen when given instructions?"

He looked up sharply, a little spark of challenge in his eyes.

"I didn't know," he declared, sticking his chin out defiantly. "How was I to know it wasn't what you wanted? Thalis said …"

"*Lord* Thalis," I corrected him, suppressing the sudden flood of fury that rose in me at the thought that Thalis had taken it upon himself to converse with my son.

"Lord Thalis said that half breeds like my mother were dangerous," he went on. "He said they were vermin, that they …" He paused, thinking hard, then continued, stumbling over the words, "that they diluted the purity of the blood. He said that if I wanted to show that I was a true heir of the blood, then I should prove that I wasn't inferior, like her."

"And do you know what Lord Thalis meant when he said that?" I asked, biting down hard on my anger.

Malim shook his head. "I thought it was what you wanted," he repeated stubbornly. "I thought you would see that I have pure blood, like you. I don't see why you want her. Lord Thalis said …"

I shot to my feet, and with a sweep of my hand sent the plate in front of him spinning into the wall with a crash.

"I do not wish to know what Lord Thalis said!" I hissed, leaning on the table, my nose an inch from his face.

"No, Lord," he stammered, trembling with fright.

I sat down again, thinking hard. Thalis's behaviour was intolerable, yet what he had told Malim could not realistically be challenged. He could always protest that he had no idea that my son would take his comments so literally, although of course he must have known of the possible consequences. At the same time I felt a glimmer of hope that perhaps the boy had acted out of some mistaken sense of duty. He was young, I repeated to myself. He would learn.

I was silent for a while, lost in thought, and when I looked up again I saw that Malim had fallen asleep, his head resting on

306

his arms. As I watched him, his mouth curled in a slight smile, a stray lock of golden hair falling across his face, I softened a little. There was an innocence about him, as there was in any sleeping child, an illusion of beauty that I wished could stay with him when he woke. I sighed, and rapped the table sharply. He jumped awake at once, and the illusion was gone.

"You may leave," I said. "Lord Sevrian has prepared a place for you to sleep. Go to his rooms and Nyran will show you. He will also inform you of your duties for tomorrow."

"Yes, Lord," he said, getting up reluctantly, trying to blink the sleep out of his eyes. At the door he remembered to bow, another cause for hope, I thought. When his weary footsteps had faded down the corridor, I sent out a call for Thalis.

CHAPTER 30

Perhaps it was a mistake. Looking back, I think that there was nothing I could have done. The blood had worked in Malim with a cruel irony, and had produced a creature that would have posed a problem even for my father, who would have thought him perfect. Yes, he was beautiful, even by our standards. The more he grew, the more beautiful he became and that, in some respects, was my downfall. How could I destroy a creature of such magnificence, that I had sired with such love, and who reminded me of his mother with such force every time I looked at him? There was also another, even greater reason for my forbearance, but forgive me, I get ahead of my tale.

That evening after my son had gone to bed, my anger broke upon Thalis like a storm upon a loose rock. By the time I had run out of steam he was cringing visibly, grateful to still be in one piece. However, for once he seemed genuinely repentant, protesting volubly that he had not had the slightest intention of inciting Malim to such unreasonable action. That was barely plausible, as of all the things that lay within my power, my right to Sherenne was the one that irked him most. He knew the value of her blood as well as anyone else, and coveted it more than any other man in the settlement. I also got the impression that Karim had been less than pleased with the outcome of Thalis's ill conceived attempt to subvert the heir.

Once I had calmed down a little I realised that he was almost as relieved as I was that Malim had not succeeded. I also had an idea. If I kept my son away from them, it would only fuel their resentment, give them grounds for complaint. It was usual for boys of high rank to be given into the care of others, at least initially, just as I had been placed first with Morlain, and after with Estoran. The precedent had been set by my father, and it would be dangerous to break it. I could have, and with hindsight should have, given him to Sevrian, regardless of the impression it would have made. But in that moment, I made up my mind to use my son to quell any sign of dissent in my enemies, thinking that whatever effect they might have on the boy would be easily dispelled. By publicly honouring them with my faith, they would have no means of trying to influence him behind my back, and their mutterings would, for the moment, be silenced.

"Very well then," I said finally. "As you clearly make such an impression on the boy, I place you in charge of his education. Perhaps you can demonstrate to him the wisdom of the Rule, and ensure that he learns to abide by it. He will accompany you at all times until I am satisfied that he has made sufficient progress not to be an embarrassment. Naturally, as he cannot now return to the compound until such time as he receives the gift, you yourself will be unable to enter until he is released from your charge. It is therefore in your interest to give the matter your undivided attention."

For a moment Thalis stood in stunned silence. When he found his tongue it was to say, incredulous, "You are asking me to be responsible for the training of the heir, my Lord?"

"I believe that is what I said," I replied impatiently. "Does that pose a problem for you? After all, you are meant to be my advisor on matters of the Rule are you not?"

Thalis bowed at once. "On the contrary, Lord, I am deeply honoured. I will give the matter my full attention, you may be assured. You will have no cause for dissatisfaction, I guarantee it."

"I do not doubt it," I said, a little surprised by the earnestness of his tone. "I want him presentable within three months. Then, if he merits it, he will go to the horse masters."

"As you wish," replied Thalis, bowing again. "Would you like me to take him immediately?"

"No. Let the boy sleep. Begin first thing in the morning. Nyran will bring him to you just after dawn."

I dismissed him and dropped wearily onto the rugs. I could feel Sherenne's disquiet, and tried to reassure her as much as I could, although I was not totally convinced myself. Still, it was done, and I could only await the outcome of my decision, hoping that it was not complete madness to bring together the two greatest threats that the Family had so far encountered.

For the next three months I saw nothing of my son. Every fourteen days Thalis presented me with a report on his progress, and it quickly became apparent that he took his new responsibility with surprising seriousness. I was informed of every detail right down to the length of the boy's fingernails and how many swallows he took to drink a cup of water. If nothing else, my advisor was proving to be a thorough and diligent tutor. Finally I decided that it was time to see for myself the result of his labours, and ordered him to bring Malim to me at first light the next day.

The child that entered my room was hardly recognisable. He was perfectly dressed, his hair sleek and shining, properly arranged in the same manner as my own. He was nervous, I could tell, but showed not the slightest sign of it. Sevrian stood on my left, Thalis to my right, both some three paces in front of me. Behind him, Nyran guarded the door.

Despite the somewhat intimidating situation the boy held himself proudly, and coming to a halt just inside the door bowed at once and said in a clear, rather pleasing tone, "You honour me, Lord," after which he raised his head and waited quietly, his eye meeting mine with no hint of hesitation. Thalis, I thought, had done his job well. At least the boy's manners had improved, as had the care with which he presented himself. The eyes, though, still troubled me. The deep blue orbs held nothing of his mother's warmth, and stared at me unblinking, the expression giving no sign of his thoughts. That, of course, was no less than I expected of my heir, but the icy coldness of his gaze reminded me once more of my failure of duty to the future of the blood.

I returned the stare until he lowered his eyes, noting the care he took not to show the resentment that was clear in his mind, although I alone could feel it. I walked round the boy, examining him from every angle. He stood perfectly still, eyes on the ground, not even moving his head as I stepped behind him.

"You have done well," I said finally to Thalis.

"I am honoured, Lord," my advisor replied with a bow, plainly delighted at the rare praise.

"I release you from your charge," I went on. "You may resume your normal duties immediately. That is all."

I caught a fleeting disappointment on his face, quickly hidden, and with another bow he took his leave, heading, I had no doubt, for the compound and a young girl to provide some compensation for his loss. I walked back round in front of Malim and gently placed a finger under his chin, bringing his head up to look at me.

"You also have learned well," I said quietly. "You impress me, Malim."

"Thank you, Lord," he replied, bowing quite correctly. "I am honoured."

I sat, and beckoned for him to come forward to join me, at the same time sending a silent signal to Sevrian to leave, and for Nyran to bring food.

"You are my son," I said when we were alone. "You may call me 'Father' if you wish. You will address Lord Sevrian always by his title. However, Thalis is not your superior. In time, he will become your servant. You bow to me and to Lord Sevrian, and to no one else. Do you understand?"

"Yes, Father," he answered at once, his blue eyes flashing with pleasure at my acknowledgement of his efforts. Nyran arrived with bread and honey, and while we ate I questioned Malim on what he had learned from Thalis, which seemed to be a great deal including, thankfully, how to behave at table. Once again I dared to hope that what lay inside him might be driven out, given time and a good deal of mindfulness on my part. At least, I thought, unlike Corvan's father, I had the strength to control my child, make a sufficient impression on him to restrain the most undesirable of his instincts.

After breakfast I took him with me down to the stables, and watched as he trod on grass for the first time. He was as enthralled as I had once been, stooping to touch the soft ground with his fingers, staring upwards, open mouthed, at the height of the tall firs on the southern boundary. I let him enjoy his new found freedom for a little while. After all, a quarter of a year in the sole company of Thalis must have been tedious to say the least, and I saw no reason why the boy should not learn to take pleasure in the natural things around us, the things that had brought me my first taste of happiness. Perhaps he would also grow to love the horses, let them teach him the value of gentleness and patience.

I was lost in memory when I heard a footstep behind me, and Orlim's soft voice broke in upon my thoughts.

"You called for me, Lord?"

I nodded. "Sit beside me, Orlim, and tell me what you see."

"You want the truth, Lord?"

"Tell me what your gift reveals to you, no more, no less."

"I see a child of great beauty, breathing the air of the valley for the first time. Those who see him will think him a worthy son of Rendail. He will have your strength and your look about him, but he will not have your heart, nor your wisdom. He will understand neither beasts nor men, and seek only power over them. Forgive me Lord, but that is what I see."

"Thank you, Orlim. You see what I see. You are the greatest of our horse masters. Can you teach him, do you think? Perhaps the path may be changed, before the coming of the gift."

"I will try, Lord, if you command me. But I fear the path is already set and whatever is done will be too little. He fears you, but he also knows that you will not destroy him. That, I sense even now. However, I also sense his love for you, his desire to please, to be by your side. He will restrain himself in so far as he can, in order to gain your approval."

I continued to watch the boy for a minute or two. He had discovered a butterfly feeding on the heather blossom, and was trying to dislodge it with his finger in order to see it fly. Why, I thought, can he not simply wait? Was there not enough fascination in a creature at rest? It would move away of its own accord eventually. But then he would have no power over it. Its beauty meant nothing to him, only its subservience to his will. How like my father he was. I called him over to me. He looked up, but didn't move, still intent on his task of making the insect fly. I took in my breath and sent out just a little reminder of my own ability to make things move at my command – not enough to hurt him over much, but sufficient to make him jump up at once and run to me, eyes lowered, cheeks flushed with resentment.

"This is Orlim, who is in charge of my horses," I explained, in answer to Malim's stare. Orlim bowed his head.

"I am honoured, young Lord," he murmured, and I was pleased to see Malim nod his head politely in return.

"I have entrusted you to his care," I continued. "I have commanded him to teach you to ride and to hunt. I will select a pony for you. You will learn to feed, train and care for it. You will remain with Orlim until you can do all of these things to my satisfaction. You must treat him with respect, and obey him as you would obey me. Do you understand?"

"Yes, Father," he replied, and then, after a pause, "May I ask you something, Father?"

"Of course," I replied. "What is it?"

"Do you have to choose my pony? Why can't I pick one for myself?"

I had to smile. After all, he was right. Had I not chosen my own first mount, the pride of my father's herd? It would be interesting to see what my son's choice said of his nature.

"Very well," I answered. "We will go now, with Orlim. If you have difficulty he can help you."

He gave me a look, as if to say that he required no help, but hid it quickly behind a bow.

"Thank you Father," he responded, eyeing Orlim uncertainly.

We made our way to the stables, where Orlim turned out the ponies into the training field for Malim to see. The pick of the herd was, without doubt, a fine black mare, at least two hand spans taller than the others, its coat as sleek as an otter's. I lifted Malim up onto the fence so that he could see them all more clearly. His eyes lingered briefly on the black mare, and then his gaze passed on. Orlim lifted an eyebrow in surprise, but I gestured for him to remain still and both of us watched, fascinated, as my son, brow furrowed in concentration, stared intently at each animal in turn. Finally he pointed to a small, nondescript beast that stood alone at the far end of the field. It was one that I had thought to send out with Amal for trade, more suited to pulling logs than carrying the son of a lord.

"I want that one," he announced firmly, and turned to me, a look of determination in his eyes. "Can I have that one Father?"

"Why that one?" I asked, puzzled. "Do you not think it is a little small? It has not the strength of some of the others."

At once he rounded on me in a fury. "You said I could choose. You're a liar! You said I could have the one I wanted, and I want that one!"

Orlim stepped back, horrified. With an effort I restrained myself and simply replied, "As you wish." I lifted him down from the fence. "Arrange it, Orlim. I will send him to you tomorrow evening."

Orlim bowed and took his leave. Malim, sensing my anger, stood quietly, his eyes fixed firmly on the ground. I set off back up to the gate at a fine pace, a snap of my fingers bringing Malim running along behind me. When we reached my house I led him up three flights of stairs to the very top, and along a corridor to the room that had once, many years ago in my father's time, been occupied by Ilvan and Castillan. I opened the door and ushered him inside, then, without a word, locked the door and strode back down to my own rooms. How I had managed to keep my temper I do not know. I would never have dared to speak to my father so, but then, I reflected, my father had not possessed my degree of restraint. Neither, it seemed, did Malim.

By dusk I had softened a little, and called for Nyran to take the boy some supper. Sevrian joined me a little while later, and while we ate I related the episode.

"I don't understand," I said. "Why would he choose the smallest, the weakest of the herd? It makes no sense to me. And to speak to me as he did defies belief. No wonder his mother had so much trouble. I confess I don't know what to do. At least I managed to keep myself from tearing him limb from limb, but I swear, Sevrian, I do not know for how long."

314

Sevrian allowed himself a brief smile. "It is quite obvious, Lord. The boy wishes to achieve mastery without effort. A decent pony would be a challenge. It would require him to exert himself. More than that, ambition brings with it the possibility of failure. He will always seek to dominate those creatures that are weaker than himself, and his position will allow him to surround himself with many willing minions. Thalis, for example, will do his best to ingratiate himself with the boy, as will Karim, Estil and others. Malim's gift will outstrip theirs, but how he will use it remains to be seen. As for his behaviour towards you, Orlim spoke truly. He craves your love, your acceptance, but he knows that he is not worthy of it. Therefore he seeks your attention instead. You set a high standard, Lord, and he fears he cannot reach it. You will always have the greater strength. He knows it, and so will always be torn between resentment, fear and the desire for love."

As Sevrian fell silent Nyran joined us, clearly flustered over something.

"What is it?" Sevrian asked, to which Nyran made no reply, but glanced at me nervously before offering a shrug and a shake of the head.

"Come," I said. "Your Lord has asked you a question. Has everyone suddenly become infected by my son's disease?"

"Please forgive me, my Lords," Nyran replied, bowing hesitantly. "It appears … I mean to say …"

"Oh, do get on with it!" Sevrian declared impatiently, and at once Nyran bowed again, and taking a deep breath said in a rush, "The young Lord Malim did not seem hungry, Lord. That is all. It is no matter."

"That is not all," I said firmly. "What happened?"

"Well," Nyran answered reluctantly, "as you insist Lord, he threw his supper at me. Forgive me, Lord, but he does not throw very well. He missed me for the most part. I offered to help him clear the mess, but he … he asked me to leave, Lord."

I closed my eyes and forced myself to take deep breaths. The child had been in my charge for less than a day and already had pushed me almost beyond endurance. I got up purposefully, and in answer to Sevrian's glance said, "You say the boy seeks my attention. Well he has it. Perhaps, when I have finished with him, he will wish he didn't."

I strode out, leaving Sevrian and Nyran exchanging worried looks, but had taken no more than two steps along the corridor when I found myself turning on my heel and heading down the stairs and out onto the pavement. I stood for a moment or two, letting the winter night cool my temper, then, with a long sigh, walked off towards the compound.

"Stop laughing!" Sherenne had listened to my account of the day's proceedings with mounting delight, it seemed.

"Poor Nyran," she commented through her laughter when I reached the end of my tale.

"Poor Nyran? Is that all you can say? Why is it that Sevrian, even Thalis can control the boy, yet I cannot? He shows me no respect, and any effort to communicate with him he treats with contempt. It is as though he wants me to be angry. He humiliates me in front of my servants. It is unbearable."

I sighed, and poured myself a large measure of warm wine from the jug. Sherenne finally mastered herself and became serious.

"Tell me," she asked, "have you done anything so far but threaten him or send him away? You expect him to understand, yet make no effort to explain."

"You talk about effort?" I interrupted. "I can't describe to you how much effort it takes me not to break my promise to you and do the little monster a great deal of harm. What can I do with both hands tied behind me? What you ask is impossible. I seem to remember that you did not have much more success with him. He almost killed you, or have you forgotten?"

"Listen to me," she said, taking my hand, completely serious now. "He thought he was doing what was right, what you wanted. How could you be expected to understand a child? You yourself never had a childhood. Corvan never allowed it. Would you have Malim live the life you lived? I swear you did not laugh until you were at least two hundred and fifty years old."

"I did not laugh until I met you," I replied, kissing her, "and I am not altogether sure that it was a good idea. In any case,

316

I see nothing to laugh at in this situation. Malim is dangerous, and if I do not contain him he will grow to bring some disaster on us all. It is my duty to protect the blood. How can I do that if I allow this to continue? Forgive me, my love, but the more time that passes, the more I think I was wrong not to act at the moment of his birth. You know what we have to safeguard. Our lives are unimportant when set against the future of all who live. That Malim is our tragedy is of no consequence."

She sighed, poured me more wine, and despite my feeble protests loosed my hair and began to brush it out, knowing that it was the one thing that always calmed my spirit.

"You have not considered how difficult it must be for Malim," she commented, stroking the hair from my brow with her fingers. "Isn't it hard enough for him to do battle his own nature, without having to fight you as well? He has tried, you have said so. Is he not clean, presentable, and does he not strive to be well mannered, restrained? He does his best to please you, but he can't control his temper. You, of all people, should understand. You punish him for the slightest failure, you behave just as your father did, but unlike your father, you do not spend time with your son, let him know you, your thoughts, what you do. You do not instruct him, let him stand beside you and learn from your actions. Tell me, what is our son thinking now? He is alone, unsure of what you require of him. Put yourself in his position. What would you do if you were him?"

I considered a moment, then turned and kissed her again.

"I think I would probably throw my supper at my father's servant in the hope that it might bring me some enlightenment."

She smiled, and firmly fastened shut the slides that held my hair in place.

I paused in front of the door, telling myself that whatever the mess that greeted me on the other side I would remain calm, as I had promised Sherenne. I waited until my breathing was slow and regular, then quietly pulled back the bolt and walked inside. What met my eye was quite unexpected. The boy had made a valiant attempt to clean up what remained of his meal. He had even torn a strip off his blanket and tried, not very successfully,

317

to mop the spilt broth off the flagstones. The rest sat in a dusty, inedible heap in a corner. Malim himself stood in front of the fireplace, biting his lip anxiously. When he saw me he bowed at once, but did not look me in the eye.

"You were not hungry?" I asked, careful to keep my voice gentle.

"No, Father," he lied, making an intense study of the stones just beyond his feet.

"It is no matter," I went on. "Perhaps, then, I should call Nyran to clear these things away, and clean the floor."

He risked a worried glance up at me, but said nothing, and went back to his examination of the floor. I closed the door and walked up to him.

"Look at me, Malim," I said, and he obeyed, his whole body tense with fear.

"You wish to say something?"

At first he shook his head, but when I did not release him from my gaze he swallowed hard, and finally stammered, "I didn't mean it. I tried to tidy up. I will tell Nyran that I am sorry I threw things at him, I promise."

"No," I said firmly, "you will not." I took his arm and sat on the dusty floor, pulling him down beside me. "Nyran is my servant," I explained. "A lord does not apologise to his servants. Do you understand?" He nodded, but I could see his growing confusion. "Nyran does as I command him. That you did not wish to see him is not important. However, a lord should be careful never to issue a command, or perform an act towards a servant for which he later feels he should apologise. A lord behaves with dignity, and does not show his feelings to those below him. Neither does he exhibit undue emotion to those above unless they request it of him. I sent Nyran to you, having failed to make it clear to you how you should receive him. Therefore, the fault, if there is any, is mine."

Malim stared at me for a full minute, struggling to make sense of my words, then a look almost of determination took over his expression, and he answered, "Yes, Father, I understand."

There was a pause, after which he added nervously "I'm sorry, Father."

I nodded. "Good. Then I will call Nyran."

We sat in silence for a little while, until Nyran appeared and without comment made short work of clearing away the evidence of my son's earlier outburst. A moment later he returned, and with a grave bow presented Malim, to the boy's utter astonishment, with a tray laden with bread, cheese and hot milk. When the door had closed and we were once more alone, I said, "A lord should also eat. I was hoping that perhaps you would make the effort, even though you are not hungry."

He looked at me, then the food, then back to me again, a hint of suspicion in his eyes.

"I can't," he said finally, and folded his arms stubbornly.

"Why ever not?" I asked, wondering what on earth he was going to say next.

"I haven't bathed," he replied simply. "You said I was never to eat unless I had bathed first. My hands are dirty," – he held them up for me to see – "and you didn't tell Nyran to bring any water."

I began at last to understand. The boy needed to interpret everything literally. He had been hungry, and I had sent him food, yet not, in his mind, the means to eat it. He had seen my gesture as a trick. No wonder he had responded with violent rage in his frustration. Likewise, I mused, it was possible that the attack on his mother was no more than a misinterpretation of Thalis's whisperings. He had simply done what he thought was required of him. It was plain that I needed to be very careful what I said next.

After a little thought, I leaned over and whispered, "Actually, neither have I, and as I also missed my supper, I thought you might be good enough to share yours with me."

He glanced at me, then quickly back to the floor, his brow knotted in concentration as he tried to work out my intentions. Finally I saw him nod his head, although his arms remained tightly folded. I reached down and tore off a piece of bread.

"I am honoured," I said, breaking off a lump of cheese. His head came up, eyes wide, and he watched, disbelieving, as I took a bite and leaned back against the wall. He wrestled with himself for a moment, then, unable to resist any longer he grabbed a piece of the bread. It was half way to his mouth when he stopped, and said with a bow of the head, "The honour is mine, Father." He reached down for the jug of milk, poured some, and held the cup out to me. I could feel my heart starting to melt. With a nod of thanks I took it from him and drank, then refilled it and passed it back to him. At last he smiled, nervous and fleeting, but a smile that was, for the first time, mirrored in his eyes. It would not be easy, and my efforts might be doomed to failure, I knew. But at least, now, I had the means to try.

CHAPTER 31

As I predicted, life with Malim was far from easy. Not a week went by without my being presented with at least one minor crisis. Although he behaved well enough in my presence and, to a certain extent, with Sevrian, the boy seemed completely unable to control himself when out of my sight. As I had promised I sent him down to the stables the next day to begin his education in the art of handling horses. The brown pony that he had chosen had been made ready for him, and I left feeling hopeful that he would absorb himself enough in the task of training and riding it to stay out of trouble for a while. However, barely a week had gone by when a servant announced that Orlim was waiting in the reception hall and wished to see me as a matter of some urgency.

It was a rare event for the master of my horses to set foot inside the south gate, let alone request an interview at my house. Immediately I had him conducted to my room, and the look on his face confirmed my suspicion that something was seriously amiss.

"Forgive me, Lord," he said, once the courtesies were over, "but I don't know how to proceed. In all my years I have never seen such a thing. If it were not for the fact that he is the heir ..."

I took in my breath and prepared myself for yet another unpleasant revelation. Given the look of distress on Orlim's face, I thought it best to receive the news sitting down, and gestured for him to do likewise.

"What can he possibly have done that is so dreadful?" I asked, as Orlim fidgeted uncomfortably, then absently took a huge gulp of herb infusion in an attempt to calm down. "He is hardly seven years old after all. I have told him quite clearly that he is to follow your instruction. How difficult can it be to control so small a child? Even you should find it a reasonably simple task."

Orlim sighed. "He has followed every instruction, Lord. That, in part, is the problem. He does just as I tell him, no more, no less. He is capable enough, and he accomplishes whatever I ask him to do, but he goes no further. He has no affinity with the beasts, and seems to desire none. But that is not why I have come. It is one thing to order him to follow my instruction, but if I give him no command, what then? I did not think to impress upon him the need not to harm the animals – I thought it self evident. So, in a way, the fault must be mine, as I failed to be sufficiently explicit."

"What has he done?" I spoke with an air almost of resignation.

Orlim shrugged. "I don't know quite where to start. He has so little patience, you understand. To train a horse correctly requires a great deal of it, as you must know from your own experience. If the animal doesn't respond immediately he becomes frustrated, which of course makes the task even more difficult. I have tried to explain this, but if you will forgive me Lord, Lord Malim does not listen very well."

I nodded wearily. "Go on, Orlim. I doubt anything you say can surprise me."

"His pony is not yet ready to ride, yet yesterday he tried to mount the beast, and naturally it threw him off. Unfortunately he did not land well and broke a bone in his arm. There is no need for concern. I got to him quickly, and it is already almost mended. However, rather than place the blame on his own lack of skill, he turned on the pony, and last night as I slept he took a knife and cut the tendons in the animal's heels. I was woken by the commotion in the stables but arrived too late to be of any help to the pony, which was in such a state of terror that I could do nothing but send it into the void. For the moment I have confined Lord Malim to my house. I didn't know what else to do, and have come to seek your advice."

I sat for a long moment with my head in my hands. I was shaking with fury. The boy was completely insufferable. To cause such mindless damage to one of my horses was all but incomprehensible to me. I got up and paced the floor, hardly able to think, then rounded on my master of horse.

"Do to him what he did to the horse. Perhaps then he will learn to control his temper."

"My Lord?"

Orlim went quite pale with shock. When I didn't speak, but continued to glare at him steadily, he bowed, clearly stricken, and turned to leave. He was out on the pavement by the time I calmed down enough to realise that the burden I had placed upon him was quite unwarranted. Whatever my son had done, to cause harm to another, man or beast, was entirely against Orlim's nature.

"Wait," I called silently, and walked briskly out to join him. "You are right," I said as we made our way down to the stables. "Much as I wish to teach the boy a painful lesson, he will not learn to control his temper if I can't keep my own."

Orlim relaxed visibly, but remained far from reassured. An idea came to me, and I came to a halt under the south arch, so suddenly that Orlim had to check himself before he knocked me over.

"What he needs is a companion," I declared. "I remember well that had it not been for your father, my young life would have been a much greater trial. Malim is strong and determined, but he is not quick witted and is easily confused. He needs someone who can be constantly with him, to advise him. I can't spend every waking hour in his presence, and neither can you. He should have a boy of his own age to guide him, one who has intelligence and is sensitive, who will show him the right path when he is in doubt. Your son is just a little younger than Malim, is he not? And judging by his father he would be an excellent choice."

Orlim's initial relief was short lived. His brow clouded again with anxiety. "You honour me Lord, of course, but …"

"You have no need of concern," I interrupted him. "As you have seen, Malim takes all instructions quite literally. He does not seem able to interpret what he is told, nor to apply what he has learned to new situations. I hope that in time and with good example that will change. Your son will be in no danger from him, I promise you. I will make sure of that. I do not command it. I ask for your consent. Do I have it?"

He nodded, still uncertain. "If you say my son will not be harmed, then I can't doubt it, Lord. But he is very close to his mother, and I fear it will be a hard thing for her to give him up so soon. May I have your permission to speak with her, let her prepare the boy a little? At least if she knows that he will be with me it will be some comfort."

"Of course. Go now and talk to them both. Tell her that you will fetch the boy tomorrow evening. Meanwhile I will try to instil into Malim the need for civilised conduct, regardless of the kind of creatures he is dealing with."

As I expected, I found Malim standing in the corner of his room, sullenly awaiting the consequence of having once again been the cause of my fury. This time, however, my newly gained insight allowed me to see the confusion that lay behind the stubborn set of his mouth, his knotted brow. He knew I was angry, but amazingly he did not appear to know why. I decided to test my theory.

"Well?" I demanded, my voice a threatening whisper. He shuffled his feet and bowed, but did not look at me.

"I'm sorry Father," he muttered finally, with a sniff. I strode across to him and pulled his head up roughly, forcing him to meet my eye.

"Are you sorry because I am angry, or because you caused the death of one of my horses?"

At once I saw the cloud of confusion descend on him. I could almost feel the effort he was making to try to understand, to find the right response.

"Answer me!" I hissed, and at once he began to cast wildly about, as though the walls might tell him what to say. No help came, however, and making up his mind he stared back up at me, eyes flaming, and shouted, "It wasn't your horse. You gave it to me. It was mine. Why can't I do what I like with my own things?"

He was losing control again, I could see it. The issue was beyond his capability to grasp and so he responded in the only way he understood, with complete rage at his own frustration. Things were beginning to get out of hand, and so, with a silent apology to Sherenne, I slapped him hard enough to knock him off his feet.

"Is that the correct way to address a lord?" I asked sharply. It was the first time I had struck him, and it seemed to bring him to his senses. At once he scrambled up and bowed.

"No, Lord – I mean Father. I'm sorry." There was a pause, and then he looked up at me and said tearfully, "I don't understand."

No, I thought, and you never will. But even so, I had to keep trying, for everyone's sake.

"Sit," I said, and he obeyed, watching me nervously as I paced up and down, wondering how I might explain what to any other child would need no explanation.

"Do you have any idea how powerful I am?" I began finally. "Did Thalis not explain to you what it means to be in possession of the gift?"

He studied me for a moment, then answered cautiously, "Yes, Father."

I shook my head slowly. "No, Malim. I do not think you have any idea at all. If you had even the slightest notion, you would understand how dangerous it is to act so recklessly. You would understand that every creature in this place belongs to me. You have nothing that I do not allow you to have, and that includes both your position here and your life. Therefore, until I give you leave to make your own decisions, you must treat all that is yours as though it were mine. Already I have shown too much forbearance. You have caused a great deal of inconvenience to Orlim, who is very precious to me, and to deliberately damage a horse is something that no man here would dare to do without my leave. Is all this clear to you?"

He nodded his head vigorously. "Yes, Father."

I could see from the way he was trembling that my words, thankfully, were having the desired effect.

"Good," I said. "Follow me."

I made my way out into the fields and came to a halt, signalling for Malim to come up and stand beside me. He did so, full of apprehension at what was going to happen next. My own horse, a huge bay gelding, was grazing several fields away, yet it heard me searching for it even before I sent out my silent call. Malim watched, amazed, as the great beast vaulted the fences with ease and came galloping up to me.

"Would you like to come riding with me?" I asked, and saw his face light up at once, partly with excitement, partly with relief that he had escaped further punishment, at least for the moment. "Come then," I said, and lifted him onto the horse's back, then jumped up behind.

At first he was terrified, naturally, but I kept a slow pace, holding him securely round the waist and showing him how to lean back into me so that he could feel my movements. I cantered out into the valley and spent a good two hours explaining to him how I controlled the animal's movements, letting him see for himself why it was that it was necessary to be gentle, and not to expect a horse to make up for the lack of skill of the rider. We stopped at the river when I saw that his attention was beginning to wander, and sat together on the bank. He was hungry – a good time, I thought, to teach him the value of concentration and the reward that comes from achievement.

"Shall I show you how to catch a fish?"

He brightened immediately. The water was dotted with slivers of ice, yet I noted with some pride that my son took to the task enthusiastically, wading into the shallows without the slightest hesitation. After several attempts he managed to catch a huge specimen that I flipped up into the air for him, and he fairly glowed with satisfaction as we climbed back onto the bank.

I gathered him up and rode quickly to the forest's edge, where I set him to work helping to make a fire. As we sat watching the fish roasting on a spit I saw his brow furrow again.

"What is it that you wish to ask me?" I said, trying to sound encouraging.

"If you are so powerful," he asked nervously, "why do you want to get cold and wet just to catch a fish? If I was like you, I would tell the fish to swim to me, and make it die so that I didn't have to chase it."

"Tell me," I replied, breaking off a chunk of the rich, steaming meat and wrapping it in a leaf so that he would not burn his fingers, "which method do you think I would find the most satisfying?"

He thought about this for a while, then said, "I suppose it's more fun to hunt. But if it were me I would not catch fish until the summer."

I couldn't help but smile. "When I was your age," I said, "my father gave me into my brother's care, so that I would learn to ride and hunt, in preparation for the gift. I was taught then that for a man to use that power to feed himself was without honour. He must prove himself fit through his endurance and his skill in the hunt. Heat, cold, hunger – we must accept all these things with grace and without complaint, for it is the denial of comfort that in part gives us our strength. You must learn to fish in ice, to bathe in snow, to sleep curled on the back of a horse and warm yourself without fire. Because you are my son and may one day hold my power, your skill must be greater than that of any other man here, your fitness beyond question. That is why I have sent you to Orlim. He is the greatest horse master living, and he will teach you well if you both listen and watch. However, if you continue to display a lack of patience and are unable to control your temper you will learn nothing, in which case you will forfeit all claim to your position as my heir. Do you understand this?"

I kept my voice soft, my expression unreadable, and he stared at me, trying unsuccessfully to calculate my mood. Finally he replied, "Yes, Father," then, after a pause, "but I can't help it."

I nodded, and drew him closer to me, stroking his head in what I hoped was a fatherly fashion.

"I know," I agreed. "But unfortunately neither can I. Already you have twice caused me to become angry, and twice you have narrowly escaped death. Had you been my father's son we would not be sitting here discussing the point. Remember,

Malim, that you are made of my blood, and it is that which gives you your strength. If one son makes me discontented, I can sire another – as many as I wish, just as my father did, and I can rid the world of those who are not fit without a second thought. My duty is to the Family and to the blood. I can't allow any child to grow into the gift who threatens its future. If you displease me again, I may not be able to restrain my own temper, which, I promise you, is more unforgiving than you can possibly imagine. Tell me, are you not afraid of me?"

I could see that I was making an impression, as he had gone quite pale and was biting his lip anxiously.

"Everyone is afraid of you," he answered, "even Thalis and Lord Sevrian."

"Then," I responded, "you should realise how dangerous it is, even for you, to make me angry. I have decided that perhaps if you were to have a guide, a companion of your own age to advise you, then you might learn to behave as befits the son of a lord. I had such a guide when I was young, and his advice was invaluable. Do you think that is a good idea?"

He nodded energetically. "Oh yes, Father. Thank you. And Father?"

"Yes?"

"I don't want to make you angry."

"I know, Malim. That's why I have made the suggestion. Orlim has consented to allow his son to join you. His name is Arvan. You will both live with Orlim at the stables and learn the skills together. Arvan will explain to you the things that you don't understand, so that you will always be clear about what is required of you. But I must tell you now that if you should ever turn your temper on Arvan, you will raise a fury in me such as you have never seen, and if that day comes, you will not live to see the end of it. I hope that I make myself clear."

"Yes, Father," he answered, once more studying his toes. Then he suddenly looked up and asked, "Why do I have to stay with Orlim? Why can't I stay with you?"

The question took me by surprise. Thinking back to my time with Estoran, it had never once occurred to me to question my father's judgement. I had striven constantly to make myself worthy of his attention, his pride even, surrendering myself completely to the rule of my teachers in order to attain perfection in his eyes. I forced myself to remember that Malim was a very different child, and that I, for all my ruthlessness, was perhaps a very different father.

I turned to my son. "When you are fit to stand beside me," I said quietly, "I will call for you. In the meantime, know that I am aware of everything you do, and that your progress is of great importance to me. Come. It is time to return to the stables. I have asked Orlim to select another pony for you, and he will be waiting."

As we doused the fire a rabbit ran across our path, and deciding that one final demonstration was needed I let my thought stop its heart right at Malim's feet. He stared as the twitching body gradually became still, then gazed up at me, the look in his eyes showing me that the message had been understood.

"Take it," I said, "as a gift for Orlim. If it pleases him, he may show you how to prepare it. And remember, Malim, that you must always try to please Orlim, for whatever pleases him pleases me."

I stayed for a while at the stables, watching as Malim was taken to meet his new mount. Before long my son's initial wariness wore off as Orlim – who had accepted the rabbit with a grave bow – skilfully worked the animal on a long rein, bringing it right up to the boy so that he could stroke it and feed it dried apples. I allowed myself to become lost in the sweet memory of my first meeting with my beloved silver pony until, drifting back into the present, I realised that dusk had fallen and the dew was beginning to settle on my shirt. I walked thoughtfully back through the gate and into the compound, but did not go straight to Sherenne's room. Instead I entered the building and climbed the stairs to the top, turning left down the long corridor, then left again to the large communal room that served the upper floor.

The chamber ran the entire length of the south side, with three large fireplaces, and became, during the winter months, the main focus of life within the compound. There had always, even in my father's time, been an unspoken rule that this room was the exclusive preserve of the women and their children. A man might call a woman away from a discreet distance, but would not generally enter to greet or fetch her. Certainly none had done so, to my knowledge, since Corvan's death. I could hear the hum of voices falter into silence before I turned the corner, and by the time I reached the door the crackling of the fires seemed deafening. Had it not been for the motion of the dancing flames I might have thought that time had stopped. Everywhere I looked, all eyes were turned on me, wide with shock. All, that is, except the children, who peered in open fascination from behind their mothers' skirts.

Regardless of custom I had every right to be there if I chose, but nevertheless I was beginning to regret my intrusion when finally a young girl, sweet faced, little more than eight years old, popped out from behind her mother before anyone could stop her and walked up to me.

"May I be of service to you, Lord?" she asked, her clear little voice ringing out like a bell, and she made what must have been her first attempt at a formal bow. If only, I thought, my son displayed such perfect manners. Entranced, I inclined my head as I would to a favoured male servant, and at once heard a great sigh as the entire company took in its breath.

"You would honour me," I replied, "by asking Shana and her child Arvan to accompany me. I wish to speak with them."

The child nodded. "As you wish, Lord," she said and scampered off into the crowd. A moment later she returned pulling a woman by the arm, a young boy following close behind.

"What is your name, child?" I asked the girl.

"Lallia, Lord," she answered, bowing again.

"Please tell your mother that I shall remember you, Lallia, and that you have my favour."

"I am honoured, Lord," she replied, and gave me a beautiful smile which almost made me laugh, but I managed to keep my face appropriately grave, and with another nod turned on my heel, beckoning for Shana and Arvan to follow. Behind me I

330

heard the murmur of voices, and the seconds began to move by once again.

Once around the corner out of earshot I turned to the young woman.

"Orlim has spoken to you concerning your son?"

She nodded apprehensively. I had not set eyes on the boy since he was little more than a week old, and more than five years had passed since then. If he was to become my son's companion, I needed to satisfy myself that he was fit for the task. I drew Arvan to me and examined him closely. He was a small, delicate boy, but in his eyes I saw a quiet thoughtfulness, and a cursory scan of his thoughts bore out my initial instinct. Like his father he was, on the surface, nervous, compliant, but appearances belied the steady, self contained calm that rested at his heart. He had his father's natural understanding of all creatures, human or animal, and his unshakeable patience made him the perfect companion for Malim, who, I hoped, would learn from the boy's measured view of the world. I nodded my satisfaction and sent him back to join the company in the hall, leaving me alone with Shana.

"I have told my son," I said to her when I was sure we were alone "that should any harm come to Arvan at his hands, he will pay for it with his life. I came to give you my assurance that your son will be treated with care, as Orlim's child is accorded great value among us."

She bowed, more to hide her distress at the impending separation than out of deference to me I thought, but did not speak.

"I also have a favour to ask of you," I continued, and at once she looked up at me in amazement. "I know that you will seek out your child in the Dance. You will wish to reassure yourself. It is unavoidable."

Her eyes narrowed slightly. "My Lord?"

"Do not fear, Shana. I have no wish to prevent you. The opposite in fact. As vigilant as I am, my eyes cannot be everywhere. You are the boy's mother, and so I charge you with the task of keeping him in your thoughts. If you see anything that gives you cause for concern, that makes you think that Lord

331

Malim is a danger to Arvan, then I want you to inform Sherenne. If she is of the same mind then she will inform me."

It took a moment for Shana to absorb what I was asking, then she looked up at me and said, still a little surprised, "As you wish, Lord. I am honoured."

I nodded, and dismissed her, but then had another thought.

"How do you find Orlim?" I asked as she turned to go. "Does he treat you well?"

She stopped, completely confused. "Yes, Lord," she answered tentatively, unsure of the purpose of my question. "He is most careful, but …"

"Yes?"

She looked a little embarrassed. Clearly she held some affection for him, and was trying find an answer that would satisfy me without giving any cause for me to be displeased with him. She hesitated, and then went on, "But he is always thinking only of the horses."

I wanted to laugh out loud, but allowed myself only a faint smile.

"You have a good son," I said. "He furthers the blood. It pleases me for you to remain with Orlim. I will remind him that horses are not the only thing of importance and that he must take care to protect all that has been given to him."

With a brief nod I turned and walked back down the corridor, leaving Shana staring after me, nonplussed. At the same time I heard Sherenne calling to me, just a hint of reproof in her mind.

"Come," I answered her as I stepped out into the courtyard. "After such an arduous day, is a ruler not allowed to become a little playful?"

CHAPTER 32

For six years Malim stayed with Orlim. As I have said, his life there was not without frequent incident, although he managed, thankfully, to restrain himself in his dealings with Arvan. In fact, the two boys formed a surprising bond, and it was not unusual to find Arvan leaping enthusiastically to Malim's defence on the numerous occasions that the latter's behaviour overstepped the bounds of acceptability. My son's tendency towards violence was worrying even to me, as each year that passed yielded more evidence of Corvan's capricious nature in my wayward heir.

Orlim had long since given up trying to instil in him any respect for the horses. He rode well enough, and had learned to hunt with an almost savage enthusiasm, more for sport than for food, tormenting the animals in the chase, relishing the kill. He had so far had three ponies and run them all to exhaustion, always choosing the weakest of the herd so as to emphasise his domination of them. Although I observed from a distance I thought it best not to intervene, in part because I did not wish to undermine Orlim, but mostly, I suppose, because I knew that Malim craved my attention.

Each of his transgressions took on the nature of a challenge, and I was not about to be summoned by anyone, let alone by my own child. On several occasions, however, I was forced to send Sevrian to dispense such discipline as was necessary. I myself was hardly innocent when it came to fits of mindless temper, and quite apart from not wishing to set a bad example, I simply did not trust myself to remain calm and not permanently damage the boy.

The time of the coming of Malim's gift was drawing near, and I viewed the impending event with some dread. Given the trial of my own coming of age I knew that I would need to take over the responsibility of fatherhood and remain with him throughout the process. To do otherwise might pose too great a risk to any who came into contact with him. What might happen after that even I could not contemplate, but I harboured some faint hope that the changing of his eyes would bring with it a greater insight, and perhaps a more temperate manner in his dealings with the world. As my heir, it was expected that Malim would join me to begin his training in the delicate matters of the blood. That, I thought, would be an interesting challenge for both of us.

As it turned out, I didn't have long to wait to satisfy my curiosity, for less than a turn of the moon was past when I received the message that the blindness was descending on my son, and that Orlim was bringing him to my house. I bade servants make ready the small room right at the top of the house, the furthest from my own, and charged Sevrian with the task of watching over the boy until I was ready to relieve him of the burden.

"He is asking for you, Lord."

Nyran was becoming tired of repeating himself, and I was becoming tired of hearing him repeat himself. I could sense his concern for Sevrian, who had been attending Malim in the upstairs room for the best part of a day and a night, while I stayed morosely in my own quarters wrapped in my increasing irritation. I kept reminding myself that the stormy arrival of my own gift must have driven well nigh the entire settlement to distraction, let alone my father, whose volatile temperament had been pushed to the limit by the outpourings of my awakening mind. Nevertheless, it was taking every ounce of my patience to stay calm in the face of Malim's raging thoughts. Sevrian, I thought, must be exhausted.

With a sigh I turned to Nyran. "Tell Sevrian I will come. Prepare hot water with just a little nightshade and I will take it to him."

Nyran bowed and left, leaving me more convinced than ever of my complete inability to master the art of communicating with children.

I paused in the doorway to the little attic room. The entire floor had been covered with soft matting, and a fire blazed in the tiny hearth. Malim was fast asleep, wrapped in furs, and I watched as Sevrian mopped the boy's brow then took his hand and stroked it gently.

"The boy has a prodigious gift," Sevrian commented as I tiptoed forward and sat beside him. "He is strong too. His eyes have already turned, but the fever is still on him. He needs you, Lord. The voices overwhelm him and I can't be of help to him any longer. Each time he wakes he asks for you, asks why his father has not come."

"I am here now," I said softly. "You have done enough, Sevrian. Go and rest. I will stay with him."

"As you wish, Lord," he replied, clearly relieved, and got wearily to his feet.
"He is very afraid," he added as he reached the door. "He needs gentleness, and reassurance."

I nodded. "I know. Don't be concerned. Send Nyran in one hour with broth, and water for him to bathe."

Sevrian bowed and went on his way, leaving me at last alone with my son. His fitful sleep would last, I guessed, no more than an hour or so, after which the mind terrors would take hold until he became exhausted again. I lifted him carefully into my arms and gazed on my dark hearted angel, so beautiful, so vulnerable, and so like his mother that it made me want to weep. He shifted in his sleep and turned into me, resting his head on my breast just as he had on the night he was born, as though the rhythm of my heartbeat calmed him. He was still sleeping when Nyran brought the things I had requested, together with scented oils and fresh clothes.

It was another half hour before Malim opened his eyes and I found myself looking into their dusky, panic filled blackness. At once the reeling of his untrained gift crashed into my senses, the noise of a thousand voices assaulting his mind and mine. As Sevrian had said, his strength was formidable, but not quite as great as mine, and I was able to envelop him with my thought, push the noise away. At the same time I sent out my silent voice, calling to him, willing him to concentrate on it and answer with his own.

335

At first he tried to speak aloud, but I put my hand firmly over his mouth, my gaze still locked on his, until at last I heard him answer, a weak, desperate cry, "Father, help me!"

"Hush," I repeated. "Hush now. Listen to my voice. Listen only to my voice and the others will fade."

After what seemed an age his breathing started to slow, although he was still tense, the effort clear in his face. Then, for the second time, I heard his silent voice.

"Don't leave me." He burrowed further into me, weeping silently, and locked his arms around my waist, clinging to me as though his life depended on it.

"I am here," I responded. "I won't leave."

All of a sudden I realised that I no longer wished to be away from him. The irresistible inner nature of the Dancer left me no room for choice, the supremacy of instinct overriding all the opposition that my mind had to offer. There I was, performing the task that should be the duty of every father, that of guiding his son into the first days of adulthood. It was the time of true bonding for our kind, and despite my reservations I could feel myself reaching out for him, drawing him to me, wanting to give him all I had to give. But I knew that I could not. He was not the true heir to my kingdom, not the one who would carry the hope of the Family with him. Rather, he was the seed of its destruction, bringing with him the risk of a return to the dark age of my father's rule. Nevertheless, I thought, I could give him the love if not the truth that was in my heart, for he was, after all, my creation, and not entirely responsible for what he was. I held him to me, understanding for the first time how privileged I had been as a child. Of all Corvan's sons I was the only one whom he had attended on the coming of the gift. The others had gone through their trial either alone or with only servants to help them.

Looking down I saw that Malim had once more drifted into sleep. I stroked his brow and sighed. 'What of my firstborn?' I asked myself. What of the one who had been so deserving and yet so denied of these precious moments, who had endured his struggle in total isolation, believing both his mother and father dead? I had never given it a single thought, but now, in the midst

336

of my own heightened vulnerability, I saw as though for the first time what had been lost to me forever and almost cried aloud.

Sherenne, feeling my disquiet, called to me softly, and in my weakened state I gave in to instinct and made my confession in a silence broken only by Malim's quiet breathing.

"It should have been Sevrian," I whispered to her in my mind. "It should have been my first, my most faithful son, the one who carries the name of the brother whose life I ended, whose mate I violated in a fit of madness."

For a long time there was no response and I sat, bereft, in the stillness. Then I felt her warmth rush over me in a wave of unexpected compassion.

"Be still." Her voice came softly into my thoughts. "You give your heart to Sevrian every day. If he knew the truth he could not love you more. He shares with you what Malim never can, so be content that your firstborn is more a son to you than your acknowledged child."

"You do not reproach me then?" I asked, incredulous.

"For the wrong that you committed against Rysha, perhaps," she answered, "but for the gift that you gave to your brother and for your care of Sevrian, how could I? Do not think of what you can't change. Take these moments with our son and give him what you can. Fate will see to the rest."

I felt Malim stir against me, and reluctantly pulled my thoughts away from his mother, sending out my protection once more to cover him. He looked up at me and gave me a rare open smile, which made him look even more deceptively beautiful. I placed a finger on his lips to indicate that we should only speak silently, then lifted him into the warm water that Nyran had brought. I bathed him, then laid him on the rugs and rubbed his skin with oil as though I were a servant and he a lord.

"Why are you doing this?" I heard him ask, his silent voice still faltering, uncertain.

"Because it is my duty as a father at the coming of the gift to his son," I answered, "and because it is my pleasure to show you my love."

Surprisingly, I meant it, and taking up a comb proceeded to smooth and arrange his hair, after which I dressed him and fed him broth from the bowl which had been kept warm in the hearth. His efforts to communicate using only his mind were tiring him, so I reverted to normal speech to let him rest.

"It will be difficult for time yet," I said as he propped himself up on the rugs in front of the fire. "It is so for all of us, but particularly for those in whom the blood is strong. It is strong in you Malim, and so you must take great care that you do not damage others unnecessarily with your gift while you are learning to use it. You will stay with me until you can control it sufficiently, and then you will be given rooms of your own. Orlim has told me that you wish Arvan to remain with you. Is that so?"

Malim nodded. "I want him to be my servant, just like Lord Sevrian's father was yours once. Thalis says that every lord needs a special servant. Arvan is special to me, so I want him."

For a moment I wondered whether I had misinterpreted him. The awakening of his body was still a little way off, although not long, perhaps three or four turns of the moon I judged. A gentle probing, however, confirmed his intent.

"Why do you think of such things now?" I asked. "You should not concern yourself with matters beyond your capability. Arvan will not receive the gift for some while, and may not be touched until that time comes."

He shrugged. "Thalis says that a man is not a man unless he can further the blood. He says that I should practice so that I will be ready for the compound, and that it is the duty of all servants to be ready if a lord should need them."

He did not need to see my expression to feel my distaste. He looked up, puzzled.

"Was Thalis wrong, then? Have I made you angry, Father?"

I could not help but think of my own first steps into manhood, and how I had treated Ilvan on that first night all those years ago. I shook my head and said, as gently as I could, "No, Malim, I am not angry with you. But you must remember that there are things that Thalis doesn't understand, and you should take care with everything he says. In a short while he will become your servant, and you will command him as I do. That is a measure of his position here, and yours. Meanwhile, if you wish Arvan to stay with you, then you must promise that you will not touch him, or do him any harm. When the gift comes to him, then the choice will be his, and if he refuses you must let him be. That is the command that I have already given, and you will continue to obey it."

"As you wish, Father," he said, then fell silent for a while, listening to the voice of his gift, which I had subdued sufficiently for him to pay attention to without being overwhelmed.

Suddenly his silent voice broke in upon my thoughts. "You are angry, but not with me. You are angry with Thalis."

I looked at him sharply. His abilities were growing stronger with every hour that passed, and he had easily read what was uppermost in my mind. There was no point in trying to conceal it, so I nodded and answered, "He takes too much upon himself. He should not have spoken to you as he did without my permission. He holds a high position here, but not so high that he can advise my son on matters for which he is not ready."

Malim sat up and reached for the herb infusion that I had placed beside his bed.

"If you don't like him, why have you given him such a high position? And why does he speak against your instruction?"

This was becoming dangerous ground, so I simply smiled and said, "In time you will understand. The Rule is greater than like or dislike, and if a man did only the things he liked, how could it be maintained? Thalis has his uses, as you will see, but at times he does not serve me as well as he should."

I sent out a call for Nyran, who appeared almost at once despite having been fast asleep at Sevrian's side. Malim watched, fascinated, catching for the first time with his gift the depth of devotion that lay behind Nyran's docile expression. I instructed my servant to rouse Thalis at once and have him attend me in my rooms, then to wake Sevrian and ask him to join us.

"Are you very tired?" I asked Malim when Nyran had gone on his errand.

He shook his head. "Not now, Father. What are you going to do?"

"Come with me and you will see. On occasion Thalis needs to be reminded of his limits. This is such an occasion."

Malim stood beside me, every sense alert, watching closely, as I had instructed him. Sevrian entered first, relaxed and impassive, hardly pausing as he nodded politely, first to me, then to my heir. With a gesture I bade him seat himself and take wine, which he did at once without question, making himself comfortable in the shadows just beyond the fire. I glanced down at Malim and noted with satisfaction that he was studying Sevrian intently, taking in the calm demeanour, the quiet control that characterised my advisor's pattern of thought.

I gave him time to absorb the detail of his first real attempt to take the measure of the mind of another, then prodded him gently with my silent voice.

"Well?"

He turned to me and nodded to show that he understood the point of my demonstration. A moment later the main doors opened, and before even a footstep was heard on the stair I saw Malim's eyes widen, his mouth beginning to curl into a smile. At a warning look from me, however, he immediately composed himself, trying to mirror my unreadable expression. Nyran appeared in the doorway and bowed deferentially.

" Lord Thalis awaits your command as you requested, my Lord."

"Show him in," I responded, "then wait outside, if you will."

"As you wish, Lord." Nyran disappeared, and a moment later Thalis made his entrance, clearly having difficulty keeping his annoyance and frustration from his face. To compensate he offered an obsequious bow and I felt Malim tremble slightly as he struggled not to burst into open laughter. Thankfully, he was able to quell the urge, but although he remained outwardly still the essence of his thought had reached Thalis, who looked up, startled, to find himself staring into a pair of eyes as black as his own.

340

For a moment he faltered, but feeling my gaze boring into him he recovered himself and reluctantly bowed to the heir before turning to me and asking, "You desire something of me, Lord?"

I gave a slight nod. "As you see, Lord Malim is now of the gift," I kept my tone light. "I have called you and Lord Sevrian here to inform you that he will soon take possession of his own rooms. I wish to consult with you on the matter of providing suitable servants for his household."

Thalis closed his eyes then opened them again, as though the action might have some effect on his hearing.

"Forgive me, Lord," he said, after a pause during which his mouth twitched several times in confusion, "but it is the middle of the night."

"So I observe," I replied, unable to prevent a faint smile as, even more at a loss, he glanced across at Sevrian. The latter responded by reaching out lazily and pouring himself more wine.

"Surely it is obvious to any man in the settlement," I went on, "that in the late hours a new gift is less troubled by noise. If Lord Malim is to listen to your advice it is better that his mind is clear, is it not?" I gestured for Thalis to join Sevrian.

"Yes, Lord, of course," he answered uncertainly, and sitting down took up a cup, unsure whether or not he should be relieved by my explanation. I guided Malim to the table and we both sat, my son completely absorbed in the task of observing the effects that my apparently innocuous statements were having on my two advisors, and from them trying to deduce my intentions.

Thalis had the cup half way to his lips when I continued, "However, the heir tells me that you have already given him the benefit of your advice – particularly with regard to the selection of servants in preparation for the furtherance of the blood."

The cup froze in mid air and was gently lowered back onto the table.

"My Lord?" Thalis knew me well enough to realise that he should now tread very carefully. Malim looked on, puzzled, as in the ensuing silence Thalis shifted uncomfortably, then said quietly, his eyes on his cup, "It is always my pleasure to be of service to the heir, Lord. I simply explained that which I believed

341

he should know, in preparation for his future responsibilities. If I have displeased you, Lord, I ask your forgiveness. I assure you it was not my intention."

"Not at all," I replied. "Your diligence in the education of my son is exemplary. In fact, I have decided that you may prove invaluable to him. Therefore I require that in addition to your present duties you should act as his personal servant, so that you can more easily avail him of your guidance in matters of the rule. Does this meet with your approval?"

Thalis at last relaxed and took a long draught of wine.

"I would be deeply honoured, Lord," he said, bowing his head both to me and to Malim. I felt Malim's puzzlement suddenly lift, and heard his silent voice, admirably controlled and audible only to me.

"Why does Thalis not see? Lord Sevrian is laughing, but Thalis does not hear."

I looked down at my son, whose face was entirely without expression. The rapidity with which he was developing mastery over his gift was astonishing, but even more so was the apparent sharpness of his perception, a thing that he had not possessed as a child. I was filled with pride and let him know it, at the same time responding privately, "Watch and listen. Thalis, as I have said, has his uses."

I gave my attention back to Thalis. "The honour is mine," I returned, with a nod. "You have rightly told my son that he needs practice, and that it is the duty of all servants to be ready if a lord should need them. As his servant I trust you will be ready at all times to attend to his needs, should he command you. As you have said, to be of service to the heir is always your pleasure."

It took a moment for the full meaning of my little speech to become apparent, and when it did the colour drained from the face of my hapless advisor, his grip on the cup turning his knuckles white. In the long pause that followed, I sensed his inward struggle for self control, and thought for a moment that he might lose it. But finally, and wisely, he mastered himself, and raising his head met my eye, his gaze perfectly expressionless.

"As you command, Lord," he whispered evenly, then, turning to Malim, "I am honoured."

"The honour is mine," Malim responded, inclining his head nicely, although unable to hold back a slight, but noticeable smile.

"Then it is settled," I said pleasantly. "I would also like Lord Malim to regularly accompany you in the course of your usual duties, as soon as he is ready. I am sure that he will learn a great deal from his observations. But you must forgive me. As you have pointed out, the hour is late, and you must be anxious to return to your rest. I thank you for your attendance, and for your generosity."

I stood up, prompting Malim to do likewise. Thalis could do nothing but respond by getting to his feet, and with a stiff bow to each of us turned on his heel and strode out.

I turned to Sevrian. "May I beg your indulgence a little longer? It is late I know, but as I said before, it is easier for my son to concentrate."

"By all means, Lord," Sevrian replied, settling back as we sat down again. "Shall I ask Nyran to bring food? I fear I am in need of a little sustenance."

I nodded my assent, and when Nyran appeared asked him to remain, motioning that he should make himself comfortable near the fire. Malim was all attention, looking up at me wonderingly, hardly able to believe that I was allowing him to be present during such intimate exchanges.

"Your opinion, Sevrian?" I asked, helping myself to bread and honey.

He chewed thoughtfully for a while, then answered, "I think that you might have been a little harsh, Lord. I feel sure that Thalis only had the boy's best interests at heart, at least on this occasion. He should have consulted you, however, before taking such matters upon himself. It is not his place to speak of your son's contribution to the blood. But if it pleases you, Lord, I would be most interested to hear what Lord Malim himself thinks."

Seeing the attention of all present turn to him, my son shuffled uneasily, and asked, "What do you wish me to say Father?"

"Exactly what is in your mind," I replied with a smile. "You are now of the gift and so entitled to your opinion. You should attend to your feelings and allow yourself to be guided by what the gift tells you. If I, or Lord Sevrian believes that you are mistaken, we will give you further instruction. That way you will learn. However, such openness must not be displayed in the company of others – only towards we two, and in time those of your household whom you come to trust implicitly. You need have no fear of Lord Sevrian, nor of Nyran, as long as you act in accordance with my will. You may place your trust in them, although it may take some time to earn their trust in return. Speak freely, and don't be afraid of us."

Malim pondered for a minute or so, then, averting his eyes, said, "I think Thalis is very stupid. He let you lead him into a trap, and he didn't realise that you were doing it. Thalis doesn't like you. He does things that he knows will make you angry, but he always thinks that you will not find out. I don't understand why you keep him close to you. When I am head of the Family I will not make advisors out of such stupid people."

The silence that followed was finally broken by Sevrian's soft laughter. At once my son's head shot up, his eyes flashing angrily.

"Why are you laughing?" He looked up at me. "Father, why is Lord Sevrian laughing? You told me to say what was in my mind. Have I said something wrong? Tell him to stop laughing at me!"

Sevrian immediately bowed his head. "Forgive me, young Lord. I did not mean to offend you. You are right, of course. Your father did indeed trap Thalis quite admirably. However, if you will allow me to say so, you should not make the mistake of believing Thalis to be stupid. Rather, your father was too clever for him. Lord Rendail is, in most circumstances, too clever for anyone, and to judge Thalis against such a master is perhaps a little unfair."

Malim looked from one to the other of us, then at his feet, as he always did when he was confused.

"I still don't understand why you have placed him so highly if he does not please you," he muttered, still pouting a little.

"Come now," I said, putting a hand on his shoulder. "Lord Sevrian does not deserve your anger. It is ill mannered to sulk, especially when you have received so handsome an apology."

He raised his head and bowed to Sevrian. "I'm sorry Father. I didn't mean to be rude. But I still want to know why Thalis is so important to you."

I felt Sevrian shift slightly, and glanced up quickly to reassure him.

"Listen, Malim," I said gently. "I have already told you that what we wish is not always what is best for this Family, nor for the blood. I value Thalis, not for his friendship but for his skill. He has many failings, as perhaps we all do, but in one thing he excels. In matters of the Rule he is more zealous than any man here, aside from myself. He and his servants safeguard the Rule and ensure that my judgements are enforced. Without him the task would be much more difficult. It is true that at times he is over zealous, that he makes errors in his haste to serve the blood. These I can overlook for the most part. However, at times it is necessary to remind him that he also is a servant of the Rule and cannot place himself above it.

"When he spoke to you he went beyond his duty in a way that could not be allowed to pass without consequence. You are my son. Your blood takes precedence, and so he must submit himself to you no less than to me. That is the Rule, and as you saw, he cannot go against it if he is to retain his position. Thalis is now your creature as much as he is mine. If that causes him to feel humiliation, it is only because he tries to step outside the Rule. Does all this make sense to you?"

Malim nodded, and was about to ask another question when Sevrian broke in, "Although Lord Rendail correctly points out that Thalis must acknowledge you as being of superior blood, I think we should also counsel you to be most cautious in your

345

dealings with him, at least until you are fully grown and have a little more experience of the minds of men. Thalis is clever in his way, cunning, and strong in the gift. He also has a tendency to violence when pushed too far. Knowing when to be cruel and when to be tender is an art that takes many years to perfect, and I mean no disrespect when I say that unlike your father, who by all accounts possessed the skill from early childhood, you have a great deal yet to learn."

"I agree," I said. "Thalis can be persuasive, and you are as yet still a boy, raw and inexperienced in the gift. Take great care how you command him, or better still send him to me for direction for the time being. When you go with him about the settlement, listen carefully to all he says, observe what he does, but do not assume that all he tells you is as if he spoke with my voice."

I might have continued, but as I spoke I saw Malim's features tighten, his mouth setting itself into a thin line, his eyes staring, unblinking, at a point somewhere beyond my left shoulder. Puzzled, I glanced across at Sevrian, who offered a meaningful look and slowly rose, saying, "If you will forgive me, Lord, I am fatigued, and would be grateful if you would allow me to go to my rest. My servant and I must wake at dawn tomorrow."

I nodded, and with a bow to each of us Sevrian and Nyran made their departure. No sooner had the door closed behind them than Malim rounded on me with unexpected ferocity.

"Why should I listen to you any more than to Thalis?" he shouted, his sudden fury making his breath come in short gasps, his whole body trembling. "One moment you say he is my servant, the next you want me to send him to you and say I can't command him. First you tell everyone that I am a Lord, I am of the gift, a man. Then you say that I am still a boy and that I am more stupid than he is. You laugh at me just like Lord Sevrian. And why should I call him 'Lord'? He is only your brother's son, yet you spend all your time with him and not with me. When I was with Orlim you never came to see me once, not even when I stamped on one of the grooms and broke his face. I only did it so that you would come, but you didn't, you just sent him, so that

346

you wouldn't have to see me. You let him beat me, and he isn't even a lord, just your servant, like Thalis." He was beside himself now, screaming at the top of his lungs, tears of rage streaming down his cheeks.

I stood up, hoping that my sheer height would give him pause, but he simply carried on, his thoughts as uncontrolled as his speech, so that I was sure the whole settlement could not help but be disturbed by the outpourings of his mind.

"Everybody says how powerful you are," he yelled, "and how clever you are. They keep telling me that I must try harder, do everything better than anyone else because I am the heir, and I have to be as good as you. But I can't. I'm not clever and I can't do things even when I try to. Arvan understands. He is the only one who explains things to me, and now you have taken him away from me because I have the gift and you think I might hurt him. If you knew anything you would know that I would never hurt Arvan. He is my friend. But you have already decided. You don't have to like me, as long as I do as you say. As soon as you can you will send me away again and pretend that I'm not there. Well I don't like you either, and I don't want to be like you and I don't want to be the heir any more. I hate you!"

So saying he flung himself at me, fists flailing, and managed to land one or two healthy punches on my chest, which were probably more painful to his knuckles than to me. He was sobbing so much he could hardly speak and just went on swinging his fists and kicking out at me, while I stood motionless, frozen with astonishment.

I had to do something. I had never seen such a display of utter rage in one so young in my entire life. That is, I had never seen it in any but myself, and as I stood there I recalled the frenzied outbursts, some fiercer even than this, that had accompanied my own coming of age. It had also never occurred to me to wonder how the boy might actually be feeling, how he might have interpreted my actions over the years. My father had called for me and had kept me close to him for a full year or more before the coming of my gift. I had learned to know him, to read his moods. And, of course, I had been given Ilvan to help me, a boy who had spent some five years in the company of Corvan and whose counsel had been invaluable.

In some ways, I had to concede, Malim was no different from the boy I had once been. He was afraid of me, yet he craved my company, my attention, just as I had craved Corvan's. Corvan, however, had looked on me as perfect, the culmination of all his efforts to further the blood. My son had no such advantages. A flawed, damaged thing, he railed against the imperfection within him, tried with all his being to defeat it, but in vain. Every way he turned he saw only how he failed me, every desperate plea for guidance resulting in his pushing himself further away from me. Now, his new abilities, his heightened perceptions served simply to bring his failings into even sharper relief, and he lashed out wildly at the cause of his misery, the one who had passed judgement on him and found him unfit. In a sudden movement I caught him by the wrists and held him at arm's length. For a moment or two he struggled like a wild thing, but realising that it was hopeless soon gave up and stood helplessly, exhausted, waiting to see what I would do.

I sat down again slowly, pulling him down beside me, then released my grip on his wrists and gently put an arm around his shoulders. I sensed yet more confusion in him. He had, understandably, expected me to be angry, and once again I had failed to fulfil his prediction. Instead, I used my gift to soothe him, letting him see that I was calm, the quiet ripples of my understanding washing over him, I hoped giving some reassurance. After a long silence he looked up at me, and seeing the same sentiment mirrored in my eyes flung his arms around my neck, completely overwhelmed. I hugged him tightly to me, forgetting for the moment the danger that, even in his innocence, he posed to all that I wished to achieve, and made the promise I should never have made.

"I will always be with you," I said. "I will never leave you, and I will look after you for as long as I draw breath." I pushed him gently away and brushed the dishevelled golden locks away from his face. "Come," I said. "Shall we go upstairs? I have already sent for Arvan, and he is waiting for you."

348

CHAPTER 33

I kept my promise. It was, in the event, easier than I expected, at least to begin with. Contrary to the beliefs of just about everyone in the settlement, Malim did have some redeeming features. Not many, it's true, and perhaps my observations were coloured a little, seeing as I did through the eyes of a father. He followed me everywhere like one of the fawning hounds that the short lived keep in their houses. His efforts to understand and follow my instruction were almost painful to watch. If he displeased me he was distraught, and when I praised him he glowed with pride. He wanted so to become what I was, to taste the power that I so effortlessly wielded. But despite his blood he did not quite have my strength, and his failings constantly threatened to overcome him.

Try as he might he could never keep his emotions from his face. Whatever his mood it was plain for all to see, a constant reminder of his lack of self discipline. He was short tempered, rage flaring up in him in an instant at the slightest provocation. When the time came for him to enter the compound I despaired, for it was among the women that he became most violent, until eventually I was forced to restrain him to prevent unnecessary deaths. Always, he would kneel before me in a state of abject repentance, and always I would forgive him, moved by the earnestness of his desire to quell the demons within him.

It was Malim's dealings with Thalis that gave me most cause for disquiet. It was my fault I suppose. I had counted on Thalis's resentment of being forced to serve my young heir to place some distance between them. Unfortunately my pronouncement only served to bring them closer together, and I came upon them with alarming frequency, discussing one aspect of the Rule or another, my son eagerly drinking in every opinion that my advisor had to offer. By the time Malim reached his sixteenth year they were bed partners, I am sure of it, but nothing was ever voiced openly. It was not my place to interfere. Malim

349

was fast becoming the more dominant of the two and Thalis, for once in his miserable life, took on the subordinate role with eager acquiescence. The standing of my advisor was not diminished as a result. Rather, his followers looked upon him with increased admiration, viewing his self sacrifice as a fair price for the favour of the heir.

In the midst of my son's excesses, however, one thing was truly remarkable. That he worshipped me I knew well enough, a proof that he was capable of some deeper feeling. But he had one other object of affection. Towards Orlim's son, Arvan, he displayed a fierce protectiveness and loyalty, never to my knowledge inflicting on him the cruelties that so often characterised his dealings with others. The boy was handsome and delicate, his gift as quiet, as subtle as his father's. One could not imagine two more unlikely companions. Yet Malim's rages never seemed to touch him, and always my heir treated him with extraordinary gentleness, becoming biddable, almost docile in the presence of the younger boy. His affection was clearly reciprocated, and sometimes I came across them together, Arvan placid and fearless as he stroked my son's brow, for all the world as though Malim were one of Orlim's tame wolves.

It was when Malim was entering his twentieth year that things took a disastrous turn. I had spent the day out with Sevrian and Orlim hunting deer before retiring to the compound where I lay contentedly, Sherenne curled up in my arms. The hunt had been strenuous and before long I was fast asleep. I dreamed seldom, at least if I did I did not remember them, but on this night I had no sooner closed my eyes than my mind was filled with a barrage of incomprehensible visions.

To begin with the images were strange enough, but more beguiling than frightening. I saw trees, but they did not grow in any fashion that I was familiar with. They were all in straight lines, like great armies of men marching across a barren landscape. I saw cattle that didn't look like any that I had ever seen – fat, wide, spotted creatures with swollen pink udders so heavy that I wondered how the animals managed to walk. I seemed to be on the land of some kind of homestead, for there were other animals – pigs, horses and fowl, all strange in their appearance, but recognisable nonetheless.

The scene shifted and night came. I was in a town, with streets and houses and lights. But what streets, what houses, what lights! Row after row of tall stone houses stretched out as far as the eye could see, the stones small and perfectly square, the angular roofs composed of little red or grey tiles. Each house had huge windows and no shutters, so that I wondered how the inhabitants managed to keep themselves warm, even in summer. The streets were equally mesmerising, and in my dream I walked along an endless road, not constructed of stone but of something dark and entirely smooth, like liquid, yet harder even than our wide stone pavements. The sound of my feet on the ground echoed horribly, as though I wore metal on the soles of my boots, and I began to be afraid that the people in the houses that towered on either side of me would hear and come out to apprehend me.

I walked for some time – I don't know how far, then, turning a corner I saw something that made my heart leap into my mouth, set it thumping in my chest. Before me stood a great stone pillar – stone, yet not stone, for when I brushed my hand against it a fine powder trickled off it as though it was made of sand, yet solid, immovable. But it was not the pillar itself that quickened my breathing; it was the thing on the top of it. Seemingly suspended on the end of the pillar, more than the height of three men above me, was a dazzling ball of light. There was no flame, no wick. It was as though the sun had come down from the sky and was lighting up the night, making my eyes hurt to look at it, the heat of it drifting down to touch my cheek. Despite the fact that something told me that this huge yellow flame that was not a flame couldn't harm me, I had a terrible urge to run from it and did just that, the noise of my feet clattering along the smooth pavement ringing in my ears.

I had gone no more than a dozen paces when I realised that it was futile, for there in front of me was yet another of the great shining beasts, and then I saw that beyond that there was another. I stared wildly around me, hoping for escape, and at that moment something else happened that was even more terrifying.

351

Suddenly I found myself sitting bolt upright, awake, or so I thought. I was gasping for breath, shivering, my body drenched with sweat. I was aware of Sherenne next to me, taking me by the shoulders to try to shake me awake, calling my name, her voice filled with panic and incomprehension. But the vision did not stop. Coming straight towards me at frightening speed were two of the impossible lights. Faster than a galloping horse they moved, and with a great roaring noise that turned my blood to ice. Closer and closer they came, the noise getting louder and louder until I was sure that they were going to crash into me and crush me to death. I almost screamed with terror, but at the last minute I somehow made my body move and leapt to one side, landing on my back on the smooth ground.

The thing, whatever it was, did n't stop, but with a piercing squealing sound shot past, the two little suns shining straight ahead, two smaller, red lights sending slivers of light like malevolent burning eyes staring out behind it as it went on, finally disappearing round another corner. Suddenly the vision faded and my eyes came back into focus. Sherenne was shouting my name, beside herself with anxiety, her hands gripping each side of my face, her eyes searching mine frantically. Breathing hard, unable to speak, I took her in my arms and squeezed her to me to let her know that I had come back to myself and she need not worry.

"Did you see?" I asked, as soon as I had sufficient breath to talk. She shook her head and offered me a jug of water, which I gulped down without a pause.

"You were awake, yet you were dreaming," she said, concern still in her voice. "I have never seen anything like it. You cried out as though you were being attacked, yet there was nothing there, only the air. I tried to see what was in your mind, to help you, but there was nothing, only a grey mist that veiled my sight. What is it? What did you see?"

I gathered myself and described to her everything that I had encountered in my vision, her eyes growing wider as I told her of the strange lights, the oddly deformed animals, the unfamiliar feel of the ground. There were the scents too, that I had not really noticed at the time – a choking thickness of the atmosphere in which the smell of grass and earth were entirely absent.

"At first," I concluded, "I thought it was a dream. But as it went on I knew that it was not, and feared that I might be going mad. It was as though I saw things that existed, but through the eyes of another. But how could that be? No such things exist in the world that I know of, and it was like no world that I have ever seen. It was a living night terror, and perhaps I am losing my mind after all."

She kissed me and stroked my brow.

"Hush now," she said, trying to soothe me. "More likely the burden of leadership has weighed too heavily on you in recent times, and you haven't taken enough rest. After all, our son is not the easiest of creatures to keep in check. You should go out tomorrow, across the valley, just you and your horse, as you used to do. Let Sevrian take care of things, at least for a day or two. He is capable enough, and Malim can't do that much harm while you are gone."

I allowed her to persuade me, and the next morning I set off, alone and troubled still, heading for the crags on the far side of the valley. I had been riding no more than three hours or so when I caught sight of a familiar plume of smoke rising in the distance. However, unlike my first sighting of such a fire all those years ago, when I had been overcome with annoyance, now my heart leapt hopefully and I urged my horse into a gallop, praying that the owner of the fire might indeed be the one I sought.

When I reached the spot I found it deserted, and for a moment my heart sank. But then I noticed a pack hung high on a branch, almost invisible to the casual eye, and hidden carefully behind it a small bedding roll, the colour of the bark against which it was stowed. The fire had been expertly damped to keep it from burning away during the owner's absence. With a smile of relief I dismounted, taking my supplies of bread and cold meat from my pack, and set myself the task of collecting more wood and building up the blaze in preparation for the owner's return. In a short while I had heated water infused with herbs and laid out my offering of food, after which I sat with my back against the trunk of a tree, dozing in the warmth.

Some time later, on hearing a faint rustle in the undergrowth I opened my eyes to find the old man standing looking down at me, his head slightly on one side. I scrambled to my feet at once and bowed.

"I hope you will forgive the intrusion," I said, noting his slightly disapproving expression. "The truth is, I am in need of your wisdom, and I couldn't pass by without asking leave to speak with you. As you see, I have tended your fire and brought food that I am happy to share."

He didn't answer, but continued to study me with narrowed eyes, his lips set in a thin line beneath his bristling beard. I bowed again, defeated.

"I will leave, then. Please forgive me for disturbing you."

I made off towards my horse, aching with disappointment, but had only gone a few paces when I heard him sigh.

"Your manners have improved somewhat, I see."

I turned, and offered a faint smile.

"Not enough it seems," I replied with a shrug.

He laughed. "Come, my boy," he said kindly. "I am just a churlish old man, and at my time of life I react badly to surprises. But now that you are here I admit I am pleased to see you, so if you will forgive my momentary rudeness I would welcome your company at dinner." He drew aside his cloak to reveal a sizeable fish. "It seems we have a feast," he commented with a smile, surveying my contribution. "I suggest we eat first and make ourselves comfortable, and then you can tell me what brings you here in such dire need of my counsel."

Afternoon had turned into evening by the time I had related all I had to tell, which was well nigh everything that had happened since our last meeting. He listened quietly, nodding or shaking his head every now and then, but not interrupting until I had quite finished, and had described the waking dream that had sent me riding out into the valley, half afraid for my sanity. I looked up at him nervously, suspecting that he might announce that I had indeed lost my mind, but in answer he patted me on the shoulder and reached for the wine skin, his look serious and thoughtful.

"You have not lost your senses," he said finally, and much to my relief.

"What was it then?" I asked anxiously. "What could cause me to have such visions, see such nonsensical things while my eyes were open and I was awake?"

He gave me a sidelong glance. "Ah. But are you sure that what you saw was nonsensical? Perhaps you are simply looking for the wrong explanation. An answer only makes no sense when you have asked the wrong question."

I laughed. "You talk in riddles. An answer can never come before a question. So how can a question ever be wrong?"

"Are you sure of that?" he responded with a chuckle. "Clearly in this instance the normal rules do not apply. You have received your answer, and can make no sense of it simply because you do not know what the question is."

"Very well then," I said, irritated. "Perhaps you can tell me what this elusive question is, as you seem to know quite well. I am a mere boy and without your experience, otherwise why should I come here to seek your enlightenment?"

"Oh, now, don't sulk," he chided, laughing again. "But I should not make light of so serious a matter. For it is serious, boy, make no mistake about that. You have been foolish, although I cannot blame you for it. I would have done the same thing had I been in your shoes. However, perhaps it was not foolishness at all, but fate that has led to this, and I judge you far too harshly. Now you must take steps to put it right and I daresay that will not be easy. No, not easy at all. Perhaps it will be the hardest thing that you have ever done, but you must do it nonetheless. I am sorry, truly I am, my boy, and I wish with all my heart that the burden had not fallen upon you. But it has, and you only have your father to blame for that. It doesn't help, I know, but there we are. It is done now and you have little choice if you are to remain true to yourself."

He patted me again and handed me a bowl filled with wine, sighing to himself and shaking his head. I had forgotten just how irritating my mentor could be.

"Perhaps, when it suits you," I exploded, almost spilling my wine, "you might let me in on the secret? I confess I have no idea what you are talking about. What is so serious, and what should I do? I came to find counsel, but if all I get is derision and accusation, perhaps it would be better if I went on my way and let things reveal themselves to me in the fullness of time. Why do you take such pleasure in tormenting me so? If I am descended into madness pray tell me so and I will trouble you no more."

At once his expression changed and he looked almost contrite.

"Oh, my dear boy, do forgive me. It is my age, as I have said, and often my mind precedes my manners, if you know what I mean. I was thinking aloud, and meant no offence. Now, listen to me. You told me, when we met before, that you took the woman, Sherenne, from Derlan's people because your father coveted a certain gift that was taken from him. Is that not so?"

I nodded. "Yes, that is so. She is the descendant of the one who crossed the Great Emptiness. But what has she to do with my vision? She was as confused, as frightened as I, and certainly she did not cause it."

"Not directly, no," the old man said. "But what of that which the two of you together have created? You have already told me the cause of her desirability. It is, is it not, the possibility that the gift your father sought might come again in any offspring she may produce? You have produced offspring, have you not? A monster of a child that should have been done away with at the moment of its birth, and whose gift now ranges far and wide, beyond even his father's control? The vision that you saw was no vision. It was your child, wandering on the far side of the Great Emptiness. The fear that you felt was his fear, the strange images the truth of life in the far future.

"Your son, boy, has fulfilled your father's ambition. He has visited the places that no other men can visit, seen a part of what we will become many centuries from now. And you, his

356

father, are his anchor. You are the thing that keeps the thread of his mind connected to this time, this place. That is why you saw his visions. When he was frightened he passed his fear on to you, and he used you to return when he was done. That is why the vision stopped. What he saw terrified him, and so he fled back to his own time. You must tread carefully now, Rendail. Your son seeks a world that he can dominate, a place where you have no control over him. This time he was cowed, but he will become used to the strangeness, and soon he will realise how easy it will be to become a lord, a master of that far time.

"You are right, he should have died long ago, but I will not place blame upon you. Which of us is strong enough to destroy our own child, especially when the full extent of that child's nature is not clear? What an error you made, but what a hard choice faced you. Success or failure, you would have suffered just the same. Still, who am I to say that your sparing of the child was a mistake? I do not know all, and perhaps it was meant to be, for some greater good that we can't yet see. Don't despair yet, boy. All is not lost, and we must trust that a way will present itself."

I sat, silent, with my head in my hands for what seemed an age. The truth of the old man's pronouncement was undeniable, and despite his advice I found myself overwhelmed with despair.

"What should I do?" I asked, raising my head, my eyes pleading with him for help. He frowned, and pondered for several minutes.

"I can see only one way out," he said finally. "You know that you can't do away with the boy now. Those you fear know of his gift. They also knows that you are aware of it. To try to destroy him would cause the very situation you have been trying to avoid. They would either protect the boy or try to avenge his death, and bring on a bloodbath that would leave no victor.

"The way I see things, you have only one choice. You must have another child, and hope that you father a son that will equal or surpass Malim. You must have another heir, one that is worthy of the name. But that is easier said than done. Can you imagine the reaction of your current heir to any usurper that comes to claim his title? Malim will not suffer such a child to live, not if he can help it anyway. Yes, you must have a son, and you must make sure that Malim does not see him as a threat, at least not until it is too late."

"And how do you suggest I do that?" I protested. "If I have a son of any power, he will be vulnerable for many years before his gift makes him Malim's equal. Besides, who is to say that another child will not be as tainted as my heir? It was my blood that made him, and my blood might very well make another just the same."

The old man laughed again. "You take a great deal upon yourself, Rendail. What made Malim was not your blood entirely. Your mate is equally tainted, as you put it, is she not? She also has the blood of Corvan running in her veins – Amala was his daughter after all. You were simply unlucky. Corvan's line came together in the two of you to create Malim, but who is to say that another mating will not produce one with Derlan's strength and Lena's heart? You must have faith. If at first you don't succeed ... eh?

"As for how you protect the child, I'm afraid I must leave that to you. Until you know what kind of creature you sire, you can't form a plan. But when you do see, then you will know. You are a strong one, Rendail. It will not be easy for you, and you will shed many tears before it is done, but you will persevere, and I think you will succeed. Yes, I am sure of it. But do not blame yourself. The responsibility may now lie with you, but you are not the cause – that was the honour of your father."

He paused, seeing that I still looked dubious.

"I have a feeling," he went on at length, his voice once again serious, "that one day you will find the peace you seek. One day, your greatness will be acknowledged, and your people will look on you with love. Perhaps you will think it too late, at least for some, but I hope I live to see it, for I have never known one so deserving, my friend. We may not meet again for many years, if indeed we meet at all, but my thoughts will be with you, and perhaps if you call for me I will hear, and I will come. Meanwhile you have your woman, and from what you tell me your first child is worth a dozen of your heir."

He offered me the wine and I took it, smiling.

"At least you no longer call me 'boy'," I said, taking a deep draught. "To have you call me 'friend' is an honour indeed, and I treasure it."

He laughed, and picked up his pack.

"I will leave you my fish, then, as a token of that friendship. Use my fire for as long as you need. You might as well, as you gathered most of the wood. My good wishes go with you, Rendail, son of Corvan. May your unborn child be all that you wish for."

"Wait," I said, rising to my feet. "You said that if I had need of you, I should call, but I don't know your name."

He cocked an eyebrow, already several paces away on the edge of the clearing.

"Actually," he said, an almost mischievous look in his eye, "it is so long since I heard it that I think I have forgotten. But it doesn't matter – I will hear anyway." With that, he disappeared down a dip in the hillside and was gone.

"Have another child?" I could see the fear begin to show itself in Sherenne's eyes. I have to admit I was no less fearful myself, given the two disasters that we had already endured.

"That is what he advised," I said lamely, wishing that I had not mentioned it in the first place. I hated to see her so anxious. "If you refuse, I will not press the matter," I assured her. "But think of this. When our daughter and our son were born, we were not joined. Our hearts did not beat as one, as they do now. I did not love you less then, but neither did I know you as I know you now. Perhaps a child that is born within our joining will be a child truly of our love, and not only of our duty to the blood. Perhaps it will be the child that is all we wished for, one to heal the wounds that the past has inflicted upon us.

"One thing is clear. We cannot leave the Family in the hands of Malim. You know what that would mean. He can cross the Great Emptiness and already Thalis guards the prize that

359

feeds his ambition. Only one of superior strength will surpass my heir, and the only chance of that is through our mating. Whatever our feelings, it is our responsibility to ensure that Malim can never take control of the workings of the gift, neither now nor in the future. I believe that we are stronger, that together we have the strength to prevent a great tragedy, even though in doing so we may bring tragedy upon ourselves."

She kissed me. "How can I refuse you?" she said. "The responsibility lies with us, and us alone. We are the only ones that can prevent the outcome that we all fear. But I have neither your strength nor your courage. It is a great deal that you ask of me, and I need time. Perhaps we both do. You must gauge the strength of Malim's gift. If it's true that you alone are his anchor, his one link to his own time, then maybe you can control him, at least for a while. You can also learn more of the places that he visits, the time in which he finds himself. He may learn of things that can be of use to you. At the very least you can't risk his hiding from you what he learns. Try to be close to him, to gain his trust. Then we may learn better how to proceed against him when the time comes."

Her words made me shudder. "We are speaking of our child," I whispered. "Monster though he is, he is our son, that we both love and have protected, whom I have sworn to care for despite his failings, for as long as I still breathe. I know you speak the truth, but still I ask myself, how much longer can I continue to cause harm to those I love? If I truly had courage I might have ended it before it began, and it is my weakness that has brought this upon us. Now I have been forced to ask you to do once more a thing that has only brought misery to us both, and I wish with all my heart that it was otherwise. What is the importance of the furtherance of the blood to me if it drives me away from you, places you in danger? I would put all thought of offspring from my mind if it meant that we would be safe, and that I could hold you in my arms, as I do now, forever."

At this she sighed, then smiled and hugged me closer. We lay together in silence for a while, and then she said, "It is not only our offspring that hold promise of the gift. Amala's blood is

360

in my father too, and who knows what may come of it if he decides to mate again. Perhaps we don't fight alone, but will one day have allies who can follow our son to the other side of the Great Emptiness, perhaps even match his strength."

That was something I had not thought about for a long time, and I wondered if perhaps the idea had occurred to Malim, possibly even to Karim and Thalis. It was another complication, but as Sherenne rightly said, one that could not be altogether dismissed. Derlan's tribe was immensely strong, although not quite with the power we possessed. That was not to say, however, that the situation would not change given time and a propitious mixing of the blood. Once, I might have been horrified by the thought, but now I was strangely comforted, despite the fact that no love was lost between our two peoples. At least, when it came to it, we were not alone, and my brief contact with Sherenne's grandfather Rolan all those years ago had been enough to tell me that his family would no more countenance a future ruled by Malim than would I. Giving her a final squeeze I got up.

"Where are you going?" she asked, anxious again.

"I think," I replied with a smile, "that it is an appropriate moment for me to disturb my son at his pleasure. It is late, and if I am fortunate I may be saved the trouble of waking Nyran to send for my advisor."

CHAPTER 34

The door was opened by Arvan, the sight of whom was always a pleasure to me, his gentle grace and calm expression making it almost impossible to believe that he was not yet quite nineteen years old. He bowed shyly.

"You wish me to fetch Lord Malim, my Lord?"

"In due course," I replied. "I am sure he knows that I am here, and I think that he might appreciate a few moments to prepare himself."

Arvan, quite rightly, made no reaction to my comment. "As you wish, Lord. May I bring you wine?"

"Thank you. And for yourself, if you will."

He complied without demur, and at my command conducted me to his own room to wait. For some twenty minutes we talked together, about his father, whom he clearly adored and whose love of horses he had inherited, and about his life with Malim, of whom he spoke with plain affection. I found his company soothing, and was almost disappointed when I heard a firm tread coming towards us in the hallway. The tall, lean figure of my son appeared in the doorway. Arvan rose and bowed at once.

"Your visit honours me, Father." Malim nodded and dismissed Arvan with an imperious wave of the hand. "You wish to speak to me?"

"You and your lover both," I answered, at which Malim blushed slightly and shuffled his feet. "I would also like Arvan to remain, if you have no objection."

"None, if it pleases you," my son lied. I had noticed over the years that his relationship with Orlim's son was somewhat of a jealous one. They had never shared a bed together to my knowledge, yet Malim was loath to allow Arvan into the presence of any but himself, man or woman. It was as though he feared that the intervention of another might break the fragile bond that held them together. At least, I thought, it was evidence that he

362

was capable of some form of love, even if it was one that was in keeping with his character. Arvan deserved better and I resolved to address the issue while I had the chance.

Thalis arrived, looking well presented but a little flustered. I let them remain standing.

"You have something to tell me?" I asked, my gaze passing from one to the other of them. Thalis immediately opened his mouth, but at a gesture from Malim he closed it again. My son hesitated, but then said, all in a rush, "Yes, Father. I wasn't sure at first, but now I am." He paused, and drew in his breath excitedly. "I have crossed the Great Emptiness! I have seen what is to come. It is just as Lord Corvan predicted. I see my mother's value now, and why I am here. I have the blood, and I can use it. It is such a wonderful thing Father, and I have done it, no one else. You should be proud that at last the gift has come, and I will make this Family great. I will take the name of Corvan to the far future, and our line will live forever."

I let the silence following this little speech hang in the air for a moment, then said quietly, "I think, Malim, that it is for me to decide of what and of whom I should be proud."

His face coloured immediately, and he swallowed hard. "Yes, Father," he replied in a whisper, furious that I should speak to him so in front of his servants.

I turned to Thalis. "You knew of this?"

Thalis nodded. "The first time it happened, Lord, I was with him. I saw everything. But we were not sure ..."

"And when," I interrupted, letting just a little fury of my own creep into my voice, "were the two of you likely to see fit to inform me of this extraordinary development? Or did you think to try to keep it to yourselves? If so, I would suggest that you are both perhaps a little more foolish than I thought."

Thalis took a step forward. "Of course not, Lord. It was simply that Lord Malim was not certain at first. Then, when we became sure we tried to find you, but Lord Sevrian informed us that you had gone riding alone. No one knew where you were, Lord. That is the truth, I swear it."

His hand trembled slightly as he spoke. I fixed him with a stare until he bowed his head.

"You may leave," I said finally, and he scuttled away with as much haste as he could muster without being downright impolite.

As soon as Thalis had gone Malim jerked his head up and protested, "You are being unfair, Father. Thalis spoke the truth. We tried to find you. Why are you angry? You should be pleased that I have brought you this treasure. You should be thankful that I serve you with the strength of my blood."

He got no further, for without moving from where I sat I lashed out with my gift, sending Malim sprawling to the floor writhing in pain.

"I was going to tell you, I was!" he squealed pathetically.

"Be silent!" I hissed, at the same time releasing him, and he raised himself to his knees, sobbing with pain, rage and humiliation.

"The gift is only as strong as the one who wields it," I said. "As for what I should and should not do, I have already told you, that is for me to decide."

He nodded, trying to wipe the tears roughly from his cheeks. "Yes, Father."

"Before we discuss this further," I went on, "there seems to be another matter in which you have been remiss." He glanced at me, confused. "The blood of Orlim's line is valuable to me. You know this, yet you have made no arrangement for its enhancement. You are responsible for the servants in your household and, as my heir, also for the furtherance of the blood. Can you explain to me why it is that you have not requested that Arvan enter the compound?"

His expression dissolved into one of complete despair. "Please, Father," he begged, crying again, "I'm sorry. I will do whatever you wish. I promise."

"I have no need of your promises," I replied. "You will do as I wish in any case. Arvan, do you know your way through the compound?"

The youth, who had stood rigidly in a corner throughout the whole proceeding, came forward. "Forgive me, my Lord, I do not. I have never had cause to enter."

"You do now," I said, rising at last and placing a reassuring arm around his shoulder. "Enter the main gate, cross the courtyard, and knock on the last door on the east side. Tell Sherenne that I have sent you, and that I wish her to take you to someone suitable. She will make a good choice. Go now." Arvan cast a worried glance at Malim. "Don't be afraid." I smiled. "My son will still be here when you return. I'm sure that he desires only your happiness. Is that not so Malim?"

Malim looked up at Arvan and nodded, completely crushed. "You must go," he managed to say weakly. "It is a great honour."

Arvan bowed, and made his departure without another word.

"Get up," I snapped, as soon as we were alone, "and stop behaving in such a shameful manner. Go and fetch more wine and then we will talk."

Malim bit back a protest and did as he was told. He poured me wine with a shaking hand, then, unable to contain himself he flung himself on his knees, tears once again welling in his eyes.

"Please, Father. Do anything that you wish to me, but please don't take Arvan away. I shall die, I know it, if he is not with me. Please, I beg you Father, let me have him back."

"You should be careful what you wish for," I replied coldly. "For had I done what I wished to do I would have whipped you in front of your entire household for your deceitfulness. But perhaps it is as well that I restrained myself, as it seems I have hit upon a more telling punishment after all. Now, get off your knees and sit quietly. Tell me what it is about Orlim's boy that leaves you so bereft without him. He speaks of you so well that I wonder whether he might not have confused you with someone else. That, at least, is something in your favour."

He fidgeted and stared at his feet, a habit that had plagued him since childhood. After several attempts he said, "I don't know if I can explain properly. Arvan is so much better at explaining things. I'll try, but please don't be angry again, Father. I am trying as hard as I can, truly."

I softened at once. "I won't be angry Malim. I promise. Try to tell me. I will listen."

He took a deep breath, searching for the words. "He stops the madness," he declared at last, looking up at me apprehensively. I nodded encouragingly.

"That's good, Malim. Now can you tell me how Arvan does this? Does he advise you? Does he use his gift? Try to describe to me what he does."

There was a long silence, during which I waited patiently, sensing that my son was doing his best to form an answer that he thought I would understand.

"He talks to me differently from everyone else," he began finally. "When we were at the stables together he always understood what I was supposed to do, and he would take me aside and explain to me. When he explained everything made sense. When I was angry he would come and hold me until I wasn't angry any more, then he would talk to me, give me nice things to eat, and keep talking until I felt safe. Sometimes Orlim or Lord Sevrian would come and say I'd done things that were wrong, but when I tried to listen to them I could never understand what they were asking of me. Then Arvan would come and talk to them. Often they would leave me alone then, but sometimes one of them would beat me anyway, and I didn't know why. I'm sorry Father. I am not explaining very well."

I put a hand on his shoulder. "It's all right Malim. Go on. What about now?"

"People kept saying that I would understand more when I got older," he went on, drawing up his knees and resting his chin on them. "I got older, but nothing changed. Then the gift came and Lord Sevrian came to fetch me. I knew that without Arvan I would be all alone, and I begged Lord Sevrian to allow Arvan to come with me. I lost my temper and I fought, but it didn't do any good. I was frightened until you said that Arvan could come and stay with me, because I knew I wouldn't manage to please you by myself. Now he can use his gift to help me as well as his voice.

"I make a lot of mistakes, but if it weren't for Arvan I would make mistakes all the time. I try, Father, but the gift makes it worse, and it's like a great fog in my mind all the time. Trying to see through it makes my head hurt. Then Arvan comes and shows me the way through. He watches over me, and things don't seem so dark."

He shrugged and burst into tears yet again. "I didn't know it was wrong, Father. Thalis said it was right to be sure, to wait. He talks to me like Arvan does, but not as well. When he speaks what he says seems so reasonable, the right thing to do. I first crossed the Great Emptiness almost a turn of the moon ago. I told Thalis that I should go to see you straight away, but he said no, that I had only gone a short way for a few moments, and that you would be better pleased if I practiced first so that I could show you properly. He said I needed to go a long way, and be there for enough time to tell you exactly what it was like when I returned. So that's what I did. Then, last night, I told Arvan. He said that if I listened to Thalis I would be in trouble, and that I should run to tell you at once. But when I did Lord Sevrian said you were gone away and that nobody knew where you were. Arvan didn't know anything about it. You won't be angry with him will you Father? It was him that told me to tell you. Thalis was wrong, but I didn't know that, and now that you have sent Arvan away, I don't know what to do next."

I had listened quietly to everything he had to say, and as I had done so the dreadful truth had revealed itself to me, becoming clearer with every word that he had spoken. I needed to speak to Arvan again, but now it would have to wait until morning. Meanwhile, I looked at my son in the light of my new knowledge and my heart went out to him.

"It's all right, Malim," I said gently. "Arvan will be with you no later than two hours after dawn tomorrow. You can wait until then can't you?"

He raised his head, relief all over his face.

"Thank you, Father. I am grateful," he said, and would have fallen on his knees again if I hadn't stopped him.

"But," I went on, "you must learn to do without him for an evening now and then. He is of our blood, and it is his both his right and his duty to go into the compound. You must not prevent him. Is that clear?"

"Oh yes," he replied. "I will make sure that he goes as often as you wish, Father. I promise."

"And what of Thalis?" I asked. "What will you do about him?"

"Do you want me to stop seeing him?" my son replied eagerly. "I will if that is what you want. He won't like it though. I will have to tell him you said so, and he won't be pleased with me."

I shook my head. "No, I don't want you to send him away. But if Thalis advises you, you must seek Arvan's advice before you decide to do anything. You are not to tell Thalis that I said so. In fact, do not tell him that we have had this conversation at all. What has been said is private, between the two of us, father and son, yes?"

He nodded. "Yes, Father, of course. I will tell no one."

"One other thing," I said. "You must understand that whatever you do, I know about it. You can't keep anything from me, and it is not advisable to try. You learned that for yourself tonight. I don't want to find I have to come to you for information again. If that happens I will be very angry. If you had told me about Arvan earlier, I would have understood, and that might have saved you a great deal of trouble. As for your gift to cross the Great Emptiness, I can tell you, between us, that I am very proud of you. It must have been a frightening thing. Would you like to tell me all about it?"

Until dawn, Malim happily described to me, as well as he could, his journeys into the future. The last one, of course, I had seen, but made no mention of it to him. I thought it best to keep that piece of information to myself, at least for the present. Aside from the visit in which I had been an unwilling participant he had made the crossing just three times. In the first he had jumped

368

forward just a few hours, and described seeing himself searching for me out by the river. On the following two occasions he had gone a little further, but still within his own lifetime, just for a few minutes, and had observed nothing of note. The final journey, however, was of most interest.

It was impossible to guess just how far into the future his gift had taken him, but it was clearly to a point well beyond his own death. He described waking, naked, in a great tomb-like cave. For several hours he had wandered, trying to find a way out, until at last he had come to a path with a stone blocking the way. On pushing the stone he found that it moved easily, and had emerged from the cave into open countryside. After walking for a long time – he could not remember how long – he had found a dwelling, and the inhabitants being asleep had availed himself of some strange clothing and some bread and cheese. There was more walking, after which he had come upon a town, the description of which left me in no doubt that this was the part of his journey that I had seen the evening before. What he saw had frightened him, and in a panic he had jumped back to his own time.

"But I will go again," he said excitedly. "Next time I know what to expect, and I will learn more about the strange things I saw, and who lives there."

"Then next time," I said firmly, "You must tell me when you intend to make the attempt. If, as you say, your mind leaves you when you travel, then it means that your body is vulnerable. You can't risk its being injured while you are gone from it. I will make sure that you are protected and that no harm comes to you. Someone must watch over your body until you return to claim it, otherwise you may not be able to return at all."

He smiled, happy to be sharing his experiences with me at last. "Thank you, Father. I will tell you, I promise, even if Thalis says not to."

"Come then," I said. "Let me embrace you. It is almost dawn and I must go to find Arvan."

He flung his arms around me and I hugged him to me, at last understanding what I should have understood from the very beginning.

Sherenne greeted me with a smile. "Arvan is a sweet child," she said, drawing me in and handing me a cup of herb water. "He was so nervous I swear he almost fell down when I opened the door. I sent him to Callenna, but first I gave him leave to visit his mother. I hope you don't object."

"Not in the slightest," I answered. I searched my mind for a moment, plucking forth an image of a slight, dark haired young girl, pretty, with a shy smile. "Callenna is a good choice," I said. "I have a feeling though that the two of them did little together last night but talk."

She laughed. "And what is wrong with that? But you are hiding something from me. You are troubled. You want to tell me something, but can't find the right words."

I nodded. "Until I speak to Arvan I can't be certain. I think, however, that I know what he will say." I made her sit by me and held her as I explained my suspicions. When I finally fell silent there was a tear in her eye.

"What will you do?" she asked. "It changes everything."

I shook my head. "It changes nothing except, perhaps, our understanding. But until I have spoken to Orlim's son I can't decide how to proceed. Don't worry. I will protect him somehow, for as long as I am able."

I kissed her and walked out into the courtyard just in time to see Arvan emerging from the central doorway.

"Forgive me, Lord," he said, as soon as we were safely within my own rooms, "but Lord Malim will be anxious. I should return in case he needs me."

"He can wait another hour," I reassured him. "I promised that you would be with him two hours after sunrise. I have ordered him to see no one until then, so he will be quite safe."

Arvan relaxed a little, and I bade him sit and take breakfast with me. He looked very tired, but what I had to say could not wait.

"Before we talk," I said, wanting to put him at his ease, "I need you to be aware that I have spoken with Malim, and he has described to me all you do for him. But as you know, he can't use words very well, and I want you to help me to better understand his situation. I want you to answer my questions truthfully, for his sake as well as for yours. Will you do that?"

"Yes, Lord, of course," he answered. "If Lord Malim has already spoken to you, then I have no reason to keep anything hidden."

"Then if you would, describe to me exactly how you find my son. Tell me what you see in his mind, and how you came to know it."

He hesitated, struggling with himself, then said, "Malim is … damaged, Lord. I have known it since we were small children together. He cannot reason as we do – I think, Lord, that he will never understand what it is to be a man."

Arvan's stark confirmation brought tears to my eyes, but I choked them back, and nodded. Seeing Arvan's fearful expression, I said, "Don't worry, Arvan. You tell me only what I already know. But why is it that he holds you so dear to him? You are, it seems, the only one to escape his rages, and when he speaks your name, I see only softness in his eyes. What skill do you have that I do not?"

He shrugged. "I use my gift, just as I would with any other creature. I think, because I make things simple for him, he understands."

Suddenly, everything became clear. Arvan, like his father, had the skill to tame all manner of beasts. Why not my son, who's mind was no more developed than that of a child, or a horse or, more apt, I thought grimly, a wolf.

"Is that it?" I asked. "You use your gift to calm him – it is that simple?"

"Yes. There is something else, but Lord Malim made me promise to say nothing to anyone. When he is particularly troubled, there is one thing that I find calms him, even more than my thoughts."

"Tell me," I said. "What is it, this thing that calms him more than anything else?"

He took a breath and looked me in the eye. "Forgive me, Lord, but I gave my word. I promised Lord Malim that I would tell no one of it. I beg you not to ask me to betray his trust."

I sighed. "I would not ask if it were not vital to me," I replied. "I have no words to thank you for your faithfulness to my son, just as no words can describe the debt I owe your father. But Malim is my son, and I love him no less because of his affliction. I confess this to you even though I know that in doing so I go against the Rule. I beg you to show me what it is that gives him peace, so that I can come to understand him. I value your loyalty, and if you refuse I will accept it as your choice, but I ask you to consider that as his father it is my duty to help him if I can."

Arvan looked at me as if measuring how far he could trust me, but finally recognising the pleading in my eyes he nodded, and slowly drew a little bag from a string at his belt and placed it on the table before me. I stared at it, then picked it up and opened it. I could hardly believe what I saw. Inside lay a cluster of sweet nuts, boiled in honey and left to dry over a fire until they became brittle. They were treats that some women made for the little children, only ever seen inside the compound. Outside they were considered frivolous, not in keeping with the way of the Family, and done away with the moment a boy left his mother.

I looked questioningly at Arvan. He blushed and said, "When you asked for me to be sent from my mother to be your son's companion, my father knew how much it pained her. Whenever he visited her she would give him a packet of sweet nuts, and he would bring them back for me. I would share them with Lord Malim at night, when all the men had gone to sleep. I soon found that I could calm him without a word simply by giving him a handful of these nuts to eat. A spoonful of honey does almost as well, but these work best of all. I told my father that they were for me, and so he has continued to bring them home each time he visits my mother. Last night, though, I was able to get some for myself, and if you allow me to continue to visit the compound I will keep a supply for Malim so that he always has them when they are needed."

I very nearly laughed. "Oh, Malim," I breathed, almost to myself. "My poor child."

What an irony it was that one so feeble had inherited the greatest gift. And how dangerous it was. Despite the tearing of my heart I could not forget that my imbecile son, my child in the body of a man, was capable of the destruction of entire worlds. It did not help to know that he had not the slightest idea of what he might accomplish, that he might bring death upon us all and not even realise he had done anything wrong.

I sat, deep in thought, for a long time. Arvan waited patiently, somehow understanding the struggle that was running through my mind, just has his father had understood my dilemma over Ilvan years before. At length I found my voice.

"May I take some of these?" I asked. "You are free to enter the compound whenever you wish, and to visit your mother if you have the need. If Callenna pleases you, take her. I know you will treat her well. If my son needs anything you may get it for him. Most of all I ask you to stay with him, and not to abandon him. He needs you, more than he needs me, and I beg you to continue to help him as you have these past years, to try to make his life more bearable. Now that I understand I will do my part. If you have need of me I am here. You only have to call and I will come."

Arvan bowed his head. "Please, Lord, take them all. I have more. You do not need to ask me to stay with Lord Malim. Forgive me, but I would not leave him even if you ordered it. I could not bear the thought of him all alone. We have spent our lives together, and I will remain with him until the end comes, for either one of us."

I got up and bowed to the boy. "My son and I are indebted to you, Arvan, son of Orlim. You honour us, and if I can ever be of service to you, you have only to ask."

Arvan stumbled to his feet, flushing with embarrassment.

"The honour is mine, Lord. May I have your leave to return to Lord Malim? He will be worried if I am late."

I nodded, and my son's protector hurried away.

Several hours later Sevrian found me still sitting, the little bag of sweet nuts in my hand. At his questioning look I tipped one out onto the palm of my hand and held it out to him. He took it wonderingly, and before I could say anything put it in his mouth, then smiled with delight, an expression I don't think I had ever seen him use before.

I must have frowned, because he said, "Please forgive me, Lord, but I have not tasted one of these since I was a small child. My nurse used to give them to me sometimes, I remember, when I couldn't sleep. Of course, as one grows, one no longer has need of such foolish things, but it is strange how the memory returns with the taste. Tell me, where did you get them?"

I shook my head. "It doesn't matter." Then, after a pause, I confessed sadly, "I have never eaten one. My mother did not allow me such things."

He studied me for a moment, his head slightly on one side, then reached over and took the bag from my open hand. Very carefully he took out a nut and placed it in my palm.

"Even a great Lord," he said with a smile, "should find time for childish pleasures now and then."

CHAPTER 35

As time went on, Malim's sojourns on the other side of the Great Emptiness became longer and more frequent. I discovered that I could not share in the experience entirely. It was only when he was ready to come home that I would begin to see through his eyes, just for the few moments before he returned to his own time. Then all of my senses became alert and it was as though I stood in that strange country in my own body.

I felt it too dangerous to let his body lie in his own house – even with Arvan standing watch over him he was vulnerable. I relieved Thalis, much to his annoyance, from any duties involving Malim's dangerous gift. I was then safely able to conceal my son in the great chamber underneath my rooms, where his almost lifeless body could stay entombed, away from curious eyes, in the centre of Corvan's secret maze.

More than a year passed thus, and during that time Sherenne and I both knew that soon the matter of our third child must be addressed. The idea terrified us, yet we knew that the old man had spoken the truth, and that if we did nothing the future would fall into the hands of Thalis and Karim, with Malim as a helpless figurehead, manipulated at every turn by those who lusted for wider power.

I could do nothing to prevent it. Even had I taken Malim's life it would have made no difference to the conflict that was to come. The only course, if I was to save the Family from itself, was to sire a powerful heir, one who would be accepted by all and who would have the strength to join with me to rid our people of the threat. How Sherenne and I longed for a perfect child. We hoped against hope that our joining, our love for each other, might bear the most precious fruit of all. On the night of our second son's conception we lay together afterwards, our hearts pounding with fear, praying that the child of our love would also be the child we had dreamed of.

Even before he was born Malim was consumed with jealousy and envy. I did not know it at the time, but Malim had seen, in one of his many forays across the Great Emptiness, what the child would become. He had seen a man, tall, proud and with all the attributes that he knew so painfully well that he would never possess. Thankfully he did not see all, but what he saw was enough.

Sherenne was hardly showing evidence of the pregnancy when I caught Malim in a vile fury trying to knock down her door, a knife in his hand, wanting to stop the new life before it had begun. At first I could do nothing but stare in horror as he screamed and kicked, oblivious to the growing crowd of men at the gates, all of them open mouthed with shock at his embarrassing display of emotion. As they became aware of my presence they parted to let me through. Karim, I noticed, was at the forefront, looking a little less surprised than the others. I had no time to investigate his contribution to my son's outburst though, as Malim had caught sight of me, and launched himself in my direction with a venom that even I found frightening.

The power of his gift poured out of him, wild, incoherent, and out of the corner of my eye I saw one of the watchers fall dead. At the same time the force of his anger hit me, and it was all I could do to stay on my feet. It was only then that I realised just how dangerous his rages had become. I sent out a bolt that knocked him flat, but still he raged on, calling his mother the vilest names, shouting that I had betrayed him. I wanted to kill him, but instead, in desperation, sent out a call for Arvan. Then, I pulled Malim to his feet and slapped his face so hard that his nose started to bleed.

At once, he stopped shouting and stared at me as if he had only just realised I was there. There was a dreadful silence, broken a moment later by the sound of his pathetic weeping as he sank to his knees, clawing at my boots. I flicked a glance backwards and the group of watchers turned away, not daring to look at me. A moment later, Arvan arrived, looking distraught.

"See to him," I managed to whisper, not trusting my voice to remain steady. Arvan nodded, and gently prised Malim away.

As I strode past and into Sherenne's room I saw Arvan gather him up and gently lead him away, every so often reaching down to the bag of sweet nuts that hung at his belt, feeding them to Malim as if to a young foal. When I finally closed the door and collapsed into Sherenne's arms, I broke down and wept.

No reassurance I could give to Malim was enough. He knew as well as I that as long as the child lived he would never again be my true heir. What he hated most was that he would have to share me with another, and he could not bear the thought. He wanted my love to be for him alone – his child's mind could not conceive of a love that could be great enough to extend beyond one individual. That is why he guarded Arvan so jealously, and flew into a rage each time his lifelong friend left him to spend an evening in the compound with Callenna. Poor Malim. The birth of my second son brought him as much pain as it brought me joy. And it was a joy such as I had never known, not even on the night that Sherenne first accepted me.

I didn't rush to see him as I had when my first son was born. I was too afraid to even think of it. For seven days I kept to my room, thinking to myself that at least if there was to be another tragedy I could delude myself for a little time, and not know until the day was forced upon me. When I took him in my arms on the eighth day my hands were trembling so much that I could hardly hold him. Sherenne dared not look as I passed judgement on his fitness but stood, her eyes closed, as still as stone, her fingers locked together so tightly that her knuckles were white. But I needed no gift to see. One brief glance at his face was enough to show me that I had sired the most magnificent of creatures, a son that would shine out like a beacon on a moonless night.

How beautiful he was – how strong and how perfect! I wanted to laugh and shout and weep with joy and gratitude for what had been given to us at last. When Sherenne and I were finally left alone we sat for hours, speechless, gazing down on the tiny miracle cradled at her breast. We named the child Arghel – it simply meant 'light'. He never cried, even then. The bond that he shared with his mother was such that she knew before he made a sound what it was he needed. Every night I would come by the secret way to hold him, talk to him, feed him warm honey water if Sherenne needed to sleep. Had it not been for his brother I might have been the happiest man in the entire world.

I knew that my contentment could not last. Arghel's birth was driving Malim more and more to madness. The more he crossed the Great Emptiness the more he learned, and he saw nothing to contradict his notion that he had been cast aside. I still went to visit him often, taking small gifts and sweet things to soothe him, but whenever I got up to leave he would hold on to me, weeping, until Arvan came to prise him away. Then he would fall into a rage and cry that he was abandoned long after he heard my footsteps die away across the pavement to my own house.

I became so concerned that I placed a guard on constant watch outside Sherenne's room. The task was overseen by Nyran, and Sevrian's son, Aloran, his only child at that time. I so clearly remember the joy of those times. I remember that I sat with Arghel, doing things that any normal father might do – things which had been denied to me for all those long centuries. I lifted him high above my head to make him laugh, built castles out of honey bread and polished round stones until they shone for him to roll along the floor. I remember the kisses that I showered upon him and, my greatest reward of all, I remember how my heart leapt at the way he ran eagerly to greet me as soon as he could walk. He looked at me then with such innocence, such trust, that I almost believed myself free of my past life. He was safe with his mother where Malim could not reach him, and he would remain protected until he was strong enough to fend for yourself.

So things were for just over four years, until I was woken in the night by Sherenne, calling to me in my mind, telling me to come, that something ailed our precious child that she didn't understand. I rushed down into the tunnels at once, and when I arrived I saw that he was curled into a tiny ball, shivering but silent. He sensed my presence and held his arms out to me, and it was then I realised that he couldn't see. He was blind, but it was no ordinary blindness. It was the blindness of the gift, and he was barely four years old. I gathered him up and sent out my gift to cover him, then sat the whole night, his mother looking on in fascination, the first woman I think to ever see the process since the Family was formed.

By morning the fever had left him and his sight had returned. His eyes gazed up at me as black as jet, the first male child in the long history of our kind to receive the gift in childhood. If that were not extraordinary enough, there was no sign of the chaos and confusion that all of us suffer at the time of transition. He lay in my arms, silent, curious, listening to the murmuring of his new world, but he was not afraid. It was as if the myriad voices made perfect sense to him, and he understood naturally how to separate one from another, give his attention to those that interested him, disregarding the rest. He behaved as though he had been within the gift his whole short life, and only now was able to give voice to it.

And give voice he did – silently and perfectly, but it was as much the words he gave me as the skill itself that made me almost drop him with the shock. His gaze was as placid as ever, and he reached out to grasp my hand, his tiny fingers curling around my palm.

"It is the end," he said.

I looked down at him and stroked the thick dark curls that set him apart from all of us – marked him, as far as the Family was concerned, with the taint of Derlan's tribe.

"No," my hidden voice answered. "How can it be the end? It is only the beginning."

Without any hesitation he replied, his silent voice so strong, so knowing, "I feel him. He will never let me live."

I could not answer, but held him to me, etching on my memory every detail of him as though I might forget. I knew he was right. I also knew that he could not stay in the safety of his mother's rooms. His eyes had changed and he must leave the compound, child though he was, to face the clear dangers that would surround him in the world outside. Sherenne realised it at the same moment and took my hand, not knowing what words had been silently spoken, only fearing for us both.

I looked down at him again, and asked simply, "How will you protect yourself?" In answer he drew down the veil of silence that he had inherited from his mother, and his mind was closed to me.

I got to my feet and embraced Sherenne, turning my head away so that my child would not see my tears. I knew then that I would not let him die, and that the saving of his life might cost me everything. I drew myself up, and taking his hand said, in a voice I hardly recognised as my own, "This boy is forbidden to come here any more." I turned, and led him out under a sky that was as grey and as empty as my heart.

That was the beginning. In the early days, when Arghel's gift was new, he ran after me, tried to find me wherever I went. He opened his mind to me, he couldn't help it, such was his love for the father that was about to betray him. Every time he let his thoughts run loose he gave notice of his presence to every man inclined to listen. Of course that included his brother Malim, and nothing could have been more dangerous to him. He knew that as well as I, yet his longing made him heedless of the danger. I suffered no less despair. His every cry rent my soul, drove me almost to madness. But he was a child, and I had to be strong for both of us. I placed his life above the happiness that we could have shared, dreaming that perhaps, one day, in a different world, we might freely share it once again.

Trapped by our fate, unable either to control Malim's gift or to destroy him, Sherenne and I formulated a plan to keep Arghel safe. I drove him away as cruelly as I was able so that Malim would think him beneath my notice and therefore not a threat. I let it be known within the settlement that I judged him tainted, a product of Derlan's inferior line. His striking head of curls only lent truth to the lie, making my contempt all the more easy for Malim, Thalis and their followers to accept.

I did not leave him unprotected. I called for Amal, the only other man I knew who possessed the gift of silence, and begged him to help me watch over my child. He had no love for me, yet he agreed, knowing that ultimately his ambition lay with mine. I placed Arghel within Sevrian's household, where he, his son and

Nyran were never more than a stride away, ready to ward off any attempt by Malim to do the boy harm.

Soon, where once Arghel had run to me with pleasure in his eyes, he began to show me only fear. In desperation he used his gift of silence to run to the comfort of his mother's arms as often as he could. I knew of it, of course, and heeded Sherenne's warnings to stay away at those times, so that I could not be accused of allowing a breach of the Rule. Knowing that he was able to take those brief respites in the safety of her room was one of my few comforts – at least it was until the day that Malim discovered the secret.

It was seven years to the day since the birth of my most beloved son. I knew that he had gone to his mother and I was glad of it. I was in my room alone, my mind, as it often was lately, in another place, another time. The spectre of the chain that had dominated my infancy haunted me still, now and then, and I was reflecting sadly on the irony of my current situation, that I, who had never known a mother's love, found it the only gift I had left to give my youngest child. The remembrance of the day of Arghel's birth was not something that affected me alone. Malim remembered it too, but for a different reason. On these anniversaries he went wild in his hatred of his brother, causing Sevrian and Nyran to remain even more alert than usual to the danger.

I was pulled out of my reverie by the sound of Sevrian's swift tread on the stair. With no more than a cursory tap at my door he flung it wide and rushed in, his consternation clear on his face. He opened his mouth to speak, but at the same moment I heard Sherenne's cry in my mind, and realised with horror that she was in fear of Arghel's life. I needed no further explanation and leapt to my feet, my heart thumping in the wake of her terror. I heeded nothing but her panic, and thrusting Sevrian aside raced out and down towards the compound gate.

Her door was open, and as I reached it I slowed, not wishing to startle Malim into further madness. The scene that met me as I stepped across the threshold almost froze my blood. Malim was in a fury, pacing up and down in front of the doorway, cutting off any escape. Little Arghel cowered in the far corner behind his mother, who stood, her feet planted squarely on the stone flags, both hands curled round a heavy iron poker, her eyes blazing like an angered she-wolf protecting her cub. Malim was too sunk in his rage to notice me, but Sherenne glanced across briefly, her look half of terror, half pleading. Malim saw her distraction and darted forward, but at once Sherenne swung the poker with all her strength and drove him back. He stopped, breathing heavily, and then he turned and saw me.

I watched as the elder of my sons sought, with an effort, to control himself. Still shaking, he sent me the silent words, full of hatred and challenge, "The Rule is broken. What will you do?"

I ordered him back with a gesture, and thankfully he obeyed. I tried to think quickly. Malim, and probably the entire settlement by now, knew of Arghel's crime. A small child he might be, but one with the gift, and so subject to the Rule. I had deliberately turned the boy into an object of scorn and derision within the Family and that, I knew, might now be the only thing that would save his life. But I could not do nothing and retain my power over Malim's, or rather Karim's faction. I locked eyes with Sherenne, and in the few seconds that it took for me to take a slow pace forward I conveyed my secret thoughts to her.

"I will strike you, and take him. Don't be afraid. I will beat him, that is all. But he will not be able to come here again."

I saw the despair in her face, but at the same time she gave a slight nod, understanding the terrible danger that we were all in, with Malim watching, conveying all he saw, I had no doubt, to Thalis. I spoke aloud, keeping my voice soft, as intimidating as I could.

"Come, Sherenne. You know the boy is forbidden to come here. He is mine now. Give him to me."

"No!" she hissed back, girding herself up and tightening her grip on the poker. I took another step forward, and as she raised her weapon I leapt at her. She swung it hard, but too late, and I knocked it out of her hand, at the same time dealing a heavy blow to the side of her head. For a moment I thought I might have hit her far too hard, as she slid across the floor and came to rest with a thump as her shoulder hit the wall. I was distracted only for a second, but it was enough. As I turned back I saw that Arghel's fear had transformed itself to fury on seeing his mother attacked, and before I had time to balance myself the child had somehow lifted the heavy poker and brought it down on my temple with such force that I was knocked to the floor, half senseless.

I remember his cries as Malim dragged him along the floor, out and through the courtyard. Sherenne was screaming to me, urging me onto my feet, her voice shrill with panic. Then Sevrian was there, his hand searching for the wound, bringing back clarity to my vision. I had no time to speak to him, but without a word dashed away, seeking Malim out as I went, following him through the east gate and down to where the watch fires burned on the boundary of the settlement.

Arghel was on the ground, struggling and kicking, the light from the watch fire illuminating his small body, held helpless by Malim's boot across the back of his neck. As I ran for my son's life I saw Malim take something out of the fire – the poker from Sherenne's room. It glowed almost white as he raised it and brought it down with all his strength. I saw the little body buck and twist under the blow, but Arghel made not a single sound. Then my child went still, and for one awful moment I thought that he was dead. Malim raised the poker a second time, too far away for me to reach him, and I shouted with all the authority I could muster, "Enough!"

Malim hesitated and turned to look at me, the flame of madness in his eyes. He turned back and made to strike again, but the brief hesitation had been all I needed and I was with them. I caught Malim's wrist a split second before the blow fell, and stopped the burning metal an inch from Arghel's flesh.

"I said enough!" I spat, enough venom in my voice to make Malim founder. "I would not have him die."

For a long moment Malim and I stared at each other, both breathing hard, and then I saw the fire in his eyes go out, the madness recede, to be replaced by an almost childlike contrition.

His arm relaxed and he dropped the poker onto the grass, then turned and ran, too afraid to face my anger.

I crouched in front of Arghel. He was trembling, his nails dug deep into the earth, the livid trace of the burn reaching from his left shoulder down his back and then round onto his stomach where he had twisted to try to avoid the blow. He still made no sound except for the chattering of his teeth from cold and shock. I reached down and lightly touched his silky curls.

"Brave little Arghel," I whispered, half to myself. "You are worth a hundred of his kind." I choked back my tears. "But sometimes," I went on, "when I see how you suffer, I think it might be better to let him kill you just the same."

There was a silence, in which all I could hear was the crackling of the watch fire flames. Then I felt a movement, and realised that Arghel had twined his arms around my leg and was hugging it tight. His body was shaking and I heard the sound of muffled weeping.

"Why can't you love me, Father?" His voice was a tiny, anguished cry. "You love Malim – why not me?"

I could stand it no longer. I carefully took his arms and prised them away, then got up and walked back towards the compound, wishing as I had never wished before that I had never been born.

CHAPTER 36

That night at the watch fire was the night that all trace of my precious son's love for me finally died, to be replaced by an open hatred that turned my blood to ice whenever he caught my eye. I made sure that he was never left alone again. Sevrian or one of his servants remained within an arm's reach of him every minute of the day and night. To Arghel, my watchfulness was simply yet more evidence of my desire to make him as miserable as possible. By the time he reached the age of fourteen, however, he had no more need of my protection. He was strong – stronger even than I had been at that age, and with a gift the like of which I had never seen before. Only Sherenne and I and, to a degree, Sevrian, knew of it. Arghel had learned to keep himself constantly hidden behind his veil of silence, so that most in the settlement saw him as a weakling. He was universally known as 'Lord Rendail's failure', although no one ever said as much to my face.

As far as Arghel was concerned I had but one comfort left. Within his gift he had been given the ability to communicate silently with his mother in a way that had never been seen in any of our kind before, save within a joining. Their minds could reach each other over great distances, Sherenne told me, even from the peaks of the great crags on the extreme northern borders of our lands. That is where Arghel spent most of his time, away from me and from his brother, and I was happy to allow it, as at least I knew that there he would be safe.

It was when Arghel passed his fifteenth year that we realised the settlement was once more a danger to him. He had long since ceased to be threatened by Malim alone – he had become powerful, and Malim was too much of a coward to take the risk. He had, however, begun to challenge the wisdom of the Rule in ways that could not be ignored. In a fit of temper over the mistreatment of a woman he stopped the heart of one of Karim's sons, and would have admitted it openly if Sherenne had not begged him to remain silent. I could ill afford such provocations of Karim's coterie and, more importantly, neither could Arghel.

It was at that time that Sherenne told me another of her secrets, one that revealed to us the path that we must take if we were to ensure Arghel's survival.

"I have seen them, within the Dance," she said one night, as we lay together engaged in our usual topic of conversation, the child who was to be the future hope of our people. "I have seen my father and my grandfather, and have watched them since I was no more than a child. I see how they live, and I know that my father would welcome his grandson, give him all the love that you cannot. They are powerful people. They would give him their protection, and in time he will give them his strength. He will be safe there, and he will learn all he needs to know, so that when he returns, no one will have the power to stand against him."

Once I had recovered from the surprise and, I had to admit, a little churlishness at the fact that she had kept the information hidden from me, I had to agree that her suggestion was perfect. When he made his escape I would of course make a public attempt to hunt him down. One of his blood would never be permitted to leave the Family, particularly if it were known that the gift that ran in his veins might fall once again into the hands of Derlan's people. But Arghel was powerful enough to withstand any that I might send against him – more powerful, in fact, than even I realised at that time. We agreed that Sherenne should use all her powers to persuade him, and I left her the next morning feeling a little lighter of heart than I had been for more than a year.

Our plan was a good one – the only one we had. But the months went by, and Arghel showed no sign of attempting his escape. Worse, his behaviour was starting to become outwardly provocative, and several times it had taken all my ingenuity to save him from the worst penalties that the Rule had to offer. Twice I had been forced to order him flogged at the east gate, arguing against the demand of some others that he be strung out and left for the wolves. His blood, I reminded Thalis, contained the seed of the gift to cross the Great Emptiness, and we couldn't

386

afford to waste it. I knew, however, that I couldn't use that reasoning for ever, and time was running short.

"Why will he not go?" I whispered to Sherenne as I paced the floor of her room. "Surely he knows what is at stake? You have explained to him – why can you not persuade him?"

She knew. The plain truth was that he loved his mother. He had seen her danger as well as his own, or at least that is how he perceived things. Despite her reassurances that she would be safe with me he did not believe her, and he would not leave without her. She was as desperate as I, but he would not listen to her. Finally, she spoke the words that were to send me to a fate worse than any I had ever imagined.

"If I am not here," she said, so calmly that the meaning of her words was almost lost, "then he will have nothing to stay for. If I am dead, he will go."

I refused to listen to her. I forbade it. I lashed out in my terror and struck her, threatened her, did everything I could to put the thought from her mind. And still Arghel was in more danger with every day that passed. When I was exhausted with fury and weeping, I held her and wept some more. But I knew that she was right. If our son did not go he would die. And without him the future only held the deaths of thousands more. The blood that harboured Corvan's madness could not be destroyed, it could only be contained, and we were no more than players in a great dice game, throwing the stones for the stake that was our future.

At last she gave me a choice. "If you love me," she said, "you will give me what I need. If you refuse I will find another way, and you will not know until it is too late."

I brought her the herbs that she needed. I held her in my arms as she drank the cup I prepared for her, and wept until I had no more tears as I felt her life start to slip away.

"Leave now," she said to me, near the end. "I will fetch him to me. Then he will go."

I sat alone in my room feeling the last of her warmth leave me forever. That last moment with her I gave to my son, so that at the final breath his arms surrounded her, his was the final kiss. But still he did not leave. For days he stayed, cradling her body in his arms, the door bolted and kept shut by the force of his gift. At last, when I could stand it no more I took Sevrian and others of my household to beat down the door, and tore her from him. The look he gave me as I entered the room that day was one I will never forget. The next morning, when the settlement awoke, Arghel was gone.

For me it was as though time stopped. I heard nothing, saw nothing, felt nothing. No one dared to enter my rooms, not even Sevrian, and so it remained for what might have been months or years. I have no recollection of time passing. I learned later that Sevrian had held the doors closed, allowed no one to see me, and it was just as well. I hardly ate and never spoke, and if any had laid eyes on me they would have thought me already dead. The settlement was in Sevrian's hands, and thankfully all accepted it. At last, though, the fog began to lift, and I could feel again. What I felt was a pain so raw that it made me long to die.

Then Sevrian came, and said, "My Lord, you must come and see your son."

I followed him down into the great chamber, to where Malim's body rested when he made his journeys across the Great Emptiness into the far future. I saw his frame laid out in rugs on the stone table, the steady rise and fall of his chest the only confirmation of the life that still rested within him. Sevrian's brow was troubled, his expression grim.

"How long?" My voice trembled, as it had on the day in Morlain's house when I had first spoken aloud.

"More than a year," he replied. "He has found his place, and he has gone."

I felt as if I had been struck the final, fatal blow. Malim was gone, out of my reach, to a future beyond our understanding. He had embarked upon his flawed dream, to create his own twisted empire in a world that had no defence against the madness in his blood. I had failed. Arghel had been born too late, and now our future lay in the hands of a madman with the power to shape the world in his own image.

"All is lost," I said, and waved Sevrian away so that I could grieve alone.

I sat beside my elder son, hollow, empty, unthinking. I had but one course left. I took my hunting knife from my belt, held it to the neck of the son who, for all his faults, I still loved, and prepared to do what I should have done all those years ago, when I had seen the taint in him and had not had the power to act. I had ceased to think. All other considerations were nothing to me now. He would die, and I would lie beside him. We would welcome death together. I shifted my grip and closed my eyes, then went to slash the blade across his throat. But my arm did not move. I was held by a force so much stronger than my will that I could hardly breathe, and I stood paralysed, unable even to open my eyes. I felt the knife taken easily from my grasp, and a moment later I was sitting on the ground, my heavy eyelids lifting to reveal a long, greying beard, beneath which lay a slight but comforting smile.

He took me in his arms and I wept. I sobbed as a lost child might cry for his mother and father, clinging onto him with all my strength, my tears soaking into the fabric of his shirt. At last, when my grief subsided, he pushed me away a little, and stroking my dishevelled hair from my forehead he said softly, "It is not over."

I blinked at him, red eyed and still sniffing. "You know the future as well as the past then, old man?"

He smiled at me and passed me a rag with which to blow my nose.

"I know what I am told, no more," he replied. "But I know enough. I am glad you called for me."

"I called for you? When?"

He laughed. "Your heart called for me, my boy, and I came. I came to remind you of what you were told. Do you remember the words that your brother spoke to you? If not, then you would do well to search your memory now."

"My brother?" For a moment I was confused, but then, out of the distant past I heard Rolan's voice come to me, and I remembered our conversation in the firelight as I recovered from my fever. 'If our Family is to survive,' he had said, 'it will do so only by your strength and your sacrifice. You are destined to lose all that is most dear to you, but you must trust in those you love.

389

The way is long and dark, and filled with pain. But if you stand firm and keep your faith, then all that is taken from you will return, and at the end you will see your dreams fulfilled.' Those words, I remembered, had come from the future – from the issue of the child of my child and the child of Rolan's child – a message of hope sent back to me from a far place, and not a dream of what might come to be.

The old man was looking at me intently, and when he saw my eyes widen he nodded.

"You have done your part," he said, "but it is not over. You cannot take this child's life now. If you do, you will change all that is to be. You must stand firm, my friend, and wait. The forces gather, and the battle is about to begin. I do not know the outcome any more than you. The signs are too hard to read, even for me. Perhaps it is too soon – the path of time is rarely clear, and there is a limit to my sight. All I know is that you cannot intervene, that the future is now in the hands of those you have sired. They are the Lords of Time, far beyond your reach or mine. One will die, that is certain. Let us hope, my boy, that it is the right one."

I wept again that night, and the old man held me until dawn broke over the crags. Before he left, he put his hand on my forehead and let his dream voice give me peace. And this time, he did not just disappear. He said, "Farewell, Rendail, my friend – until we meet again."

THE END

BIOGRAPHY

Following first degrees in psychology and pure science, Jo went on to gain a PhD by research at the University of Bristol, specialising in behavioural psychology and brain physiology. She worked for seven years as a research associate/lecturer, working on the interaction of genetic and environmental factors. Jo has twenty research publications in academic journals from that period. She then went on to become a full time lecturer in further and higher education, writing and delivering training materials for teachers in addition to lecturing work. She still lectures in brain physiology for the Open University, and works part time as a freelance educational consultant, writing and delivering training courses for teachers.

Jo was winner of the Daily Telegraph Travel writing award 2008, and has had short stories published in Mslexia magazine and the recent Bookshed anthology, 'Short Fuses'.

The Tyranny of the Blood was voted the most popular adult fantasy of the year on the Arts Council sponsored website YouWriteOn, and was a runner-up in the all-genre 2008 YWO book of the year awards.

The novel went on to win an 'Apprenticeship in Fiction' award (www.adventuresinfiction.co.uk) supported by the Arts Council and a grant from the Oppenheimer John-Downes Memorial Trust.

Lightning Source UK Ltd.
Milton Keynes UK
07 November 2009

145912UK00002B/4/P